# LORD TEMPTATION

REBECCA HAGAN LEE

AMBER HOUSE BOOKS

## PRAISE FOR REBECCA HAGAN LEE

"Rebecca Hagan Lee warms my heart and touches my soul. She is a star in the making!" — Sabrina Jeffries, *New York Times* bestselling author

"Tender, enthralling romance straight from the heart!" — Eloisa James, *New York Times* bestselling author

"Rebecca Hagan Lee taps into every woman's fantasy!" — Christina Dodd, *New York Times* bestseller

"Rebecca Hagan Lee is a writer on the rise!" — *Romantic Times*

## BOOKS BY REBECCA HAGAN LEE

***The Charlotte Society***

*Lord Temptation*

*Lord Dare*

*Lord Rogue*

***Gold Coast Bride Series***

*The Treasure Bride*

*The Silk Bride*

*The Heiress Bride*

*The Irish Bride*

***Free Fellows League Series***

*Barely a Bride*

*Merely the Groom*

*Hardly a Husband*

*Truly a Wife*

*A Bachelor Still*

***Mistresses of the Marquess***

*Once a Mistress*

*Always a Lady*

*Ever a Princess*

***Borrowed Brides***

*Golden Chances*

*Harvest Moon*

*Something Borrowed*

*The Counterfeit Bride*

*Twice Blessed: A Borrowed Brides Novella*

*A Hint of Heather*

*Whisper Always*

ISBN: 978-1-943505-77-7

Cover design by Control Freak Productions

Cover Photo © Period Images

Cover Background © Unholy Vault Designs (Used under license from Shutterstock.com)

Published by Amber House Books, LLC

http://www.amberhousebooks.com

For more information, contact publisher@amberhousebooks.com

❀ Created with Vellum

*This book is dedicated to my dear friend,*
*Staci Bea La Mere*

*Friends from schooldays to adulthood*
*Through thick and thin*
*Through sunshine and shadow*
*Through decades of shared confidences and dreams*
*And thirty acres of peanuts...*

*Thank you, Staci, for gift of your friendship.*
*And for sharing my 10,000 steps a day.*

*And, thank you to my hero, Steve*
*For sharing my life.*
*With love.*

*Journal Entry of Major Anthony Carlisle*
*Belgian Countryside*
*Wednesday, 16 August 1815*

*Bonaparte is gathering his forces for one last great battle for Europe. The French have converged along the border between France and Belgium. He has retaken Paris and sent the Bourbon king scurrying to safety. Wellington and the coalition are determined to put an end to Bonaparte's triumphant march before the whole of the French army turns against the king and rejoins Napoleon. So far, every command sent by Louis XVIII to repel him has gone unheeded. The French army has forsaken the French king and bestowed their allegiance on Bonaparte once again.*

*Wellington has ordered me to find the main arm of the French army—to find Bonaparte—and report his location and that of the troops moving to join him. I pray our new recruits will be up to the task when they meet his seasoned soldiers...*

*I pray I shall be up to the task...*
*Carlisle*

# PROLOGUE

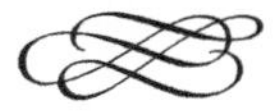

*"A coward turns away,*
*but a brave man's choice is danger."*
—Euripides, 486-406 B. C.

*16 June 1815*

The door to hell opened on the road from Brussels to Charleroi at Quatre Bras.

The road had seemed virtually deserted and unprotected when they'd left the town limits of Brussels in the early morning hours to confirm or repudiate the rumors that Bonaparte was heading toward the city. But it was teeming with activity now.

Major Lord Anthony Carlisle, third Earl Carlisle, watched from his observation point on a hill just outside the settlement of Quatre Bras—four houses—sitting at the intersection of the Brussels to Charleroi and the Nivelles to Namur roads. Reaching out, he smoothed his hand down the neck of his horse, who was anxiously snorting and prancing in anticipation of the coming confrontation. "Sorry about this, Ajax. I was hoping the dispatches were wrong."

But the rumors flying through the city and the intelligence report Wellington had received in the morning dispatches, along with an invitation to the Duchess of Richmond's ball, were correct. The main force of Bonaparte's army was heading up from Charleroi, not for Mons as expected, but toward Brussels. All that stood between the French army and the city was Tony's reconnaissance unit of fifteen and a small force of Orange and Saxe-Weimar soldiers, who had discerned Bonaparte's intent and rushed to guard the crossroads at the first hint of French troop movement.

Tony dismounted, removed his leather notebook from his dispatch pouch, and quickly scrawled three words to Wellington: *Dispatch confirmed. Carlisle.* He folded the note, sealed it, and returned it to his leather dispatch pouch before signaling Corporal Holman to join him.

The young soldier rode up beside him.

Tony handed him the dispatch pouch and Ajax's reins. "Take the dispatches to Wellington."

"Sir?" The corporal looked down at the reins in his hand.

"Change mounts. You take my horse. I'll ride yours."

The corporal's eyes widened in surprise. "But, sir, nobody can ride Ajax except you."

"You can try."

He did. The corporal dismounted and tried valiantly to mount Ajax. Corporal Holman managed to get his foot in the stirrup twice. And twice, Tony's horse forced him to remove it. Ajax pranced and danced, laid his ears flat, and snorted at the young corporal. He finally went so far as to rear and paw at him.

"It's no use, sir. He's not having it," the corporal said. "He won't leave you."

The corporal was right. Tony was the only man who had ever ridden Ajax. The only man Ajax would allow to ride him. There was no use wasting time arguing about it. Taking the reins from Holman, Tony stepped up on the horse. "All right, Ajax," he murmured in a soothing tone. "Let's hope we made the right decision." Turning to

Corporal Holman, Tony said, "You have your orders, Corporal. Good luck and Godspeed."

Corporal Holman saluted. "Thank you, sir. Good luck to you, too, sir."

After dispatching the corporal with the message confirming Wellington's intelligence reports, Tony began the task of readying his remaining men for the coming battle. He was duty-bound to keep as many of his men alive and able-bodied as possible, but they were cavalry and Tony knew they would be attached to the larger force of allied cavalry occupying the area around the crossroads once the fighting began. He didn't know any of the Dutch cavalry commanders by name or by reputation and his knowledge of the language was limited at best.

He'd feel better if Lord Uxbridge or Lord Ponsonby arrived with British cavalry to lead the charge, but if his fate and the fate of his men lay in the hands of the Orangemen, Tony could only pray the officer in charge was an experienced field commander who wouldn't offer them all up as cannon fodder for the French.

# CHAPTER 1

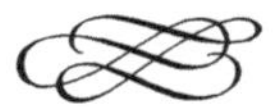

*"When the hurly-burly's done;*
*When the battle's lost and won."*
—William Shakespeare, 1564-1616

*04 July 1815*

He jolted awake to the sound of screaming. Of men and horses. Of the wounded and dying. He awoke to the sound of fierce fighting. Of curses and prayers, of cannon and rifle fire. He heard the boom of cannons and the whistle of rifle balls whizzing through the air, heard the thud as they met human and animal flesh, as they slammed into trees and earth. He recognized the peculiar swooshing and the clang of sabers exchanging blows and the acrid smell of gunpowder and gore, of blood and puke, of excrement and earth.

His senses on high alert, Tony felt the rapid pounding of his heart. He was alive and in a fierce battle, but something was dreadfully wrong. He should be galloping across the field, saber drawn, charging into the French artillery. Fighting raged all around him, yet he lay on the ground, his back pressing into the damp earth. His brave war horse lay atop him, crushing him beneath its dead weight. Tony squeezed his eyes shut to halt the sudden sting of tears.

Poor Ajax.

Men chose to go to war. Horses did not.

Neither man nor horse had chosen this one.

Slipping his hand beneath Ajax's black mane, Tony caressed the slick hair of the beast's neck as he said a silent prayer for his noble horse. Tony didn't know if God listened to the prayers of men engaged in the wholesale carnage of their fellow men, but he knew that any god worth praying to would listen to a prayer for a brave and selfless animal. If horses had souls, Ajax had surely had the most noble and generous. And courage to match any men on the field... He deserved a better fate...

Moving to slip free of his stirrup irons and retrieve the saber that had fallen beyond his reach, Tony gasped as white-hot pain coursed through his body. Perspiration beaded his forehead as he fought to retain his grip on consciousness. He could manage the pain if he lay still and didn't move, but if he lay still and didn't move, he would die pinned beneath Ajax.

He would die of his wounds or putrefaction or exposure or be trampled by the men and horses and wagons and caissons still engaged in the battle or die at the hands of deserters and looters scouring the battlefields when darkness fell and the fighting ended.

Glancing down, Tony realized he was covered with blood and gore and unable to see his right leg. It was under Ajax beyond his line of vision. He thought it must still be attached to his torso because the pain he felt when he tried to move it was excruciating, but he'd seen too many men who had lost their limbs swear the pain in their missing arms and legs was almost beyond bearing. No matter. He must move or die. Pressing his hands against Ajax's withers, Tony shoved with all his might.

A hoarse scream tore through the air. Recognizing it as his own,

Tony knew he'd officially entered the ranks of the wounded and dying.

~

WHEN HE AWOKE ONCE AGAIN, HE WAS LYING ON A COT. OPENING HIS eyes, Tony blinked up at the profusion of angels and cherubim above him and wondered if he had died. It took him a foggy moment to realize he was staring up at a frescoed ceiling. A cracked frescoed ceiling. He was in a building—a church or palace or some other place with a need for a frescoed depiction of heaven. He was sure it wasn't the real heaven because he hurt from the top of his head to the tips of his toes.

*Tips of his toes...*

He tried to flip off the blanket covering the lower half of his body and swing his legs over the side of the cot, but nothing happened. Rolling his head against the pillow, he looked to his right and saw a person sitting on a chair beside his cot. *Barnaby.* Tony recognized his batman. "Barnaby." His lips were dry and cracked and his throat raw and hoarse.

"Here, Major."

"Legs? Where?" Tony struggled against his pillow, trying to push himself up.

"Easy, sir." Barnaby leaned over Tony's cot. "You've still got them." He took a deep breath. "I had the devil's own time convincing the surgeon to let you keep 'em, but they're still attached." Barnaby met Tony's gaze, clearly recognizing the fear and uncertainty in it. "You're safe, major. You're in a hospital in Brussels. Not to worry. I won't let anybody cut off your legs unless you say so." Reaching over to a small bedside stand, Barnaby retrieved a cloth from a wooden bowl and began dabbing Tony's parched lips with cool water. "You were wounded, sir, and gravely ill."

"How?" Tony tried to take a deep breath but found the exercise beyond him.

"Your horse was shot out from under you as you were leading your third charge. You broke three ribs, both legs and a hip when Ajax fell on you. You also suffered a head wound and a bayonet wound to the chest before we found you."

Tony squeezed his eyes shut, hoping to block out the memory of Ajax and his last disastrous charge. Twin tracks of tears seeped between his lashes. But Tony didn't feel them. He didn't weep for himself. He wept for the loss of his noble horse and for the loss of the plans Tony had had for him. He wept for the waste of life because his beloved horse should never have been in the war at all. "Ajax."

Barnaby bowed his head. "I'm sorry, sir."

"How…long…" He gritted out the question one word at a time, doing his best to ignore the pain that came with every breath. "Here?"

"It's been nearly three weeks since the battle. You were brought here eighteen days ago."

"Eight days…" He breathed the word, letting it trail off before he could finish it.

"*Eighteen*, sir," Barnaby corrected. "*Eighteen* days."

"Who?"

After serving as Lord Carlisle's friend, confidant, and batman and sharing his living quarters for the last four and a half years, Barnaby understood Tony's truncated questions. "Neither side, sir. The Battle of Quatre Bras was a draw, but we held our ground and two days later, Wellington and Blücher won the day outside the village of Waterloo."

"Bonaparte?"

"Beaten. The war's over, sir. Old Boney abdicated. He is being held in British custody while the coalition governments find a place to put him. Wellington sent word to the French king requesting that he return to Paris."

"Men?"

"Eight wounded at Quatre Bras, sir, including you. Three killed at Waterloo."

Tony sighed.

"The surgeons say the wounded men should all recover, sir."

Tony gave a slight nod, relaxed a moment, then asked, "Me?"

Barnaby hesitated. "It's a bloody miracle you're alive, sir. You've been unconscious since we found you and so gravely wounded the surgeons all gave up on you." Tony's batman snapped to attention. "I did not give up on you, sir. I swore an oath to see you through this war and take you home to England just as soon as you're strong enough to travel..."

Tony frowned. "And?"

"It may be a while, major. Your legs were crushed. You may still lose them..."

"No." Tony shook his head.

Barnaby took a deep breath. "If you don't succumb to infection or poison of the blood or inflammation of the lungs, if there's no fatal damage to your internal organs, and your hip and your legs heal reasonably well. If none of the marrow in your broken limbs seeps into your blood. If nothing else goes wrong, one surgeon believes you might survive a return to London."

That was a bloody mouthful of ifs. With no guarantees. Carlisle couldn't say he liked his odds.

Anthony Carlisle squeezed his eyes shut once again, too weak to keep them open. He'd slept for eighteen days while Barnaby watched over him. He had survived the Battle of Quatre Bras, but he might yet become its casualty.

The war had ended, but battles remained. He was *still* fighting for his life.

"Home," he whispered. "Promise...whatever...happens... Home."

# CHAPTER 2

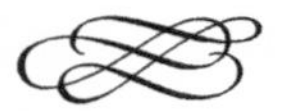

*"'Tis not enough to help the feeble up,*
*But to support him after."*
–William Shakespeare, 1564-1616

*18 March 1816*

"Caro! Caro!" Lady Phoebe Osborne rushed into Lady Caroline Blessing's morning room, breathlessly untying her bonnet ribbons as she went. "I'm sorry I'm late for the meeting, but you'll understand when I tell you I have the most amazing news! I was in Hookham's Circulating Library returning the books I'd borrowed when I heard several ladies of the ton gossiping about it and I simply had to stay and listen to the latest…"

Pouring chocolate for her other guest, Caroline looked up as Phoebe burst into the room, fairly vibrating with excitement. Her eyes were bright, her cheeks pinked with color. "I thought you gave up gossiping at Hookham's for Lent."

Phoebe refused to take umbrage at the disappointment she heard in Caroline's voice. Her news was clearly too exciting. "I didn't gossip. I listened. And, Caro, *he's* back. *He's* returned from the continent and is back in London." Phoebe removed her bonnet, scattering hairpins as her long, baby-fine blond hair escaped its confinement. She tied the ribbons together, then hung it on the row of brass hooks mounted by the door before bending to collect her hairpins.

"Who's back?"

"*Carlisle*," Phoebe breathed, straightening to her full height and pocketing her hairpins.

The world seemed to stop, and the house became so quiet the sound of another pin dropping would have rattled the rafters.

"What Carlisle?" Caroline did her best to sound only moderately interested, but her hands shook and her face lost color at Phoebe's stunning announcement. There was only one Carlisle who mattered.

"*Anthony*," Phoebe confirmed, "third Earl of Carlisle."

Dulcie Tennant, the other member of their little triumvirate, leaned closer in her chair, and placed her hand on Caroline's, quickly rescuing the delicate bone china chocolate cup rattling dangerously against its matching saucer. "But he was..."

"Presumed dead," Phoebe confirmed. "Yes, I know, but it seems Caro's dashing earl has returned from the grave."

Caroline gasped, nearly dropping the chocolate pot before managing to set it down on the table without spilling the contents across the snowy white linen cloth. "Anthony Carlisle was never *my* earl," she replied in a low, wobbly voice.

"He could have been," Dulcie reminded Caroline.

"*Should* have been," Phoebe added, almost simultaneously. "You and Carlisle were the talk of the town before he left for war."

Caroline blushed. "We could not have been. We were careful and very discreet."

"Caro, everyone knows Lord Temptation was mad about you. The rumor was that he planned to offer for you right before your wedding announcement appeared in the *Times*," Phoebe continued, using the name town gossips had given Anthony Carlisle years earlier. Carlisle had been highly sought by London's marriageable young ladies and their mamas and with his height, athleticism, and extraordinary good looks, *he* had been more tempting than his title or his fortune. But he'd been taken by Caroline Hardage the moment he saw her. Lord Temptation had never considered anyone else.

"He asked me to marry him," Caroline said. "But he never offered for me. Lord Carlisle had never officially asked her father for her hand in marriage. He hadn't entered into negotiations with her father and the solicitors and hadn't signed any marriage contracts binding him to her.

"He was going to offer for you," Dulcie said.

Caroline shook her head. "My father would have told me."

"Your father never gave him the chance. He accepted Lord Blessing's suit before Lord Temptation had the opportunity to offer for you," Phoebe insisted. "But Carlisle wanted you, Caro."

"How can you possibly know that?" Caro demanded.

"Unlike you," Phoebe pointed out, "I paid attention to the gossip surrounding your sudden nuptials to a man more than three times your age *and* the rumors about Lord Temptation. And the talk was that Carlisle made an appointment to speak with your father on a matter of utmost importance."

"Why didn't you tell me? Why didn't you say something?" A tear slipped down Caroline's cheek. She scrubbed it away with the heel of her hand before pinning Phoebe with her fierce gaze. "I spent years agonizing over him. Years wondering why."

Phoebe glanced at Dulcie, clearly distressed by the realization that their silence had hurt their dear friend. "We never mentioned it because the announcement of your betrothal to Lord Blessing appeared in the papers the day after I learned of Carlisle's appointment with your father. And you made us promise never to mention Lord Temptation's name in your presence ever again." Phoebe withstood Caroline's gaze without flinching. "A promise we kept until a few moments ago."

Caroline settled back into her chair with a defeated sigh. Phoebe was telling the truth. It would be utterly unfair of her to be cross with Phoebe or Dulcie about anything. They had been loyal friends, standing beside Caroline as she exchanged vows with Lord Granville Blessing and became his marchioness. Caroline *had* made her friends swear to never mention Anthony Carlisle's name in her presence. Even now, the thought of him was like a jagged splinter driven into her already aching heart. She had blamed him for failing to approach her father, for leaving her trapped in a loveless union to a man she barely knew. Caroline took a deep breath, slowly released it, then turned to Dulcie.

Dulcie slowly nodded. "It's true, Caro. Everyone knew Carlisle intended to offer for you. Rumor was that he had purchased a betrothal ring from Dalrymple's Jewelry to present to you."

Caroline knew Tony had planned to ask her father for her hand in marriage, but her father had never given her any indication that he had followed through on that promise. And neither had Tony. "Well, if he *did* talk to my father, he must have been easily dissuaded from his task. Because he joined the army instead." Caroline knew her tight-lipped smile didn't fool either of her two closest friends. Somehow, it hurt even more to know Tony must have calmly accepted her father's decision. That he had chosen to fight for his country instead of for her. "Besides, it was all a long time ago." *A lifetime ago.*

Phoebe and Dulcie exchanged knowing glances. Caro had married Granville, second Marquess of Blessing, five seasons ago. And five seasons wasn't long enough for Caro to have forgotten Anthony Carlisle. He was, after all, Lord Temptation.

And Phoebe and Dulcie found it impossible to believe Carlisle had forgotten Caro. The rumors around town were that Lord Temptation had gotten drunk after Caroline's wedding and had done his best to drown her memory in a veritable *ocean* of spirits.

Caroline caught a glimpse of the looks her friends were exchanging and understood the meanings behind them. She knew Phoebe and Dulcie as well as she knew herself. Tall, blond, blue-eyed Phoebe looked like a cool, calm Nordic princess. But appearances could be deceiving. Outspoken and opinionated, the energetic Phoebe tended to act first and think later. Tiny, doll-like Dulcie, with her big brown eyes and mass of dark auburn curls, was the opposite. With her dark red hair, she might easily be mistaken for a fireball, but there was nothing flighty about her. Dulcie was careful and deliberate. She weighed each decision and considered each word before speaking. Caroline knew her friends were also remembering that season, five years ago, when she had been madly in love with the dashing young Earl of Carlisle.

Unfortunately, her papa hadn't felt the same way. Lord Rushton didn't put any faith in romantic love. Her papa was politically minded and ambitious. He subscribed to the theory that affairs of the heart were best left outside the bounds of marriage. Marriage was reserved for the most important matters of state—to secure political alliances and increase the family coffers. Her papa was a belted earl, the ninth Earl of Rushton, and as such, Lord Rushton believed the best thing he could do for his family was marry his daughter to a wealthier, higher ranking peer…a more powerful peer.

Anthony Carlisle was wealthier than Lord Rushton and came from a long and ancient lineage of noblemen. Caroline had thought that would be a mark in Tony's favor when he asked her father for permission to marry her. But Tony was an earl like Papa and Caroline knew Papa wanted someone with a more exalted title and stronger political connections for her.

The Carlisles were not political. They were not courtiers. They were soldiers, sailors, and explorers, men of action, and men of property. Caroline had hoped Papa would ignore Tony's disregard of political connections. She hadn't thought it would matter.

Caroline hadn't realized her papa had had a very different suitor in mind.

The Marquess of Blessing's fortune wasn't as great as Carlisle's, but he'd possessed all the other qualities Papa wanted in a son-in-law —the loftier title, advanced maturity, and a hereditary position at Court. Lord Blessing came from a long line of political puppet masters and Lord Rushton heartily approved of the marquess.

Although the marquess was older than Papa, they were of like mind where marriage was concerned and took close interest in the affairs of government and life at court. Her papa had been flattered when the widowed marquess chose her to be the next Marchioness of Blessing. The Marquess of Blessing was everything Lord Rushton could have asked for as a suitor for his only daughter.

If only her papa could have married Lord Blessing instead of her.

For a young lady forced into a marriage with a difficult, volatile man more than thrice her age, three years had been an eternity.

"It *was* a long time ago," Dulcie said softly, her expressive brown eyes aching for her friend. "For you and for Carlisle."

"You've both spent years in a purgatory not of your own making," Phoebe said. "But you're both free now."

"I'm a widow," Caroline reminded them.

"A widow whose year of mourning is over," Dulcie pointed out.

Caroline glanced down at her gray frock, then over at the calendar on the wall. Dulcie was right. Her year of mourning for the husband she could never love, but had tried her best to tolerate and respect had ended months ago.

Caroline could have put away her mourning. She could have donned colors again and resumed her place in society. No one knew that she had remained in mourning—not for Blessing—but for Tony, who had been presumed dead on the day her mourning for her husband concluded. She focused all her attention on Phoebe. "You are certain he's alive? You are certain the gossips are correct? You are certain it's Tony?"

Phoebe nodded.

"Oh, God..." Caroline's voice began to quaver. She leaned back in her chair. "All those years I tried not to think about him. I did my best not to hope... Not to hope that I would be set free and Tony might take me back... But I couldn't help it. I lit candles on his birthday and prayed that God would watch over him and keep him safe." She looked up at Phoebe once again. "I even wrote to him while he was away. I asked him to write to me in care of you or Dulcie."

Her friends were surprised.

"I didn't tell you," Caroline admitted. "But I knew I could trust you. I knew you would understand. I knew you would see that I got his letters." She bit her bottom lip. "But he never wrote back. Not once.

And then, I saw his name on the casualty lists printed in the newspapers. Lord Anthony, third Earl of Carlisle, Major, His Majesty's Own 11th Blues. I made inquiries at the War Office. There was no mistake."

"But there was," Phoebe assured her. "The reports were wrong. Someone *did* make a mistake. Your prayers were answered. I heard the news from several exceptionally reliable gossips."

Caroline frowned. "Did you see him with your own eyes? Did you see Tony?"

"In Hookham's?" Phoebe was shocked by the suggestion that a man like Lord Anthony Carlisle might be found browsing the shelves at the circulating library frequented almost exclusively by ladies when he had a magnificent library of his own at his Park Lane town house. "Of course not. But the town is all abuzz with the news. He isn't dead, Caro. Lord Anthony Carlisle is alive and home from Belgium."

Caroline smiled her first genuine smile in ages. Her features brightened and she suddenly felt lit from within. "We'll need to choose another name for our aid society. We cannot go with my first choice."

"Why not?" Dulcie asked.

"As our purpose is to offer comfort and aid to returning soldiers, I intended to name our group the Saint Anthony Society," Caroline confessed. "In memory of Tony, who was born on Saint Anthony's Day and who lost his life at Quatre Bras. But with Tony returned from the grave..."

"We would do well to come up with another, more appropriate, name," Dulcie finished Caroline's thought.

"Indeed." Caroline shivered with anticipation and beamed at her two closest friends. "I can hardly believe it! He's alive. Tony has come home. Alive and well."

Phoebe frowned, then bit her bottom lip and quickly turned her attention to the contemplation of the tips of her half-boots.

"What is it, Phoebe?" Caroline furrowed her brow. "What's wrong? What else did you hear?"

Phoebe hesitated.

"Tell me!" Caroline demanded. "Please."

Phoebe looked up and met her friend's gaze, a pinched look of dread on her face

Caroline exhaled, wringing her hands beneath the folds of her skirts, preparing herself for whatever bad news Phoebe had to reveal. "I know there's more. I can see it on your face. What haven't you told me?"

"Lord Carlisle has returned from the dead." Phoebe met Caroline's unwavering gaze. "There's no doubt about that. But he hasn't returned unscathed. He was injured."

Caroline gasped, covering her mouth with her hand. "Badly?"

"I'm afraid so," Phoebe said.

"How?" Caroline was suddenly incapable of forming complete sentences. The most she could manage was a word at the time.

"He was crushed beneath his horse," Phoebe said softly. "The gossips were saying he is unable to walk."

Caroline sat without moving for long minutes, as if she had lost the use of her own limbs.

"The ladies at Hookham's were discussing the fact that Lord Temptation was carried home in a closed sedan chair and has refused to receive callers since his return," Phoebe added. "Carlisle has retreated to his Park Lane town house and withdrawn from society and everyone in it."

"Then I suppose I shall have my work cut out for me," Caroline pronounced, her lips tightening once more, this time with determination.

"I don't follow..." Phoebe blinked in confusion.

"We decided that providing money and charity items were not enough, that our society should provide personal encouragement and support..." She looked at Phoebe, then at Dulcie for confirmation.

Both of her friends nodded. Dulcie's dark auburn curls bounced at the motion and another pin slipped from Phoebe's hastily resecured bun. "That's right," Dulcie added. "We agreed that the best way to begin our work is for each of us to adopt a returning soldier and become acquainted with him and his special needs." She blushed, making the sprinkling of freckles across the bridge of her nose and her cheeks even more prominent.

"Have either of you found a soldier yet?" Caroline asked.

Phoebe glanced at Dulcie before answering. "Not yet."

It had sounded simple enough when Caroline proposed the idea for an aid society that did more than simply provide money. But choosing a soldier recently returned from the battlefields of Europe in whom to take a personal interest was not as easy as one might think for unmarried ladies with reputations and positions in society to consider. Their adopted soldiers need not be officers or titled gentlemen, but they must adhere to a certain standard of behavior so no one would look askance at ladies of quality taking a personal interest in their plight. Phoebe and Dulcie hadn't given the notion a second thought when they'd helped Caroline plan the society, but in the past few days the two unmarried members of the society had become keenly aware of the restrictions placed upon them and their charitable associations.

"But we haven't given up," Dulcie assured Caroline. "It's only a matter of time before we find the perfect candidates."

"Well..." Caroline rubbed her hands together. "That settles it. Lord Anthony Carlisle shall be the first beneficiary of our little charity."

"But, Caro, Lord Carlisle is a wealthy man," Dulcie pointed out. "He doesn't need our charity."

"I won't be offering charity," Caroline explained. "I'll be offering care."

"He won't accept it," Phoebe warned. "He's refused all invitations and all callers."

Caroline lifted her chin a notch higher. "He won't refuse. He won't have a choice. He cannot refuse a visit from a representative of the queen."

"What representative?" Phoebe asked.

"Me." Caroline grinned.

"But you don't represent the queen," Dulcie insisted.

"Yes, I do," Caroline replied. "And so do you." She glanced from Dulcie to Phoebe and back again. "We all do." Reaching out, Caroline lifted a parchment document from the table and showed it to her friends. "Queen Charlotte has agreed to sponsor our charity. I received the patent yesterday."

"From the queen herself?" Dulcie asked, her eyes widening with both shock and delight. "Caro, however, did you manage it?"

Caroline shrugged. "I petitioned the queen and Her Majesty replied. She specifically requested that our society, 'render all necessary aid and provide solace to members of His Majesty's Own regiments for the good of king and country.'" She pointed to the wording of the patent that had not appeared in her original petition. "As far as I'm concerned, that's tantamount to a royal command."

"If you're going to pass yourself off as a representative of the queen, I think it would be best if we call ourselves after the words of her patent. The Charlotte Society," Phoebe suggested.

"Agreed," Caroline replied. "We are the Charlotte Society, dedicated to the care and solace of His Majesty's Own and as one of His Majesty's Own, Tony will be the first to benefit from our care."

Phoebe frowned, still worried about the damage Lord Carlisle could inflict on her friend's tender sensibilities. "Caro, are you certain? He won't welcome you. He's aloof, withdrawn, sullen, and angry."

"He's hurt and frightened," Caro said. "He needs me."

Five years ago, Lord Anthony Carlisle had been a superb figure of a man, commanding respect from his peers and standing head and shoulders above most of the ton. He was energetic and athletic and had sat a horse with a grace and skill and beauty rarely matched by members of the ton. Caroline knew that for Tony, confinement would be a living hell he wouldn't care to have her witness.

"He has his pride," Phoebe pointed out.

"She's right, Caro," Dulcie agreed. "It might be best to wait until—"

"Until his bitterness festers and his bones and sinew have knit so firmly that walking again will be out of the question?" What her friends said was true. Tony had enough pride for a dozen men. His sense of pride and his innate confidence had been two of the qualities that had initially attracted her to him. She had loved the fact that

Anthony Carlisle was his own man. Not a political lackey. Or a royal one. He was a man who knew what he wanted in life and dedicated himself to it. But his pride could work to his detriment. Caroline knew that better than anyone. *Pride goeth before a fall.* She shook her head. "I can't."

"But, Caro..."

"I became Lord Blessing's wife because my father signed a contract that bound me to him and forced me to accept it," Caroline explained. "I spoke the words to Lord Blessing, but in my heart, I said my vows to Tony. For better or for worse. I chose him then and I choose him now."

# CHAPTER 3

*"And dar'st thou, then,*
*To beard the lion in his den,*
*The Douglas in his hall?"*
—Sir Walter Scott, 1771-1832

"I am Lady Blessing," Caroline announced, presenting her calling card with a flourish to the butler who had swept open the massive oak front door of the Park Lane town house. She had completed all but one of her morning calls, leaving her calling card at the homes of hostesses to whose functions she'd been invited and sharing "at homes" with her acquaintances.

This was the last call of the morning and Caroline was visibly nervous about paying it. Morning calls were paid to ladies. Never gentlemen. She knew she should not call upon an unmarried gentleman at his place of residence during her morning calls—or at any time if she wanted to maintain her unimpeachable reputation—and she most certainly should not call upon a gentleman when unaccompanied by a maid or companion or lady friend, but she couldn't wait a moment longer. She *had* to see him.

Caroline took a deep breath that did nothing to steady her nerves. She was about to break society's rules. She was about to flaunt a lifetime of teachings. But she was a widow now, and widows were not bound by the same strict rules of polite society as unmarried girls or married ladies. Or so she'd heard... Or so she *hoped*... "I've come on behalf of The Charlotte Society. Please inform Lord Carlisle that I am here."

The butler frowned, doing nothing to hide his dismay at finding an unaccompanied lady on Lord Carlisle's front steps. "I'm afraid there's been a mistake, Lady Blessing. We are a bachelor household. There are no ladies present for you to call upon."

Caroline's heart skipped a beat at the news. *We are a bachelor household. He* remained unmarried. "There has been no mistake," Caroline told the butler. "I'm here to see Lord Carlisle."

"Lord Carlisle is not at home, milady."

"He is *physically* present, is he not?" Caroline asked, fighting to keep the edge of panic she was feeling out of her voice.

"He is in residence, ma'am," the butler admitted, "but he is not receiving any callers."

Caroline inhaled, trying to calm her racing pulse, and prayed her wobbly legs would continue to support her. Tony was at home, just not at home to callers. "I'm sure he will see me if you tell him I am here."

"His Lordship instructed me to inform all visitors that he is not at home to them. And even if he were at home to visitors, it would be highly improper for Lord Carlisle to receive a lady in this manner."

Caroline nodded her head in sympathetic understanding of the butler's orders. "I'm sure you're quite right, Mister..."

"West, ma'am."

"That's right. I remember." She gifted the butler with a smile. "I'm sure you're quite right, West. It would be highly improper for Lord Carlisle to receive me if I had come here representing myself, but I've come as a representative of The Charlotte Society, a benevolent society sponsored by our most august majesty, Queen Charlotte, in order to render aid and provide solace to members of His Majesty's Own regiments. And as I'm most certain that Lord Carlisle would never deliberately request that the queen be turned away at his front door, I'm sure he wouldn't ask that the queen's representative be turned away, either. So, kindly inform His Lordship I am here to see him. I'll wait in the salon." She stepped over the threshold.

West moved back to avoid colliding with her in the doorway. "This is most unusual, ma'am."

"Yes, I know." Caroline glanced back at him over her shoulder as she marched through the entry and down the short hall to the salon. She had never been in Tony's house, but she'd paid calls at the ones to the right and left of him and knew that the Park Lane town houses were virtually identical in design. "It's a most unusual day."

~

*"Is Her Majesty with her?"*

The angry demand rumbled through the house, shaking the rafters and setting the crystals on the massive chandelier hanging above the marble entranceway vibrating. The tinkling sound of crystal striking crystal filled the hallway.

Seated on one of the matching striped satin sofas in the blue salon below, Caroline cast the ceiling an apprehensive look, recognizing Anthony Carlisle's voice. She had never heard him raise that voice in anger, but she still knew every nuance of it. She'd heard it thousands of times in person and in her dreams. It was Tony's voice, and even angry, the sound of it recalled a million different memories and sent a warm wave of awareness throughout her body.

"I beg your pardon, milord?"

"Is Queen Charlotte and the rest of her so-called benevolent society in the blue salon with Lady Blessing?" Lord Carlisle's voice rose slightly in volume as he carefully enunciated each word as if his butler was slow of thought as well as hard of hearing.

"No, milord."

"Then kindly remove Lady Blessing and her damned benevolence from my house."

"How, milord?"

*"How?"* Tony repeated. *"How?* I don't care how. You're bigger than she is. Pick her up and carry her out for all I care."

"Milord!" West was clearly shocked. "It would never do for a man in my position to manhandle a lady!"

"You let her in, you get her out," Tony ordered. "Do whatever it takes, West, but get that female out of my house. If you don't want to manhandle the lady, send Barnaby to do it. He's guarded me against Napoleon's minions for years. He can certainly handle Lady Bloody Blessing."

Caroline's eyes narrowed. She had already heard through society gossip that after Lord Carlisle's army batman had brought him home from Belgium, the man had stayed on to become Tony's personal manservant.

"Milord, you sent Barnaby to the chemist for more pain medication an hour or more ago. He should be returning any moment, but..."

*"Damnation,"* Tony swore. "A moment is too long to wait to have Lady Blessing removed from the premises. Call the footmen, then. Have them remove whatever article of furniture she's sitting on with her on it. Roll her up like Cleopatra in the Turkish carpet. Dust the marble floor with her pretty little backside. Drag her out by her heels. Open a window and shove her through it! I don't care how you accomplish the task, just do it."

"But, my lord..." West began.

His anger and his breath abruptly spent, Tony suddenly lowered his voice so that Caroline had to strain to hear it. "I would do the deed myself but..." He paused. "For God's sake, West, get her out of here. Don't let her see me like this."

Caroline couldn't hear the end of his tirade, but she had heard enough to recognize the lay of the land. Tony had made himself quite clear. He wanted nothing to do with her. He knew she was there in his house and had refused to see her. He knew she was there and had rejected her out of hand.

Caroline stiffened her spine and swallowed the lump in her throat. She rose from the sofa as West entered the blue salon. "You needn't worry about devising a believable fiction to explain Lord Carlisle's refusal to see me." She managed a small self-deprecating smile. "Or worry about removing me with the furnishings, dragging me about by my heels, dusting the marble floor with my backside, rolling me up in the Turkish carpet, or shoving me out the nearest window... I heard it all. Indeed, I am certain many of Lord Carlisle's Park Lane neighbors heard it as well. I shall spare you the need for violence and remove myself from his residence today, but you may inform Lord Carlisle that I shall return—with Her Majesty if needs be—but I *shall* return. I will not give up on him and he will not be rid of me quite as easily in the future..."

Drawing herself up to her full height, Caroline looked the butler in the eye, making it clear she meant every word. She would return. And she would keep returning until Tony agreed to see her. And if it took bringing the queen along to persuade him, then somehow Caroline would manage to do that. She wouldn't stop until she saw him, and it was only right to give his butler fair warning.

But today it was enough to know Tony was alive and upstairs. Today it was enough for Caroline to hear his voice—even if he was using that voice to dismiss her and have her removed from his house. She could withdraw from today's battle in order to fight again another day. "Good afternoon, West." Exiting the blue salon, Caroline made her way to the front door.

West opened the heavy oak door for her, then stepped back to allow Caroline to cross the threshold. "Good day, Lady Blessing."

Her spine was straight, her head held high, but her knees were quaking in reaction as Caroline walked the short distance down the path and through the gate to her coach parked beside the pavement.

"Where to, ma'am?" her coachman inquired as she climbed inside, settled onto the plush velvet seat, and closed her eyes.

"Home," she told him. "I want to go home." Home. Where she could reflect on her failure to get past Tony's defenses. Home. Where she could come up with another idea, another way to capture his undivided attention. Home. Where she could lick her wounds and console herself with the knowledge that the only witness to her complete and utter rejection and humiliation was Tony's butler...

# CHAPTER 4

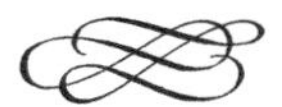

*"The virtue of Prosperity is temperance;*
*the virtue of Adversity is fortitude."*
—Francis Bacon, 1561-1626

"What the devil is she doing now?" Lord Anthony Carlisle scowled out the window, watching as Caroline made her way through the hole in the brick wall at the back of the garden. He watched her from the window just as he had watched her retreat to her carriage on the first day she'd come to call. Just as he'd watched her walk down the path and out through his front gate every day since.

Barnaby leaned forward to peer over Tony's shoulder. "It looks like she had the gate separating your garden from the one behind it removed." Barnaby couldn't quite keep the note of admiration out of his voice. Lady Bloody Blessing, as the major called her, was nothing if not persistent. The major had had his butler turn her away from the front door every day for the past fourteen days until this morning.

This morning she'd abruptly changed tactics and begun an assault on the back gate.

And this morning, the major had left his bedchamber for the first time since his return to London in order to gain a vantage point at a window overlooking the commotion in the garden behind the house. He had only moved from the window in his bedchamber to a window in the suite of rooms adjoining it, but after weeks of self-imposed exile in his bedchamber, any movement was progress....

"I can see that!" Tony shoved his chair away from the window, narrowly avoiding Barnaby's toes as he wheeled around to face him. "What I want to know is *why.*"

"Well, she wasn't getting anywhere with the front door," Barnaby said. "And she promised West she'd be back."

Tony snorted. "Caroline was always good at making promises..." The memory appeared unbidden as it always did when he least expected it.

*"Marry me, Caro. Promise you'll be my wife, share my life, and love me always."*

*"Oh, yes, Tony! I'll marry you. I'll be your wife and I promise to love only you for as long as I live."*

Caroline had promised to love and to marry him. She had done neither. And Tony had never managed to come to terms with her betrayal.

Barnaby cleared his throat. "People change, sir."

"Not *that* much."

"She's been here every day for nearly three weeks."

"What difference does it make if she comes here every day for the next five years?" Tony demanded. He'd kept track of time. He had been marking days off a printed calendar since the physician in Belgium—Doctor Guillory—had predicted his fate. "I'm not interested in her or her charitable society."

"You certainly appear interested in what's going on in the garden," Barnaby mumbled. "Interested enough to get yourself out of bed, washed, dressed, and in here."

"Why shouldn't I be interested?" Tony demanded once again.

"After all, it is *my* garden. And who can rest with all the racket? What the devil is she doing over there anyway? And who in the bloody hell gave her permission to trespass or demolish my garden gate? I don't recall her having any connection to that property. The last I heard it belongs to Viscount Selby."

"The old viscount died last winter," Barnaby told him. "Last *I* heard his heir suffered heavy losses at the gaming tables and put the estate up for sale."

"What?!" Tony exclaimed. "When? Why hasn't he come to me about it? I loaned the old man money on several occasions. I'll be happy to take the place off his hands." Carlisle hated to learn of the old viscount's death. Tony had been genuinely fond of the rakehell and had always considered him a friend and a good neighbor. Tony didn't know Rupert's heir at all. He supposed he might have been introduced to him at some ball or club, but if he had, the young heir had failed to make an impression.

Tony *had* known that Rupert Selby had concerns about his great-nephew. Bent over the chess board after supper one evening, the older viscount had expressed the fear that his young heir might squander his inheritance.

*"London holds many temptations for a wide-eyed young man from the Midlands." Selby had given Tony a rueful look. "I know. I was a wide-eyed lad from the Midlands myself when I came to town during the reign of the second George."*

Tony shook his head. It appeared Rupert Selby's concerns had been valid. The young viscount had managed to lose prime Park Lane property within six months of inheriting it. Vowing to make further inquiries into the property and the young heir's current situation, Tony turned his attention back to Barnaby. "I'll have my solicitor make an offer."

"No need, sir," Barnaby told him. "Lady Blessing has already purchased it."

Lord Carlisle arched his eyebrow in query. "Purchased? Lady Blessing bought Selby's house?"

Barnaby nodded.

"When?"

"The first of the month, sir. Rumor has it that she's had her man of business searching for suitable Park Lane or Park Lane Mews property since she learned of your return. She purchased the Selby house *before* it came on the market."

"How do you know this?" Tony was curious. Barnaby had been on the continent and away from town longer than he had. "Where the devil do you come by your information?"

"Servants talk, Major. And I've got ears. All I have to do is listen." Barnaby shrugged. "The estates share the back wall, so the gate is as much hers as it is yours. She isn't trespassing and she doesn't need permission to demolish it."

"She *is* trespassing," Tony replied. "She's on *my* side of the wall. And even if she weren't, the proper thing for her to do would be to consult with me about the shared wall before she demolished the gate and made a hole in the wall large enough to drive a loaded dray and a team through."

"Maybe that's what she's been trying to do." Barnaby's observation was calm and matter of fact. "Lady Blessing has been paying calls and leaving calling cards every day for the past weeks. Maybe she's been trying to tell you she planned to buy the Selby estate and renovate the garden—or the garden gate. You've only yourself to blame for refusing to see her."

Tony scoffed at Barnaby's rationale. "Then why didn't she write a letter informing me of her intentions? I may not be able to walk, but I'm still able to read and the post runs twice a day."

"Maybe she believed you'd ignore her letter the way you've ignored everything else." Barnaby didn't elaborate, but they both knew the major had received letters from Lady Blessing during his war years. Letters the major had never opened.

Tony pinned Barnaby with a hard stare. "Whose side are you on?"

"Are we taking sides, sir?" Barnaby blinked innocently at him. "Because we've just fought a war together and if we're siding up to fight another one, you ought to know by now that I'm on yours."

Tony knew his batman was right. His frustration at Caroline's persistence was no reason to question Barnaby's loyalty. He just didn't understand why Caroline seemed so determined to get his attention now when she had turned her back on him and married Granville Blessing.

Wheeling his chair back to the window, Tony watched as half a dozen workmen followed Caroline through the breach in the wall, trailing along behind her like obedient hounds as she made herself at home in *his* garden, pointing out statuary, flower beds, the open ground between the summer house, and the reflecting pool filled with goldfish. Leaning forward in his chair, he frowned. Caroline was up to something—something more than destroying the back gate between his garden and the one that, up until quite recently, had belonged to Viscount Rupert Selby and his heir. The question was what?

Tony exhaled, releasing a long breath. Her persistence was unexpected and completely out of character. She should have retreated and left him alone weeks ago.

Caroline Hardage wasn't a fighter. Not the Caroline Hardage he'd known. She'd retreated at the first sign of conflict and hadn't done so much as put up a favorable argument when her father refused his suit in favor of Lord Blessing's. She hadn't fought for the love he had believed they shared. Tony speared his fingers through his hair. She hadn't fought to hold onto him five years ago. So why the devil was she fighting now?

Why didn't she just go away and leave him alone?

What kind of game was she playing?

Why didn't she leave him in peace? Whatever peace he could find?

Tony gazed out the window. "She's guilty of trespassing now, Barnaby. And she's not by herself. She's brought her retinue into *my* garden without *my* permission." He sat up straighter and leaned closer, watching as a trio of Caroline's workmen removed a statue of Artemis from her pedestal and carried her away. "What the devil?" He turned to Barnaby in disbelief. "She just took *my* Artemis off her pedestal and absconded with her."

"Lady Blessing lifted a statue off a pedestal? By *herself*?" Barnaby leaned over his employer's shoulder to look out the window.

"Not Lady Blessing," Tony snapped. "Her bloody workmen. Look!" He pointed to the trio of workmen carrying a stone statue of the Greek goddess through the hole in the wall to Selby's estate. "Now, she's going after Apollo." He turned to his former batman. "My great-grandfather fancied himself a Greek scholar. He added the reflecting pool and those statues of Greek gods and goddesses to the gardens when he became earl. Lady Blessing has no right to direct her workmen to steal them."

"She might not be directing the men to steal them, sir," Barnaby pointed out.

"What would you call it?"

"She could be *borrowing* them."

"Borrowing?" Tony snorted. "Who the devil borrows antiquarian Greek statues? For what purpose?"

"Maybe she's redesigning the Selby House gardens and wants to show the gardeners and the stone masons what she wants. Or maybe she plans to turn Selby House into a museum."

"You think so?"

"I don't know, sir," Barnaby admitted. "But it's possible."

"Is it?" Tony didn't bother to hide his disbelief. "Why don't you go find out before Calliope disappears?" He pointed to the workmen standing at the head of the queue of Muses surrounding the reflecting pool.

"Me, sir?" Barnaby was once again the soul of innocence. "I'm a former batman. Shouldn't you send Gerald? He's the head groundskeeper?"

Carlisle spun his chair in a tight half-circle to face his batman.

Barnaby took a quick step backward to avoid the chair's wheels.

"Do you see Gerald anywhere?" Tony demanded. "Is he anywhere in sight?"

Barnaby took note of the men working below. "No, sir."

"She has a crew of workmen removing *my* statues from *my*

garden," Tony said. "Right under the head groundskeeper's nose. How effective would you say Gerald has been in dealing with Lady Blessing?"

"What about West? He's the head of your household. Lady Blessing listened to him."

"I've *been* sending West for a fortnight," Tony reminded him. "She may have pretended to listen to him, but West has been as ineffective as Gerald. Clearly, Lady Blessing hasn't *heard* a word he's said."

"What makes you think she'll listen to me?" Barnaby asked.

"I don't." Tony threw up his hands in exasperation. "But there's nobody else to send. And you're my personal manservant."

"That's right, sir. I'm your personal manservant." Barnaby repeated, emphasizing his status in the household.

Tony fixed his gaze on his former orderly. "As my personal manservant, you're closer to me than anyone. If any man knows my mind, it's you. She may listen to you once you explain your position in my household."

Barnaby looked skeptical.

Tony gave him a knowing smile, then spread his hands in a gesture that encompassed his wheelchair and the fact that he was confined to it. "I'd go myself if I could."

Barnaby's expression grew more skeptical. After avoiding the woman for days on end, the manservant doubted Lord Carlisle would willingly confront her—even if she *was* absconding with his great grandfather's statues.

Tony didn't miss his batman's expression. "I would," he assured him. "If the situation was different. If I wasn't confined to this chair."

The two men faced each other. If the situation was different. If Tony could get out of his chair, he wouldn't have spent all this time avoiding Lady Caroline Blessing. Or manipulating his manservant and butler into facing Lady Blessing for him.

"I'm not ordering you to go out to the garden," Tony said. "I'm asking you as a friend to volunteer to satisfy my curiosity and find out about her so-called charity and what that little schemer is about."

Barnaby watched as his employer followed the action in the garden from his position at the window. He hadn't seen the major this animated since before the Battle of Quatre Bras. He didn't dare show it, but Barnaby was looking forward to meeting the young woman who had finally penetrated Lord Anthony Carlisle's shell of bitterness and pain.

# CHAPTER 5

*"I like to convince people rather than stand on mere authority."*
—Duke of Wellington, 1769-1852

"Do you want us to move this one too, ma'am?" The workman standing before the statue of Calliope tugged at his forelock as he addressed the Marchioness of Blessing.

"Yes, that one, too," Caroline said, gazing up at the face of the goddess. "I want you to move all of them."

The workman pointed at each statue as he counted. "You want us to move all nine of them?"

Caroline graced him with her warmest smile. "The nine Muses and Hermes, Pan, and Eros." Seeing the workman's frown, she indicated the three smaller statues at the centers of three different sections of the formal rose garden.

The workman groaned.

Caroline could understand him not wanting to move three additional chunks of marble through a rose garden, but she was paying top wages for the job. "If moving all the statues is more than you wish to take on, I'll contact the staffing agency to make other arrangements..." She let her voice trail off.

Caroline didn't want to threaten the workman with unemployment or be forced to return to the staffing agency to hire other workmen, but her mission was more important than the complaints of the workmen. And she would do what she had to do to get what she wanted done.

"No need, your ladyship." The workman gave a deferential nod. "We'll get these statues moved for you right away."

"I'll be most grateful," Caroline told him.

"You must be Lady Blessing."

Caroline turned at the sound of her name spoken in a voice she didn't recognize. She watched as a tall, heavily built man with the rigid posture of a career soldier left the flagstone terrace at the rear of the town house and walked toward her. "I am," she said. "And who might you be?"

"Barnaby, ma'am." He gave a slight bow as he reached her. "I'm a member of Lord Carlisle's household."

"Mr. Barnaby," she repeated warmly. His voice was rough, not coarse but low and gravelly. He didn't sound like a servant and he wasn't wearing a wig or the knee breeches, stockings, and buckle shoes of household livery, nor was he dressed well enough to be a valet. She drew her brows together as a thought occurred. "Don't tell me Lord Carlisle sacked his butler for failing to roll me up in the carpets and toss me out?"

"No, ma'am." The corners of Barnaby's mouth turned up in a barely distinguishable smile. "Mr. West is still with us."

"That's a relief," Caroline said. "I was afraid I might have placed him in a difficult situation with his employer."

"No need to worry, milady. Mr. West's position is secure. He's been with the family since Lord Carlisle was a boy."

"And you?"

"I'm a more recent addition to Carlisle House."

Caroline laughed. "You must have drawn the short straw."

Barnaby shook his head. "As a matter of fact, I volunteered for this mission."

Caroline appreciated his forthrightness. "All right, Mr. Barnaby," she said. "You wish to speak with me?"

"Yes, ma'am."

"About?"

"The assault on Lord Carlisle's back wall."

Caroline glanced at the gaping hole in the fence between the grounds of the house she'd purchased from the current Viscount Selby and Anthony Carlisle's estate. Although it wasn't what she had intended, Caroline had to admit her destruction of the gate and the wall did resemble an assault. Crossing her arms over her chest, she settled into a defensive stance. "I've attempted to discuss my plans with Lord Carlisle and have been summarily turned away at the front door since my very first visit. Did Mr. West send you to challenge my presence here?"

"No, ma'am." Barnaby glanced up at a first-floor window overlooking the garden. "*He* did."

Caroline followed Barnaby's gaze. She didn't see a man at the window, but the movement of the drapery offered proof that someone had been there. "Lord Carlisle?"

"Yes, ma'am."

"Tell me, Mr. Barnaby, what exactly do you do in Lord Carlisle's household?"

"It's not *Mr.* Barnaby. Just Barnaby," he said. "I serve as His Lordship's batman. And I generally do whatever His Lordship requires me to do."

Caroline knew, from her recent association with military men, that Army officers were assigned batmen, sometimes called orderlies, to see to their needs, to act as valets and as head of the officer's household. Batmen oversaw the setting up and the taking down of the officer's headquarters and of the officer's pack horse and kit. "Have you been with Lord Carlisle long?"

Barnaby stood at attention. "A bit under five years. My service with the major began when he joined the regiment."

"And continued after he left it," Caroline murmured. "I suppose you're very loyal to him."

"Very, your ladyship," Barnaby confirmed. "Although the major might disagree at times."

Caroline looked up at Barnaby from beneath her lashes. "I don't suppose you would ever entertain the idea of disregarding his orders..."

"Not directly," Barnaby said.

"Did he order you to remove me from the premises?"

"Not at all."

"Because I've paid a call at his house every day since I learned of his return," Caroline said. "And he has refused to speak with me."

"He hasn't changed his mind, milady."

"If he didn't send you to get rid of me, what does he want you to do?"

Barnaby smiled a genuine smile. "He sent me to satisfy his curiosity."

"About what?"

"You, Lady Blessing."

"Me?" Caroline gave an unladylike snort. "I'm no mystery to Lord Carlisle. We are well acquainted."

"Once, perhaps," Barnaby told her. "But you appear to have changed."

Caroline studied Tony's manservant, a quizzical expression on her face. "You and I have never met. How can you know whether or not I've changed?"

"I don't know anything about your personal life, Lady Blessing," Barnaby said. "But I recognize a change in tactics when I see one and you've changed your tactics."

"I had no choice." She straightened her shoulders. "Since my frontal assault wasn't working, I decided a change was in order."

"As any good soldier would," Barnaby agreed. "When his previous tactic is unsuccessful."

"I don't know if this one will work any better," Caroline admitted.

"It already has," Barnaby said.

Caroline's expression was skeptical.

"You got his attention," he told her. "His Lordship hadn't entered that room of the house since we returned to London. Until he heard the commotion this morning..."

"I suppose he's watching to see if you'll be as successful at convincing me to retreat from the premises as his butler has been."

"He's watching," Barnaby admitted, "because he wants to know why you're stealing his great-grandfather's statues."

Caroline bit her bottom lip. "I suppose it may seem that way to His Lordship, but I'm not stealing his statues."

Barnaby lifted an eyebrow in query.

"I'm temporarily *removing* them for safekeeping. They'll be returned once the project is completed. I can assure you it was never my intent to *keep* them."

"He'll be relieved to hear it." Barnaby rocked back on his heels. "But the fact is that you have no right to remove them for safekeeping or otherwise without His Lordship's permission, milady. The statues have occupied space on his property since the time of his great-grandsire. They belong to him."

"His Lordship refused to give me his permission," she pointed out, "when he refused to speak with me."

"It's doubtful he would have given permission for your project if he *had* spoken with you," Barnaby told her. "Now, he'll be wanting to know why you've disregarded his rightful share of ownership of the back wall, trespassed, and removed the statues to begin a renovation on his property."

"Knowing Lord Carlisle, he'll want to know how I managed to purchase the property from Lord Selby in the first place," Caroline said.

"He does."

"Then he'll have to satisfy my curiosity."

Barnaby frowned. "How, milady?"

She smiled. "If Lord Carlisle wants to know how I came to possess Viscount Selby's property, he'll have to ask me himself."

"And the destruction of the gate and the garden?"

"He will have to ask me about those as well."

"I'll relay your message." Barnaby turned to leave.

His sudden retreat surprised Caroline. "You're not going to try to stop me?"

Barnaby gave her a conspiratorial look. "Not my place to stop you."

His answer gave her pause. "Will Ton—will His Lordship?"

"One can only hope."

Caroline smiled. "Will he be angry with you?"

Barnaby nodded. "Most likely."

"Angry enough to dismiss you?"

"No, ma'am," Barnaby said. "He'll be angry for sure, but it won't be the first time His Lordship has lost his temper with me. And it won't be the last. But he's not one to hold a grudge."

Caroline suspected she might be the exception when it came to Tony's failure to hold a grudge, but she didn't say it. "I'm delighted to hear it."

Barnaby turned to leave again.

"Barnaby..."

"Yes, ma'am?"

She glanced up at the window. "Is this the first time Lord Carlisle has watched me? Or has he been watching me all along?"

"Not from there," Barnaby replied.

"But he's watched me from other windows." It was not a question, but a statement.

"Only one."

"Which one?"

"The one overlooking the front walk and the street beyond."

Caroline sighed. She would have sworn she'd felt his gaze on her several mornings when she'd left his house. The feeling had been so strong, so real, she had shivered in anticipation. But when she had looked back at the window, he was never there, and Caroline had begun to doubt. "Then I didn't imagine it," she murmured.

"No, your ladyship. You did not," Barnaby said solemnly.

"I've never been past Lord Carlisle's drawing room. I'm not

familiar with the arrangement of the rooms in his house." She glanced up at the window once again, hoping to catch a glimpse of Tony, but the drapery remained still. "That room overlooks the back garden, not the front. So, tell me, Barnaby, is that Lord Carlisle's bedchamber?"

"No, ma'am." Barnaby scratched his head. "His bedchamber overlooks the front walk. The room he's in this morning is one of the suites of rooms used for entertaining and fancy parties."

"The ballroom?"

"That's the one."

Caroline frowned. That must be bittersweet. The Anthony Carlisle she had known had been welcome in every ballroom in town. He was an excellent dancer and as a most eligible bachelor, he'd been in great demand as a partner. Now, he was peeking at the world from behind the draperies. "The only ballroom I've ever known Lord Carlisle to avoid is Almack's Assembly Rooms on Wednesday nights during the season even though the patronesses were always trying to persuade him to attend."

"That was before he left for the war, wasn't it, ma'am?"

"Yes, it was."

"War changes a man." Barnaby followed her gaze to the window high above them. "Some more than others."

"Then the rumors I heard in town are true." Caroline drew herself up to her full height, took a deep breath, and looked Barnaby in the eye.

He didn't pretend not to understand. "That depends on what rumors you heard."

"I heard Lord Carlisle's legs were crushed and that he's confined to an invalid chair." She raised her chin a bit higher. "I want to know if it's true."

"He was confined to bed." Barnaby didn't look away and he didn't mince words, but was careful not to betray the major's trust. "He's progressed to the wheeled chair. This morning was the first morning I didn't help him out of bed and into his chair."

Caroline drew her brows together. "I'm not sure I understand what you mean..."

"When I arrived to assist him with his morning ablutions, his bedchamber was empty. I found him in the ballroom washed, shaved, dressed, and sitting in his chair, watching you directing your workmen in the removal of his ancestor's tributes to the Greek gods from the window overlooking the rear gardens." Barnaby grinned at her. "As far as I'm concerned, that's progress. So if it's all the same to you, your ladyship, I'm going to tell the major you refused to explain your actions to me or to halt what you are doing unless he personally tells you to do so."

"That's exactly what you *should* tell him," Caroline said. "Because it's true."

"It's also sure to upset him," Barnaby added.

"Enough for him to take action." Caroline expelled the breath she hadn't realized she'd been holding. "I hope."

"He's stubborn, ma'am. And bitter." Barnaby's rough voice held a note of concern. "He won't thank you for interfering. Are you sure you know what you're doing?"

"I'm not sure of anything, Barnaby. Except that if I don't do something, Lord Carlisle will wither away and die in that wheelchair."

# CHAPTER 6

*"It is the nature of the nobility to desire to dominate."*
—Machiavelli, 1469-1527

"You're back." Major Lord Carlisle's surly observation greeted his batman as soon as Barnaby entered the room. "But she's still out there directing her workmen." Tony watched as two workmen lifted Calliope off her pedestal. "There goes Calliope."

"That was fast." Barnaby moved close enough to peer out the window and watched as the statue disappeared through the hole in the back wall and out of view. "She didn't waste any time."

Irritated by the note of admiration in Barnaby's voice, Tony glared up at his batman. "*She* didn't. I'm not certain I can say the same about *you*."

"You misjudge my efforts, major." Eyeing the empty medicine bottle beside the major's coffee cup, Barnaby refused to take exception. The major had suffered through an uneasy night.

Ever since Lady Blessing had taken it upon herself to knock down the back gate, the major had begun working harder, insisting Barnaby manipulate his long-atrophied muscles and limbs, forcing them to move for longer periods of time each morning. But with the major's exertion came pain. And with increased pain came the consumption of larger doses of laudanum to ease it. The bottle that had held several doses of medicine last night was empty this morning.

"Perhaps," Tony conceded. "At any road, I would never have expected it of you, Barnaby."

"Expected what, sir?"

"Betrayal."

"I haven't betrayed you, sir."

Tony snorted. "What would you call it? I thought I sent you to get rid of her."

"And I thought you sent me to find out what the '*little schemer was up to*'," Barnaby countered.

"Did you?" Carlisle demanded.

"Did I what, sir?"

"Find out why she's trespassing in my garden and stealing my statuary?"

"She's not stealing the statues, sir," Barnaby said.

"All evidence to the contrary," Tony replied, watching as the workmen lowered Terpsichore from her pedestal and began wrapping her in sheets of canvas.

"She doesn't intend to keep them. She's having them removed for safekeeping during the renovations."

"What renovations?" Carlisle asked through gritted teeth, struggling to keep from shouting.

"To the gardens."

"*My* gardens? Or *hers*?"

"She didn't say, sir."

Tony glanced at the ceiling, then slowly counted to ten. "What *did* she say?"

"Lady Blessing said she would have discussed her plans with you, but you refused to see her, so she wasn't able to enlighten you."

"I don't need enlightening," Tony snapped. "*She* does. She's the one breaking the law. Not I." He followed Terpsichore's journey from the reflecting pool through the hole in the back wall, where she was hopefully reunited with her sisters. Wheeling his chair around to face his batman, Tony skewered Barnaby with a look. "And what the devil did she do with Gerald?" Tony's head groundskeeper had been conspicuously absent from his duties all morning. "Did she remove him for safekeeping as well?"

"I don't know." Barnaby shrugged. "She didn't mention Gerald, sir."

"Well, go back and find out where he is and why he isn't protecting my gardens from her assault. Tell her I'll have no part of her plans or her renovations. Tell her she's to remove her workmen and herself from my garden forthwith. And—"

"I can't do that, sir," Barnaby said.

Carlisle widened his eyes at that. "Why not?"

"Lady Blessing refuses to take orders from me."

"Balderdash!" Tony exclaimed. "Caroline Hardage takes orders from everyone." The girl he had known had been entirely biddable and obedient. If she'd ever refused to take orders from anyone, Tony wasn't aware of it. She'd certainly never defied her father.

"I don't know Caroline Hardage," Barnaby said. "I only know Lady Blessing."

"They're one and the same," Carlisle said.

"Are they, sir?" Barnaby queried. "Because she said to tell you if you want her gone from your gardens, you'll have to tell her yourself. Face-to-face."

Tony recoiled. "That's impossible. I won't have her in here and I have no way to get out there—"

"Major, Kirby and Fielder..."

"Without assistance, Barnaby." Tony forced the words through clenched teeth. "Without being carried. I refuse to be carried and placed, like a supplicant, at Lady Blessing's feet."

"But, sir..."

Tony glared at him. "I will not allow her to see me that way. Sitting perhaps," he relented slightly. "But never carried by a footman like a babe in arms." He glared at his former batman. "If I face her at all, it will be from a position of strength. Not weakness. Do you understand?"

Barnaby ran his hand over his closely shorn hair before nodding.

"You want to negotiate from a position of strength. I understand, sir."

"Good." Tony rubbed his hand over his face before pinning Barnaby with a stern look. "Because I'm not certain I could bear the look of pity on her face when she realizes I can't stand on my own. It's difficult enough for me to face servants who've known me all my life. But Caroline? What kind of man would do that to the woman he..." Unable to continue, Tony gave the empty medicine bottle a glance.

"Those are Lady Blessing's terms, sir."

Tony heaved a heavy sigh before reaching up to tug the draperies closed. He slumped forward in his chair. "I suppose it's time the gardens *were* renovated. Everything else about home has changed. Why shouldn't they?"

CAROLINE GLANCED DOWN AT THE TIMEPIECE PINNED TO THE LAPEL OF the pinafore she wore to protect her dress. She'd dismissed the workmen a half hour earlier after securing their promise to return at half-past six in the morning. The work crew had removed seven of the nine statues from Tony's garden and sent them to the stone mason to be cleaned and stored until the renovations were completed.

The workmen had accomplished a great deal, but their work was far from done. There were two Muses, three lesser gods, four sundials, two fountains, and six stone benches with which to contend. Not to mention the goldfish in the reflecting pool.

After the workmen left for the day, Caroline had spent an hour wandering the gardens taking stock of what must be done before the next phase of the renovations began, hoping Tony would appear.

But her hopes were dashed.

All her efforts had gone for nil. She hated to admit it, even to herself, but she'd been counting on her latest tactic to work. She strolled the gardens, taking longer than she wished to marshal her resources and pull herself together. Now she had no choice but to rush so she wouldn't be late for the weekly progress meeting of The Charlotte Society.

"Caro, tell us. We've been on tenterhooks waiting to hear all about it. Did it work?" Dulcie bombarded her with questions as soon as she entered the foyer of Blessing House.

Caroline spared a glance for her friends, then removed her bonnet and gloves and handed her duster to the butler. "I'm sorry I'm late," she began in a rush. "Inspecting the gardens with the head workman took longer than I expected. Did Tyson see to your comforts?"

"Yes, of course," Dulcie confirmed, nodding toward the Marquess of Blessing's longtime loyal retainer and head of household. "He was most hospitable."

"Miss." Tyson bowed slightly to acknowledge Dulcie's compliment, then turned to Caroline. "Ma'am, now that you've returned to entertain your guests, I'll see to your refreshments. If you and the young ladies will remove to the Petite Salon."

Caroline frowned. "I prefer the morning room."

"I beg your pardon, ma'am." Tyson's bland expression didn't so much as flicker. "But the morning room is unavailable. The Petite Salon has been made ready for you and your guests."

"Make the morning room available, Tyson."

"That's not possible, Madam."

"Then deliver the tray to the Petite Salon. We'll collect it there."

Gesturing for Caroline, Dulcie, and Phoebe to precede him, the butler ushered them into the little salon, then backed away, closing the doors behind him.

"Caro, how long are you going to keep him on?" Phoebe demanded once Tyson retreated.

"He's a loyal family retainer," Caroline said. "I can't dismiss him. He's lived and worked here most of his life."

"But to ignore Tyson's blatant disregard for your wishes," Dulcie continued. "Lord Blessing is dead and buried, as are all the Blessings before him. It is *your* house now. You should be able to have your household run to suit you, not your dead husband."

It was no secret to her friends that the staff of Blessing House rarely recognized her as mistress of the house. During her marriage, Lord Blessing's word had been law. His bride had been regarded as too young and inexperienced to run a household. Tyson and Mrs. Tyson ran the house as they had always run it—without regard to Caroline's wishes.

The new Lady Blessing's activities had been confined to the rooms of the house her husband designated as appropriate for ladies—the Morning Room, the Petite Salon, and the Music Room. The use of the other rooms—including the library and the formal dining room—had been forbidden to her unless her husband granted permission for her to enter them for a specific purpose or invited her to join him in one of them.

She was allowed to enter the dining room to oversee the table settings and the flower arrangements when guests were expected, but guests were infrequent. Lord Blessing had generally entertained his contemporaries at his club or his favorite restaurant. The exception to that rule was her father. Lord Rushton dined at Blessing House every Wednesday evening. On all other nights at home, Lord Blessing dined on a tray in the library and Caroline dined on a tray in her room.

She had thought herself confined as an unmarried girl in her father's house, but she'd been free to use the entire house—including the library—and free to receive and entertain guests and to go about her usual activities. The same could not be said of the time she'd spent as Lord Blessing's wife. Caroline sighed. Her husband had been dead nearly two years, yet his butler still adhered to his dictates, routinely disregarding her wishes in favor of her late husband's.

But that was about to change.

Caroline had had no reason to upset the household routine after her husband's death. No reason to impose her authority as the marchioness and insist on changes while she and the household were in mourning. Widows were excluded from society during their period of mourning. While members of the ton attended the funeral and sent notes of condolence, no one paid morning calls or issued invitations to dinners or fetes or dances she could not attend. For nearly two years, her only callers had been Phoebe, Dulcie, her father, and her husband's solicitor.

Caroline smiled. Phoebe and Dulcie had come to see *her*. Even her husband's solicitor, who had come to the house to discuss business, inquired about her well-being. But her father did not. He questioned her about her business dealings, but never once had he asked about her. Or about how she was coping with the loss of her husband.

Her father probably believed, or hoped, she was too grief-stricken over the loss of her husband to notice that all her father's visits, with the exception of his regular Wednesday evenings, had come on the heels of her solicitor's. But Caro was very much aware of Lord Rushton's machinations and his desire to control the property and the fortune her husband had bequeathed to her even more than he wanted to reassert his control over her life.

Hearing Tyson's approach as he returned with their refreshments, Caroline placed her finger against her lips, gesturing for her friends to hold their questions and comments until the butler left the room.

Phoebe was practically bouncing in her seat as Tyson delivered the tea and cakes. He set the butler's table down beside Caroline. "Shall I pour, ma'am?"

"No, thank you, Tyson," Caroline replied. "I'll see to it."

The butler pursed his lips in a show of disapproval, but refrained from commenting.

"I'll ring for you if we require anything more. Otherwise, you may collect the tray and the dishes in one hour."

"But, madam..."

"That's all, Tyson."

His eyes narrowing slightly, Tyson gave her a barely discernible bow and withdrew from the room.

Caroline counted to ten, then picked up the butler's table. "Dulcie, open the door."

"Where are we going?" Dulcie asked.

"To the morning room."

Phoebe smiled at Caroline. "I thought the morning room was unavailable."

"Not to me." The china rattled as Caroline secured her grip on the heavy table, carrying it through the doorway and down the corridor to the morning room. She set the butler's table beside her favorite chair and began pouring tea for Phoebe and Dulcie. "Not anymore." She smiled at her friends. "I've been the Marchioness of Blessing for five years. It's time I put the title to use."

"Huzzah!" Dulcie proclaimed, executing a perfect curtsey.

"I'm making changes," Caroline told them. "Starting today."

"So, you did it," Phoebe said. "You purchased Viscount Selby's town house."

"Yes, I did."

"What was it like?" Dulcie asked.

Caroline took a moment to reply. "It's larger than this house and although the gardens have been badly neglected since the old viscount died, they are beautifully designed around a spectacular fountain."

"No," Dulcie said. "What was it like to buy a house for yourself? What was it like to go against society and break the rules?"

"Thrilling," Caroline admitted. "And terrifying. I've always done the expected. Always obeyed the rules. Doing the unexpected is somewhat unnerving. At times, I wasn't certain my limbs would support me."

"But you did it," Dulcie reminded her.

"Yes, I did." Caroline gave a decisive nod of her head. "And there's no going back. Now, I have to go forward."

"So, tell us about the house," Phoebe said. "Was it what you expected?"

"It could use some modernization. The old viscount hasn't made any changes since George the Second's reign, so it's a bit old-fashioned and dark with heavy draperies and mahogany furniture. But it has wonderful windows and a beautiful orangerie paved with Spanish tiles. And I have some ideas."

Dulcie set her cup on its saucer. "For what?"

"For brightening it up and making it more comfortable and cozier."

"Are you planning to live there?"

"I'm considering it." Caroline poured them each a cup of tea, set a plate of tiny frosted cakes on the settee cushion beside Dulcie, helped herself to a cake, and began relating the mornings events, starting with her arrival at her newly acquired town house and ending with her solitary tour to check the progress on the Carlisle House grounds.

"I think you should live there," Dulcie said firmly. "It would be more convenient."

"I would be much closer to the gardens."

Dulcie heaved an exasperated sigh. "You'd be much closer to *Carlisle*."

"I don't know if that's an advantage or a disadvantage," Caroline admitted. "He's not happy about the destruction of the back gate or the removal of his great-grandfather's Greek statues." Caroline gave a small smile. "Of course, I'm going to put everything back after the renovations are finished."

"Did you tell him that?" Phoebe scooted to the edge of her seat. "What did he say?"

"He didn't say anything." Caroline's stomach growled and she automatically selected another cake and bit into it. She had been so excited this morning she hadn't broken her fast and so busy at the noon hour, she hadn't given a meal any thought at all. "But I know he's not happy."

"How do you know?"

"Barnaby told me."

"Who's Barnaby?" Phoebe asked.

"Tony's former batman." Caroline repeated her conversation with Barnaby.

"Did you see Carlisle?" Dulcie asked when Caroline finished speaking.

Caro reached for her cup and took a sip of tea. "No. All I saw was the flutter of the curtains at the window."

"Oh, Caro..." Leaning closer, Phoebe reached over and squeezed Caroline's hand. "I'm so sorry."

Caroline straightened her spine and met her friend's gaze. "Don't be. If he had seen me today, Tony would have asked me to leave. And might have barred me from setting foot on his property again."

"You think so?" Dulcie asked, helping herself to another cake.

"I know so. He would have no choice. He has to maintain discipline and reestablish authority over his household." Caroline shrugged. "After all, I had his head groundskeeper working on *my* side of the fence."

"You had *his* head groundskeeper working for you? And you thought it was a good idea to issue an ultimatum to Carlisle?" Phoebe gave a delicate shudder. "That was rather bold, Caro."

"I had to do *something* to get his attention," Caroline said.

Dulcie giggled. "I'll bet you've got his attention now."

"Maybe. Maybe not." Caroline chewed at her bottom lip. "But I had to try."

"You certainly have broken out of the old Caroline's shell." Dulcie giggled harder.

Caroline pinned Dulcie with a fierce look. "You're the one who's been telling me I need to speak up for myself and to be more assertive. Ten minutes ago, you were urging me to dismiss Tyson."

"I thought you'd start with small steps," Dulcie confessed.

"I did," Caroline said. "When I started the Charlotte Society."

"And we're glad you did," Phoebe told her. "But, Caro, the whole thing might have blown up in your face."

"It still might," Caroline admitted. "But that's a chance I'm willing to take."

"You're going back?" Dulcie was genuinely surprised. Despite Caroline's protestations of turning over a new leaf, Dulcie found it hard to believe that Caro would really do it. She'd always been so obedient, so *dutiful,* so *predictable.*

"I have to return." Caroline smiled. "I've destroyed the back gate and a portion of Lord Anthony Carlisle's garden. I've no choice but to see this project through to the end."

"Carlisle is sure to object," Phoebe replied.

"I expect him to," Caroline said.

"How are you going to convince him to let you help him, Caro?" Dulcie asked. "When he's refused to see you every time you've paid a call. And sent his butler and his batman to remove you from his property."

"I'm going to ignore his demands," Caroline said. "He can have me removed from his property, but I'll be next door and I'll keep returning until I wear him down," Caroline replied, a stubborn set to her chin. "I'm not going to accept any orders that come from his staff. Eventually, he'll have to see me."

Her friends were looking at her as if she had taken leave of her senses. "Caro, you know Carlisle wants you gone," Dulcie finally said. "You said you heard him that first day."

"He wanted me gone one day almost three weeks ago," Caroline insisted. "I didn't hear him say anything today."

"His batman told you what Carlisle said," Phoebe said.

"But did he mean it? Tony could have demanded I abandon the garden himself. He had every opportunity to open a window and shout down at me. But he didn't. So I'm going to continue the renovations until Lord Anthony Carlisle tells me to not to himself."

"But, Caro, you're being so..."

"Unreasonable? Obstinate?" Caroline met Dulcie's gaze with an unflinching one of her own. "You're right. The old Caroline never protested authority. Never fought back. Never defended what she believed in. Never said anything. Never *did* anything that might cause her family embarrassment or displeasure or jeopardize her chances for an advantageous marriage." Caroline squared her shoulders and sat up straighter on her chair. "But I'm not the old Caroline any longer. For the first time in my life, I am going to be my own person. And for that alone, I'm grateful to Lord Blessing."

He hadn't liked it, but Lord Blessing had agreed to the only demand Caroline had made during her marriage. In exchange for being his dutiful and scandal-free wife, Lord Blessing had prevailed upon Parliament and the Crown to grant letters of patent and a royal warrant with a special remedy for Caroline to become the Marchioness of Blessing in her own right.

And the Prince Regent, acting in his father's stead, had granted the request. The title of Marquess of Blessing had been placed in abeyance for the nine months following Lord Blessing's death to prevent the possibility of disinheriting a legitimate heir in the event Lady Blessing should give birth to a child during that time.

One month later, the title was terminated, and Caroline Hardage Blessing was created *suo jure* Marquess of Blessing with all the hereditary rights and honors the title entailed. Without benefit of, or interference from, a legal guardian. The arrangement was highly unusual, but Lord Blessing had been a powerful man at court and a close advisor to two kings and a Prince Regent who valued his services.

Phoebe heaved a put-upon sigh. "Caro, you were miserable living here with Lord Blessing."

"Under the circumstances, I would have been miserable anywhere," Caroline agreed. "I was not happy at the prospect of becoming the Marchioness of Blessing."

"And nothing has changed," Dulcie reminded her. "You're still miserable. So miserable you purchased another town house across the park rather than continue to live in this one."

"That's true," Caroline agreed. "But it's not the only reason. Purchasing Selby House is a necessary part of my plan. And Lord Blessing made it possible for me to do what I need to do to help Tony."

"Lord Blessing never did anything to accommodate you, Caro," Phoebe reminded her. "He humiliated you at every turn while he was alive."

"In your own home." Dulcie fixed her gaze on Caroline. "In front of the servants, who continue to disregard your instructions and your wishes two years after his death."

"That's also true," Caroline cheerfully admitted.

Dulcie rattled her cup against her saucer as she set it down with more force than necessary. "How can you be so—so—infuriatingly *congenial* about it?"

"There's no point in being anything else," Caroline pointed out. "What's done cannot be undone. Lord Blessing's regard or lack of regard for me is over. He's dead and buried. There's no sense holding a grudge now. And how ungrateful would I be if I did?"

"How can you deceive yourself into believing you *should* be grateful to a man who held you in such low regard?" Phoebe was clearly shocked at Caroline's choice of words. "How could you possibly be anything but ungrateful to him?"

Caroline drew her brows together. "Lord Blessing and I came to an understanding after my father signed the marriage contracts. I lived up to my end of the agreement and Lord Blessing lived up to his."

"You, by becoming all but invisible," Dulcie concluded. "Him, by dying."

"However it came about, he kept his word," Caroline's tone forbade further argument. "And in so doing, he gave me the greatest of gifts. He gave me my personal and financial freedom. And although I didn't know it at the time, something much more valuable..."

"What?" Phoebe asked.

"A title." Caroline grinned. "And as marchioness, I outrank my father *and* Earl Carlisle."

Dulcie thought for a moment, then cleared her throat before she spoke. "You outranked them both the moment you plighted your troth to Lord Blessing."

"Which means I no longer have to answer to either one of them," Caroline continued. "Lord Rushton can't run roughshod over me. Nor can he choose another husband for me. And Anthony Carlisle can get as angry as he likes at what I am doing to his gardens, but he can't stop me unless he's willing to bring suit against me and cause a scandal."

Phoebe frowned. "What about the scandal you're going to cause when word of this gets out? Have you thought about that?"

"Of course I've thought about it," Caroline said. "If my purchase of Lord Selby's house causes a scandal, there's very little I can do about it." She gave a Gallic shrug. "It's done. And if my moving into that house once it's refurbished causes a scandal, there's nothing I can do about that, either." She met Phoebe's worried gaze. "I'm sure I'd cause more scandal by moving into Tony's house."

Dulcie's eyes widened in shock. "Is that what you intend to do?"

Caroline shook her head. "Eventually..."

"Eventually?" Dulcie repeated. "Caro, you cannot be serious!"

"I've never been more serious about anything in my life."

"But the scandal..." Dulcie began.

"Hang scandal!" Caroline said. "I intend to do what I should have done years ago."

"What's that?" Phoebe asked.

"Change," Caroline said. "I'm going to be a vastly different Lady Blessing than I was when I was married. I'm going to live my life the way I see fit. And I am going to see to it that Anthony Carlisle can do the same. Whether he likes it or not."

# CHAPTER 7

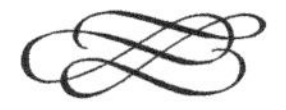

*"Friends share all things."*
—Pythagoras, 580-500 B.C.

Caroline waited for the arguments she expected her two dearest friends to make, the arguments best friends always make, declaring there was no need for her to change her ways. Arguments assuring her that everyone else was the problem and that she was perfect as she was. But neither Dulcie nor Phoebe said a word.

That could only mean one thing. Her two best friends were in agreement with her. It was time for sweeping changes. For all of them.

Setting her plate aside, Caroline refilled her teacup, then brushed her palms together. "Now that you've heard my report on my choice of soldier, I think it's time I heard from the two of you." She nodded at Phoebe. "Care to go first?"

"Yours was easier," Phoebe muttered, remembering the half dozen men she'd served tea and cakes to at the Returning Soldiers' Hospital at St. Martin-in-the-Fields earlier in the day.

"My choice might have been easier," Caroline replied. "But finishing my task won't be. So tell me how your search is going. Have you found anyone?"

Phoebe took a deep breath. "I served tea and cakes to five soldiers this morning."

"Any likely candidates?" Dulcie was curious about Phoebe's eventual choice. Unlike herself, Phoebe had been betrothed once. To her childhood sweetheart. But the marriage had never taken place because Phoebe's young lieutenant had died in the Peninsular Campaign two months before their wedding. Dulcie wondered if Phoebe would choose a man similar to her young lieutenant.

"I'm not sure." Phoebe frowned. "Perhaps."

"Tell us about them," Caroline encouraged.

"Two of the men were married..." Phoebe began.

"Strike them off the list," Dulcie said. "Our rules forbid the adoption of married men."

"Strike the next one off, too," Phoebe said. "Corporal Garland. He's betrothed to a girl from a good family in Sussex. And he has a living awaiting him at a vicarage in the village of Tunbridge Wells as soon as he's ready to leave the hospital."

"Off the list he goes." Caroline lifted Phoebe's cup and saucer and carefully filled the cup with tea. She offered Phoebe another sweet. "What about the other two?"

Phoebe refused the cake. "One was *Belgian*." She didn't have anything against Belgians. The Belgians had been British allies in the war against Napoleon. Nor was she purposefully dismissive of the Belgian cavalry officer. Phoebe was practical. "Lieutenant Ryskamp. He's returning to Brussels as soon as he's released from hospital." The young lieutenant was attractive and ambitious, but selecting him as her soldier made no sense. Not when he would be in Brussels and she'd be in London. "The last one appeared more interested in the cakes than in me or why I was there."

"That's a shame," Dulcie commiserated. "Two married. One betrothed. One foreign. And one who wanted cake. Maybe you'll have better luck next week."

"There was another man..." Phoebe began.

"You said you served tea and cakes to five soldiers. Another man equals six," Caroline pointed out. "Not five."

"I invited six." Phoebe's lips turned up in the merest half-smile. "The last man is a rude, churlish Scotsman who refused the tea and cakes *and* my offer of charity."

Caroline sucked in a breath. "You didn't make the mistake of mentioning charity?"

"Of course not, Caro," Phoebe assured her. "Those were his words, not mine. I offered him the same thing I offered the other soldiers—tea and cakes and conversation. When he refused my 'charity', as *he* called it, I suggested that he might like me to write letters to his kin or read letters or newspapers to him." She released a heavy sigh.

"And he refused that as well," Caroline concluded.

"Yes," Phoebe confirmed. "Quite disagreeably. By informing me that he was a Scot, not a savage. And despite the arrogant condescension of the British who believed otherwise, he was perfectly capable of reading for himself and writing his own letters." She sighed. "I offered kindness and he called it pity. I offered refreshments and he called it charity."

"That was a shame on both counts. Your handwriting is lovely and your speaking voice is most agreeable." Caroline nibbled at a pink rosebud of icing on her bite of cake. "And your cook's cakes are delicious. They're a treat that shouldn't be missed."

"I know," Phoebe agreed. "Unfortunately, he was the most interesting of all the men I've met so far."

"Interesting?" Dulcie repeated.

"*Intriguing*," Phoebe elaborated.

"Just how intriguing?" Phoebe's answer piqued Dulcie's curiosity. It had been a long time since Phoebe had expressed any interest in a man. "What was he like? Other than disagreeable?"

"Forceful," Phoebe said. "Frightening. Thrilling. Angry."

"At you?" Dulcie's voice held an indignant note.

Phoebe shook her head. "At the world. And everyone in it. And because I was there, I was included."

Caroline was thoughtful. "He's a Scotsman. I'm not personally acquainted with any Scots, but I've heard they're very proud people. Maybe he is ashamed of his weakness. Ashamed of being injured and confined to a hospital." She frowned. "Are his wounds serious?"

"Not the ones I could see," Phoebe said. "He was shot and suffered several saber wounds."

Caroline shuddered. "How awful." Lifting the teapot, she refilled Dulcie's cup, then placed another small cake on her friend's plate.

"The surgeons attending him say he's healing well," Phoebe continued.

"That's good," Dulcie said softly. Her brother had died in the recent war. Phoebe's betrothed had died in the war. And until three weeks ago, they had believed Anthony Carlisle had also perished in the war. England had lost far too many of her fine, young men. She could not afford to lose any more.

Wondering if Phoebe's intriguing soldier might be acquainted with, and a source of information on Tony, Caroline asked, "Was he Foot or Cavalry?"

"Foot. He was in a Highland regiment fighting in America under Sir Edward Pakenham," Phoebe replied.

"Oh. America." Caroline couldn't keep the disappointment out of her voice as she began collecting Phoebe's empty tea things and stacking them on the tray.

"Yes," Phoebe confirmed. "He's only recently returned from there."

"That explains some of his anger," Dulcie said. "Major General Lord Pakenham lost a skirmish in the swampland of Louisiana near a place called New Orleans at a cost of many men, including the near entirety of the Highland Regiments."

Phoebe leaned closer. "How do you know that?"

"I read *The Times*. The Duke of Wellington gave the eulogy for Lord Pakenham and in it, he blamed Admiral Cochrane for failing to do his duty and causing the defeat," Dulcie told them. "I clipped the obituary and the Duke's eulogy from the newspaper to paste in a book to save for posterity. I started clipping newsworthy items when my brother, Geoffrey, left for the war so he could catch up on the news when he got home..." Dulcie let her voice trail off. Her brother hadn't come home. He'd been killed in Spain. She glanced from Phoebe to Caroline and back again. "I still do it. Even though Geoff..." She shrugged. "I suppose it's become a habit. I have the book at home. I can bring it to our next meeting if you'd like to see it."

Reaching over, Phoebe squeezed Dulcie's hand. "I'd like that very much."

Seeing the shimmer of tears in Dulcie's eyes, Caroline abruptly changed the topic. "Does he look like a Scotsman? Is he ginger-haired, blue-eyed, with a ruddy complexion?"

"Not at all," Phoebe recalled. "He's tall and broad-shouldered with thick, dark hair and dark brows over sparkling emerald green eyes that flash with emotion."

"Dark and dangerous," Dulcie murmured. "Like Byron. Mad, bad, and dangerous to know."

"And intriguing." Caroline studied Phoebe. "Are you sure you want to take on the challenge?"

Phoebe met her friend's unwavering gaze. "Are you certain you want to continue yours?"

Caroline smiled. "Yes."

"So am I," Phoebe said.

Caroline set her napkin aside, then brushed her hands over her skirts. "So we're set." She turned to Dulcie. "Have you decided on anyone yet?"

Dulcie nodded. "I know the name of the man I intend to adopt."

Caroline and Phoebe both stared at her open-mouthed for a full moment before blurting. "You do?" and "Since when?"

"I've known for some time," Dulcie said, "but I haven't been able to locate him."

"Have you tried the other hospitals?" Caroline asked.

Dulcie nodded. "I've visited all the hospitals accepting returning veterans. And all the inns and boarding houses. He isn't at any of them."

Caroline and Phoebe shared a glance.

Dulcie didn't miss their look or the meaning behind it. "He's not among the wounded or the dead. At least, not in the War Office reports. Or in the casualty lists or obituaries published by *The Times*. I know because I've kept them in my book."

Phoebe drew her brows together. "How do you know this man, Dulce?"

"I don't know him." Dulcie pushed her chair back. "I know *about* him."

Recognizing an evasion when she heard one, Caroline pinned her friend with a question. "How? Who told you about him?"

"My brother." A shadow crossed Dulcie's face. "He was one of Geoff's close friends. They served together. Geoff wrote me all about him."

"If Geoff told you all about him," Caroline said. "He must have told you the man's name."

"He did," Dulcie said.

"But you aren't going to tell us?" Phoebe ventured.

"It's not that I don't *want* to," Dulcie told them. "I would gladly tell you, but Geoff made me promise not to tell anyone about the man until I've had a chance to meet him." Dulcie bit her bottom lip in consternation. "And I daren't risk having my uncle find out what I'm about before I have a chance to meet him."

The youngest of the three friends and founders of the Charlotte Society, Dulcie shared her family home with her Uncle Guilford Tennant and his pregnant wife.

The current Lord Tennant had inherited the title of Viscount Tennant from her brother, Geoffrey. And upon her uncle's inheritance, Dulcie had been reduced to living as an interloper in her own home. Geoff's premature death had made Dulcie's life more difficult than either of them could have ever imagined.

Dulcie had never expected the man who had appeared to be a loving uncle when her parents and her brother were alive to become a virtual tyrant determined to marry off his only niece to the highest bidder at the earliest possible moment. And as much as she wanted to escape her uncle's guardianship, Dulcie refused to be sold to the highest bidder in order to do so. But her uncle had issued an edict. If Dulcie failed to find a husband by the end of the season, her uncle was going to choose one for her.

Phoebe reacted instantly, clutching at the fabric covering her heart. "Caro and I would *never*..."

"Oh, Phoebe, I know that." Dulcie hastened to reassure her. "I trust you and Caroline more than anyone. It's just that I gave my word to Geoff..."

"But, Dulcie, we may be able to help you," Caroline reminded her.

"Not with this," Dulcie said. "Remember, the rules of the Charlotte Society say we're responsible for choosing our soldiers on our own."

"We made the rules," Phoebe reasoned. "We can change them."

"No." Dulcie remained adamant. "Once I find him, I may need your help. But I must do that on my own. I don't want to involve you—either of you—in the search. If my uncle were to get wind of it, he might forbid me to see you." She gazed at her two friends. "And I couldn't bear that. You are my dearest friends. I don't know what I would do if I couldn't come here. Time spent with the both of you is my refuge."

Phoebe reluctantly accepted Dulcie's terms. "All right, Dulcie. Whatever you think is best."

But Caroline wasn't ready to give in. "If you won't let us help you directly, let us help you indirectly."

"How?" Dulcie asked.

"I know someone who might be able to help you locate your soldier," Caroline said. "He has connections in the War Office and he's very trustworthy and discreet. I'll send him a note, asking him to pay a call here at his earliest convenience."

"It isn't your father, is it?" Dulcie dreaded the thought of meeting with Lord Rushton for any reason. "Or one of your father's friends?"

"Oh, heavens no!" Caroline exclaimed. "Lord Rushton has none of the sterling qualities of this man. Lord Rushton isn't discreet, trustworthy, or helpful."

"How do you know the man?" Dulcie asked Caroline the question Phoebe had asked her moments earlier.

Caroline smiled. "He's my godfather. He and my mother grew up together in Hertfordshire. Their families were close and always hoped they would marry, but they both chose other partners. His choice worked out beautifully. Mother's choice did not. So she asked her life-long friend to be godfather to her firstborn child—especially if that child turned out to be the heir. I turned out to be a female, but he's looked out for me all my life." She frowned thoughtfully. "He's never said so, but I suspect he wielded his influence on Lord Blessing to persuade him to petition the crown and parliament for the change in the Blessing warrants so I could inherit."

"Who is he?"

"Lord Weymouth," Caroline told them.

"The Earl of Weymouth is your godfather?" Phoebe was awestruck. Although, no one knew quite what Lord Weymouth did at the War Office, people whispered that he was essential to its success. Weymouth's name instilled the same sense of respect and admiration as the Duke of Wellington's. He was a force with which to be reckoned.

"Yes," Caroline confirmed.

"He's your godfather and you never asked him to verify Carlisle's death?" Phoebe asked, clearly still reeling from the revelation.

"On the contrary," Caroline said. "I begged him to. And he did. But every battlefield report he received listed Tony as killed in battle at Quatre Bras. Thank heavens, the reports were wrong."

"Do you think he would help me?" Dulcie asked.

"Yes." Caroline broadened her smile as hope lit up Dulcie's face. "If I ask, I feel certain Lord Weymouth will do what he can to help you in any way he can now that he's back from the Continent."

Dulcie beamed at her, grateful tears welling in her eyes. "Thank you, Caro."

Caroline swallowed the lump in her own throat. "What are friends for if not to help each other? Write your soldier's name on a notecard and seal it." She pointed to her writing desk. "I'll give Lord Weymouth the sealed note when he pays his call."

"Oh, Caro..." Fresh tears shimmered in Dulcie's eyes.

"You won't be betraying Geoff's trust because no one will know the name except you and Lord Weymouth," Caroline continued. "I'll send a message to Uncle Trevor this evening."

# CHAPTER 8

*"An Englishman's home is his castle."*
—English Proverb

"The workmen are back again." Tony wheeled his chair away from the window overlooking the back garden to face his batman as Barnaby cleared the doorway. "*She's* back again."

"I know, sir. The workmen have been here since sunup. Lady Blessing arrived shortly before nine o'clock."

Tony frowned. He had been watching the activity below for the past hour, enjoying the spectacle of Caroline directing the workmen. But he'd found the sight of her standing beside the reflecting pool, netting the carp who lived there, entrancing. He couldn't help but hope the slippery fish would present more of a challenge so Caroline would be forced to tuck up her skirts and wade into the pool to collect them.

Unfortunately, Barnaby's appearance on the lawn had interrupted her in the task.

"The purchase of Selby's house. All these workmen. All this

destruction." Raising his spyglass, Tony studied the activity taking place beyond the missing back gate. "All this rearranging must be costing her a fortune."

"I understand Lady Blessing has a fortune, sir."

Tony lowered the spyglass and turned his attention back to Barnaby, pinning him with a sharp look. "Whatever fortune she has, her husband controls."

"No, he doesn't, sir," Barnaby corrected.

"If Blessing doesn't control it, who does? Her father?"

"She does, sir."

"*What?*" Barnaby's pronouncement took Tony by surprise. The Caroline Hardage he had known had a legacy income from her mother, but it was hardly enough to buy Selby's house, much less renovate it. "What can she accomplish with a thousand pounds per annum?"

"A thousand pounds a year, sir?" Barnaby frowned, clearly puzzled.

"Her income from her mother," Tony explained.

"Lady Blessing's income is far greater than a thousand pounds per annum," Barnaby told him.

Tony's frown deepened. "And you know this how?"

"Lady Blessing has been the topic of downstairs conversation since she purchased Selby House," Barnaby said. "The staff at the house next door is buzzing with excitement at having a fabulously wealthy mistress."

"Of course they are." Tony wiped his hands over his face. He had half-hoped that eventually his body would heal enough for him to resume the life he'd led before war. Before Quatre Bras. Before Henry Hardage, Lord Rushton, had accepted Granville Blessing's offer for Caroline instead of his own. Before Blessing married her. Before he'd found himself in the cavalry and at war on the continent, Tony had dreamed of returning to England a hero. He had dreamed of showing Caroline what she'd given up. But Tony had never imagined returning home a broken hero.

"She inherited Lord Blessing's fortune."

Tony snapped his head up to focus on Barnaby's words. "What did you say?"

"Lady Blessing is a widow, sir," Barnaby said. "A fabulously wealthy widow."

Tony exhaled. "How is that possible?"

"Lord Blessing died, sir. She inherited."

"Widows inherit a widow's portion. One-third of their husband's estate," Tony said. "Generally, they do not inherit their husband's *entire* fortune. Not when there are male heirs in the family."

"The marquess didn't have any male heirs." Barnaby told him.

"How long has the marquess been dead?"

"Nearly two years," Barnaby said. "Lady Blessing was made a marchioness in her own right."

*Two years. She'd been a widow for two years while he was lying in a hospital flat on his back dreaming of her.* Tony heaved a loud sigh to cover his sense of relief at learning Caroline hadn't given Blessing an heir. Thinking of her sharing a bed with an old man had nearly driven Tony mad in the days and weeks and months following her marriage.

"As marchioness, she has the income to purchase Selby's house and to renovate to her heart's content." Tony pinned Barnaby with a sharp glance. "But her title doesn't give her the right to renovate *my* gardens. What does she have to say for herself? What's going on?"

"The workmen are here to complete the removal of the statues." Barnaby walked to the fireplace on the near wall where a fire was burning in the grate to keep the worst of the morning chill at bay. "After that's done, they're going to remove the rest of the stonework."

"What's she going to do while the workmen finish removing my statues?" Tony demanded. "Reward them with my goldfish?"

"She didn't say." Barnaby collected Major Carlisle's breakfast dishes and stacked them on the tray. For the past two days, the major had bathed, shaved, and dressed himself without assistance and had spent an inordinate amount of time at the window, observing the work in his garden.

"She didn't say?" Tony repeated. "You were down there with her for two-quarters of an hour." He made a circuit of the room before returning to the window.

Barnaby glanced at his employer. "Lady Blessing was issuing instructions to the workmen. I wasn't included in the conversation."

Tony shoved his fingers through his hair. "Carol—Lady Blessing—didn't say *anything* to you?"

"She said, 'Good morning, Barnaby, will Lord Carlisle be joining us today?'"

"And?"

"When I told her you would not, she politely refrained from further conversation." Barnaby glanced at the major's breakfast tray, relieved to see that Carlisle's appetite was returning. The major had eaten everything on his plate for the first time since his return to London. "Shall I remove your dishes now or would you care for more coffee?"

"No more for me." Tony shook his head. "But feel free to help yourself."

"Thank you, sir. I think I will." Barnaby poured himself a cup of coffee.

Tony wheeled himself as close to the window as possible and picked up his spyglass. "Is that Gerald?" He speared Barnaby with a glance. "Is that *my* head groundskeeper at Selby's? Helping her direct the workmen?"

Barnaby carried his cup and saucer to the window and stood behind Tony. "I can't be sure at this distance, sir."

Tony handed his batman the spyglass.

"It looks like Gerald to me, sir," Barnaby confirmed.

"Go tell him I want to see him. I want to know why he's been helping her and what she intends to do in my garden."

Barnaby took a swallow of coffee. "Now, sir?"

"If it won't be too much bother," Tony snapped.

The batman set his cup and saucer on the breakfast tray. "Of course not, Major. I'll attend to it straight away."

Watching Gerald in the garden taking orders from Caroline, Tony instantly regretted his sharp tone. Barnaby didn't deserve his show of frustration. "Wait, Barnaby."

"Sir?"

"Gerald's not going anywhere anytime soon. And neither am I. Whatever I have to say to Gerald can wait until after you finish your coffee." Backing away from the window, Tony began circling the room, deep in thought. "First, I need to find out what she's planning to do. Then I need a plan of my own."

"For Gerald?"

Tony snorted. "Not for Gerald. For Lady Blessing." He was silent for a time, rolling his chair back and forth in short strides, before suddenly snapping his fingers. "I've got it!" Tony rolled out of the ballroom and returned moments later with an ivory vellum note card. "When you go to collect Gerald, please give this to Her Ladyship."

Barnaby drew his brows together.

"And send West to me. We have a great deal to do."

"If I may be so bold as to inquire about your plan, sir."

Carlisle gave Barnaby a slight smile. "You'll find out soon enough."

Barnaby grinned, then snapped to attention. "Yes, sir, Major sir." For the first time in long months, Major Lord Anthony Carlisle sounded like the commander he'd been before Quatre Bras.

"WHAT'S THIS?" CAROLINE REMOVED HER GLOVES, STUFFING THEM INTO the pocket of her pinafore as Barnaby offered her a cream-colored vellum envelope sealed with the Carlisle family crest.

"From Lord Carlisle, your ladyship," Barnaby said.

Caroline's hand trembled as she took hold of the envelope. Her name was scrawled across the front in Tony's bold hand. *Caroline, Lady Blessing.* Looking up, she met the batman's gaze. "Do you know what it says?"

Barnaby shook his head. "No, ma'am. He wrote it in private and handed it to me sealed."

Caroline pressed the envelope to her heart. She had waited five long years for a letter from Tony. But she'd waited in vain. It seemed Tony had dismissed her once the announcement of her wedding to Lord Blessing had appeared in the morning papers. He'd left London that same evening, having secured a commission in the cavalry. He'd joined His Majesty's Own Eleventh Blues serving first as a lieutenant squadron leader on the Peninsula and later, as a scout for Wellington in Belgium.

Caroline had written to him every week, but all of her letters had gone unanswered. And unreturned. It hurt Caro to think Tony hadn't considered her worth the cost of franking a letter. Gripping the ivory vellum, she pressed the note closer to her breast.

"Are you going to read it, milady?" Barnaby asked.

"I'm almost afraid to," Caroline admitted. "It's probably a written invitation to leave the premises."

Barnaby laughed. "He wouldn't write a note for that. He'd send me."

"And here you are," Caroline pointed out.

"Yes, ma'am." His laughter ended, but a trace of his smile remained. "Here to deliver that note and to inform Gerald, Lord Carlisle's head groundskeeper, that the major wishes to speak with him."

"Lord Carlisle wishes to speak with him?" she repeated, not quite sure she'd heard Barnaby correctly.

"Yes, your ladyship."

"Is Gerald in trouble?"

"If he is, I'm not aware of it," Barnaby said.

"But he's going to meet with Lord Carlisle..."

"There's nothing untoward about that, milady. Lord Carlisle is his employer."

Caroline sighed. "You'll let me know if I've caused Gerald trouble, won't you?"

"Of course, milady."

"Perhaps that's what this is." She tapped the envelope against her lips.

"Open it and see, milady," Barnaby suggested, turning his back so she could have a bit of privacy in which to read the major's note. "Then you won't have to fret about it any longer."

Caroline rubbed her lips across the Carlisle family crest, then broke the wax seal on the envelope. Smoothing her fingers over the vellum, she read:

*My Lady Blessing,*

*Please accept this invitation to an alfresco dinner on the grounds for you and your workmen at noon on this day.*

*Carlisle.*

Caroline pressed the note to her lips again before carefully tucking it inside her bodice. It pained her that he didn't address her by her Christian name, but she was thrilled to have received a hand-written note from him. Caroline glanced up at the window overlooking the garden, hoping to catch a glimpse of him watching her. But the draperies remained still. She gently touched Barnaby on the shoulder. "Lord Carlisle has invited us to dinner on the grounds today at noon."

"Are you going to accept?" Barnaby asked.

"How can I refuse?" She bit her bottom lip. "He's invited all the workmen. I can't deprive them of the treat."

"Of course, you can," Barnaby told her. "The workmen will never know about His Lordship's invitation unless you tell them. If you refuse it now, there will be no food or tents or any sign they were offered."

"What about Lord Carlisle?" she asked. "Won't he be disappointed if I refuse his invitation?"

"Does the invitation say he'll be joining you?" Barnaby asked.

Caroline hadn't thought about that. She'd assumed that since Tony had issued the invitation, he would host the gathering. "No." Caroline glanced up at the window and this time, she caught the slight flutter of a drape. "He didn't say anything about joining us."

Barnaby paused, clearly considering how much he should reveal. "Then I wouldn't count on it, milady. Stairs present a challenge for the major."

"I plan to attend to that soon." Caroline smiled a mysterious smile. "Until then, please collect Gerald for Lord Carlisle and tell him, for me, that he has a ready situation at Selby House should Lord Carlisle dismiss him. With or without references. And when you speak with Lord Carlisle, please inform him that while I appreciate His Lordship's concern for the workmen and his gracious invitation, I must decline." She turned her attention to the gap in the back wall where several tents were going up in the garden. "As you can see, I've already made arrangements to provide dinner *alfresco* for the workmen at Selby House. Please see that Gerald doesn't miss it."

TONY GROANED WITH THE EFFORT OF BRACING HIMSELF AGAINST THE arms of his wheelchair as he pushed himself out of the seat. His hands were pale from the strain, ropy veins on the back of them thrust into prominence each time he tightened his grip. Beads of perspiration dotted his brows and his top lip and soaked the hair on the nape of his neck.

The white linen shirt he wore clung to his back and shoulders. Staring at the mantel clock, Tony counted the seconds. One. Two. Three. Four. His legs wobbled beneath him and Tony sat down hard on the seat of his chair.

Five seconds.

He'd made it.

Tony had barely managed to stay upright for three seconds the day before.

He should be elated that his legs had supported him, but all he felt was exhaustion. Swiping at the perspiration running down the side of his face with the back of his hand, Tony exhaled a shaky breath, then gritted his teeth against his quaking muscles and the pain radiating through the injured nerves, muscles, and healing bones of his legs. Suddenly, he was very much afraid the surgeons and physicians had been right when they told him he would never walk more than a step or two on his own or sit a horse again.

Tony didn't recall much of the time he'd spent in the hospital in Brussels. But he remembered that. The army surgeon who'd fought to amputate his limbs had made his diagnosis abundantly clear. The surgeon believed Tony to be a colossal fool. He could live without his damaged legs, the surgeon had assured him, but he'd be riddled with pain and dead of gangrene or putrefaction within a year if he kept them.

Tony had kept his legs. He fought the pain with regular doses of laudanum. And counted the days he had left to suffer.

Despite the bitter pill he had been forced to swallow, Tony had held out the hope that he could manage a miracle. He had hoped, that with time, he'd be able to stand on his two feet long enough to feel like himself again.

Tony squeezed his eyes shut. Long months had passed since Quatre Bras, and his stamina had yet to return. Was it possible the surgeon was right? The longest he'd spent on his feet was five seconds. A meager five seconds that had cost him dearly. It would be hours before he recovered.

He'd never make it down the stairs on his own at this rate.

Unless he scooted down them on his backside as he'd done as a small child. And if he resorted to that, he might reach the bottom, but he would never be able to stand up when he got there.

Tony shoved his fingers through his hair, raking it into a semblance of order. In the weeks since he'd arrived in London in a closed sedan chair, hidden from curious eyes and battling fever and delirium, Tony believed he'd made progress. But all he'd gained from his painful effort was five seconds of weakness on legs as wobbly as a newborn colt's.

He was weak. But he wasn't going to look weak in front of the staff. The household staff or the small army of gardeners and groundskeepers who tended to the outside of the house. Certainly, not in front of Gerald or the workmen ripping up his gardens.

And never in front of Caroline.

No one in London, no one from his life before Quatre Bras, would ever be allowed to see the extent of the damage he had suffered. Or his weakness.

Except Barnaby. And West. Because he trusted them. Barnaby, because Barnaby had fought beside him, defended, and taken care of him. If it weren't for Barnaby, he wouldn't have legs to pain him. If it weren't for Barnaby, he wouldn't be alive.

And West, because the butler had served his mother and father before him and was a member of the family.

Wheeling himself to the full-length mirror, Tony finished tying his cravat into his usual barrel knot, buttoned himself into his favorite brocade waistcoat, and gritted his teeth against the agony in his legs as he shoved his feet into his top boots. Removing his superfine coat from the mahogany clothing stand, Tony slipped it on, and summoned his butler.

"Please send Kirby and Fielder to collect me," Tony instructed as soon as West entered the ballroom, naming the two strong, young footmen charged with carrying him up and down stairs. "Clear the staff away from the staircase and the entry hall until I've reached my study." He met his butler's forthright gaze. "Barnaby will be returning shortly with Gerald."

"Gerald, sir?" West sounded puzzled.

"Our head groundskeeper, Tom Gerald," Tony enlightened him. "We'll be meeting in the study. I'll need a few moments to get settled before you admit them and I prefer to do that away from prying eyes."

"Of course, sir," West said.

"We'll require coffee and refreshments for three in my study."

West acknowledged Lord Carlisle's instructions. "Cook has freshly baked gingerbread and a plum cake cooling as we speak, sir."

"Thank you, West." Tony gave the man who had served his family for as long as he could remember a grateful smile. "That would be most welcome. Oh, and bring the household accounts ledger to the study."

"Of course, my lord." West returned Tony's smile with brisk nod. "I'll see to it right away."

LORD CARLISLE WAS SEATED BEHIND THE MASSIVE OAK DESK IN HIS study when Barnaby and Tom Gerald entered the room. Barnaby stood at attention. Gerald pulled his forelock, then stood studying the scuffed toes of his worn work boots and gripping his cap in his fist as he faced the earl.

Tony set the accounts book he'd been reviewing aside and turned his attention to his head groundskeeper. "Well, Tom, I see you've been keeping busy."

Gerald swallowed hard before answering. "Yes, your lordship."

"The shrubbery and flower beds at the front of the house and beside the front gate are immaculately maintained," Carlisle said. "As are the lilies and tulips planted along the pavement."

The groundskeeper's stomach growled loudly as Gerald glanced at the side table laden with plates of gingerbread and slices of plum cake, cups and saucers, spoons and forks, cream and sugar, and a pot of steaming hot coffee.

Carlisle gestured toward the table. "Please, help yourself." He spared a glance for his batman. "You, too, Barnaby."

Gerald bobbed his head. "Thankee, sir." Stuffing his cap into his trouser pocket, the groundskeeper ambled over to the table and helped himself to cake and coffee.

Barnaby folded his arms over his chest and remained where he was. He'd seen this tactic before. The major had used it several times to upbraid inexperienced young lieutenants. And to upbraid his batman upon occasion.

Watching Gerald awkwardly struggling to balance a plate of cake and a cup of coffee, Carlisle indicated one of a pair of leather chairs positioned in front of his desk. "Please, sit. Make yourself comfortable while you explain the state of the back garden and your participation in it."

Gerald swallowed a mouthful of plum cake and washed it down with a noisy gulp of coffee. "Beg pardon, my lord, but Her Ladyship said…"

"Her Ladyship?" Carlisle narrowed his gaze. "I have no wife, so by that, I assume you are referring to the Marchioness of Blessing?"

"Yes, your lordship."

"The woman who destroyed my back gate and absconded with my

ancestor's statuary." Carlisle's tone was decidedly sharper. "The woman you assisted."

Gerald looked down at the plate in his hand. "Aye, sir. But Her Ladyship assured me that you..."

Arching an eyebrow, Carlisle prompted, "That I *what?*"

"That you had granted permission for the renovations." Gerald set his empty plate on the small table between the matching leather chairs and took a final swallow of coffee before placing his cup on its saucer.

"And you began helping her dismantle my garden without consulting me?" Carlisle asked.

"Of course, your lordship," Gerald said.

*"Of course?"* Tony arched his eyebrow.

The groundskeeper nodded. "It's not my place to question a marchioness, your lordship. She told me she had purchased Lord Selby's house and that since the houses shared a back gate, you had agreed to share the gardens as well. I believed her."

"You believed a strange young woman who decided not only to rip up her gardens and lawn, but mine as well?" Carlisle pinned him with a stern gaze. "Then proceeded to assist her in the destruction?"

"I had no reason not to believe her, milord." Gerald met Carlisle's steady gaze. "I was charged with following her directions unless you said otherwise." He straightened his shoulders, pushed himself to his feet, and stood before his employer. "I've had no instructions about the grounds since you returned, your lordship. No directions as to the spring and summer plantings or maintenance. I was given to understand that you were ill and otherwise occupied. When Lady Blessing put me to work on your behalf, I was happy to oblige her. Happy to earn my wages." He paused to clear his throat. "If I'm to be dismissed for going against your wishes..."

Carlisle inhaled, then slowly expelled the air. "I'm not going to dismiss you, Tom. I simply asked you here this morning to find out what Lady Blessing has planned for the gardens." He glanced at Barnaby. "I haven't seen her—or rather, I didn't wish for her to see me—until I regained my strength..."

"That's what she has planned, your lordship," Gerald told him.

"I beg your pardon?"

"Lady Blessing is renovating the gardens and grounds in order to help you regain your strength."

Carlisle frowned. "I fail to see how destroying my gardens is going to help me regain my strength."

"She intends to turn our joint gardens into a small version of the Roman baths in Bath." Gerald's voice held a note of pride. "The hot springs at Bath are where the ill and infirmed go to heal, your lordship. Lady Blessing said there was no need to haul you all the way to Bath when we have hot springs right in our own back gardens."

"We do?" Carlisle asked.

*"We* don't," Gerald informed him. "But Selby House *does.* There's a hot spring beneath the fountain in the rear garden."

"This is the first I've heard of it," Carlisle said. "And I've lived here most of my life."

Gerald smiled. "You were a young lad away at school when Lord Selby's roses began dying. He ordered the groundskeepers and the gardeners to replant. The gardeners dug up the old roses and discovered a hot spring beneath the bed." His voice held a note of sadness. "Those beautiful old roses were drowning in hot mineral water. So Lord Selby ordered a fountain built around the spring and had the rose beds relocated." He paused a moment before resuming his story. "Lady Blessing plans to pipe the hot spring water from her fountain to your reflecting pool."

"For what purpose?" Carlisle asked. "To boil my goldfish?"

Gerald drew his brows together, a look of consternation on his face. "Oh, no, sir. The water isn't hot enough to boil them. It's more likely to poach them, but it's too hot for them to live in it."

Carlisle persisted in the playing devil's advocate. "So...Lady Blessing is simply planning to kill my goldfish."

"That's not the plan at all, your lordship."

Reaching across his desk, Carlisle refilled Gerald's coffee cup and passed him the plate of cakes. "Why don't you tell me what the plan is?"

# CHAPTER 9

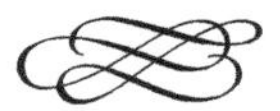

*"A single sunbeam is enough to drive away many showers."*
—St. Francis of Assisi, 1181-1226.

Caroline paused in her task, wiped her hands on her apron and checked to make certain her invitation from Tony was secure. She may have refused his invitation, but his hand-written note was precious to her. She glanced at the timepiece pinned to her bodice, then at the gravel path leading to the front door of Carlisle House. Nearly an hour had passed since Gerald had accompanied Barnaby into the house to meet with Lord Carlisle.

She was worried. It didn't take three quarters of an hour to enumerate your head groundskeeper's transgressions. Or to dismiss him. What were they doing in there? And why was it taking so long?

Unable to stand the suspense a moment longer, Caroline emptied the fish she'd netted, dropping four koi into a bucket of water for the workmen to collect and pour into waiting barrels to transport to the temporary fish pond they had dug for the duration of the renovations. She shrugged out of the oilskin she wore over her cape and draped it over a wrought iron bench, grabbed the net she had laid aside, and holding it like a staff, marched through the back garden to the front door of Carlisle House.

Lifting the brass knocker, Caroline banged on the wooden door as hard as she could. She was still knocking on it when the front door swung open and she all but fell inside.

Tony's butler stepped out of the way as she regained her balance. West eyed the fish net warily and his voice held a note of dread when he uttered her name. "Lady Blessing."

Raising her chin to its most authoritative angle, Caroline returned his greeting in like manner. "Mr. West."

"His Lordship is not receiving guests."

"I'm not here to see His Lordship," she announced.

"I beg your pardon?" The butler was clearly nonplussed.

"I'm not here to see Lord Carlisle," Caroline repeated. "I'm here to discover what he's done to Mister Gerald."

"Mister Gerald?" West parroted.

"Lord Carlisle's head groundskeeper. He accompanied Mr. Barnaby to a meeting with the earl." She met the butler's stern look without flinching. "But Mr. Gerald is needed to attend to the project in the gardens straight away..."

"Meeting, ma'am?"

Caroline narrowed her gaze. "Don't pretend ignorance, West. It doesn't become you or your position in Lord Carlisle's household. I know Mr. Gerald was called before Lord Carlisle this morning and I'm fully prepared to interrupt the meeting..."

"Madam, I cannot allow that." West blocked the entrance. "Lord Carlisle has instructed me to refuse you entrance to this residence."

Squaring her shoulders, Caroline looked the butler in the eye. "Unless you're prepared to forcibly remove me, the Marchioness of Blessing and a peer of the realm, you cannot prevent it."

~

Tony looked up as West entered the library without knocking. "I believe I asked that we not be disturbed."

"You did, sir," the butler admitted. "I apologize to you and the gentlemen, but it's imperative I speak with you."

"Now?"

"Yes, sir," West confirmed.

"And?"

"There is a caller at the door," West said.

"Did you explain to the caller that I am not receiving guests?" Tony asked.

"No, sir."

"Why not?" Tony focused his gaze on his butler. "I asked that we not be disturbed until we finished our meeting." Carlisle turned his attention to Gerald and Barnaby. "Gentlemen, have we reached the conclusion of our meeting?"

Barnaby shook his head. "Not yet, sir."

"Send the caller away, West," Tony commanded.

"I would be happy to, sir," West said. "But she's threatening to interrupt your meeting unless I relay a message to Mr. Gerald."

Tony sat straighter on his chair. *"She?"*

"Lady Blessing, sir," West replied. "She's in the entry hall, brandishing a weapon and threatening to interrupt your meeting unless I relay a message to the groundskeeper."

Tony nodded toward Barnaby, who opened the library door to reveal Lady Blessing standing in the open front doorway holding a long-handled fishing net. Barnaby turned to Carlisle.

"Well?" Tony demanded.

"She's standing on the threshold."

"Any sign of a weapon?"

Barnaby smiled. "A fishing net, sir."

Tony bit the inside of his cheek to keep from smiling, recalling the sight of Caroline scooping his goldfish out of the reflecting pool. He pinned West with a look. "Any other weapons?"

"Only the net, sir," West replied. "But she wielded it like a weapon."

"I don't doubt it a bit." Tony gave West a hard look. "Especially if you're a member of the carp family."

West blinked. "I beg your pardon, sir."

Tony took a deep breath. "As well you should, but as you've already interrupted our meeting, you might as well relay the message to Gerald." Tony nodded toward the groundskeeper.

West turned to the groundskeeper and did as the earl instructed. "Lady Blessing asked me to inform you that you are urgently needed in the gardens."

Gerald looked to Lord Carlisle. Tony turned to West. "Please inform the marchioness there is no need to storm the library. Gerald will be out momentarily."

West firmed his lips in a rare display of disapproval before exiting the library to perform the onerous task of approaching Lady Blessing.

"Are we concluded, your lordship?" Gerald rose to his feet.

"If you've nothing more to add," Tony said.

Gerald shifted his weight from one leg to the other. "I've told you all I know about the lady's plans for the grounds."

"Then we've concluded our business," Tony told him.

"Have I your permission to pursue Lad—your neighbor's plans—for the gardens?"

The earl shrugged. "If she wants to waste her money landscaping my gardens—"

"It won't be a waste, your lordship," Gerald said. "She's hired Capability Brown to design the landscaping and John Nash to design the structures."

Lancelot "Capability" Brown and John Nash were two of the foremost landscaping and building architects in the country. They did magnificent work that would greatly enhance the reputation and value of Carlisle House. If nothing else, Caroline, Lady Blessing, had excellent and expensive tastes.

"Well, if that's the case, I see no reason to stop her." He met his groundskeeper's gaze. "Or you."

"Thankee, sir." Gerald doffed his cap, then turned and exited the library.

~

"THE GROUNDSKEEPER WILL BE HERE MOMENTARILY." WEST DELIVERED Lord Carlisle's message before adding one of his own. "You may put aside your weapon and return to the out of doors, your ladyship."

"Not until I see Mr. Gerald."

"He's on his way."

"I'll wait." She leaned the fish net against the wall inside the door.

"Suit yourself," the butler grumbled, then turned and left her standing in the doorway, waiting for Gerald.

She didn't have to wait long.

"Your message said I was needed in the gardens, milady." Gerald removed his cap and held it in his fist as he approached Caroline.

"You are," she said. "The noon meal is being served in the Selby Gardens if you'd like to join the other workmen."

"Thankee, milady." Gerald excused himself and moved to step around her.

"Gerald, did you speak with His Lordship?"

"Yes, ma'am."

Caroline swallowed hard. According to the downstairs gossip flowing from house to house around town, Tony had refused to see anyone except a few select members of his household staff. He'd refused to meet with his solicitor, his man of business, the caretaker of Carlisle Court, his country house in northwest Yorkshire, and he'd repeatedly turned her away from his door since she'd learned he was alive and back in London.

But he'd asked to meet with Tom Gerald and as much as she hated to admit it, that stung her pride. And her heart. Caroline was desperate to see him. Desperate to find out how he looked. How he felt... Taking a deep breath, she swallowed her pride and asked, "How did he..." Catching herself, she changed in midstream. "Did he dismiss you?"

"No, ma'am," Gerald replied. "Just the opposite."

"The opposite?" Caroline repeated the word as if she'd never heard it before.

"Lord Carlisle gave me leave to continue my work with you on the gardens and grounds."

"Thank heavens." She briefly closed her eyes, then opened them again. "Had he dismissed you, I would have offered you immediate employment," she said, "but I hoped it wouldn't be necessary. I didn't want to be the cause of your dismissal from longtime service with Lord Carlisle."

"You needn't have worried on that account, Lady Blessing," Gerald assured her. "He's a fair man. Lord Carlisle would never have dismissed me for following your orders." He pulled a face. "He was more likely to dismiss me for not assisting you."

She frowned. "I don't understand."

"You're a marchioness, ma'am. Lord Carlisle would dismiss any member of his staff who refused the orders of a peer of the realm on Carlisle property."

Caroline chewed at her bottom lip. "I suppose you knew that when you agreed to help me." Responsibility to the workmen she had hired to do her bidding and to Tony's staff weighed heavily on her shoulders. Her title carried great weight among the common people and she suddenly realized her good intentions might have unintended consequences for the people around her.

"I counted on it, your ladyship," Gerald said. "I've known the earl a long time. I apprenticed under his father's head groundskeeper at Carlisle Court before I came to London to become head groundskeeper under His Lordship, the present earl."

"I apologize to you, Mr. Gerald," Caroline said. "I never meant to put your livelihood at risk."

"Of course not, ma'am." He smiled at her. "Now, if you will excuse me, I'll be helping myself to the fine feast you've provided for us next door. Lord Carlisle has already kindly treated me to coffee and cakes."

Caroline lingered in the doorway after the groundskeeper departed, waiting to see if West would return to ask her to remove herself from the premises. But West had retreated down the hall and did not reappear to escort her out of the house.

Hearing the low murmur of men's voices, Caroline took advantage of the only opportunity she was likely to get and followed the sound, making her way down a short corridor.

The door to the room on her left was open. Caroline moved closer. Moments later, she was standing on the threshold, drinking in her first sight of Anthony Carlisle in five long years as he sat behind a massive oak desk in a room surrounded by walls of leather-bound books.

She didn't think she made a sound, but she must have. Her heart beat a rapid tattoo beneath her bodice and her breath seemed to catch in her throat. She listened. Not to his words, but to the warm rumble of his deep voice.

His voice recalled a thousand memories. A thousand tender moments. Moments she had cherished. Moments she still dreamed about. Caroline watched the play of sunlight on the crown of his head and longed to run her fingers through his thick, unruly black hair the way she had years ago when she'd teased him and called him her dark knight.

A mysterious smile played at the corners of her mouth. Anthony Carlisle was English through and through, but he bore the dark hair and silvery gray eyes of a long dead ancestor from the south of France, who had come to England with the Conqueror.

Caroline admired his unusual coloring and the way long hours on horseback had burnished his skin and sculpted his body. She had believed she remembered every detail, every nuance of his face and form, but she'd forgotten how striking his features were. She'd always considered him handsome, but now she realized handsome didn't begin to describe him. She adored the shape of his mouth, his nose, his ears, the tilt of his head as he gave his full attention to the man with whom he was speaking.

Her breath quickened. Tony was thinner than she remembered. His face and jawline sharper, his eyes bracketed by a network of fine lines that hadn't been there when she'd last seen him. The scars were also new.

He carried a curved scar at the corner of his right eye that bisected his brow. Another scar marred his forehead at his hairline. Yet another marked the center of his lower lip. Her heart ached for the pain those wounds had caused, but none of the scars detracted from the masculine beauty of his face. If anything, the marks on his face enhanced his extraordinary good looks, giving him an edge of danger that hadn't been there before.

Caroline focused her gaze on his mouth—his beautiful, tantalizing mouth. The scar on his bottom lip was different. So was the way he pressed his lips together into a firm line, as if he were in in pain. Glancing at the hands he kept resting on the desktop, she saw they were fisted so tightly his knuckles were white.

Caroline knew she should walk away, but she was frozen in place, transfixed by the sight of him. She wanted so much to run to him, to throw herself into his arms and press her cheek to his chest to listen to the steady beat of his heart. She wanted to feel his arms around her and be surrounded by the warmth of his body, enveloped in the heat and scent of him. She wanted to touch him and to keep touching him for as long as he allowed. But she stood where she was. Unable to move. Unable to take her gaze off of him.

The conversation between the two men suddenly died.

Barnaby cleared his throat.

Tony looked up and saw her.

Their gazes collided and held. His, dark silver and unfathomable. Hers, bright blue and shimmering with emotion.

Caroline felt the impact in her bone marrow. Anthony Carlisle wasn't known as Lord Temptation for nothing.

They might have been the only two people in the room, the only two people in the world. The air seemed to thicken, shrouding them in a world of their own. Caroline felt as if they stared at each other, absorbing the essence of each other, for hours, but it couldn't have been more than a few seconds before Tony broke the spell. "Lady Blessing."

His low baritone sent shivers up her spine. "Lord Carlisle." Caroline's voice was a husky whisper.

Barnaby stood up to leave, but Tony stopped him. "No need for you to leave, Barnaby." He waved his manservant back onto the chair. "Lady Blessing won't be staying."

"Won't I?" she asked.

He shook his head. "As far as I'm concerned, you've wandered far beyond your purview," Tony said. "The garden is that way, madam." He pointed in the direction of the back lawn.

Suddenly nervous, Caroline moistened her lips with the tip of her tongue. "I came for Mr. Gerald."

"He isn't here." Tony's tone turned dismissive. "He left a few moments ago."

"Yes, I know," she said. "I spoke with him as he was leaving."

Tony inhaled. "Then, you've no reason to be standing in my doorway."

"I have reason."

"Oh?" He sounded surprised.

"I wanted to thank you."

"For what?"

"For not dismissing Mr. Gerald."

"There was no reason to," he said. "Gerald does an admirable job as head groundskeeper."

"I'm glad you think so," Caroline said. "He's been doing quite a bit of rearranging."

*"Unauthorized* rearranging."

"It was authorized." Caroline smiled an impish smile. "Just not by you."

Barnaby coughed to disguise what sounded suspiciously like a chuckle.

Tony drew his dark brows together in a mighty frown. "You've thanked me. I've assured you Tom Gerald's position as head groundskeeper at Carlisle House is secure. As far as I am concerned, our business is concluded, Lady Blessing."

Caroline refused to be dismissed. "I fear you are mistaken, Lord Carlisle. As far as you're concerned, our business together is far from concluded."

Tony gaped at her. "*You* are mistaken, Lady *Blessing*," he emphasized her surname. "I have no further need of you."

"You have great need of me," she contradicted.

"You found your way in. So I believe you can find your way out without my assistance." He glared at her, his dark eyes flashing.

"You are correct, my lord Carlisle," she agreed. "But can *you* make your way to the front door and the gardens beyond without mine?"

"What makes you think I can't?" he snapped.

"Your lack of manners."

"*My* lack of manners? You barged into my house uninvited."

"Yes, I did," Caroline said. "And for the first time since I've known you, you failed to stand when I entered a room."

Carlisle's frown grew deeper, fiercer, as he bit out his words. "That wasn't a lack of manners, *madam*. Forgive me if I've forgotten proper protocol, but I've spent little time in the company of women these past few years. Refresh my memory, Lady Blessing. Am I expected to stand for a marchioness? Or kneel at her feet?"

Caroline gasped. Searching his thunderous face, she recognized his anger and frustration for what it was. Her heart ached for him. But her empathy did nothing to blunt the pain he inflicted with his words.

"What? No witty repartee?" He didn't wait for her to reply before pinning her with his hard stare. "Well, good day, *madam*."

Tears stung her eyes. She blinked them away. "Good day, *my lord*." Squaring her shoulders, Caroline turned and walked away. *My love.*

# CHAPTER 10

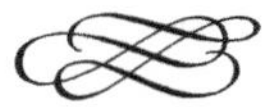

*How doth the honeybee*
*Improve each shining hour*
*And gather honey all the day*
*From every passing flower!"*
—Isaac Watts, 1674-1748

Tony pinched the bridge of his nose, then covered his face with his hands. He sat at his desk holding his head in his hands for long minutes after the Marchioness of Blessing departed for the gardens. Five years had passed since he'd spoken to her. Five years had passed since he'd seen her up close, since he'd heard her voice, smelled the scent of her perfume. Five years since he'd held her in his arms and kissed her.

He inhaled, filling his lungs, before slowly exhaling. Trying to dispel the tension that had filled the room from the moment he had looked up and saw her hovering in the doorway.

Watching her from a distance had been a distraction from the boredom of confinement and the unrelenting physical pain he suffered. A pleasant daydream. Observing her from a distance had kept him safe. After watching her day after day, Tony had convinced himself that he was cured. The spell Caroline Hardage had cast over him was broken. He'd convinced himself that he was over her. Over her betrayal. He'd fought a war to get over her and her betrayal. If he'd returned from war whole, things might have been different…

But now that he'd seen her again, spoken with her again, Tony knew just how wrong he'd been. She'd been lovely before, but she was beautiful now. She'd been a girl when they'd parted. And she had grown into a beautiful woman. Tony had carried the memory of a lovely girl to war with him, hoping to get over her.

It would take more than a war for him to get over her now. He suspected nothing short of death itself would do it. And even then, Tony had his doubts.

Caroline Hardage was buried as deeply inside him as the bits of shrapnel he had carried in his leg and hip since Quatre Bras.

"Major? Are you all right?"

Carlisle lifted his head from his hands. Barnaby's concern was etched on his face. "I've been better."

"How long since you last saw her?"

Tony pinned him with a sharp look. "Five years." *Five years, one month, two weeks, three days, and—he glanced at the mantel clock—four hours.*

"Before you became a lieutenant in the cavalry. Before you were attached to Wellington's staff."

Tony nodded. "A day before I found myself commissioned in the army."

"She told me you were well acquainted," Barnaby said.

"*Well acquainted.*" Tony snorted. "That's how she described us?"

"Yes, sir."

"Well acquainted," Tony mused. The idea stung. While he believed her to be the love of his life, Caroline considered him an acquaintance. He managed a rueful smile. *Well acquainted.* "Somehow I thought we were much more than that."

"How so, sir?" Barnaby asked.

"I asked her to be my wife." Tony's answer was flat and unemotional.

Barnaby widened his eyes in surprise. "She refused you?"

"She accepted me," Tony corrected. "Lord Rushton refused me."

His manservant frowned. "Lord Rushton?"

"Her father," Tony elaborated. "The family name is Hardage. His title is Earl of Rushton."

Barnaby bobbed his head. "Lord Rushton refused your offer for the young lady's hand in marriage."

"Twice," Tony said. "I increased my original offer, but Rushton turned me down a second time by telling me quite plainly and emphatically that his daughter favored security and a certain position in society over sentimentality and youthful good looks. He told me that as the daughter of an earl, she had no wish to be the wife of one. Her ambitions went higher. Rushton told me I was too late. Caroline had made her decision."

"Did you believe him?"

Tony gave a caustic laugh. "Not a bloody word." He swiped his hands over his face, then opened his eyes and met Barnaby's gaze. "I demanded to speak to Caroline."

"Did you?"

"No." Tony shook his head. "Rushton summoned three footmen and had me removed from his library."

Recalling the major's condition when he'd joined his cavalry regiment, Barnaby asked. "What happened?"

"It took the three of them and Rushton to remove me. I was beaten to a bloody pulp, thrown into a carriage and driven here." He spread his arms to encompass the interior of Carlisle House. "The announcement of her nuptials to a man more than thrice her age appeared in the *Morning Chronicle* and *The Times* the following morning."

"Lord Blessing."

"Yes." Carlisle nodded. "Granville Blessing, Second Marquess of Blessing."

Barnaby could tell from the bitterness in the major's words there was more to tell. "What did you do, sir?"

"I went to Blessing and informed him that I had already offered for Miss Hardage and she had accepted. I told him the proper thing for him to do, as a gentleman, was to withdraw his suit." Tony squeezed his eyes shut. "But I miscalculated. Blessing took one look at me and laughed in my face. Laughed at my naiveté at not understanding the perfidy of women and in believing a man as ambitious as Rushton would ever accept a mere earl—even a wealthy one—as his son-in-law." He paused. "Blessing seemed so civil. He poured brandy for us both as he discussed the necessity of his marriage to Caroline. He and Rushton had plans. Political ambitions that could only be met by a union between the two families." Tony shoved his hands through his hair once again. "Blessing desperately needed an heir. Caroline was his hope of gaining one."

He looked at Barnaby. "I threatened to take Caroline and make a run for Scotland. Blessing advised me to cut my losses and find another girl to marry or risk another thrashing." Tony took a deep breath and slowly blew it out. "Once again, I was removed from a house."

"I'm sorry, sir."

"I don't remember much of anything else. It's all a blur." Tony shrugged. "I somehow acquired a commission in His Majesty's Own Eleventh Blues and sailed for Portugal." Tony's memory wasn't a blur. It was non-existent. He had no memory of how he came by his commission or how he had come to be on the transport. He only knew that when he awoke, some four days later, he had a commission in the Eleventh Blues and had been summoned to the quartermaster's office. Tony speared Barnaby with another sharp glance. "You know the rest. You were there."

Barnaby had been assigned as batman to the newest young lieutenant during the Peninsular Campaign in the spring of 1810. When they met, the young lieutenant had still been sporting a nasty cut above his black eye, a split lip, and an assortment of ugly bruises.

Barnaby saw to Lieutenant Lord Carlisle's household, setting up and tearing down their temporary quarters as they fought their way from Spain and Portugal, around France, and into Belgium where

Major Lord Anthony Carlisle had been attached to Wellington's staff as a scout. "What about Lady Blessing?"

"What about her?" Tony reached for his coffee cup only to find the beverage had grown cold. His hand shook and the cup rattled against the saucer as he replaced it.

"You never spoke with her?" Barnaby knew she had written to him. The major had never opened the letters. But instead of destroying them, Carlisle had kept them bound by a leather cord in the bottom of his army kit. "Never wrote her?"

"What was there to say? She was married. She had made her choice and there was no undoing it."

"Did she make the choice? Or her father?" Barnaby posed the questions that had haunted Tony for five years. Had he been mistaken? Had Caroline chosen Blessing? Or had she been as much a victim of her father's ambition as he had been?

"Either way, the decision was made," Tony insisted. "She chose Blessing."

"She chose you first when she accepted your proposal," Barnaby reminded him. "And now, she's chosen you again."

"Now that she's a wealthy widow and a marchioness in her own right." Tony's words were bitter. "Now that I'm confined to this bloody chair for the rest of my life. Now that I'm of no use to her at all." He glanced at the calendar on the wall and slapped the arm of the hated chair.

"She's dedicated to helping you, Major," Barnaby said.

"She's dedicated to making me a recipient of her blasted crippled soldiers' charity," Tony said.

Barnaby scratched his grizzled head. "I don't believe she sees you as a cripple, sir."

Tony snorted. "She hasn't seen me attempt to stand." *For longer than five seconds.*

"She intends to, sir." Barnaby walked to the library window, opened the drapes, and gestured toward the lawn. "That's what all of this is about."

Tony followed Barnaby's gaze and saw the new wooden construction taking place in the garden. "What is it?"

Barnaby faced his employer. "Since it's being constructed of wood, I think it must be a temporary ramp for your chair."

"A *ramp*?" Tony repeated. "Gerald didn't say anything about a ramp."

Following the Great Fire of London, large wooden structures had been outlawed in the city. Nearly all modern residences were constructed of stone or brick, but wooden structures were allowed in gardens, provided they were temporary and near water.

"He must have forgotten to mention it," Barnaby said. "Lady Blessing is having the workmen construct a new summerhouse and a ramp from the orangery through the garden to the reflecting pool."

"How do you know this?" Tony demanded.

"I asked about the cartloads of lumber and the carpenters she hired."

"Apparently, Gerald isn't the only one who forgets to mention things." He pinned Barnaby with his sharp gaze.

"I didn't forget, Major. I didn't mention it before because I thought you might object to its construction if you knew about it."

"You thought right."

Barnaby returned Tony's sharp gaze. "Why, sir?"

"Lady Blessing is changing things she has no business changing. She's usurping my authority.". *She was interfering with his normal routine. Creating chaos and unrest. Occupying too many of his thoughts. Making him want things he could not have. Making him want her.*

"She ordered the building of the ramp so you will be able to go from the house to the back gardens unassisted."

*"Unassisted?"* Tony glanced down at his lap as he sneered the word. "Are you blind, man? Or is she some sort of miracle worker? Is she going to order my limbs to support me as well?" He turned to his faithful batman. "You've seen my legs. You were there when the surgeon tried to saw them off. You heard the physician describe my fate. You know the eventual outcome."

"No, sir, I don't," Barnaby said. "And neither do you."

Tony arched an eyebrow. "But Lady Blessing does?"

"I don't know, sir," Barnaby admitted. "But she has good ideas and wants to help you. What harm will it do for you to sit in the garden and enjoy the sunshine while the work is going on?"

"Sunshine?" Tony complained. "When have we seen sunshine? It's nothing but rain and this interminable fog."

"It won't rain every day," Barnaby predicted. "And if it does, you can sit in the belvedere and watch it."

"And catch my death of cold."

Barnaby gave him a mighty frown. "Self-pity doesn't become you, Major."

Tony heaved an exasperated sigh. "All right. I'll sit in the garden, in this blasted chair. But until the ramp is completed, no one will be allowed to witness my humiliation at being carried down the steps. I intend to be there before she arrives and stay until she leaves. And she must never know the extent of my injuries."

"She already knows, my lord," Barnaby said. "Or weren't you paying attention when she departed?"

"She knows I don't stand in her presence," Tony corrected. "She doesn't need to know any more."

# CHAPTER 11

*"Knowledge itself is power."*
—Francis Bacon, 1561-1626

"Good evening, my dear." Lord Weymouth stood up and opened his arms as Caroline entered the room. "You look lovely."

"Thank you, Uncle Trevor." Caroline walked into his embrace. "You look as handsome as ever. Just like a proud new papa."

He squeezed her tightly. "The proudest." Brushing her forehead with a kiss, he added. "Of both my sons. And my precious grandchildren."

"I can't wait to see them. I want to be the first visitor once Aunt Cicely is feeling well enough to receive me."

Trevor and Cicely Abernathy, the Earl and Countess of Weymouth, weren't her true aunt and uncle. They were her godparents. *Aunt* and *Uncle* were honorary titles she'd bestowed on them when she was a small child. Caroline also considered their eldest son, Griffin, her honorary cousin.

Uncle Trevor and Aunt Cicely had welcomed another son six weeks ago. Thirty-one years after their first one. Griffin and his wife, Alyssa, had welcomed twins—a daughter and a son—only hours before Aunt Cicely presented Uncle Trevor with Nathan.

"I'll see that you are," Lord Weymouth promised.

"How are Aunt Cicely and Nathan?"

Trevor Abernathy, Lord Weymouth, beamed. "He's happy and healthy and growing like a weed. They're still at Abernathy Manor with Griff and Alyssa and will be for some time. I don't want them traveling in the damp and cold. Cicely is recovering nicely—not as quickly as Alyssa—but she's regaining her strength thanks to Alyssa, who doesn't believe in bloodletting. She refused to allow the physicians to bleed Cicely during her confinement. And for that, I am deeply grateful."

"How are Griff and Alyssa and the twins?"

"Cicely and Nolan," Lord Weymouth supplied the names of his six-week-old grandchildren. "Cicely after her grandmother and Nolan after Griff's junior officer, Nolan Hughes, who was killed on the Peninsula in the engagement where Griff was injured."

Caroline nodded. "I'm so happy for all of you."

"Cicely and Alyssa adored the gifts you sent. They asked me to relay their personal thanks, in addition to the formal thank-yous they sent."

"They are most welcome." Caroline ushered Lord Weymouth to a comfortable chair close to the fire. "Would you like tea or coffee? Or something stronger?"

"Coffee with brandy if you have it." He made a wry face. "I'm not as young as I once was and the trip to London gets rougher each year."

Caroline gave the bell pull a tug. When Tyson appeared, she ordered coffee and brandy for Lord Weymouth and tea for herself and an assortment of small sandwiches, biscuits, and cakes. "I know you've had a long journey from Abernathy Manor, Uncle Trevor. I appreciate your taking the time away from your family for me."

"You are welcome, my dear. It was no hardship to come visit my only goddaughter. I haven't seen you since Blessing's funeral. You look much better. There are roses in your cheeks once again and I'm particularly glad to see you have given up your widow's weeds."

Caroline blushed. The blue frock she was wearing was most becoming and the time she'd spent in Tony's gardens had put the roses in her cheeks. That, and her frantic rush to change out of her work clothes and into the blue dress before her guest arrived.

Weymouth's eyes sparkled with amusement when he spoke. "You seem to be adjusting well to your new circumstances."

Caroline smiled. "Circumstances I believe I have you to thank for."

"No thanks are necessary." Weymouth shrugged. "Suggesting that Blessing abide by the terms of the agreement he made with you was the extent of my involvement in the matter." *That wasn't entirely true. But Caroline didn't need to know the leverage Weymouth had used to force Blessing to keep his word.* "I did hope Blessing would do his utmost to protect you from your father's further ambitions."

"Uncle Trevor, you've been a wonderful godfather to me in every way."

"I'm only sorry I couldn't protect you from Rushton." He smiled at Caroline. "When I read your wedding announcements in *The Times* and the *Chronicle*, I was hoping you would escape them by eloping with young Carlisle."

She had hoped that, too. But Tony hadn't come for her.

"That's one of the things I wanted to talk to you about," Caroline said.

"I'm listening," Weymouth replied.

Hearing Tyson's approach with the tray table, Caroline put a finger to her lips to caution her godfather that the staff wasn't as loyal to her as they had been to Lord Blessing.

Knowing Granville Blessing as well as he had, Lord Weymouth immediately understood Caroline's warning. He lifted a copy of *The Times* from the side table and pretended to peruse it while Caroline admitted the butler and took command of the tea tray.

After Tyson withdrew from the room, Caroline poured coffee and brandy for her guest and tea for herself, then set out the plate of light confections. Weymouth laid the newspaper aside and accepted the glass of brandy she offered. "I don't quite know how to begin," she confided. "When I sent the note, I was doing a favor for a friend."

Weymouth took a sip of brandy. "One of your Charlotte Society friends, no doubt."

His comment shouldn't have surprised her, but it did. Weymouth had a reputation for knowing everything that occurred in London—especially anything involving the military. "I wasn't aware our little organization had become common knowledge."

"It isn't common knowledge," Weymouth told her. "But it was made known to me when your name appeared on the royal patent."

"I suppose you think it's an impractical idea."

"On the contrary." Weymouth shook his head. "I think it's a very personable and compassionate idea. Far too many of our soldiers suffer from a lack of understanding from family and friends when they return home from the battlefields. I appreciate what you and your friends are attempting to do, but I must caution you against your method of selecting soldiers at random." He tapped his temple with his index finger. "Wellington was right about the common soldiers. Many of them *are* the scum of the earth. I suggest you be careful and base your choices on logic rather than sentiment."

"I think you will find Phoebe, Dulcie, and I will be quite sensible in our choices."

"Have you made them?" Weymouth asked.

Caroline smiled. "I've made mine and Miss Tennant has made hers. Miss Osborne has yet to make her final decision. But I'm sure you know that already."

Weymouth laughed. "As a matter of fact, I didn't. May I inquire as to whom you've chosen?"

"My choice is Major Lord Anthony Carlisle, Earl of Carlisle."

"I was notified he had returned from the dead," Weymouth said, arching his brows in admiration of her boldness.

"And returned to London," Caroline added.

"I'm pleased to hear it." Weymouth's answer was sincere. He liked the young earl and admired his service. "I was glad the battlefield reports of his untimely death were incorrect." He took a finger sandwich from the tray. "I was given to understand that the surgeon who tended his injuries reported him dead based on his profound belief that young Carlisle would succumb to his injuries within hours. The subsequent reports failed to correct the surgeon's assumption."

"He was badly injured," Caroline said. "And he's yet to fully recover from his injuries. He returned to London in a closed sedan chair and he refuses to receive any visitors. Including me."

"I suppose one of the reasons you purchased the Selby estate is its convenient proximity to Carlisle's." Weymouth washed down the finger sandwich with his last swallow of brandy.

"How long did you say you'd been in London?"

"I didn't," Weymouth replied. "But the answer is one day."

"One day and you've already learned most of what I planned to tell you." She met his gaze with an admiring one of her own. "I don't know how you do it."

"Do what?" No choirboy had ever looked as innocent as Trevor Weymouth.

"Discover so much information in such a short amount of time." She sighed. "You always seem to know everything before anyone else does."

"I receive dispatches from the War Office every day. Rain or shine. At war or at peace. Whether in the country or in town. I'm kept informed."

"I'm glad." Caroline refilled his coffee cup. "Because I am in need of information."

Weymouth helped himself to another sandwich. "Well, Caroline, what can I do for you and Miss Tennant?" He fixed her with his gaze. "Or is it Miss Osborne?"

"It's Miss Tennant," she acknowledged. "See? Right again."

"Process of elimination, my dear. Only two of you have selected your soldiers. I know who you've selected so that leaves Miss Tennant."

Caroline took a sealed envelope out of her skirt pocket and handed it to Lord Weymouth, who slit the seal with his thumbnail.

"No." Caroline held up her hands to stop him before he could unfold the paper. "Please don't read it in my presence."

Weymouth looked at her askance.

"I'm not privy to his name and I promised Miss Tennant that only the two of you would know it until she is ready to reveal it."

"I understand." Weymouth pocketed the note. "I'll read it when I'm alone. You have my word on it."

"Thank you."

"You're welcome." Lord Weymouth took her right hand in his and patted it before letting go. "What does Miss Tennant need to know about this fellow?"

"She needs to know where he is," Caroline replied. "She's looking for him. He's not listed on the casualty lists—the wounded or the dead. She's searched every hospital and lodging house in London open to veterans, but he's nowhere to be found."

"How does she know this man?" Weymouth propped his elbows on his knees and steepled his fingers.

"She doesn't know him—yet. But she promised a close relative—" Caroline caught herself before she revealed too much of what Dulcie had told her.

"Her late brother. Geoffrey, Viscount Tennant," Weymouth surmised.

"Yes," Caroline confirmed. "Her late brother. Dulcie promised Geoffrey she would contact the man whose name is on the card I gave you if the worst should happen to Geoffrey and she found herself under the new viscount's control."

"And your friend, being female and unmarried, finds herself under the dominion of the current viscount, a relation who doesn't appear to have her best interests at heart," Weymouth concluded. "It seems Geoffrey Tennant was well aware of the current viscount's nature."

"Exactly." Caroline smiled at Lord Weymouth. "You were the only person I knew who could help her."

"I'll do what I can for your friend," Weymouth said. "Now tell me what I can do for you."

Caroline scraped her bottom lip with her teeth before answering.

"I want Lord Carlisle's medical reports and the names of the surgeons and physicians who've tended him."

*"What?"* Weymouth didn't surprise easily. He was too well informed. But Caroline's request took him aback.

"You know about my charity, Uncle Trevor. You know how it works."

He gave a sharp nod. "I know the aim of your society is to help the veterans returning from war regain their places in civilian society as quickly and seamlessly as possible."

"I can't help Lord Carlisle unless I know how badly he was injured."

Weymouth grinned. "I take it Lord Carlisle is an unwilling recipient of your charity."

*"Most* unwilling."

"A man has his pride," Weymouth warned her.

"Too much of it, I fear." Caroline sighed. "There is such a thing as cutting off one's nose to spite one's face."

"I'll see that you get his medical reports along with his physician's and surgeon's names and recommendations for care."

Caroline frowned as a new thought occurred. "You won't say anything about this to Papa, will you? I don't relish his reaction."

Weymouth gave an exaggerated shudder. "Heaven forbid. There is no love lost between the two of us. I only speak to him when protocol or the Prince Regent demands it." Weymouth rose to take his leave, then bent unexpectedly to press a kiss against Caroline's forehead. "Good luck, my dear. I'll be in touch."

"Thank you, Uncle Trevor."

"Don't mention it. The only thing I relish more than putting a spanner in your father's machinations is watching a young man lose his heart in a battle of wills with a determined young woman." He touched the tip of her nose with his index finger. "Like my beautiful goddaughter, Caroline."

# CHAPTER 12

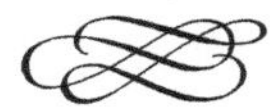

*"He is the very pineapple of politeness."*
—Richard Brinsley Sheridan, 1751-1816

Lord Anthony Carlisle was sitting at a table beneath a tent beside the reflecting pool in his garden, wrapped in a heavy great coat, sipping coffee when Caroline entered through the hole in the wall from Selby House. He turned in his seat and watched as she paused along the way to issue instructions and greet the workmen by name. She stopped short when she saw him.

"*Tony.*" She breathed his name. "What are you doing here?"

"I live here," Carlisle replied. "This happens to be my garden. Your garden is that way." He pointed toward the gaping hole in the back wall where the gate had been.

She had the grace to blush. "What's a gate between neighbors?"

"Indeed." He lifted the pot and poured coffee into a mug. "Join me?"

Caroline eyed him warily.

"Go on. Take it." He extended a steaming mug of the brew. "There is no hemlock."

After accepting the mug, Caroline wrapped her hands around it and took a sip of the steaming brew. She grimaced at the strong taste, but appreciated the warmth that penetrated her gloves and spread through her body.

She tried to hide it, but Tony recognized her expression of distaste. He sympathized. He had learned to drink coffee black and strong in the cavalry. "You don't like it?"

"I never acquired a taste for coffee," she admitted. "I prefer chocolate in the morning."

He patted the seat next to him, inviting her to take a seat.

Caroline shook her head.

"I beg your pardon." His voice held a note of disdain. "It's been a long time since I entertained a lady in my garden. I'd forgotten that ladies generally drink tea or chocolate. I wasn't prepared."

"How could you be prepared?" she asked. "After yesterday, I'm sure you weren't expecting to see me this morning any more than I was expecting to see you."

"I expected to see you." A mysterious half-smile lifted the corners of his mouth. "I wouldn't have come down here if I hadn't." His voice took on a husky note and the look on his face made Caroline intensely aware of him. "I knew you would never be satisfied with painting the gardens..."

*"Painting?"* A quizzical look crossed her features.

"You know—paper, watercolors, palette, brush, easel..." He mimicked the act of painting. "The delicate talent all proper young ladies are encouraged to pursue." His tone was sardonic, charming, and the Tony she remembered so well.

"What good would my painting a watercolor of your gardens do for you?"

"I could frame it and mount it on the wall and view my gardens the way they used to be. The way my ancestors planned them. The way I chose to maintain them."

"I paint about as well as you write." Caroline thought of the invitation she'd tucked between the pages of *The Complete Works of Shakespeare* for safekeeping and all the letters she had written to him over the years. All the letters that had gone unanswered while she desperately hoped for a reply from Tony to read and treasure during her years at Blessing House. Caroline had cherished her secret love. Lord Blessing might have laid claim to her body, but he couldn't control her thoughts or her feelings. Or Tony's.

Tony could have addressed his letters to Phoebe, as Caroline had suggested, and Caroline would have had something from him, something of her own to treasure the way she had read and re-read his note last night.

She would have liked to have known Tony's thoughts during the war. She would have liked to share his experiences. But he had denied her even that small comfort when he refused to correspond with her.

Tony blinked in surprise. "After everything that happened, you expected me to write?"

"I hoped you would," she murmured. The truth was that Caroline had done more than hope. She'd prayed. She'd begged. And she'd made bargains with God. Promising to be the best wife in the world if only Tony would write one letter to her.

"It's most improper for a bachelor to correspond with a married lady," he reminded her. "Especially one married to a powerful, jealous, and vindictive old marquess." He pinned her with his silvery gaze. "Since you chose to end our brief *acquaintance* to exchange vows with the marquess," he emphasized the word she'd used to describe their relationship, "I thought it most imprudent to resume it by post after your nuptials." Tony's blood ran cold at the thought of what Blessing might have done to her had he intercepted letters from him. "I considered the consequences." He met her gaze. "Even if *you* did not."

Caroline gasped, nearly overturning her mug in her haste to get up from the table. "Thank you for the coffee, Lord Carlisle." She gave him a coldly polite smile. "I won't detain you any longer."

He inclined his head. "As you wish, Lady *Blessing*."

"It seems the marquess wasn't alone in his jealousy or his vindictiveness." She glared at him with all the frost she could muster. "I would have thought you above that, Tony."

*She had no idea.* "No man is above that, Caroline," Tony said. "Not when it concerns his woman."

"And no woman is above doing what she deems necessary to help her man." Caroline looked him in the eye.

"Would that be me? Or Blessing?"

"You, you ass. But you are too blind to see it."

"I saw your wedding announcement. And that was all I needed to see."

"You can't see anything," she accused. "Because you insist on living in the past. Look around, Tony. Things can change."

He glanced down at his legs. "They certainly can, Lady Blessing. And some of us live in the past because the past is all we have."

"Only because you refuse to see that you have a future."

"Do I?"

The look she gave him fairly crackled with anger. "And let me tell you this, Lord Carlisle. If I *could* paint, I wouldn't paint your gardens. Why would I waste my talent? They've looked the same for over a hundred years."

"It's called succession," he said. "That's what I love about it. It's home. It never changes. It's always the same."

"Then I'm truly sorry. For trying to expand your world when you're determined to shrink it."

"It wasn't your decision to make. Changing the gardens and grounds to expand my world is a decision for my wife to make."

"Have you a wife?" Caroline asked, her heart pounding in her chest as she awaited his answer.

He firmed his lips and gritted out the words. "You know I don't."

"Have you asked anyone else to be your wife since you asked me?"

"No."

"Then, I was right to assume I could use my authority just as if nothing had changed between us," Caroline said. "Because it didn't."

"You married someone else," Tony reminded her.

All activity in the garden seemed to stop except the air around them. It sparked, crackling like lightning in a summer thunderstorm. Building off the heat they generated as they continued to wound each other with sharp words and lingering, smoldering looks.

Caroline inhaled. "I had no choice."

"Oh?" Tony arched one eyebrow. "I heard differently."

"I don't know what you heard," she said. "But nothing between us changed."

"Everything changed," Tony said harshly. "You overstepped your bounds, Lady Blessing. You assumed too much. But I expected you would. Marchionesses always do." He held her gaze. "The only thing I didn't expect was for you to come unarmed."

"Unarmed?" It took a moment for Caroline to grasp his meaning. "The fish net?"

"The one you used to terrorize my unsuspecting goldfish—" He managed a smile. "And my poor butler."

"I didn't terrorize your butler with the net." She squared her shoulders and raised her chin a bit higher. "I had it in my hand when I decided to see what had become of Gerald. Your butler mistook my intentions."

"The same way the French nobility mistook the intentions of the peasants storming the Bastille with pitchforks, scythes, and poles."

Caroline bit her bottom lip to keep from smiling at the picture he painted of her storming Carlisle House like French peasants storming the state prison in Paris. "How did you get down here anyway? The ramp isn't finished yet."

"So, it appears," he said. "Yet, I managed to make my way just the same."

He hadn't answered her question, but Caroline decided to let it go. "The work has been going on for over a fortnight," she said. "Why haven't you made an appearance before today?"

"It was foggy." Tony swallowed a mouthful of coffee.

"It's London," she retorted. "I should think you'd be accustomed to it by now." She gestured toward his great coat.

"I am well acquainted with fog." Carlisle met her gaze. "I spent an interminable night in a penetrating fog in Belgium once. I don't care to repeat the experience."

"I don't imagine you do," she murmured. She knew nothing about his night in the Belgian fog, but Caroline knew it had to be far worse than Tony made it sound.

She couldn't possibly imagine, Tony thought. Nobody who hadn't been there could. The night he'd spent in the mud and gore and the heavy fog would always be with him. He carried the scars from it. He could steer clear of mud and gore now that he was home, but London was a foggy town. He couldn't avoid the fog forever, even if the cold and damp proved as detrimental to his health as his physician had predicted. "What are your plans for today now that the Muses are gone and the goldfish have been captured?"

"Your Muses are safe," Caroline said. "They're at the stone mason's on Southwark for cleaning and polishing. They'll be restored to their former glory and returned when the renovations and the new constructions are finished. As for your goldfish..." She met his gaze. "I didn't finish my task yesterday. There are still fish to be captured." She set her empty mug aside, lifted the hem of her skirt, and extended her foot to show him her galoshes.

"Gerald told me you planned to boil my goldfish."

"I'm not planning to boil your fish!" she exclaimed. "I'm planning to boil *you*."

Tony lifted an eyebrow at that.

Caroline gave an exasperated sigh. "Not boil you exactly. I just want to deepen the pool and heat it so *you* can use it."

"What makes you think I want to use it?"

"Why wouldn't you want to relax and soothe aching bones and muscles in hot water?" Caroline glared at him.

"What about the fish?"

"We're building another pond for the fish at the center of the maze." She pointed toward the maze. "I'm trying to save your blasted fish by moving them to safety while we drain and rebuild the reflecting pool." Caroline made a face. "The trick is to catch the slippery things."

"At least you came prepared." Tony indicated the hooded cape she wore over her pinafore and muslin dress. He ignored her waterproof overshoes, but paid close attention to her slender calves and her exposed knees beneath the fine lace of the leg of her muslin drawers.

"Not quite." She laughed. "I forgot my net."

"I didn't." Tony pointed to the fishnet propped against the railing of the belvedere.

Caroline glanced at him from beneath her lashes. "Are you planning to help me remove the fish, my lord?"

"Of course not." He gave a mock shudder. "As a belted earl and a gentleman, I'm here as a spectator only. I can't be seen working alongside laborers."

"I'm a marchioness," she reminded him. "I outrank you. If I can do yeoman's work, so can you."

"We only have one net," he pointed out.

"You use it," she said as she removed her cape and tucked up her skirt and pinafore in preparation. "I'll wade in."

"I won't hear of it," he protested.

"All right." Caroline conceded. "I'll use the net and *you* can wade in."

Tony opened his mouth to speak, but his words wouldn't come. How could he protest when he knew he was unable to wade in? He glanced down at his feet and realized he was wearing new boots.

"What's the matter?" Caroline followed his gaze. "Surely you aren't afraid of ruining your boots?"

He didn't care about his boots. He could afford to ruin dozens of pairs of boots by strolling into the reflecting pool if he chose. If truth be known, he'd enjoy the opportunity. If only he could... Tony flexed his ankle, gritting his teeth against the agony in his calf muscles as he did so. "As it happens, I am. Mr. Hoby just delivered these boots. I'd prefer to oil them again before I test the leather by wading in." He shrugged. "And as you pointed out, you outrank me. And you're wearing galoshes." He paused for dramatic effect. "So have at it. Ladies first. You herd the fish. I'll net them..."

# CHAPTER 13

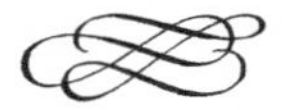

*"Give a man a fish and you feed him for a day.*
*Teach a man to fish and you feed him for a lifetime."*
—Chinese Proverb

Tony watched as Caroline took the last koi from the pocket of her pinafore, dropped it into the water barrel, and disappeared through the missing back gate. He waited a minute longer to make certain she wouldn't reappear before taking a linen handkerchief from his pocket and waving it in the air.

The two footmen stationed by the door of the conservatory hurried forward at the sight of the prearranged signal.

"G-get m-me i-inside." Tony fought to keep his teeth from chattering and failed. "I-I'm f-freezing."

Fielder, the taller of the two footmen, blocked the view from the back gate while Kirby, the stronger, lifted Tony from the chair and carried him inside the conservatory. After clearing the housemaids and other footmen from the rooms along the way from the conservatory to Lord Carlisle's bedchamber, Barnaby opened the hothouse door for Kirby and the major and began issuing instructions. "Take him straight to his rooms."

"Yes, sir, Mr. Barnaby."

Barnaby matched them stride for stride, opening doors and removing impediments along the way, until they reached the master suite. "I've drawn a bath for you, sir."

"Thank you, Barnaby." Tony firmed his lips to stop the chattering.

"Put him there." Barnaby pointed Kirby to a leather reclining sofa. "And leave us."

Kirby gave a slight bow as he and Fielder withdrew from the chamber.

Barnaby assisted Tony as he began removing his clothes. "You took long enough, sir. I was beginning to think you were going to stay outside all night."

"I stayed until she left for the day." He shuddered as the warm air in the bedroom penetrated the chill that permeated his clothes and his very bones. "The woman works from dawn to dusk and beyond. I was afraid I was going to turn into a bloody iceberg."

"No wonder." Barnaby tugged Tony's boots off and placed them near the fire to dry, then took the gloves Tony handed him and draped them over the top of the boots. "What happened to your great coat?"

Tony shrugged out of his jacket, untied his cravat, and unbuttoned his waistcoat. "I gave it to Lady Blessing after she slipped and fell in the reflecting pool."

"She stayed out in this weather wearing wet clothing?" Barnaby asked.

"She had a velvet cape," Carlisle told him. "But it offered little warmth when she pulled it on over her wet clothes."

"Lady Blessing is a healthy young woman; you are otherwise," Barnaby reminded him.

"I should hope so." Tony gave Barnaby a wry look.

Barnaby's cheeks reddened. "I meant that you are not as healthy as you once were. And are particularly susceptible to the cold and damp." He handed the major a length of flannel.

Working together in the manner that had become second nature,

Tony lifted his hips so Barnaby could tug his breeches down his legs. "I had to give her my coat." He covered his groin with the flannel as Barnaby exposed his nakedness. "After I failed to go to her aid when she slipped in the pool and came up drenched from head to toe." He raked his hand through his hair. "It was the least I could do for my ungentlemanly behavior."

"I'm sure Lady Blessing didn't consider your lack of assistance ungentlemanly. She knows you're confined to a chair." Barnaby began moving Tony's legs through the series of exercises he performed twice a day. "She suggested the construction of the ramp to enable you to enjoy the out of doors."

"No doubt she's a virtual paragon of dutiful sacrifice," Tony snapped as a muscle spasm tore through his leg. He reached down to grab his calf. "The surgeon might have been right. Amputation might have been a better option."

"Bite your tongue, major," Barnaby scolded. "After everything we've been through, I'll not listen to that blasphemy." He began massaging the major's painful calf. "Tell me about your time in the gardens. What did you do today?"

Tony forced himself to ignore the pain and focus on relating the day's events. "You should have seen the look on her face when she arrived to find me drinking coffee under the tent in the garden."

"I'm sure the sight of you was unexpected." Barnaby completed his massage, then moved to the bathtub and bent to test the temperature of the water before adding more hot water.

"Quite unexpected," Tony agreed. "Especially since the ramp she ordered built hasn't been completed."

"Did she ask how you came to be there?" Barnaby scooped Tony from the sofa and carried him to the bath.

"She asked. I didn't answer." Tony expelled his breath in a hiss as Barnaby guided his descent into the tub. "Are you trying to boil me, too?"

"Too?" Barnaby pretended ignorance of the major's meaning.

"You heard Gerald relate Lady Blessing's plans to boil me in the reflecting pool by piping the water from the hot spring in Selby's garden into it."

"Lady Blessing is trying to help you," Barnaby said. "And the rest of us as well."

Tony arched an eyebrow.

"You've lost two or three stone during your convalescence, but you're far from a featherweight. And I'm not as strong or as young as I once was."

Tony snorted. "You could still outdo any man in the regiment."

"All the same, a heated bath adapted for your use would be a welcome addition. You could bathe unassisted." Barnaby gave him a mischievous smile. "And when you're not bathing in it, I intend to avail myself."

"It's not even built and you're already planning to borrow it?" Tony teased.

"Indeed, I am, sir."

"You're welcome to it." Tony sighed as the warm water dispatched the chill in his bones and soothed his sore muscles and the aches and pains brought on by a day spent in the raw weather. "In fact, you're welcome to avail yourself of it first. In case she does make good on her threat to boil me."

Barnaby chuckled. "I doubt Lady Blessing would go to all the trouble to transform the goldfish pond into a heated bath to help you if she planned to boil you."

"Maybe not boil me." Tony chuckled. "But she wouldn't mind scalding me. And dare I take the chance?"

"Fortune favors the bold," Barnaby quoted.

"Does it?" Tony's question held a bitter edge. "Once upon a time I was a bold lad." A dark shadow crossed his face as he glanced down at his scarred legs.

"You survived, sir," Barnaby reminded him. "Many bold lads did not."

Tony covered his face with his hands, sluicing water over it to soothe his suddenly burning eyes. "You're right, Barnaby. Battle and disease have decimated a generation of bold lads. It's time I cease feeling sorry for myself and do what I can do for as long as I can do it."

"I agree, sir." Barnaby glanced at the major, who wiped his face, then rested the back of his head against the rim of the tub. "As long as you're sensible about it. No more sitting in the damp and cold for hours on end without your coat. No need to tempt fate."

"That reminds me," Tony said. "I'll need one for tomorrow morning. Lady Blessing wore mine home. And although I'm certain she'll return it, I've no idea when." He grinned. "She won't return it until it's as good as new. And it may take a while to get the fishy smell out of it."

Barnaby snorted. "If the odor comes out."

"It will come out." Tony grinned his first real grin in months. "It will have no choice against her. She won't give up until it does. You should have seen her, Barnaby, wading in the reflecting pool, forcing the koi fish into the net."

"I cannot believe Lady Blessing waded into the pool rather than have someone else do it."

"The hired men were engaged elsewhere," Tony explained. "I couldn't do it. She was wearing rubber overshoes, so she elected to do it."

"Who was wielding the net?"

"I was," Tony replied proudly. "I may not be able to walk, but there's nothing wrong with my arms." He ran a soapy cloth over his upper arm, surprised to find that his broken arm had not only healed, but regained the muscle he'd lost. And more. "She drove them into the net and I landed them." He demonstrated the wrist action he'd used to net the fish and drop them into the water barrel. "What we couldn't net, she caught by hand and pocketed."

"In your great coat?" Barnaby was appalled by the idea of the pockets of the major's wool great coat holding fish.

"No. In the pockets of her pinafore."

Barnaby imagined Lady Blessing's lady's maid being equally appalled at the idea of fish in her mistress's pinafore pockets.

Tony's lips turned up at the corners at the memory of Caroline stuffing goldfish into the large square pockets on the front of her pinafore before carrying them to the water barrel for transportation to the temporary pond. "Everything was running like clockwork until she lost her footing and went under." Frowning at the way his heart was pounding as he recalled the moment Caroline had slipped and gone under the water, Tony kept a white-knuckled grip on the edge of the tub.

He'd been terrified she might have hit her head on the bottom of the pool.

For the second time in his life, Anthony Carlisle had felt real fear. The fear that Caroline might drown before the footmen he had standing by could reach her. Tony could swim. But he couldn't stand. Seated as he was, on a chair, beneath the tent, there was no way for him to get to her, except belly crawl.

Until he remembered the long-handled net…

It seemed an eternity before she grabbed hold of it. Forever before she pushed herself into a sitting position and gulped a mouthful of air. She was soaking wet from head to toe and shivering like she'd never get warm, but as far as Tony was concerned, Caroline Hardage had never looked more beautiful.

She was alive and breathing and, despite her blue lips, chattering teeth, and straggling hair, undaunted and scrambling to keep the koi from escaping. "Blast it, Tony! Use the net! Use the net! Don't let them get away!"

Tony grinned. The girl emerging from the water, like Aphrodite arising from the foam of the waters of the Paphos on the island of Cyprus, was the girl he remembered. Not the high-handed Marchioness of Blessing, who had created chaos in his garden, but the girl he'd asked to marry him.

"Happy memory, sir?" Barnaby asked.

"How did you manage to miss it, Barnaby? I thought you were watching from the window."

Barnaby didn't have to ask which window. "I wasn't in constant attendance, sir," he said. "I watched off and on while I was tending to my duties."

"No doubt relieved to be rid of my constant demands for the day." Tony's comment carried no bitterness this time. It was simply an observation, not an indictment of his situation.

"Fishing for compliments, sir?" Barnaby set a glass of whisky on the table beside the bathing tub.

"No." Carlisle laughed at Barnaby's play on words. "Just recalling the day's events. I'll never forget the sight of Lady Blessing stuffing goldfish in her apron pockets. Or the look on her face when she sat up in the water and realized the fish were escaping. She was so determined to keep them from swimming away she was shouting at me to net them." He rolled his head from side to side along the rim of the tub. "She was wet and disheveled and so beautiful it hurt to look at her. It reminded me of..." *The sudden spring shower at a friend's garden party when he and Caroline had taken shelter in the gazebo in the center of the maze and had spent the downpour kissing as if their lives depended on it.*

Tony let go of the edge of the tub and covered the length of toweling preserving his modesty with his hand. "It reminded me of things better left forgotten."

"Good memories need never be forgotten, sir." Barnaby turned to leave. "Sometimes they are all we have."

*His thoughts exactly.* "Barnaby?"

"Sir?"

"It occurred to me that most of your waking hours are spent tending to my needs and wants and that you might relish a day to yourself."

"I've been taking care of young cavalry officers for nearly twenty years." Barnaby scratched a gray patch on his grizzled head. "I wouldn't know what to do with free time. I wouldn't know what to do with myself." He gave Tony a stern look. "Call when you require my assistance, sir."

"I will," Tony said. "And thank you, Barnaby."

"Don't linger after the water cools," the manservant advised before adding another log to the fire. "You've already spent the day in the cold and damp without your coat."

"I barely felt the cold," Tony told him.

"You barely felt it the last time, too," Barnaby drawled, "and it nearly killed you."

"The weather didn't nearly kill me," Tony corrected. "The broken bones, the bayonet wounds, and the failed cutthroat did." He rubbed the scar on the underside of his jaw where the young scavenger had cut his throat, but failed to nick the jugular vein.

"Next time, the cold and damp weather might."

Tony let Barnaby have the last word because he knew his friend was right.

The Belgian physician who had attended him in the hospital in Brussels had made certain Tony understood the extent of the damage his lungs had suffered. As the physician had explained in his halting English, "the terrible British weather could do what the enemy soldiers and scavengers had failed to do." Until he regained his strength, Tony would be highly susceptible to pleurisy.

Parting with his great coat had been foolish. But he didn't regret it. At the time, Caroline had needed his coat more than he did. Tony hadn't been able to do much to help her as she scrambled in the water, but he could offer her a dry garment and protect her from the weather and the stares of the men working in the garden.

Tony couldn't regret the best day he'd had since that day in the rain so long ago. Once he had spent nearly every waking hour planning ways to steal a few moments alone with her. He couldn't regret the time he'd spent alone with Caroline today.

Closing his eyes once again, Tony recalled every detail of her face —her blue eyes with the flecks of gold in the irises that made them look green at times, her creamy ivory complexion with the light sprinkling of reddish freckles across her beautifully sculpted cheeks and the bridge of her perfect nose. And her mouth—with its slightly fuller lower lip and the bow of her upper one. Her lips were so tempting he'd wanted to kiss her on the spot. Tony groaned. He'd always loved the softness and the sweetness of her lips... So much so that he'd had to curl his hands into fists to keep from smoothing a strand of her light brown hair away from the corner of her mouth and following his impulse to taste her.

She was five years older now. With a pair of frown lines on her forehead that hadn't been there before. But Caroline Hardage was every bit as beautiful now as she had been the last time he'd held her in his arms.

Tony sluiced warm water over his face. The soap he'd been using stung his eyes. Blinking furiously, he fought to keep his eyes from watering. He'd spent five years reminding himself she was married and beyond his reach. Five years of hating the lucky old man she married. What was he going to do now that she was a widow and he was half the man he'd once been? Now that she was further beyond his reach than ever?

Five years ago, he had told himself she'd married the Marquess of Blessing rather than settle for becoming the Countess of Carlisle. During five years of war, he'd managed to stay angry at her. Tony had believed he always would be. Until a day ago, he believed he'd succeeded. But he was mistaken.

If he'd kept his distance—kept *her* at a distance—he could have held onto his anger. But seeing her up close... Hearing her voice again... Remembering the way it caught in her throat when she was nervous or excited... Seeing the little pulse beat at the base of her throat. Smelling the intoxicating scent of her soap and perfume. The fragrance of roses in her hair...

Tony squeezed his eyes shut. She was a marchioness in her own right. Why the bloody hell was she wasting her time with him? He had offered her the world before. Now he could offer her nothing...

Opening his eyes, he reached for the glass of whisky and drained it.

# CHAPTER 14

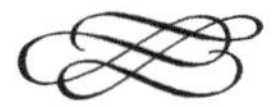

*"Some are weather-wise, some are otherwise."*
—Benjamin Franklin, 1706-1790

"Good evening, madam." Tyson greeted Caroline as she entered through the front door.

"Good evening, Tyson." Caroline returned her butler's greeting, crossing the entrance hall on her way to the stairs. "I left my galoshes on the front steps. Please see they're dried and returned to my room by morning."

Tyson curled his upper lip in distaste at the distinct odor of fish emanating from her. "May I ask if madam has been near the fish market at Billingsgate?"

Caroline stopped before the butler and shrugged out of the great coat she was wearing. The hem of her cloak, and the hems of her dress and canvas pinafore, were dripping wet and she reeked of carp. She was also thoroughly soaked and half-frozen from hours spent in the reflecting pool and in the thick mist shrouding Tony's gardens. She was in no mood to explain her appearance or her whereabouts to a contemptuous butler. "Billingsgate?" She huffed with disdain. "Household staff shops at Billingsgate. Marchionesses do not. If I carry the odor of fish, it's not because I waded through the gore at Billingsgate, but because I've been fishing at the finest estate in Mayfair." She shoved the coat at him. "Please see that this is also cleaned and dried."

Tyson blinked at her. "I beg your pardon, madam."

"It's about time."

Clearly shocked at her tart tone, Tyson gaped as she started up the stairs. "Madam?"

"See that the gentleman's coat is dried, cleaned, and brushed by morning so I can return it to its owner."

"Madam, I must protest your questionable behavior."

"If you must," she replied. "But before you do, perhaps I should explain..."

"Please do," Tyson invited.

"Before you question the coachmen and the footmen about my whereabouts, you should know I've already explained myself to the footmen and the coachmen."

"In what way, madam?" Tyson sniffed, clearly affronted by Caroline's breach of household protocol.

In traditional households, the butler's authority extended to the coachmen and grooms. Protocol demanded that the master or mistress of the house express his or her pleasure or displeasure with the service of the coachmen or grooms to the butler, who would then relay it to the appropriate person.

"I explained that the Marquess of Blessing is no longer master of this house." She stopped a third of the way up the stairs and turned to gaze down at the butler from her superior vantage point. "I am. I hold the title. I hold the keys to this house and to employment within it. I explained that my comings and goings are *my* business and that reporting them to you was no longer required or warranted." She took another step up, then swung back around to face the long-time family retainer. "How long have you been in service here, Tyson?"

"Thirty years, madam."

Caroline nodded. "That's a long time to be in service to one household." She met Tyson's gaze. "If you wish to continue in your current position, I suggest you treat me with the deference I've earned during my five years as marchioness. Think on it."

Leaving the butler standing open-mouthed at the foot of the stairs, looking just like one of the fish she had netted earlier, Caroline turned and marched the rest of the way up the steps.

Caroline made her way to her bedchamber, calling for her lady's maid. "Susan!"

"Here, milady." The maid came running, halting abruptly as she caught a whiff of the fishy smell coming from her mistress's clothes.

Caroline shed her hooded cape, wool gloves, and pinafore, dropping them in a heap on the parquet floor. "I require a hot bath."

"Aye, that you do." Susan pulled the bell pull, then held her breath as she bent to gather the discarded clothing. "Your clothes smell of fish."

"So I've been told," Caroline said.

Susan looked surprised.

"Tyson objected to the way I smelled when I walked in the door."

"I can't say I blame him." Susan wrinkled her nose. "I'll take these downstairs to the laundry and send up the maids with the buckets of water for your bath."

"Leave them for a moment," Caroline said, fumbling with the tiny buttons. "My hands are so cold I can't manage these buttons and ribbons."

"Lord have mercy, ma'am." Susan brushed her mistress's shaking hands aside and began tackling the row of tiny buttons and the bright blue ribbon fastening the bodice of her gown. "Your hands are like ice. What have you been doing?"

Caroline shimmied out of the dress, letting it fall to the floor, kicked off her slippers, then sat on the edge of a chair, and rolled her white stockings down her legs. "I went wading."

"Wading?" Susan retrieved Caroline's velvet robe and handed it to her, then bent to stir the fire. "In this weather? Why would you do such a foolish thing?"

Caroline shrugged. "That's where the fish were."

"You went fishing?"

"In a manner of speaking." Caroline repeated Tony's earlier phrase as she wrapped the robe tightly around her and moved closer to the fire.

"Did you catch any?"

"Dozens." Caroline sounded triumphant. "But they're fast and hard to grab."

Susan frowned. "What did you do with them? Take them to the kitchens to cook for supper?"

"Of course not," Caroline told her. "They're carp. They're too beautiful and expensive to be eaten."

"Carp?" Susan wrinkled her nose. "There's nothing beautiful about a carp. Unless you're hungry and it's presented on a platter."

"These are koi. From Japan. They're for looking. Not eating," Caroline explained.

"Tell that to the kitchen cats."

Caroline smiled at her maid's sharp-tongued wit. She and Susan had grown up together. Her lady's maid had moved with her when she'd married Lord Blessing and was her closest ally in the household. Susan was as close to her as Dulcie or Phoebe. And in some cases, much closer. Susan lived in Blessing House. She knew all but the most intimate details of Caroline's life there. Dulcie and Phoebe did not. "I doubt the cats would listen. They seldom do."

"You'd be right about that," Susan said. "The gardeners find the skeletons of dead fish outside the kitchen fishpond all the time." Susan finished bundling Caroline's clothes to take to the laundry and caught another whiff of the odor. "These things are sopping wet."

"Water is wet." Caroline turned her backside to the fire, hoping to warm it as she fought to keep her teeth from chattering. "Fish live in water."

"I never see any wet cats."

"They're quicker and more agile than I am." Caroline chuckled, recalling Tony's laughter and his derisive comments on her efforts to drive the fish toward his net. Urging her to move faster. To scramble. To cut off the fish who swam over, under, or around his net. And the comments she'd flung back at him, daring him to do better if he could. Tony had put up a good front, but Caroline knew better than to believe it. He had failed to stand in greeting for the second time in as many days. She'd dared him to wade in a half a dozen times and he had failed to accept any of her dares. Nor had he jumped in to rescue her when she'd slipped and fallen.

Susan clucked her tongue. "And smarter. Cats have sense enough to stay out of the water. And here you are wanting to get into *more* water."

"I want to get into *hot* water," Caroline clarified. "As soon as possible."

Susan pushed the chair closer to the fire and gave her mistress a wry look. "It appears to me you're already in it."

"Ha. Ha."

"Sit there," Susan ordered, "And get warm, while I see to the hot water."

"And tea," Caroline added. "And a supper tray."

"And tea," Susan confirmed. "And a supper tray." She shook a finger at her mistress. "I warned you that society of yours would get you into trouble... Staying out in the cold fog all day alone with a man..."

"I wasn't alone with a man. There were forty-three men working there today..."

"Good heavens." Susan fanned herself with a handkerchief.

"Not counting the servants watching from the windows," Caroline continued. "My society isn't going to be trouble for me; it's going to save me."

"If you don't lose your good name or catch your death of pneumonia first."

CAROLINE WAS STILL SOAKING IN THE TUB, UP TO HER NECK IN HOT, scented water, her head lolling against the rim, when Susan returned to the bathing room, carrying a heavy brocade robe.

"Sorry to interrupt, ma'am, but Lord Rushton is here for supper. He's waiting in the marquess's study."

Frowning, Caroline sat up straight in the tub. "My father is here? Now?"

"Yes, ma'am." Susan held the robe open, waiting for Caroline to step out of the tub. "He's insisting you invited him to supper this evening."

"I did no such thing," Caroline said, scowling. "I planned to eat my supper and go to bed."

"I know, ma'am," Susan replied. "I brought your supper tray when the maids brought the last pail of water. It's on the table in your bedchamber."

"Thank you." Caroline stepped out of the tub and shrugged into the flannel-lined robe, belting it tightly at the waist. "Why in heaven's name did Tyson let him in?"

Susan shrugged. "You know Tyson, ma'am. He's not one to refuse Lord Rushton entrance to Lord Blessing's house."

"It isn't Lord Blessing's house any longer. It's *my* house."

"And Lord Rushton is *your* father."

"Who is here uninvited." Squaring her shoulders, Caroline pulled herself to her full height, stepped into her slippers, and headed toward the door.

Susan was shocked. "You can't greet your father dressed like that!"

Caroline glanced down at her brocade robe. Only the most discriminating of men would know she was wearing a robe and not a dress. "I'm perfectly presentable."

"For someone else, maybe," Susan said. "But not for Lord Rushton." She gave Caroline a pointed look. "You're a marchioness now. On your own accord. If you want to get the better of Lord Rushton, you need to look like one."

Caroline took a deep breath, then exhaled it. *Only the most discriminating.* That described her father perfectly. Lord Rushton was nothing if not discriminating. Even Lord Anthony Carlisle hadn't been good enough to become a member of Rushton's family. "All right. Find me something suitable to wear and help me look like a marchioness in my own right as quickly as you can."

"No." Susan shook her head, the wicked sparkle in her eyes deepening. "Not quickly. Make him wait. You're a marchioness. Your father is only an earl. He should learn to wait for his betters."

"His betters? Me?"

"Of course, you, ma'am," Susan said. "According to court precedence, he follows you. That means you are one of the earl's betters."

"You're right." Caroline gave Susan an impulsive hug. She had announced her independence from her father and the Earl of Carlisle in an impassioned statement to her maid two nights ago. But a lifetime of jumping to do her father's bidding had Caroline falling into the same old pattern of obedience. Patterns so ingrained Caroline had already forgotten there was no reason for her to fear his temper. Lord Rushton no longer had any dominion over her. "What would I do without you?"

"You can't," Susan replied. "I'm the only ally you have in this house."

Caroline smiled. "Right again. So take all the time you need. I'll go downstairs when I'm ready. Not a moment before."

Susan did as her mistress suggested, taking her time with Caroline's toilette. She finally pushed the last hairpin into place, fastened a sapphire necklace around Caroline's neck, and handed the matching earrings to her mistress to put on.

When Caroline had finished, she stood up and smoothed the front of her gown. "You forgot the sapphire tiara."

She was teasing, but Susan took her comment seriously. "It's locked in the safe in the study. I didn't want to risk running into your father in order to get it."

"Neither would I," Caroline agreed. "And a tiara is a bit much for supper at home."

"You don't need it." Susan dropped into a deep curtsey. "You are every inch a marchioness in her own right, milady. And now, you look it."

"Thank you." Caroline took a deep breath to steady herself. She had managed to control her anger, but it was still there, simmering beneath the surface, as she prepared to face her father.

~

"It's about time you came downstairs," Lord Rushton said when his daughter crossed the threshold of the room that had once been her husband's private domain. "Cook has been holding supper for three-quarters of an hour."

"For whom?" Caroline asked, lifting her chin to a regal angle.

"For us." Rushton hurried to the door to prevent Caroline from entering the room he considered his private sanctum now that Lord Blessing was dead. "It's Wednesday. My club doesn't serve supper on Wednesday evenings." He began to elaborate on the shortcomings of his club choosing not to prepare and serve Wednesday evening meals.

"And here I thought you showed up every week to see me," she murmured. Her sarcasm was lost on her father who continued his litany of complaints.

Lord Rushton suddenly broke off his conversation. "What's that you said?"

"I pointed out that you took it upon yourself to intrude upon my evening uninvited," Caroline said. "Because my kitchen is open and your club is not."

"Uninvited?" Rushton was indignant. "I didn't come uninvited. I've been dining here every Wednesday evening for the past five years."

"You were invited to dine here when my late husband was alive," Caroline corrected. "You've continued to do so *uninvited* since he died."

"I come for a pleasant supper with my daughter." Lord Rushton reached for Caroline's arm.

Caroline stepped out of her father's reach. "Then I'm afraid you'll have to grace some other household with your presence on Wednesday evenings." She looked her father in the eye. "I've never considered your suppers here pleasant. And at any road, I prefer to dine alone on a tray in my room."

"I don't." Rushton offered her his elbow, then nodded to Tyson. "Inform Cook that we're ready to dine."

Caroline refused to allow her father to escort her into dinner. "Tyson, tell Cook to pack my father's supper in a hamper. He won't be staying."

"The devil you say!" Her father rounded on her. "I am dining here just as I always do!"

Caroline stood firm. "No, you are not."

The butler looked to her father for confirmation.

"Tyson, inform Cook I want supper served immediately." Lord Rushton snapped at the butler, then turned back to his daughter. "I am a belted earl. And your father. I demand obedience and respect."

"And I am the Marchioness of Blessing." Caroline lifted her chin a notch higher. "In my own right, made so by royal warrant and a parliamentary patent. This is my home. I decide when I dine. Where I dine. And with whom."

Lord Rushton's face turned an angry, mottled red. "If it hadn't been for me, you wouldn't be Marchioness of Blessing."

"That's right, Lord Rushton." Caroline had spent a lifetime trembling at the smallest threat of her father's wrath. But she wasn't trembling now. "If it weren't for you, I'd be the Countess of Carlisle."

"So *that* is what this little display of independence is about." Her father sneered his words. *"Carlisle."*

"As a matter of fact, it is," she said.

Taking a folded newspaper from his coat pocket, he waved it at her. "So all of this is true?"

"I have no idea." Caroline turned to leave. "Goodnight, Lord Rushton."

"Not so fast, missy." He glared at her. "Page four. *The Ton Tidbits* column."

"I don't read it," she said.

"You should. It concerns you." But instead of handing her the newspaper, Lord Rushton began reading aloud. *"There's quite a buzz going through Mayfair as of late. It begins in the Earl of Carlisle's gardens, which are currently being besieged and renovated by the Marchioness of*

*Blessing, who put away her mourning clothes for the late marquess mere days ago. Whatever could be taking place between our recently returned war hero and the widow of the late Lord Blessing? Has our hero rekindled his long-ago romance with the marchioness? Will there be a garden wedding soon?"* Lord Rushton slapped the newspaper against his thigh. "Well?"

"It's news to me," Caroline said. "I don't read gossip columns. And I don't carry tales."

"Is it true?" her father demanded. "Because that would explain your callous disregard for traditions. And what the devil are you wearing?"

"It's called an evening gown, Lord Rushton. I'm sure you've seen one before."

"Not on a woman in mourning," he snapped. "That gown is blue. Widows don't wear colors. Or *ostentatious* displays of jewelry." He sneered the word. "You're a widow."

"My husband is dead, Lord Rushton. I am not."

"You've been giving a good imitation of it for over a year," he retorted. "Refusing to put aside your mourning for any of the gentlemen I suggested you receive. Yet you threw off your mourning and got yourself written about in the newspaper as soon as you got wind of your former lover's resurrection."

"I put aside my black for my husband on the first anniversary of his death," Caroline reminded him. "I donned fresh mourning for Anthony Carlisle the following day."

"You allowed people to think you were grieving for your husband. You allowed *me* to think you were grieving for your husband."

"I cannot control what people think. They will believe what they will," Caroline said. "You, of all people, should have known better."

Rushton turned on his daughter. "Don't think I don't know all about the little charity you formed with your circle of spinster friends. I also heard you had your man of business purchase Selby's estate from his simpleton of an heir. Long before this came out." He shook the newspaper at her.

"I wonder where you heard it." Caroline glanced from her father to her butler and back again. "And from whom."

"Never you mind about that," Lord Rushton said. "I have my sources…"

"You call them sources. I call them informers."

"They are people looking out for your best interests."

"Really? I thought they were looking out for *your* best interests."

"No matter." He dismissed her comment. "They were right to tell me. As your father, it's my duty to protect you from your own female idiocy. I have a right to know what my daughter is doing."

"You no longer have any rights over me. Certainly not the right to rearrange my life to suit your needs, to choose the guests I receive, or to bully me in my own home."

"*Carlisle.*" Lord Rushton shook his head. "Bloody hell! I thought I'd succeeded in getting rid of him. But not only has he returned from the dead, he's returned a war hero."

Caroline sucked in a breath.

"So…you didn't know about that." Rushton gave an ugly laugh. "The War Office is giving him a bloody medal for his heroic actions at Quatre Bras. He can no longer sit a horse, but they're making him a lieutenant colonel in the cavalry and awarding him the Army Gold Cross."

"I am well aware of Lord Carlisle's injuries," Caroline informed her father. "And an injured Anthony Carlisle is worth a hundred uninjured lords you would toss my way."

Lord Rushton raised his hand to strike her.

But Caroline didn't flinch.

He dropped his hand and glared at his wayward daughter. "You would throw your life and Blessing's good name away over *him.*" He practically spat the pronoun. "Him with no ambition to speak of. Carlisle hasn't made an appearance in the Lords since his maiden speech."

"Carlisle hasn't made an appearance in the House of Lords, because unlike most of your acquaintances, he was fighting Bonaparte. Tony was *doing* instead of *talking.*"

"He might have been fighting Bonaparte, but it wasn't because he was doing instead of talking." He huffed. "Carlisle didn't have enough initiative for that. You should thank your lucky stars I intervened, *Lady Blessing*. Carlisle was never good enough for you."

"No, Lord Rushton," she retorted. "He was never good enough for *you*. I loved Anthony Carlisle. He was all I ever wanted."

"And you wonder why I look out for you." Turning his back on his daughter, Lord Rushton headed into the dining room. "Come along, Caroline. Supper is getting cold."

"Yes, it is," she said. "Mine is getting cold upstairs on a tray. Yours is getting cold in a hamper in the kitchen." Caroline gave her butler a quelling look. "Retrieve Lord Rushton's supper and show him out."

"Madam..." Tyson protested.

"Tyson, you have your instructions." Caroline didn't mince words. "I'm going upstairs. Lord Rushton is going home. If you allow him to dine under my roof, you may pack your personal belongings and leave with him."

"Lady Blessing..."

"Caroline!"

Ignoring them both, the Marchioness of Blessing left her father and her butler standing open-mouthed while she marched upstairs to where her supper tray was waiting.

# CHAPTER 15

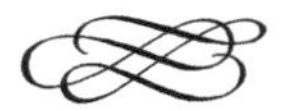

*"She is clothed with strength and dignity,*
*and she laughs without fear of the future."*
—The Bible, Proverbs 31:25

"Anything else you need, sir?" Barnaby asked as he ducked beneath the garden tent where Major Carlisle sat on a chair at the table.

Tony folded his morning newspaper and surveyed the breakfast spread out before him. "A pot of hot chocolate."

"I beg your pardon, Major." Barnaby bent closer to hear over the din of the workmen beginning their day. "Did I hear you say a pot of hot *chocolate?*"

"Yes." Carlisle kept his voice low, then dipped his head to keep the blush that suffused his face from showing. "Chocolate. I want a pot of hot chocolate for breakfast."

Barnaby blinked, taken aback by the request. "I apologize, Major. I didn't realize you were fond of chocolate."

"I'm not," Carlisle replied stiffly. "Lady Blessing is. She doesn't care for coffee. She prefers chocolate for breakfast."

"Oh." Barnaby bit the inside of his cheek to keep from smiling. "Right away, sir." He glanced at Kirby. "Please ask Cook to prepare a pot of hot chocolate for Lord Carlisle's breakfast."

While Kirby hastened to do Barnaby's bidding, Fielder, the other footman, filled two heavy brass footwarmers with hot coals and placed each of them on a platform of paving stones set beneath the table.

Barnaby had argued against the major spending another day in the frosty weather while he put him through the strengthening exercises his master had endured twice a day every day since he'd been strong enough to push himself into a sitting position. But the major had insisted. He had dressed for the occasion in layers of flannel and silk beneath his linen and buff breeches and wore a heavy great coat lined in beaver fur over that. He'd also requested that fur-lined lap robes from his carriage be brought to the tent.

"I don't like this, sir," Barnaby said. "Two days out of doors in this weather is dangerous for you."

Tony gave his batman a wry smile. "Who is going to direct the workmen this morning?"

"Lady Blessing," Barnaby replied. "As always."

"Look around, Barnaby," Tony said. "Do you see her?"

Barnaby glanced around, taking note of the different groups of workmen scattered around the gardens awaiting orders. Lady Blessing was nowhere to be found. "No, sir."

Tony nodded. "I've been watching for her since sunrise. The workmen began arriving half an hour ago. She's late. And she hasn't been late since she began this enterprise." He looked up at Barnaby. "Find Gerald and send him to me. If Lady Blessing hasn't arrived by eight o'clock, I'll send Fielder around to Blessing House to make certain she didn't suffer any ill effects from her fishing expedition."

"She's a strong young woman," Barnaby assured him. "She may contract the sniffles, but I'll wager she'll be fine." He gave the major a hard look. "She can handle the damp and cold. Unlike you, sir."

Tony shook his head with a bemused smile. "And they say women are the weaker sex."

"Don't you believe it, sir," Barnaby said. "My mum gave birth to seven children. It was pure agony for her each time. It was a miracle she survived it. But she did. I don't know that I could have done the same."

"I'll send Fielder to check on Lady Blessing all the same."

"I'll go, sir," Barnaby volunteered.

"No." Tony held up his hand to halt Barnaby's arguments. "I need you here to be my legs."

Barnaby nodded. "Understood, Major."

"Good," Tony said. "Now go find Gerald for me. I'll be fine until you get back."

"Aye, sir." Barnaby snapped a brisk salute, then hurried through the garden to find the major's head gardener.

CAROLINE AWOKE WITH A START. SUSAN HAD FAILED TO COMPLETELY draw the drapes and a sliver of daylight peeked through. Glancing at the small ormolu clock on her bedside table, Caroline saw that it was approaching eight o'clock in the morning. Sighing, she snuggled deeper into her pillow.

She'd dreamed of Tony, dreamed of the times they'd spent together —their 'accidental' meetings on Rotten Row during their early morning rides. He, on his magnificent stallion, Ajax, and she on her sweet, little dapple-gray mare, Mira.

It had been such a lovely dream. Full of heartfelt sighs and caresses and sweet words and kisses. *Kisses.* Caroline had nearly forgotten how it felt to be touched and kissed. She'd nearly forgotten how lovely those carefree days had been. And how much they had meant to her. And she'd almost forgotten Mira…

Caroline squeezed her eyes shut. The day the announcement of her impending wedding to Lord Blessing had appeared in the newspapers, Lord Rushton had sent Mira to the horse sale at Tattersall's.

The Marquess of Blessing didn't approve of females riding in the park or to the hounds, or in any way except by wheeled conveyances. So, her beautiful little mare had been sold. Caroline had never seen her again. Except in her dreams...

Caroline longed to linger in bed and return to her dreams, but carpenters were scheduled to arrive at Selby House at seven to complete the work there. And stone masons, bricklayers, and engineers were scheduled to begin deepening, rebuilding, and piping the fishpond for Tony's use.

She was already late.

Flipping back the covers, Caroline swung her legs over the side of the bed. She shoved her feet into her slippers, grabbed the brocade robe lying across the foot of her bed, and rang for her lady's maid.

Susan appeared almost immediately.

"Help me," Caroline ordered as she sat down at her vanity table and began hastily pinning her long plait into a bun at the back of her neck. "I overslept. I'm late."

"Sorry, ma'am," Susan apologized. "The household is in an uproar this morning. Mr. Tyson and Mrs. Tyson were up most of the night deciding whether to stay at Blessing House or leave."

Caroline untied the ribbon at her neck and stepped out of her nightgown, then pulled on her chemise and drawers. "And the verdict?"

"They decided to remain at Blessing House."

Caroline arched an eyebrow in query.

"They were all set to go with Lord Rushton, but he refused to replace his butler and housekeeper with Tyson and Missus Tyson. It's very touchy downstairs. Mr. Tyson has been out of sorts this morning and everything is running behind schedule." Susan paused to take a breath. "Cook is upset because the scullery maids hadn't finished washing up from last night's supper in time for her to begin breakfast. And most of the regular deliveries are late—including the butcher's and the milk and eggs."

Caroline sighed. "So Tyson decided to stay."

Susan shrugged. "It's better to stay where he is than to take a lesser position in Lord Rushton's household."

"You mean it's more *prestigious* to remain in service to a marchioness than to serve an earl," Caroline said.

"Yes, ma'am."

"Tyson should have known my father would never replace Birdwell or Mrs. Palmer." Caroline pursed her lips. "I wonder if Tyson will still collect payment from my father for spying on me. Or if that association ends with Tyson's failure to subdue his ambition and accept my father's less-than-flattering offer to become Under Butler at Hardage House."

"If he's being paid by you for his service as butler at Blessing House and by your father for spying on you, I can't believe he would even consider leaving his position here to become Under Butler there," Susan said. "Lord Rushton must have offered him a considerable increase in wages."

"Lord Rushton?" Caroline scoffed. "Not on your life."

"Then why would Mister Tyson consider leaving?"

"He didn't consider it until I suggested he should." Caroline raised her arms above her head so Susan could drop a flannel petticoat and her dress over it.

"You didn't!"

"I did," Caroline said. "I made him choose between continuing his service here or going into service for Lord Rushton or anyone else he considered worthy of his service."

Susan frowned. "I wouldn't drink any wine Mister Tyson decants if I were you."

"Do you honestly think he would try to poison me?"

"Not enough to murder you." Caroline had asked a rhetorical question, but Susan gave it serious consideration. "But enough to make you ill."

Caroline smoothed her dress into place and met Susan's worried gaze. "Keep that in mind if I become unexpectedly ill."

"It's nothing to jest about, milady," Susan warned. "Perhaps, we should retain the services of a food taster."

"So that I might have *his* illness on my conscience should Tyson be willing to poison the wine enough to make me ill?" Caroline sniffed. "I think not."

"Better a food taster become ill than you," Susan muttered.

"Not if you're the food taster," Caroline said. "Besides, we've no idea whether Tyson would ever consider poisoning anyone, much less me."

"I'm just saying it's worth considering," Susan insisted. "Of course, you may not need poisoning to become ill. Your determination to remain out of doors in this weather may be enough."

Caroline pulled on her stockings and stepped into her half-boots and overshoes. "That reminds me. I must return Lord Carlisle's great coat to him. Is it cleaned and dry and free of the odor of fish?"

"Yes, milady," Susan said. "I'll fetch it straightaway along with your hooded pelisse."

Caroline glanced at her maid. "My hooded pelisse?"

Susan flushed with embarrassment. "Yes, ma'am. I tried to get your cape dry and odor-free, but the gentleman's great coat took so much work..." She met Caroline's gaze. "Your velvet cape is still too damp to wear. I'm sorry, ma'am, but I knew you would want the gentleman's garment to be ready."

"You were right to concentrate on the great coat. I promised to return it this morning. But I forgot we no longer have a valet in service."

After the marquess's funeral, there was nothing for his valet to do. Caroline had thanked Slater for his years of service to the marquess, written him a glowing reference, and released him from service at Blessing House so he could pursue his profession in a gentleman's household. "And that you would have to care for both our garments." Caroline bit her bottom lip in consternation. "I apologize for my thoughtlessness. Did you get any sleep at all?"

Susan bobbed a curtsey, then quickly covered a yawn. "Enough, ma'am."

Caroline wasn't fooled. "I'll be out of the house all day today. See that you get a long rest while I'm gone. Use my bed so the housemaids don't disturb you."

"Oh no, ma'am," Susan protested. "I couldn't do that."

"Of course, you can," Caroline told her. "You have my permission. Sleep here where it's warm and comfortable instead of the dressing room." When her maid would have protested, Caroline insisted. "I'll make certain Tyson and Mrs. Tyson know..."

Susan looked stricken. "Oh no, ma'am, please don't say anything to them."

Recognizing the look on Susan's face, Caroline nodded. "All right, but be sure to lock and bolt the door. I'll be home before supper."

"Yes, ma'am." Susan handed Caroline her gloves. "Shall I fetch your chocolate and toast now?"

"Oh, no. I'm frightfully late as it is. And there's no need to bother Cook about preparing my chocolate."

"No bother," Susan assured her. "I'll make it myself."

Caroline was tempted. Tony's coffee was horribly bitter and strong and not at all to her liking.

Seeing her mistress waver, Susan urged her to reconsider. "You have to eat something, ma'am. Chocolate and toast the way you like it will be just the thing."

"I *am* hungry." Caroline smiled at her lady's maid. "And I'm already late. A few more minutes won't make any difference..."

A HALF DOZEN MEN IN CHARGE OF THE GARDENERS, LANDSCAPERS, carpenters, plasterers, and stonemasons were gathered beneath the tent set up by the reflecting pool, sharing coffee and tea and tea cakes and scones when Caroline reached them.

"Ah," Tony said, looking up. "Lady Blessing, you've arrived just in time. I was consulting with the workmen on their instructions for the day."

"So I see."

She didn't sound happy about it, but Tony thought she did a fair job of hiding it. "I hope you don't mind."

"Of course not," Caroline replied. "It's your garden, after all."

"Please. Join us." Tony gestured for her to take a seat at the table. "Gentlemen, make way for the lady."

The group of men parted like the Red Sea before Moses. There was a general murmur of 'Good morning, your ladyship' as Caroline made her way to Tony's side.

"I'm returning your great coat." She handed him the garment. "I thank you for the loan of it when I became chilled." Caroline glanced at the other men, then walked around the table and took the empty seat across from Carlisle. "Good morning, gentlemen. I apologize for keeping you waiting."

"Not at all." Tony spoke for the group. "We've been enjoying refreshments." He gestured toward the tea cakes and scones. "Would you care for a cup of—"

Caroline braced herself to accept a mug of strong coffee.

"Chocolate."

"Chocolate?" she repeated.

"Or tea if you prefer."

Caroline met his gaze. "Thank you, my lord. I prefer chocolate."

"Excellent." Carlisle picked up a linen napkin and waved it.

A liveried footman hurried to his side. "Milord?"

"Lady Blessing is ready for her hot chocolate now."

"Right away, milord."

Carlisle waited until the footman hurried away, then smiled at Caroline, looking very pleased with himself. "I didn't want to risk scorching it." He pointed to the candle in the pot warmer. "So we've been keeping it warm for you in the kitchen."

Caroline glanced down at the table, then back up at him. "There was no need for you to go to all this trouble for me, Lord Carlisle. I'm perfectly happy with whatever you and the other gentlemen are having."

Tony's gaze met hers. "We both know better than that, my lady." His voice became a low, almost intimate, rumble. "And it's no trouble," he said when his footman returned and set a silver chocolate pot over the warmer and a cup and saucer on the table close enough for Carlisle to reach. "Thank you, Kirby."

"Shall I pour, sir?"

"No, thank you. We'll manage." Gathering his great coat, Carlisle caught a whiff of Caroline's favorite roses-and-orange blossom fragrance wafting from the wool collar. His body reacted immediately and predictably. Leaning close, Tony buried his face in the silk lining and breathed in the scent of her.

Watching him, Caroline responded. "I assure you it's clean and dry and minus the fishy odor."

Tony slanted a look at her. "I was checking to make sure it would meet Barnaby's standards."

"Of course, it does," Caroline said. "It's the same as when you gave it to me to wear. My staff saw to that."

*It wasn't the same at all. His great coat no longer bore the scent of his shaving soap and cologne. Now it smelled like Caroline, and as far as Tony was concerned, was in better condition than when he placed it around her shoulders.* "I appreciate it," he said, his gaze never leaving hers. "Thank your valet for me."

"I don't have a valet," Caroline said.

Tony frowned. "Who…"

"My lady's maid," she said. "Susan."

"She does excellent work," Tony said as he handed the heavy garment to Kirby. "Please ask Barnaby to take care of this."

"Yes, sir." Kirby grabbed Carlisle's coat, then turned and headed toward the door to the conservatory.

Carlisle waited until Kirby was out of earshot before continuing. "Would you care to do the honors, Lady Blessing? Or shall I?"

"Please." Caroline nodded. Once again, Tony had failed to stand when she'd approached, but he poured chocolate flawlessly. She watched as he twisted the silver knob on the hinged lid, frothing the chocolate before he poured, as if he'd done it a thousand times before, just for her pleasure.

"Cream?" He offered her a dollop of fluffy cream.

"Please." Caroline shivered as the look in his eyes and the low rumble of his voice roused feelings she believed were lost. She didn't normally add cream to her chocolate or indulge in more than one cup in the morning, but he was trying so hard to please her, Caroline couldn't find the will to refuse him.

Tony set the pot aside, then carefully placed a spoonful of cream on the chocolate before he handed her the cup and saucer.

"Thank you, Lord Carlisle." Her fingers brushed his as she accepted the cup and saucer.

His eyes spoke volumes. "My pleasure, Lady Blessing."

Gerald broke the spell by loudly clearing his throat. "Thankee for the tea and cakes, your lordship. Begging your pardon, but it's time we returned to our duties…"

"Yes, of course," Carlisle responded to his head gardener without removing his gaze from Caroline's. "Lady Blessing and I will continue our discussion of the plans for the outbuildings and gardens. We'll be sure to alert you immediately should the plans change."

Gerald tugged his forelock. "By your leave, your lordship." He turned to Caroline. "Milady."

"Mr. Gerald. Gentlemen," she murmured as the workmen withdrew from the tent and returned to their assignments. Feeling Tony's unwavering gaze, Caroline gazed into her cup of chocolate.

"They are, you know," Tony said.

Surprised, Caroline took a careful sip of the hot chocolate, then another bigger one. "They?"

"The workmen," he said. "They are true gentlemen. More so I think than a good many of our class of so-called gentlemen are."

"I agree," Caroline said.

"Do you?"

"Of course." She nodded at the laborers unloading stone from the dray. "Men like those build the foundations that provide and secure our lofty existence."

"Surprising."

"What is?" she asked.

"Common ground."

Caroline took another swallow of chocolate, savoring the taste and the warmth it created. Although the hot chocolate couldn't match the heat that had suddenly flared in Tony's cool gray eyes.

He fastened his gaze on the cream mustache crowning her upper lip. "Is it to your liking, *Caroline?*"

The sound of her name on his lips, spoken in that intimate tone, snapped her gaze back to his. "Very much. Thank you."

"Seeing to your comfort this morning was the least I could do after watching you nearly drown yesterday." *The least was an understatement. Kirby had spent three quarters of an hour and two pots of chocolate teaching him how to froth and pour the stuff and add the perfect dollop of cream.* Reaching across the table, Tony ran the pad of his thumb over her upper lip, then touched his thumb to his lips, tasting the cream he'd swiped from her mouth.

Intensely aware of him, Caroline's whole body tingled from the emotions his provocative gesture evoked. "I was never in danger of drowning," she whispered. "Not with you nearby."

"You might have hit your head," he said, giving voice to the fear he'd felt.

She heard it. "I didn't."

"You could have. And I would have been of precious little use in helping you."

"But you did help me," she insisted. "You pulled me to the side of the pool and helped me regain my footing." Struggling to retain her composure, Caroline glanced at the reflecting pool and noticed all the fish were gone and the water drained. "It's empty."

"I asked the workmen to complete the task we started. They finished just before you arrived," he explained. "I was meeting with the foremen, reviewing the work plans. They gathered beneath the tent because I invited them for morning refreshments."

"That was very thoughtful of you, Tony."

"I couldn't very well walk over to speak to them, now could I?"

Caroline chose to ignore what he was implying. "It was still very thoughtful of you and much appreciated on a morning like this." She cradled her cup between her hands, allowing its warmth to penetrate the leather of her kid gloves.

"Four years of war taught me the value of good men." He squeezed his eyes shut, pinched the bridge of his nose, then raked his hand through his hair. "It was a hard lesson to learn and one I'll never forget."

Recognizing the pain in his voice, Caroline reached out to touch him.

Sensing it, Carlisle quickly moved his hand out of reach. "Did you suffer any ill effects from your unexpected dunking yesterday?"

His abrupt withdrawal hurt. Caroline fought to keep from showing it. Cradling her cup in her hands, she focused her gaze on his dark hair. Looking her fill, noting the changes in his appearance while his eyes were closed. His hair was longer than he'd worn it five years ago. The ends, curling against his neckcloth, were less tamed and more unruly.

Caroline realized she'd never seen him even slightly unkempt. When she had run her fingers through his hair years ago, it had fallen back into place. He had kept it clipped shorter on top. She'd had no idea his hair was so thick and wavy. She liked it. The devil-may-care style suited him. Caroline itched to run her fingers through it to feel how it suited her.

"Caroline?"

"Hmm?"

"I asked if you suffered any ill effects from your fall yesterday?" He'd opened his eyes and was staring at her.

Lost in her reveries, Caroline realized she had never answered him. "Nothing a hot bath, a warm fire, and a comfortable bed couldn't cure." When she spoke, her voice came out lower, huskier, than she intended.

Tony's eyes darkened at the sound. "I was concerned when you failed to show up early this morning."

"Thank you for sending your carriage. It saved me from having to order mine. That would have made me even later."

"I'm glad I could be of some service, my lady." Tony refilled his coffee mug, adding two drops of brown liquid from a bottle he removed from his coat pocket. He grimaced as he took a swallow.

She gave him a sharp look. The irises of his gray eyes were huge, but without the hazy, unfocused look common to poppy users. "Brandy or laudanum?"

"My, how observant you are." He met her gaze without flinching. "And how curious." He saluted her with his empty mug.

"You didn't answer my question," she pointed out. "And it occurred to me that you wouldn't carry brandy in a glass vial." Caroline gave the sapphire stickpin securing the intricately tied linen around his neck a knowing glance. "You'd carry it in a silver flask. So…that leaves laudanum."

"What do you know about laudanum?"

"More than you might think," she retorted. "I was married to an old man for three years."

"Don't remind me."

"Then don't remind *me*," she said. "I recognize a tincture of laudanum bottle when I see one. Lord Blessing used it to ease the pain of his final illness."

Tony pinned her with his gaze. "What did *you* use, Lady Blessing?"

Caroline jumped up from her chair. "Why are you doing this?"

"Doing what?"

"Deflecting my questions. Turning my words against me every time I get close to you…to the truth. Purposely wounding me."

"My apologies, Lady Blessing, if I wounded you." He quirked his eyebrow at her. "I wasn't aware I retained that particular power."

"You retained it, Tony. And you wield it heartlessly." She swallowed the tears that threatened to choke her.

"Heartless? How have I been heartless to you, Lady Blessing?"

"By blowing hot and cold. Showing me kindness one minute and cold disdain the next." She searched for a handkerchief as she battled the quaver in her voice. "Why bother being nice to me? Why help me out of the water yesterday? Why give me your coat? Why go to the trouble of having hot chocolate prepared for me this morning?" She searched his handsome face for some clue to those mysteries.

"It's called chivalry."

"Is it?" she challenged. "Because it seems to me you can't make up your mind whether to forgive me or torment me. I don't understand the game you're playing. Unless the laudanum makes you..."

"Makes me what?"

"Short-tempered." She took a deep breath. "Short-tempered and mean. I don't recall you ever being short-tempered before. And you were never mean to me."

"I never had reason to be," Carlisle said. "*Before.*"

"I suppose I deserve that." Caroline stood up to leave. "I know you despise me. You made it plain the first day I called on you."

"Then why did you keep coming back?" Tony caught her by the elbow as she turned to flee. "When you know I have no need of your misguided charity?"

"Because." She focused her gaze on the ground before looking up and meeting his unflinching gaze. "Because I couldn't stay away."

"Why not? What happened to your pride? Why come where you know you aren't wanted?"

She blinked back tears. "Because the only thing I ever wanted was here."

"And what was *that?*" He raked his gaze over her, then focused his attention on the renovation taking place around him. "My gardens?"

"No."

"What then?" he repeated. "Tell me."

"You," she said. "The only thing I ever wanted was *you.*"

# CHAPTER 16

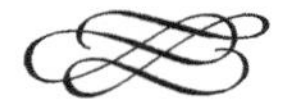

*"Waste not fresh tears over old griefs."*
—Euripides, 486-406 B.C.

Tony immediately loosened his grip and let go of her arm, recoiling as if she'd run him through with his own sword. His pain and his guilt warred with one another. Guilt won out when he saw the tears that had rimmed her blue eyes were slowly rolling down her face.

*"Bugger me!"* He swore like the soldier he'd been.

Caroline kept her shoulders straight and her head high. She didn't make a sound when she cried, but fat, heavy tears rolled unabated down her face.

"Stop that." Carlisle almost wished she'd cry aloud. Her silent tears made his guilt far worse. He almost wished she would yell and scream and sob uncontrollably. But Caroline didn't throw a fit. She didn't do the expected. She simply stood frozen in place while tears rolled down her face. He softened his tone. "Don't, Caro. You don't want them"—he nodded toward the hired men— "to see you like this."

His words did nothing to slow her tears. "I don't care how they see me."

"I do."

"Too bad," she said. "It's been a horrid day."

"The day has barely begun, Caroline," Tony reminded her.

She fixed her gaze on his face. "And we're already fighting."

Tony reached out and brushed a strand of hair off her cheek and gently tucked it behind her ear. "We're not fighting."

"What do you call it?"

"I call it me being exactly what you called me. A boorish ass."

"I didn't say boorish."

"I added it," he said. "Because it's true. There are times I lash out at anyone and everyone in range. I admit it. I get angry and frustrated. And—" Tony fought to keep from choking on the word he had never admitted aloud—even to himself. "Jealous."

She gazed up at him, her eyes wide, as the tears flowed over her cheeks and dripped off her chin onto the front of her pelisse. "*Jealous?* Of me?" She scrubbed her cheeks with the heels of her hands.

Reaching into his waistcoat pocket, Tony pulled out a handkerchief and awkwardly dabbed at her eyes and cheeks before thrusting the square of monogrammed linen into her hand. "Jealous of your freedom. Jealous of anyone who is able to do what they want to do. Anyone able to go about their daily business without restrictions. And without needing this—" He held up the laudanum bottle.

"And here I am crying over it." Caroline dried her eyes and blew her nose on his handkerchief before pocketing the linen. "After I promised myself I wouldn't shed any more tears over you."

"You shed tears over me?"

"Who else?" she snapped.

"Blessing." His green-eyed monster made another appearance.

Caroline glared at him. "Jealousy is beneath you, Tony. You're better than that."

"Apparently not," he muttered.

She inhaled. "There's no reason for it. It serves no purpose. Everyone has restrictions of some sort." Her words were so softly spoken, they came out as a whisper. "From King George to the lowest street urchins in the land."

He lifted an eyebrow, silently challenging her to prove her point.

"King George is confined to a single suite of rooms in his palace because he's ill. You are confined to a chair—for the moment—because you suffered an injury in war. Street urchins are confined to a life of poverty because they lack the education and the wherewithal to do better. But none of those conditions have to remain permanent."

Tony lifted his mug in a mock toast. "From your mouth to God's ears."

Caroline glanced down at her cup. "I'm sorry. I had no right to judge you so harshly. I've never suffered pain that required laudanum."

Carlisle shook his head. Street urchins might have a chance to escape their lot in life. King George's madness and his own inability to walk might well be permanent.

But Caroline had no way of knowing that.

"What about you, Lady Blessing? Have you escaped your restrictions now that you're a widow? And a marchioness in your own right?"

Caroline had expected his bitterness. She'd been prepared for anger and hostility. But Tony had surprised her with his kindness. After weeks of refusals, insults, and rebuffs, he'd surprised her with his thoughtfulness. She hadn't been prepared for it. But she would be —from now on. She'd be ready for his lightning-swift mood changes. He wouldn't catch her unawares again. This time there was no sarcasm in his tone, just sincerity. "One would think."

"But one would be wrong?" he guessed.

She released the breath she hadn't realized she'd been holding. "Last night, Lord Rushton came to Blessing House expecting supper because it was Wednesday and his club doesn't serve supper on Wednesdays."

Taking note of the fact that Caroline referred to her father by his title, Tony waited for her to continue. "And..."

"I was soaking in a hot bath to warm up after my unexpected—"

"Fishing expedition?" The mischievous light was back in Carlisle's silvery gray eyes.

Seeing it, Caroline smiled through the trails of her tears. *"Dunking.* I had arranged for my supper to be sent up to my room on a tray so that I might dine in comfort and retire early." She sighed. "Lord Rushton was neither invited, nor wanted."

"So your butler did what West has been doing to you for weeks and turned him away at the front door."

She shook her head. "My butler not only admitted him, he *welcomed* him."

Carlisle arched his eyebrow at that. "Against your wishes?"

"A tradition at Blessing House."

"Welcoming visitors?"

"Ignoring my instructions. Going against my wishes. I may be a marchioness in my own right, but nothing at Blessing House is mine. Everything belongs to Lord Blessing. Including the staff."

"It sounds as if you need to sack the butler and hire a new one."

"It isn't just the butler, it's everyone except Cook and my lady's maid. And it's not as easy to get rid of the household staff as you think. They're attached to the house as well as the family. It's their home as much as it is mine. More, really." She was thoughtful. "They were born to it. I was not."

"It doesn't matter," Tony told her. "I was born to this house, but when I die, a cousin I've never met will become the fourth Earl of Carlisle. The house will belong to him and the staff here will be just as loyal to him as they are to me." He glanced up at the window overlooking the back garden and gave a wry smile. "With one exception."

"Your cousin is a man, part of your family, and your blood heir," Caroline said. "I'm a woman who married into the title."

Tony gazed at her, surprised that she thought so little of her accomplishment. "However it occurred, you're the woman who kept the title from becoming dormant. That's reason enough to expect loyalty from the household staff."

"Apparently, not," she said. "And in a day or two, when the refurbishing is complete, I'm moving into a home of my own."

"Selby House?"

Caroline smiled.

The fact that she'd taken the place off the hands of the debt-ridden new viscount was no secret. Barnaby had told him that. But Carlisle hadn't realized she planned to move into the house that shared his garden wall.

"We'll be neighbors." She waved her hand to encompass the gardens. "We'll be sharing all this."

Carlisle raised his left eyebrow and his voice held an ironic tone. "*Will* we?"

"Of course, we will."

"For how long?" he asked.

"For as long as it takes."

"To do what?"

Caroline gazed out at the different projects going on in the gardens—the wooden ramps and walkways defining the garden boundaries, the partially completed summerhouse over the fishpond, the underground pipes bringing hot spring water from the Selby House gardens to Tony's gardens, the new fishpond in center of the maze—then looked Tony in the eye. "To finish what I started."

Blessing House was still in chaos when Caroline returned home shortly before supper as promised. She assumed—and rather hoped—the chaos was due to the imminent departure of Tyson and his wife, but as soon as Caroline entered her bedchamber, Susan blurted out, "Oh, ma'am, did Mr. Tyson tell you?"

Caroline shrugged out of her pelisse, removed her gloves, galoshes, and half boots and made her way to the fire in her stocking feet. "Tell me what? Tyson is only speaking to me when I address him directly." Gathering her skirts in one hand, Caroline backed up to the fire. "You look much better, Susan. Were you able to rest?"

"Yes, ma'am," Susan said. "I slept in your bed like you told me to do. And when I awoke, I changed the linens and re-made the bed for you."

Caroline smiled. "Thank you." Reaching over her shoulder, she began unfastening the hooks at the back of her dress.

"You're welcome, ma'am." Susan curtseyed. "It was a good thing I did. Everything has been topsy-turvy since you left. The whole household has been getting ready for his arrival."

"Whose arrival?" Caroline froze, her brows furrowed in a deep frown as an unwelcome thought occurred. "Don't tell me Lord Rushton is making a return visit, hoping to secure an invitation to supper."

"No, ma'am." Susan took a deep breath, then began speaking in a rush. "He's not coming for supper. He sent word right after you left this morning that he's leasing his town house to Lord and Lady Something or Other for the season and taking up residence here."

*"What?"*

"Lord Rushton has decided to take the gold suite. His valet has been unpacking his trunks all afternoon." Susan hesitated, clearly reluctant to reveal the rest of her news. "Lord Rushton said he intended to stay here in order to prevent you from dragging your good name—Lord Blessing's good name—through the mud and plunging the family into scandal." Susan met her mistress's gaze. "Supper is at seven. Shall I draw your bath now?"

"No." Caroline sprang into action. "Hook my dress back up. I have no intention of bathing and dressing for supper. Because I have no intention of staying in this house while my father is in residence. And I absolutely refuse to sit down to supper with him." She looked Susan in the eye. "Pack our things. We're leaving."

"How much should I pack?" Susan began gathering up Caroline's pelisse and gloves.

"Enough for a day or two." Caroline sat down to pull her boots and galoshes back on. "We'll send for more later."

"I was hoping you would say that." Susan plunked two heavy satchels down beside Caroline's chair. "I packed as soon as I heard the news."

"Good thinking." Caroline rose.

"Where are we going?"

"Home."

"Back to Hardage House?" Susan wore a mutinous expression.

"Heavens no." Caroline shuddered. "We can't go there if he's leased it to someone else. And even if we could, going to Hardage House would defeat the purpose of leaving here."

"Where are we going to stay? An inn?" Susan was clearly dismayed by the thought of staying in an inn and sharing a communal sleeping mat with other lady's maids.

"No." Caroline shook her head. "We're going to a house down the lane and across the park."

# CHAPTER 17

*"Now's the day and now's the hour."*
—Robert Burns, 1759-1796

"Are we expecting visitors?" Tony sat gazing out the window of his bedchamber following his bath.

"No, sir." Barnaby added another scoop of coal to the fire and stirred the coals. "Word has gotten around that you refuse all visitors. Why do you ask?"

"Two people just alighted from a cab at our front gate." Tony leaned closer to the window. "Two females from the looks of them."

"Females? At this time of night? Shall I inform West?" Barnaby finished his task and dusted his hands on the seat of his breeches as he straightened to his full height.

"No, I thought for a moment..." He let his words drift off as he caught a glimpse of a light-colored garment trimmed in darker fur pass beneath the puddle of light from the carriage lantern. "One of the females is wearing a coat like the pelisse Lady Blessing was wearing today." Swinging his chair around, Tony wheeled himself out of his bedchamber and across the hall to the window overlooking the gardens, where he took up his spyglass. "Bloody hell!"

"Sir?"

"Lady Blessing and her companion are creeping through the gardens, heading toward Selby's house," he called to Barnaby from across the hall.

Barnaby entered the room carrying a glass of whisky and the tincture of laudanum. He set the tray on the small side table in front of the window, pulled the cork from the bottle of laudanum and tilted the bottle over the whisky glass.

"One drop tonight, Barnaby."

"But, Major..."

Over the months, they'd learned that two to three drops of laudanum in a glass of whisky was enough to help ease the pain and allow Carlisle to sleep. Any more and he was besieged with nightmares. Any less and he was wracked with pain.

"One, Barnaby." Tony ignored his batman's disapproval and braced himself for the long night ahead.

Barnaby added one drop of laudanum to the whisky and set the glass on the table within Tony's reach. "Better drink it down, Major, before the pain gets too bad."

"I'll wait a while yet." Tony glanced at the glass of whisky before returning his attention to the window. Because he feared addiction to the only pain killer he had, Tony forced himself to wait to take it on occasion, just to prove he could.

"But, Major..." Barnaby leaned over Tony's shoulder, peering at the two figures hurrying across the back lawn. "Who's that with her, sir? A maid?"

"Looks like," Tony confirmed, watching as the second figure, struggling with a large bag, bumped into Caroline's back and nearly sent her sprawling. Stopping, Caroline exchanged bags with the maid, taking the larger one for herself and giving the smaller one to the maid.

"What do you make of that, sir?"

"She said she was moving in," Tony told him. "But the way she said it, I didn't expect it to be tonight." He watched as Caroline disappeared through the hole in wall.

"Major, she can't take up residence there tonight!"

"Why not?" Tony shrugged. "It's her house. She bought it."

"That may be, sir, but the work on the house isn't finished and the staff is on holiday. It's empty."

"No staff at all?"

"None."

Tony's pursed his lips as a thought occurred. "Who's been preparing the noontime meal for the workers?"

"Hired caterers who come in to cook and serve, then clean up and leave."

Tony studied his batman, an expression of awe on his face. "How do you know this?"

"I told you before, Major." Barnaby rubbed his hand over his head. "Servants talk. Most nobles pay no attention to the people who serve them. They forget servants have eyes and ears and mouths. I pay attention to what they have to say. And how they say it." He met Tony's gaze. "Our kitchen maids were whispering about the Selby House staff being given a week off with wages as a holiday. If those two women we saw sneaking through the garden are taking up residence in that house, they'll be all alone."

"She had to know that," Tony said. "She mentioned this morning that the house wasn't ready for occupancy."

"It doesn't make sense for her to go home this evening and come sneaking back to an empty house," Barnaby said. "When she could have easily gone to the house next door when she finished in the gardens instead of going across the park to Blessing House." He met the major's gaze. "Why would she do such a thing?"

Tony considered Barnaby's question carefully before he realized Caroline had revealed the reason during their morning conversation. "She did it to avoid an uninvited guest."

"Who?"

"Her father." Tony said. "She told me Rushton showed up at her door uninvited last night expecting supper." He repeated the story

Caroline had told him about the situation at Blessing House. "The only reason she'd sneak out of her own house to take up residence in an empty one is to escape her father's latest machinations."

"What are we going to do about it, Major?"

"If we were smart, we would back away from this bloody window and mind our own business," Tony muttered. "And leave Lady Blessing to manage her own affairs."

Barnaby frowned. "Are we going to mind our own business?"

"No." Tony took a deep breath, then slowly let it out. *Where she was concerned, he couldn't. He wanted to mind his own business, but he'd learned years ago, in a gazebo in the rain, that* she *was his business. And it appeared she always would be.* "Would that I could. We're going to let people think we're minding our own business, but we're going to do what we can to help her."

"Thank goodness," Barnaby breathed.

"We're going to start by asking Cook to pack a hamper with supper for our new neighbors." Tony watched as Caroline hung her lantern beside the kitchen door, took a ring of keys out of her pocket, and began awkwardly fumbling with them, trying each one in the lock. Tony glanced at the mantel clock. "She has to be hungry. She scarcely had time to get home, let alone eat or rest or bathe. And all she had this morning was toast and chocolate."

Barnaby gave him a knowing look.

Tony ignored it. "Send a footman with the hamper and instruct him to light fires and do whatever the ladies need him to do."

"I'll go myself, sir," Barnaby said. "She knows me."

"No." Tony shook his head. "Send a footman. I need you to pay a call at Blessing House and find out if my theory is correct. Find out if Rushton is there."

Barnaby met his employer's gaze and a look of understanding passed between them. "How do you suggest I go about it?"

Tony smiled. He wasn't surprised by Barnaby's question. His former batman had spent four years helping him gather valuable information from within the ranks, going so far as to don disguises when necessary. Tony understood Barnaby was asking what disguise would work best in Mayfair, where most of the inhabitants were unknown to him.

"A cab driver seeking a fare," Tony said. "Take my unmarked hansom and go to Blessing House. Tell the butler you're there for Rushton. If he's there, the butler will notify him."

Barnaby nodded. "And if he refuses?"

Tony sighed. "You're to become a destitute soldier needing food and shelter. Go to the trade entrance or the stables. Lady Blessing is the founder of the charitable Charlotte Society. Her household should willingly offer help." He frowned, considering. "I haven't heard of veterans seeking help in this part of town. Hospitals and churches, yes, but not private homes in Mayfair. At least, not yet. A carriage driver seeking a passenger in Park Lane is a better idea." He winked at Barnaby. "But either should work. You know how it's done."

"Aye, I do," Barnaby said. "So I'll be a coachman first. At the front door. If that doesn't work, I'll become a needy former soldier and try the back door. What are you going to do until I get back?"

He waved his spyglass. "I'm going to watch until she's safely inside."

"Is she house breaking?" Barnaby's voice held a note of alarm.

"Not yet." Tony lowered the spyglass. "She's got a ring of keys. And it's apparent she's never unlocked a door before."

"She's a lady, sir," Barnaby reminded him. "She's always had household staff and a butler to open doors for her."

Tony agreed. "Until she bought Selby's, I doubt she's ever used the tradesman entrance of any house." He lifted the spyglass to his eye once again. "But she's a fast learner."

"I thought you were tired and eager to retire for the night," Barnaby said as he quickly tidied the room, placing everything the major might need close at hand.

"I was." Tony pinched the bridge of his nose. His eyes stung from lack of sleep. Truth be told, he was tired to the bone and more than ready to seek his bed. But there was work to be done and Tony wasn't about to abandon his post until he learned why Caroline and her companion had sneaked through his back garden to gain entrance to the late Selby's town house instead of driving up to the front door.

"I see." Barnaby nodded. "And our policy of isolation?"

"I'm a bloody fool to relinquish it. But I'm an officer and a gentleman," Tony drawled. "I can't allow two vulnerable women to go unprotected. What do we know about the household staff at Blessing House."

"Not enough, sir."

"Then find out everything you can." Carlisle paused to look through the spyglass. "They've made it inside." He lowered the spyglass and gave his batman a meaningful look. "Get going, Barnaby. I'll take first watch."

# CHAPTER 18

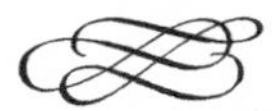

*"He that can have patience can have what he will."*
—Benjamin Franklin, 1706-1790

"I don't like it, ma'am," Susan complained as soon as Caroline opened the door and ushered her inside the dark kitchen. "Someone should have met us at the door. You've never had to unlock a door before." She set her satchel on the floor by her feet. "I don't think there's anyone here."

"There isn't." Caroline stepped inside the room behind Susan and placed the lantern on the kitchen worktable along with her heavy bag. Locating another lamp, Caroline lit it and made her way through the kitchen and up the stairs to the front of the house, carefully shielding the light until she was certain the windows facing the street were shuttered.

Her maid balked. "What do you mean there's no one here?"

"I mean there is no one here except us," Caroline confirmed.

"I thought we were going to stay with one of your friends. Miss Osborne or Miss Tennant."

Caroline struggled to hide her surprise. "We can't stay with Phoebe or with Dulcie any more than we could stay at Hardage House."

"Why not?"

"We haven't been invited." Caroline said the first thing that popped into her head, but the truth was that Dulcie was no longer the lady of her house. Her uncle's wife was the viscountess now that her uncle had inherited the title Dulcie's brother had held. Dulcie had become her uncle's ward, and as such, she couldn't extend invitations to friends to visit without permission from her aunt and uncle.

Phoebe was in a similar situation. She lived with her mother and great-aunt in her great-aunt Augusta's town house. Because Lady Augusta Nesbitt controlled the purse strings, and because Phoebe and her mother were considered the poorer relations, Phoebe wasn't at liberty to invite overnight guests, either.

"But they're your friends."

"It doesn't matter. We cannot go where we're not invited. It's simply not done."

Her maid glanced around the kitchen and sniffed with disdain. "We don't appear to have been invited to stay here either."

"We don't need an invitation to stay here," Caroline explained. "This is *my* house."

Susan was skeptical. "I hope you didn't pay good money for it."

"Of course, I did." Caroline bit the inside of her cheek to keep from laughing at Susan's expression. "Don't look so glum. It's a wonderful place. You're just not seeing it in its best light..."

"I'm not seeing it in any light," Susan grumbled.

"No matter," Caroline said, dismissing her maid's pessimism. "You'll love it once it's completed. It looks this way because the renovations aren't finished yet."

"We're spending the night in an unfinished house?" Having been in service all her life, Susan couldn't believe her ears. Earls and marquesses did not stay in empty houses, town houses, or palaces.

"That's the beauty of it," Caroline explained. "Rushton will never think to look for me here because he can't conceive of any peer of the realm staying in a house without staff. Especially a woman."

Susan looked at Caroline as if she'd taken leave of her senses. "I hate to agree with Lord Rushton on anything. But he's right." She met Caroline's gaze in the candlelight. "No peer would. Except you."

Caroline smiled. "I *am* unique in the peerage."

"Not entirely," Susan reminded her. "The current Duchess of Sussex is also the Marquess of St. Germaine, a marchioness in her own right.

"Miranda St. Germaine inherited her title from her father. I inherited mine from my late husband. No marchioness in her own right has done that," Caroline said. "Therefore, I'm unique in the peerage."

Susan dropped into another curtsey. "I stand corrected, Lady Blessing. You *are* unique in the peerage." She heaved a dramatic sigh. "You don't truly intend that we stay the night here, do you?"

"Yes, I *truly* do."

Susan glanced around the empty kitchen. "Where?"

Caroline gave her lady's maid another reassuring smile. "There are servants' quarters on the third floor, family suites and guest rooms on the second, two boudoirs, and two drawing rooms on the first floor. The entrance hall, the staircase hall, the library, dining room, serving room, and the former morning room are on the ground floor and behind the kitchen is the scullery." She gave a nod toward the doorway. "The laundry, and the enclosed yard and kitchen gardens are through there. In front of the kitchen are the butler's room and butler's pantry, the housekeeper's room, the deed room, wine cellars and dish rooms, still room, servant's hall, and other domestic rooms."

"But do we have a place to sleep?" Susan was skeptical. "Are the bedchambers habitable?"

"Everything upstairs is. Including my bedchamber and dressing room and your room. The only rooms that aren't ready yet are down here. There's still clean-up to be done on what used to be the morning room and the common areas on this level. But the bedchambers upstairs are all nicely appointed and quite lovely," Caroline assured her. "I toured the house and inspected the rooms this afternoon."

"With whom?" Susan asked, giving an exaggerated glance around the empty room.

"With the laborers who've been working here for the past ten days."

Susan swiped a finger along the tabletop and frowned at the dust that had collected there. "Where's the staff? From the looks of the kitchen, they haven't done much cleaning."

"I gave the domestic staff a few days off while the construction was underway."

Susan rubbed her hands up and down her arms in a futile attempt to ward off the chill in the room. "When will they be back?"

"The day after tomorrow."

"Who's going to clean all this?" Susan waved a hand to encompass the whole of the basement rooms.

"The workers I hired. They'll be here tomorrow. They're responsible for cleaning up the mess."

"Thank goodness." Susan sagged with relief. "Can they cook and light a stove, too? Because I trained as a lady's maid. Boiling water for tea and making chocolate and toast is the most I can manage. I've never worked in a kitchen."

"No need to worry, Susan," Caroline assured her maid. "You don't have to learn to light the stove or learn to cook. Everything is going to be all right."

"How?"

"Someone will come to our aid." Caroline pulled out a chair and sat down to wait.

"Who?" Susan frowned. "A fairy godmother? Nobody knows we're here."

Caroline focused her gaze on the worried expression on her maid's face. *"He* knows."

*"Who?"*

The knock on the back door startled them both.

Susan let out a shriek and Caroline nearly jumped out of her skin. Pushing herself out of her chair, Caroline grabbed the lantern with a shaky hand and peeked through the shutters at the silhouette of a large man standing at the door.

"Your ladyship," he called through the door. "I beg your pardon for frightening you."

"Who are you?"

"Fielder, ma'am. I'm a footman for the Earl of Carlisle. He sent me to help you get settled into the house for the night." Fielder held a lantern very much like the one Caroline was holding up to his face so she could see him. He gave her a few seconds to identify him before he lowered the lantern and held up a large hamper. "Cook packed some provisions for you."

Recognizing the man wearing Carlisle livery as one of the two footmen she'd seen waiting attendance on Tony for the past few days, Caroline reached for the bolt on the door.

Susan grabbed her arm. "Ma'am, do you think you should?"

"Of course, I should," Caroline replied. "You heard him. He's the answer to our prayers. Carlisle sent help. I'll wager he's watching us now." She gazed at the windows of Carlisle House across the gardens. "Nothing escapes him. He's always watching."

"That's comforting," Susan said, meaning it. She didn't like big, empty houses. "It's like having a guardian angel."

"I suspect he's more recording angel than guardian," Caroline muttered, picturing Tony gleefully recounting all her transgressions. But even as she said it, Caroline knew she was wrong.

*"Seeing to your comfort this morning was the least I could do after watching you nearly drown yesterday."*

Tony's words came to mind unbidden. He had watched her slip and disappear beneath the surface of the water of the fishpond and feared she might drown, but he'd also managed to save her. Just as he'd sent this footman to her door to help. Caroline didn't want to admit it—even to herself—but she knew that despite his anger and resentment at her marriage to Lord Blessing, Tony *was* her guardian angel.

The only time Tony Carlisle had ever failed her was on the day she married Lord Blessing.

"Maybe so, ma'am." Susan gnawed at her thumbnail. "I wish there was some way to know. Anyone could knock on the door and say he's a footman for Lord Carlisle. How do we know he is?"

"He's wearing the uniform of the Carlisle footmen, Susan. And I've seen him with Lord Carlisle. He's one of the sentinels."

Susan stared at her mistress. "Sentinels?"

Caroline felt her face redden. "It's my private name for the two footmen always in attendance to Lord Carlisle. They flank the doorways like sentinels whenever the earl is about." She unbolted the door and stepped back to allow Fielder inside the kitchen. "Come in, Fielder. And thank you."

He bowed. "No need to thank me, your ladyship. His Lordship saw your light and thought you might be needing some assistance seeing as how the staff is still on holiday." He set the heavy oak basket on the table beside the two satchels and went around the kitchen lighting lamps before he began unpacking the Carlisle cook's offerings. "Cook said to tell you the food isn't fancy. There's no garlic or leeks or cabbage in the stew—on His Lordship's orders—but it's hot and filling."

"Hot and filling is greatly appreciated and all we require." Caroline caught a whiff of freshly baked bread as Fielder set a cloth bag and a covered crock on the table. Her mouth watered in response. "It smells delicious."

"Yes, ma'am." Fielder's chest practically puffed with pride at Caroline's compliments on the Carlisle cook's supper. "Fresh bread, butter, mutton stew and pudding for dessert." He named the dishes as he placed them on the table.

"I'm sure everything will taste every bit as good as it smells," Caroline said with a grateful smile. "Please relay our thanks to the cook and her kitchen staff."

"Cook also sent a pot of tea."

Susan stepped forward, gave Fielder a long, appraising glance, and said, "Once we wash up, we'll be happy to sit down and eat supper. You—" She pointed a finger at the footman. "Light the stove and fetch water to heat for bathing. I'll finish unloading the provisions and set the table."

After giving Susan an equally frank appraisal, Fielder took the pail she offered and looked around for the pump.

Caroline came to his rescue. "Through there." She nodded toward the scullery. "We have cold water piped in from the cistern and hot water piped in from the natural hot spring in the garden. You can fill the pails from the taps. We'll still have to boil water for tea and for cooking, but not for bathing. It comes out hot enough for that right out of the taps."

Susan stared at her, dumbfounded. "Hot water comes from a tap in the scullery? I knew Selby House had a hot spring in the garden, but I had no idea the water was piped into the house."

"When the hired men showed me around the place this afternoon, they explained how everything works. The cistern and the hot spring are one of the main reasons I bought the house. I think having hot and cold water at the turn of a tap is wonderful."

"Having hot and cold running water in the house *is* wonderful," Susan said dryly. . "But I'm not sure you should have bought this place just to get it."

"Having hot and cold water piped in wasn't the only reason I purchased the house."

"Oh, I'm certain of that," Susan drawled. "I'll wager hot water isn't nearly as wonderful as the reason next door."

Caroline felt the color rush to her face. "Susan!"

Susan grabbed two mugs out of the kitchen cupboard and set them on the table, then lifted a steeping pot of tea, a crock of fresh cream, and a bowl of sugar out of the hamper while Fielder lit the cook stove and filled the kitchen basin with hot water for washing up. As soon as Fielder completed the task, Susan pointed to the two leather traveler's bags on the table. "Carry those upstairs to the mistress's bedchamber and light the fire. And don't forget to heat a brick for her bed."

Fielder looked as if he might balk at taking orders from a lady's maid when he obviously had prior orders from the Lord Carlisle, so Caroline stepped into the breach to diffuse the tension in the air. Lifting the lantern, she turned to the footman. "Thank you, Fielder. I'll lead the way while Miss Brown sets the table for supper."

~

TONY PUSHED HIMSELF UP FROM HIS CHAIR AND LEANED AS CLOSE TO the window as he could, watching as Fielder entered the rear door of Selby House, carrying a large hamper. Tony's arms began to quake from the strain, but he forced himself to remain upright for the count. "One. Two. Three. Four. Five." His elbows bent and he nearly sat down, but he refused to give into his weakness. "Six. Seven."

His strength deserted him between the counts of seven and eight. Arms quivering and legs wobbling, Tony sat down hard on the seat of his chair. A thin sheen of perspiration beaded his upper lip and stuck his linen shirt to his torso. *Seven seconds.* His injured legs had supported his body weight for a full seven seconds before they'd given way. Tony wanted to celebrate his accomplishment, but the reality of his situation prevented it.

After months of recuperation, after enduring countless hours of Barnaby's painful muscle-strengthening exercises twice a day, he'd managed to stand on his own two feet for fifty-three seconds shy of one minute. Tony shoved his fingers through his hair, pushing it off of his damp forehead. Seven seconds. He didn't know whether to laugh or to cry. Barnaby manipulated his legs twice a day, every day, morning and evening, and all that had gotten him was seven bloody seconds on his own two feet. Tony had told himself the first six physicians and the surgeons were wrong.

He chose to believe the last one—the Frenchman captured at Waterloo—who had recommended the torturous exercises twice a day rather than amputation, the physician who claimed to have had great success in restoring mobility to injured soldiers. Carlisle had believed that one day, he'd be able to walk again. But now he wasn't so sure. Now he was very much afraid he would be consigned to his wheelchair for as long as he lived.

Tony blew out his breath. The effort it took to stand had sapped his remaining strength. He stared at the glass of whisky Barnaby had left within his reach and the small brown bottle of laudanum he hadn't. Carlisle despised the feebleness his injuries had caused, despised his inability to do the things he'd taken for granted all his life.

Things like standing and walking and climbing up and down stairs and riding and sleeping without fear... Things like reaching for a bottle atop the mahogany wardrobe, the bottle containing the magic elixir that would grant him deep, dreamless sleep and end the unrelenting pain...

The pain was harder to overcome than the craving for the laudanum. He had slept for eighteen days following his injury and barely a few hours a night since. He had awakened in the field hospital outside Quatre Bras to discover the searing agony he'd suffered on the battlefield had become his constant companion. He'd tried to ignore it, tried to pretend he didn't feel the persistent ache in his bones. Tried to pretend he didn't wake up at night, drenched in sweat, and trembling in terror from the nightmares. He tried to pretend he didn't wake up writhing in agony with the metallic taste of blood in his mouth. But he and Barnaby knew the truth.

And the truth was that although he hated the fact that he had to use it, Tony needed the blessed relief, the blessed oblivion, the laudanum brought him. He not only wanted it, he craved it. Now. Hands shaking, Tony reached for the glass of whisky with the single drop of laudanum Barnaby had added to it. Cradling the glass in his hands, he swirled the golden liquid in the glass, savoring the bouquet, fighting the urge to down it in a single gulp.

Long hours spent sitting in one position in the cold, damp garden had taken their toll on him. His body ached. His legs ached. His chest ached. And he shivered with cold, despite the roaring fire Barnaby had lit for him. Tony wanted to feel the carefree warmth of the alcohol and the laudanum surrounding him, easing the pain, protecting him from the nightmares.

He was sorely tempted.

More tempted than he had been in weeks.

The desire to couch himself in the blissful nothingness of laudanum was strong, but Tony withstood the urge. Caroline was alone and unprotected in the empty house next door.

She needed him as much as he needed the laudanum and Tony felt duty-bound to see that no harm came to her. He had cared for her once. Cared enough to ask her to be his countess. He couldn't abandon her now. He had to watch over her.

And that meant denying the pain, denying the craving, long enough to do so.

# CHAPTER 19

*"The man who is prepared has his battle half fought."*
—Miquel de Cervantes, 1547-1616

"Good evening, Tyson." The Earl of Weymouth greeted the Marchioness of Blessing's butler as soon as he opened the front door of Blessing House. "I'm here to see Lady Blessing."

"Lady Blessing is not at home to visitors, my lord," Tyson said, before stepping back to close the front door.

The earl didn't budge. "She invited me to join her for supper tonight," he said before putting his hand up to keep Tyson from closing the door in his face. "I can't believe the invitation slipped her mind."

"She said nothing to me about expecting an additional guest."

"*Additional* guest?" Weymouth pinned Tyson with a look. "Are you referring to me?"

The butler nodded.

"If I'm an additional guest, who else is here? And where is Lady

Blessing? Is she avoiding guests by remaining above stairs? Is she indisposed? Or is she truly not at home?"

"Madam left earlier in the evening. She didn't offer an address or mention her intended destination to me. Good evening, my lord." Tyson attempted to close the door once again and once again, Weymouth stopped him.

Weymouth glanced over the butler's shoulder. The house was alight and full of activity. The dining room table was set for supper and footmen were preparing to serve the supper guests. "If Lady Blessing isn't here, who is sitting down to supper in her dining room in her absence?"

Tyson gave a heavy sigh.

"You tell me this instant." Lord Weymouth took a step closer, using his size and height to intimidate Tyson, who stood a head shorter than the earl. Genuinely concerned about his goddaughter, Weymouth was prepared to push his way into the house to get answers. "Or I will find out for myself." He spoke with the calm authority of a man long accustomed to issuing orders and having them followed. He was a belted earl and an important, if shadowy, figure in the government, whose manner brooked no argument from domestic servants.

Tyson slowly exhaled the breath he'd been holding. "Lord Rushton is in residence," he said. "He and Lord Merrivale are about to sit down to supper."

Weymouth fought to keep his temper in check at the mention of Merrivale. A recent widower, the thirty-eight-year-old Hansell Hogarth, the second Earl of Merrivale, was an inveterate gambler who had gone through his late wife's dowry and allowance, and his own inheritance, in record time and was in desperate need of cash. If Rushton was bringing Merrivale to Blessing House for supper, it could only mean one thing. Merrivale had something Rushton wanted and Rushton was apparently willing to sell his daughter into marriage a second time to get it.

A close companion and confidant to the Prince Regent, Merrivale had been named one of the Regent's Gentlemen of the Bedchamber the previous year. It was apparent to Weymouth that, having lost the close relationship of his son-in-law, the powerful Marquess of Blessing, to King George III, the Earl of Rushton desired the ear of the Prince Regent. "And Lady Blessing?"

"As I told you, she isn't here, my lord," Tyson told him. "Lady Blessing left the house upon learning Lord Rushton had decided to establish his residence here."

Weymouth frowned. "Lord Rushton has a house on Portman Square. Why has he taken up residence here?"

"I understand he leased his town house to Lord and Lady Digby for the season."

Weymouth didn't recall hearing any talk about Rushton leasing his house for the season. Portman Square wasn't the most desirable of addresses during the season. It wasn't as coveted as Mayfair and Park Lane, but it was considered one of the fashionable addresses. And Rushton's town house was on the most fashionable block of Portman Square. Far enough away from the charitable addresses to be entirely respectable. "Recently?"

"He signed the lease this morning."

Weymouth pursed his lips in thought. "When did Lady Blessing learn Lord Rushton had decided to relocate to her home?"

Tyson hesitated, seemingly unwilling to divulge that bit of information. "I'm not certain of the exact time. I was supervising Lord Rushton's move to the gold suite when Lady Blessing returned from her daily outing."

"What outing?" Weymouth demanded.

"If your lordship reads the *Morning Chronicle,* I'm sure you're aware that Lady Blessing recently purchased the property of the late Lord Selby." Tyson was careful not to spread the gossip from the *Ton Tidbits* column lest he be accused of doing so. But Tyson was equally careful to inform the Earl of Weymouth he was aware of everything concerning the late Marquess of Blessing—and that included his widow.

Weymouth wasn't impressed. "My understanding is that the late

Lord Selby's property is currently undergoing renovations. If that's the case, it's certainly no place for a lady alone to spend the night."

"Where else would she go?" Tyson asked.

"Visiting friends?" Weymouth suggested. "Miss Tennant or Miss Osborne?"

The butler immediately dismissed the idea. "Lady Blessing's friends come here to visit. She doesn't visit them. And she could not go to an inn without an escort. No reputable establishment would allow an unaccompanied female on the premises."

"You've no idea when she left the house?"

Tyson shook his head. "I learned of her departure shortly before you knocked on the door. But I know she didn't go alone."

"Oh?"

"Her lady's maid is missing, too."

"What about footmen? Coachmen? Grooms? They must know something," Weymouth said.

"She didn't request a coach or coachman. Or any footmen."

Weymouth's blood began to boil. "Do you mean to tell me that she left on foot?"

"As far as I was able to ascertain." The haughty tone was back in the butler's voice.

"You allowed a marchioness to *walk?*" Weymouth didn't raise his voice. He didn't need to. His softly spoken words carried an edge as keen as the sharpest knife and just as lethal. "When her vehicle is parked in your drive?" He nodded toward a hansom cab parked near the tradesman's entrance.

Tyson's face turned a mottled shade of red. "She's a marchioness. I am but a butler in her household. I couldn't stop her." He met Weymouth's angry gaze. "And I don't recognize that vehicle or the driver, but I can assure you it doesn't belong to Lady Blessing."

"Whose is it?"

"I assume it belongs to Lord Rushton," Tyson said. "Or Lord Merrivale."

"So you have no idea where Lady Blessing went?" Weymouth asked.

"None."

"Any idea when she'll be back?"

"None. But I believe she'll wait until Lord Rushton departs."

Weymouth lifted his eyebrow in query once again. "Why is that?"

"She objected to her father appearing unannounced for supper last night. Lady Blessing refused to allow him to sit down at the table. She threatened to dismiss me from Blessing House if I allowed Lord Rushton to dine here. She suggested that I should accompany him to his home if I did because I would no longer be butler at Blessing House." Tyson took a deep breath before resuming. "When I explained my situation to Lord Rushton, he offered me a position in his household as Under Butler." Tyson puffed out his chest and drew himself up to his full height. "I've been here thirty years. Twenty-three as butler to the Marquess of Blessing. I'll not be dismissed on a whim by the female the marquess married and sent to become part of her father's household. Imagine an earl offering me a situation as Under Butler."

"Yes," Weymouth drawled. *"Imagine."* He eyed the butler with distaste. "So, Lady Blessing dismissed you..."

"Not yet," Tyson said. "But she will when she returns."

*"If* she returns," Weymouth said.

"She'll be back," Tyson told him. "This is her home. And now that Lord Rushton has leased his town house for the summer, she has nowhere else to go."

"Let's find out, shall we?" Weymouth turned toward the hansom cab parked near the tradesman's entrance. The cab hadn't been there when Weymouth arrived—also by hansom cab. But it was here now. And it hadn't brought Rushton or Merrivale. They'd arrived long before Weymouth had.

Weymouth took his time as he approached the driver's perch at the back of the cab. The hansom appeared to be a vehicle for hire, but the horse pulling it bore no resemblance to any hired horse Weymouth had ever seen. In fact, the horse standing between the traces of the cab, bore a remarkable resemblance to the horses in Weymouth's own stables. The earl reached up and ran his palm over the white blaze on the horse's face. "How are you, Aeolus?"

The horse nickered in response.

"It's been a while, old boy," Weymouth whispered. "It's good to see you again." He gave the horse another affectionate pat, then walked to the driver's perch at the back of the vehicle and looked up at the driver. "Did you happen to pick up two ladies earlier this evening?"

"Are you Lord Rushton?" the driver asked.

Weymouth shook his head. "Thankfully, no. I'm the Earl of Weymouth. Rushton and Merrivale are at supper. I came to pay a call on Lady Blessing, but she left before I arrived."

"I didn't transport the lady and her companion," the driver said. "But I saw where they went. If you wish to pay a call on the lady, I can take you there."

"Thank you." Weymouth opened the door of the cab.

"My lord," Tyson called from the doorway. "Where are you going?"

"I came to see Lady Blessing," Weymouth said. "Since she isn't here, I'll be on my way. Good evening, Tyson." He climbed into the cab, settled onto the seat, closed the door, and nodded to the driver.

The driver flicked the reins and the hansom began to roll.

Weymouth waited until they turned onto Park Lane before he spoke. "You must be the former batman to Major Lord Anthony Carlisle of His Majesty's Own Eleventh Blues."

"How can you know that?" Barnaby demanded.

"I recognized Aeolus." Weymouth grinned. "I make it a point to keep track of the horses bred and foaled in my stables. Carlisle purchased this horse as a four-year-old close to six years ago. You may be driving a vehicle for hire, but the horseflesh pulling it is far superior to anything on the city streets."

Barnaby snorted his skepticism. He'd disguised himself and used an unmarked vehicle, but he'd forgotten about the horse. Weymouth was right. The major's livestock was far superior to hired horses.

Weymouth laughed at the driver's honest response. "Your reputation precedes you, Sergeant Major Barnaby. I've followed your career since you began your service in the Peninsular campaign."

"Alongside your son, Major Lord Griffin Abernathy and his

batman, Corporal Eastman," Barnaby recalled. "You're Weymouth, the wizard of the War Office."

"*Wizard*. Is that what they call me?" Weymouth asked. "I heard it was the Warlock of the War Office."

Barnaby nodded. "I've heard both."

"Among other things, I'll wager."

It was Barnaby's turn to laugh. "Where would you like me to take you, your lordship?"

"I thought we agreed you would take me to Selby House so I can conduct my business with the Marchioness of Blessing."

"I never mentioned Selby House, your lordship," Barnaby said.

"But that's where she is," Weymouth replied. "Isn't it?"

"Wizard suits you, your lordship. Your ability to ferret out information is uncanny."

"Nothing uncanny about it, Barnaby," Weymouth said. "It's simply logic and the process of elimination. And a knowledge of my goddaughter. Rushton invaded her home, so Lady Blessing vacated it in favor of the last place that arrogant, avaricious scoundrel who sired her would think to look."

"Lord Carlisle said the same," Barnaby told him.

"Carlisle knows about Rushton taking up residence in Lady Blessing's house?"

Barnaby turned onto Park Lane. "She told Lord Carlisle that Rushton appeared for supper uninvited last night, but she sent her father packing."

"She told Carlisle?" Weymouth asked. "I was under the impression he had refused to receive her at Carlisle House, that he hadn't received anyone since he returned home."

"He hasn't received anyone—except Lady Blessing and the head groundskeeper. And that only recently." Barnaby slowed the cab as they approached the densely populated area of the lane.

"How recently?"

"A day or two ago," Barnaby said. "She joined him for breakfast in the gardens this morning."

"Just the two of them?"

"Yes," Barnaby said. "Except for the forty hired men working around them."

"That's interesting," Weymouth said. "They must be getting along very well."

"I thought so," Barnaby agreed. "I thought it most interesting. He's showed more interest in the renovation of the gardens and the lady presiding over them than he has in anything since he awoke in that field hospital in Belgium. But it's not all polite and cordial."

"How is it then?"

"She's as stubborn as he is. Maybe more so. He doesn't like being told what to do. And she doesn't give an inch when she thinks she's right."

Weymouth was thoughtful. "That being the case, you might want to let Carlisle know Rushton not only returned to Blessing House, he's taken up residence and brought reinforcements."

"What kind of reinforcements?" Barnaby asked.

Weymouth paused, debating whether he should interfere or let nature take its course. "A prospective bridegroom for Lady Blessing. And I don't relish the thought of having a blighter like Merrivale foisted upon her." The shadow of a smile hovered at the corners of Weymouth's mouth. *Nature could be notoriously unreliable. Experience had taught him it was better to give nature a nudge.* "Lord Blessing was old, but at least he was more concerned with securing an heir than he was with securing her fortune. And Blessing's advanced age gave us hope she wouldn't be tied to him for any length of time. Unfortunately, Merrivale is considerably younger. And more attractive. He's one of the members of the Prince Regent's Carlton House set. Despite that kind of lifestyle, Merrivale could live for *decades*. She could be tied to him until she's old and gray."

"Lady Blessing wouldn't be renovating Lord Carlisle's gardens and constructing a heated bath for him if she was interested in marrying someone else." Barnaby steered the cab onto the drive and around to the stables.

Weymouth looked around. "Is this Selby's house?"

"No, it's Carlisle's," Barnaby informed him. "Follow the path through the garden and the back gate. It will take you to the back door of Selby House. I'll leave the cab in the mews behind Lord Carlisle's house if you need to avail yourself of it."

"Thank you, sergeant major. I'll see that it's promptly returned."

Barnaby handed him a small carriage lamp, then touched the brim of his hat. "If you hurry, sir, you might make it in time to share the supper His Lordship sent over for the ladies."

Weymouth alighted from the vehicle. "And Carlisle?"

Barnaby glanced up at the ballroom window. "He's keeping watch until I get back."

Weymouth grimaced.

"I see the major's reputation has preceded him as well."

"Indeed," Weymouth drawled. "And I would greatly appreciate it if you see that I don't get shot while I'm making my way through his gardens."

# CHAPTER 20

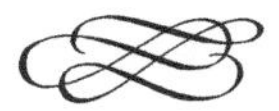

*"Better a meal of vegetables where there is love than a fatted calf with hatred."*
–Proverbs 15:17

"You're a hard woman to track down," the Earl of Weymouth said when the Marchioness of Blessing opened the kitchen door in response to his insistent knock.

"Uncle Trevor!" Caroline breathed a sigh of relief as soon as she recognized the man standing in the doorway. "What are you doing here?"

"Looking for you," he replied. "I just came from Blessing House, where I'd gone to deliver the information you asked for." He grimaced. "I had no idea Lord Rushton had decided to take up residence in your home."

Caroline groaned. "Neither did I. Until I returned home this afternoon."

Weymouth nodded. "He and Lord Merrivale were sitting down to supper when I arrived. And apparently, so are you. Are you going to invite me in? Or leave me exposed to prying eyes?" He gave a quick nod over his shoulder in the direction of Carlisle House.

Caroline stepped back and held the door wide open. "Please, come in, Uncle Trevor." She gestured toward the table. "You remember Susan Brown, my lady's maid?"

"Yes, of course. Good to see you again, Miss Brown." Weymouth nodded to Susan, then shrugged out of his coat and handed it to a liveried footman who appeared at his side.

Susan curtseyed. "Nice to see you again, too, Lord Weymouth."

"And this is Fielder." Caroline continued the introductions as Fielder, returned from lighting the fire and filling the coal hod in the upstairs bedchamber, took Weymouth's coat. "He's one of Lord Carlisle's footmen. He brought a basket of food for supper. You're just in time to join us."

Weymouth acknowledged the footman with a nod.

Caroline patted the empty chair beside her. "There's plenty. Please, sit down, Uncle Trevor."

"Shall I serve, ma'am?" Fielder asked.

"No, thank you." Caroline shook her head. "We'll serve ourselves."

"Very well, ma'am. I'll attend to my other duties," Fielder said. "If I have your permission, ma'am, I'll lay a fire in the drawing room so you and Lord Weymouth may remove there for private discussion after supper." Fielder inclined his head in a show of deference before leaving the kitchen.

Weymouth pulled Caroline's chair out for her, then proceeded to do the same for Susan before seating himself.

After enjoying their meal, Caroline and Lord Weymouth left the kitchen and made their way to the drawing room while Susan stayed behind to help Fielder clear the table.

"I'll serve dessert and coffee now." Fielder bowed and withdrew to collect the dessert tray as Caroline preceded Lord Weymouth into the comfortably elegant drawing room.

Caroline waited until the footman left before turning to her godfather and gesturing toward the furnishings, noting that the sheets that had covered the furniture when she'd toured the house earlier in the day had been removed. "I'd offer you the most comfortable seat in the room, Uncle Trevor, but unfortunately, I don't know which one that is." She shrugged. "This is only my second time in the room. I've never had occasion to sit on any of the furniture."

Weymouth laughed. "I have." He pointed to a pair of wing chairs near the fireplace. "Whenever I paid a call here, the late Viscount Selby always sat on that one. I took the other."

As they settled into the chairs, which were indeed quite comfortable, Caroline smiled at him. "Have you any information?"

Weymouth nodded. "That's why I came."

"For Miss Tennant? Or for me?"

"For both of you," he said. "Since I cannot discuss the results of my research for Miss Tennant with you, I'll have to relay it in person. I'd like you to invite her for luncheon here tomorrow."

"The Charlotte Society is meeting tomorrow."

"That's ideal," Weymouth told her.

"At Blessing House," Charlotte concluded.

"That's not ideal," he said. "Now that your father and Lord Merrivale are in residence there."

"Just what is Merrivale doing in my house?" Caroline asked, frowning.

"Plotting with your father to become the master of it." Weymouth didn't mince words.

"But Blessing House is not for sale."

"Merrivale is not plotting to buy your house, Caro, my dear." Weymouth's tone was gentle. His words were not. "He's planning to marry *you* in order to get it."

"Hansell Hogarth?" Caroline gave an exaggerated shudder. "Why, I wouldn't marry him if he came wrapped in royal purple and presented on a silver salver by the king himself!"

"He *is* young and handsome." Weymouth stressed Merrivale's two best qualities—some might say, his *only* two qualities.

"Is he?" she queried. "I never noticed anything about him beyond the fact that he's a fortune hunter who's not interested in anything or anyone except himself. Apparently, his only interest lies in improving his current mode of living with my money and property."

"Not to mention your title, Lady Blessing," Weymouth pointed out.

"My title wouldn't do him any good," Caroline said.

"On the contrary."

"But husbands don't assume the rank their wives hold once they marry."

"That's true," Weymouth said. "He wouldn't become the marquess, but a husband doesn't necessarily need to hold the title in order to exploit it. Being married to a marchioness in her own right and having almost unlimited access to her fortune and credit would greatly expand Merrivale's living and social standing, as well as his reach in less exalted quarters."

"The very idea of being tied to him is abhorrent to me."

"It isn't abhorrent to your father," Weymouth remarked. "He appears to be quite taken with the idea."

"You've spoken with my father?"

"I spoke with Tyson. This evening. While your father and Merrivale were sitting down to supper at your dining table."

Caroline smiled a mysterious half-smile.

Weymouth cocked his head to study her. "What do you find so amusing?"

"Lord Rushton and Lord Merrivale sat down to supper at Blessing's dinner table. *You* sat down to supper at mine."

"I suppose I did." Weymouth smiled back at her. "And here's Fielder returning with dessert."

Understanding her godfather's warning, Caroline held her comments and questions for him while Fielder served the pudding and beverages.

"I found coffee in the larder," Fielder said as he set a cup and saucer on the small table between the wing chairs. "And took the liberty of brewing a pot for Lord Weymouth." Fielder met Caroline's gaze. "I brought tea for you, ma'am. I'm sorry I couldn't find any chocolate."

"That's quite all right, Fielder," Caroline told him. "I only indulge in chocolate in the mornings. I prefer tea in the evening."

Fielder allowed himself a ghost of a smile as he served the pudding. "I'll collect the dishes and bank the fire when you've concluded your visit." He nodded toward the bellpull. "Just ring for me."

"Thank you, Fielder." Picking up her spoon, she took a bite of sticky pudding.

The footman turned to Lord Weymouth. "Will you be staying the night, sir?"

Weymouth glanced at Caroline. "I'm afraid not. It wouldn't be proper for me to stay with a young widow in a house without staff on the premises."

"Not proper for my godfather to visit me?" Caroline didn't hide her dismay at the ridiculous idea. "Nonsense."

"Not proper for me to stay the night alone with you, Caro," he said, using the diminutive of her name as he'd done when she was a child. "Gossips would exaggerate the situation should word of it get out."

Caroline opened her mouth to protest, but Lord Weymouth stopped her. "Word of it would eventually get out, my dear." He turned to Fielder. "I'm not suggesting that you or Miss Brown would carry tales, but the fact that I stayed the night here might come to light in other ways, even though it's perfectly innocent." He turned his attention back to Caroline. "And I wouldn't want to do anything to damage your reputation or give your father more reason to encourage Merrivale's courtship, nor would I want to cause distress or concern to my family."

"Neither would I." Caroline set her pudding aside. "Although Aunt Cicely would laugh at the very notion of us—she pointed at him and at herself—causing gossip. But the idea that Aunt Cicely might hear rumors makes me ill."

"I know, my dear." Weymouth reached over and patted her hand. "You wouldn't be the cause; others would be. But it's best if I stay at my club tonight and return here in time for luncheon tomorrow." He met her gaze. "Will that present a difficulty for you?"

Caroline shook her head. "No. Not at all. I'll need to alert Miss Tennant and Miss Osborne to the change of location. And I'll have to cut my time in the gardens short, but the caterers I hired to provide luncheon for the hired men renovating the gardens are more than capable of providing one for us."

"Good." Weymouth took a sip of his coffee. "Invite Miss Tennant to come a half hour early, so I can speak to her in private. Write the notes to the ladies tonight. As you are short of staff, and Fielder cannot abandon his post, I'll have my messenger deliver them."

"All right," Caroline said. "Finish your coffee while I write the notes."

Crossing to the writing desk in the corner of the drawing room, Caroline found writing supplies and quickly penned notes to Phoebe and Dulcie. After sanding and sealing them, she handed them to Lord Weymouth.

"Thank you, my dear." Weymouth removed a sheaf of papers from his inside coat pocket to make way for the two letters. "Now, if Fielder will kindly excuse himself, I'll get to the reason I came by."

Fielder bowed, then quietly left the drawing room, closing the doors behind him.

Caroline took a deep breath and clasped her hands together in her lap. "Are all those papers Tony's medical reports?"

"I'm afraid so."

She exhaled a shaky breath. "Have you read them?"

He nodded. "They're official War Office documents, I can't allow you to read them, but I can tell you what's in them. Understand?"

Caroline nodded. "Before you tell me what's in the reports, Uncle Trevor, tell me if you think I'm foolish for doing everything I can to help him."

Weymouth cleared his throat. "Other than having Sergeant Major Barnaby by his side to prevent the second surgeon from amputating his legs, I think what you're doing is the best thing that could happen to Lord Carlisle. I support your efforts wholeheartedly."

Caroline beamed. "Thank you for that, Uncle Trevor."

"Shall we begin?" Weymouth shuffled a few papers and pulled out two sheets of notes. "The first report is from a Belgian doctor, Dr. Rene Doucette, one of the surgeons at the field hospital at Quatre Bras. He writes that 'a young British major who lay on the battlefield a day and a half still breathes, but his body is too damaged for him to survive. In my experience, a soldier this gravely injured will not live to see another morning.'" Weymouth met Caroline's gaze. "Doucette's report is the reason young Carlisle was officially declared dead."

"Why would the surgeon declare Tony dead ahead of time? How could he give up on him?" Caroline asked, torn between fury and horror.

"Years of experience on the battlefield and knowing the damage Carlisle suffered." Weymouth read the list of Carlisle's injuries. "Concussion, four broken ribs, shattered right tibia, fractured left tibia, broken pelvis, broken right radius and ulna. Bayonet wounds, a sliced throat, and various cuts and bruises." He continued to read through the reports from the physicians and surgeons who had seen or treated Anthony Carlisle. Seven medical doctors had filed official reports on Carlisle's injuries. None had thought his long-term prognosis was good. Only one had optimistically included a schedule for his recommended treatment.

Caroline gasped, then covered her face with her hand. "Poor Tony."

"Buck up, little girl." Weymouth spoke gently, but his tone conveyed an order. "Not 'poor Tony'," he ordered. "He mustn't feel weak. He mustn't be pitied. There's work to be done and he must be strong enough to bear it."

"But what if I can't?" Overwhelmed, Caroline was suddenly, desperately afraid of the responsibility she'd taken on. "I had no idea he was so terribly injured." Unshed tears sparkled in her eyes as she looked up at Weymouth. "None of his doctors believed he would live. They all gave up on him."

"That's why you must not," Weymouth told her. "The fact that he survived at all is remarkable."

"His recovery so far has been even more remarkable," Caroline said. "And probably entirely due to Mr. Barnaby's care." She met

Weymouth's gaze. "What if what he has today is the best he can achieve?"

"If it is the best he can achieve, you live with it and help him learn to live with it. But not until you try all there is to try." Weymouth gave her a tender look. "I've related the surgeons' and the physicians' reports. Now tell me what you know."

"I know he never stands when he sees me. He always remains seated. And although I've never seen him in one, I suspect he's confined to a wheeled chair. He didn't protest when I ordered the workmen to build wooden ramps and walkways throughout the gardens." She took a deep breath, sucking in the sobs that threatened to choke her. "He can't walk and I'm not certain he can stand. Yet. But I'm convinced that with the right treatment and support, he will be able to. Eventually."

"The second Belgian surgeon to treat him disagrees with you," Weymouth told her. "The doctor, a man named Jean Guillory, recommended amputation of both legs, but especially his right leg. He believes Carlisle's chance of survival is dire unless he submits to immediate amputation."

"Do you believe that?"

"I'm not a physician. And I haven't seen him," Weymouth said. "Carlisle's butler refused to admit me. He turned me away from the house along with everyone else. But from what I've heard from you and Barnaby, I believe Carlisle deserves a chance to recover." He pinned Caroline with his gaze. "And from what I hear, you're providing him with that chance. And a reason to get up in the morning."

"Oh, no, Uncle Trevor." Caroline met Weymouth's gaze. "He has a reason, but his reason isn't me."

"Are you certain?"

"As certain as I can be," she said. "What Tony and I shared before is over. He tolerates me in his garden because I outrank him and he can't say no to me. But he doesn't like me anymore. The trust we once had is broken. We'll never be more than neighbors and acquaintances sharing a garden."

"Then why are you working so diligently to help him?"

"Because I hurt him," she said. "I accepted his proposal of marriage and a day later, the announcement of my marriage to Lord Blessing appeared in the newspapers. I promised Tony I would love only him, but I married someone else."

"Have you broken that promise?" Weymouth asked.

"He thinks I did. He believes I betrayed him when I married Lord Blessing."

"Did you love Granville Blessing?"

"Of course not," Caroline said. "You know I had no say in my marriage to Lord Blessing. My father arranged it. Without my knowledge and against my will. I felt nothing but revulsion for Lord Blessing. I didn't like him, and I certainly never loved him."

"Have you told Carlisle how you feel?"

*The only thing I ever wanted was you*. Caroline shook her head. "Not in so many words."

"Perhaps you should," he suggested.

"I don't believe that's something he wants to hear."

"Are you going to give up on him?"

"I *can't*." Her voice broke on the last word. "I can't give up on him. I owe it to him to help him regain what he was before he...before I...before we..."

"The mission of The Charlotte Society."

When she spoke, her words were fierce. "That's right, Uncle Trevor. *My* mission."

"Then perhaps I can put you in touch with a physician who might be able to help him..."

"Truly?" Caroline's face lit up. "Oh, Uncle Trevor, could you?"

"I've been following the career of a physician and surgeon in Edinburgh. Sir James McGregor. I wrote him when Griffin was injured. Griffin's convalescence was long, but he eventually healed without Sir James's surgical skills. McGregor is unorthodox and many of his theories are untried, but he's pioneering battlefield medicine and surgery with the goal of increasing survival rates." He paused a moment to let Caroline digest what he'd told her before offering more. "I'll pen a letter of introduction for you and include a report of Carlisle's injuries and treatments if you like."

"I would appreciate it, Uncle Trevor. And there's something else you might do for me to assist in Lord Carlisle's recovery, if you will."

"What is it, my dear?"

Caroline took a deep breath, blushed to the roots of her hair, then gestured for Lord Weymouth to lean close enough for her to whisper her request.

The tips of Lord Weymouth's ears pinkened at her request, but he sat up straight in his chair and gave a brisk nod. "Done. I'll write the letter and send it in the morning." He rose and walked over to Caroline's chair, then gently helped her to her feet. "The course you've chosen for yourself and for Carlisle isn't going to be easy, Caro. His physical injuries are serious; his emotional injuries may be equally serious. Or *more* serious. He isn't the same man you knew before, my dear..."

She glanced down at her feet. "I'm well aware of that."

Weymouth placed his finger beneath her chin and tilted her face up. "He went to war, Caro." He studied the expression on Caroline's face. "War changes a man. We can't pretend it never happened. He can't pretend it never happened. He'll carry the memories of it with him for the rest of his life. We don't know the whole story of what happened to him while he lay on the battlefield and Carlisle may not know everything that happened to him, either." Weymouth had a good idea of the hell Carlisle had endured. He'd heard the horror stories from survivors and had witnessed the aftermath of a battle. But there was no need for Caroline to be haunted by the realities of war. "Whatever happened to Carlisle left scars on his soul as well as his body."

The earl took a deep breath. "He may never fully recover from the experience. And there's nothing you can do about that. You can't change what happened to him, Caro. Or what happened to you. All you can do is try to replace as many of his bad memories with good ones. Recovering his strength is going to take time, patience, determination, hard work, understanding, and his desire to show you that he's every bit the man he once was."

Weymouth knew what he was talking about. Griffin had suffered similar injuries after being crushed beneath his horse during the Peninsular Campaign. But Weymouth's older son's injuries had been less severe than Carlisle's. Even so, it had taken nearly a year for Griffin to mount a horse and several more months before he could ride for any length of time. Two things had gotten Griffin through his rehabilitation—the love of his bride, Alyssa, and the desire to resume his work and ride his horses once again.

For an expert horseman like Griffin, being unable to ride had been one of the most difficult parts of his rehabilitation.

Anthony Carlisle was also an expert equestrian. His physical pain and his inability to walk had to be excruciating for him. His inability to sit a horse had to be soul-crushing. And all the surgeons' reports Weymouth had read indicated there was worse to come for young Carlisle. "It might help to provide him with an incentive, beyond pleasing you. Give him a goal to work toward."

"His goal isn't to please me. His goal is to show me he doesn't need me or anyone else to help him. His goal is to be his own man once again."

"Is it?" Weymouth asked, playing devil's advocate.

Caroline thought for a moment and realized she didn't really know what Tony wanted. And she hadn't asked. "Of course it is. Tony treasures his independence."

Weymouth fixed his gaze on his goddaughter for a moment before he pulled another sheet of paper from the written reports. "I seem to remember that you used to ride several mornings a week on Rotten Row while Carlisle exercised his mount, Ajax."

"I did." Caroline smiled, remembering early morning rides in the park alongside Tony and Ajax. "Those days were so carefree and glorious. I adored them." *And him.*

"I don't recall seeing you ride since you became a marchioness," Weymouth remarked.

"I haven't," she admitted. "Lord Blessing disapproved. He preferred carriage travel to horseback and didn't think it seemly for his marchioness to ride." She bit her bottom lip. "My father sold my mare the day the marriage announcement appeared in the papers." Caroline had been devastated by the loss of her mare and her freedom. And Tony. Nothing had hurt as much as losing Tony.

"I'm sorry."

"There's no need for you to apologize, Uncle Trevor. Rushton is my father. He had control over me. And he used it. There was nothing you could have done."

Weymouth wasn't so sure, but he didn't want to distress her by continuing to argue the point. "I should have known."

"But you didn't," she countered.

"I'm glad I know now." Weymouth flashed his disarming grin. "It gives me another reason to despise Rushton."

"You don't need another reason for that," Caroline said. "You've always disliked him."

"True." Deep in thought, Weymouth carefully considered his words before he spoke. "Did you know Carlisle lost Ajax at Quatre Bras?"

"What?" Caroline was clearly surprised. And clearly dismayed. "Are you certain?"

"I am," Weymouth said.

"Oh, no." Caroline covered her mouth with her hand as if to keep the shock and horror from escaping. "Not Ajax. Tony adored that horse." She wrinkled her brow. "I can't imagine Tony risking Ajax's life by taking him to war."

"Why not?" Weymouth asked. "Every cavalry officer wants an exceptional mount."

"But Tony loved Ajax. He planned to use him and my mare to improve the bloodlines in his stable." She smiled at the memory. "He planned to give you and Tressingham a run for your money."

Weymouth nodded. "That's what he told me. That's why I sold Ajax to him."

"Tony would never have taken Ajax to war with him. He wouldn't risk him that way."

At the time he learned of it, Weymouth had found that surprising as well. Suspiciously so. But the fact that Carlisle had suddenly turned up on the Peninsula in the cavalry was more surprising. "According to this"—he waved an official looking document in the air between them —"noble Ajax saved Carlisle's life." He gave Caroline a moment to consider what he'd told her, then read the report detailing Carlisle's heroics and his recovery from the battlefield, omitting the gruesome details of the way Ajax's carcass had protected Carlisle from looters. He had been bayoneted and had his throat sliced, but the looters had been unable to strip him of his clothes, his valuables, or his teeth because they had been unable to move Ajax off of him. "When he tires of his therapy and wants to quit—and he will—you might try tempting Carlisle with a trip to the horse sales at Tattersall's," Weymouth suggested.

Caroline wrinkled her forehead. "He arrived in London in a closed sedan chair, Uncle Trevor. Tony isn't going to appear in a public place like Tattersall's," she said. "I don't know that he's ready to be around horses. Any horses." She took a breath. "I *do* know that he'll never allow fellow horsemen, friends and acquaintances to see him in his present condition. To pity him."

"His friends will be happy to see him. They're not going to offer pity."

"Convince Tony of that," she said. "I haven't been able to."

Weymouth took a deep breath, then slowly released it. "Carlisle can't hide in his house forever. And three weeks from today, Ajax's three-year-old full brother will be coming up for sale at Tattersall's." He winked at Caroline. "There's nobody I would rather sell him to than Carlisle. You might mention *that* should you need incentive."

# CHAPTER 21

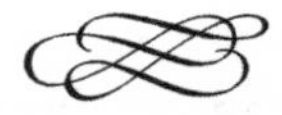

*"All things are difficult before they are easy."*
—Thomas Fuller, 1608-1661

"Was he there?" Tony wheeled around to face Barnaby as soon as his former batman entered the ballroom, carrying a silver ewer of hot water for washing.

In the days since Caroline had begun rearranging the back garden, Tony had had a table and washstand moved into the ballroom, so he could wash and shave, dress, and enjoy a light meal while watching Caroline and the workmen recreate his domain. Now, studying the shadowy structures below, he realized the buildings were almost complete. There were still flower beds to be rearranged, existing flower beds to be moved and new plantings put into the ground according to Capability Brown's design, but the renovations were essentially done.

When the work was finished, he'd be able to move about the garden in his wheelchair. But he would be alone. With her obligations to her charity done, Caroline would be free to resume her life without him.

"The house was full of people." Barnaby filled the basin with hot water, then set the ewer aside and busied himself by laying out the major's favorite soap, along with his toothbrush and tooth powder.

"What?" Lost in thought, Tony had missed Barnaby's answer to his question.

"I said the house was full of people."

Tony wheeled his chair from the window to the washstand.

Emptying the ewer of hot water onto a length of toweling, Barnaby wrung the excess out over the basin and handed the wet cloth to Tony. "Maids and valets, footmen, cooks and cooks' helpers."

Tony soaped the wet towel and washed his face. "What about Rushton?"

"He was there." Barnaby filled a glass with water, added a few drops of common mint oil to it and set the glass and the tooth powder beside the basin. "That's why the house was in such an uproar. He moved into Blessing House this afternoon and brought a gentleman houseguest with him. They were about to sit down to supper when I arrived."

Tony rinsed his face in the basin, then groped for a clean towel. He dried his face, then pinned Barnaby with a stare. "Who was the houseguest?"

"A gentleman by the name of Merrivale, sir."

"Hogarth? The second Earl of Merrivale? Are you certain? Did you recognize him?"

"I didn't hear his family name, only his title," Barnaby told him. "I'm afraid I didn't see either man. And I wouldn't have recognized them if I had. I've never been introduced to Lord Rushton or Lord Merrivale. I didn't speak to anyone in Blessing House." Barnaby laid out a fresh towel and turned to face Lord Carlisle." Studying Tony's face, the batman said, "Forgive me for mentioning it, sir, but you look tired."

Tony *was* tired. His eyes were red-streaked and his lips white-rimmed with pain.

Barnaby glanced at Tony's hands and saw he was gripping the rims of the chair wheels to hide the obvious tremors in them. When the major was tired or in pain, his hands gave him away. Turning his gaze to the side table, Barnaby saw the glass of whisky with the single drop of laudanum in it sat untouched.

Carlisle frowned. "How did you discover who was in the house? Who told you Rushton and Merrivale were there?"

"The gentleman who arrived at Blessing House a few minutes before I did told me." Barnaby kept his voice low and his manner nonchalant as he waited for the major's reaction to the information the Earl of Weymouth had shared with him.

*"Gentleman?* What gentleman?" Carlisle demanded, unable to halt the green wave of jealousy washing over him.

According to the gossip Carlisle had gleaned from the *Ton Tidbits* column, the Marchioness of Blessing had shed her widow's weeds less than a fortnight earlier. And prospective bride grooms—including Merrivale, a known fortune hunter—were showing up on her doorstep in an unseemly amount of time.

Barnaby bit the inside of his cheek to keep from smiling at the major's reaction. "The Earl of Weymouth, sir."

"Weymouth?" Tony's frown grew deeper. Weymouth was neither a fortune hunter nor a prospective bridegroom. He was Caroline's godfather.

"The Wizard of the War Office, sir."

"I know who the Earl of Weymouth is and what he's called in military circles," Tony retorted. "What I don't know is why he was visiting Caroline."

"He said he had urgent business with her," Barnaby said. "He didn't divulge the nature of the business. However, Lord Weymouth *did* tell me that Rushton and Merrivale were there. According to Lady Blessing's butler, Rushton took up residence at Blessing House this afternoon and brought Merrivale with him. The two gentlemen were sitting down to supper when Lord Weymouth arrived to pay a call on Lady Blessing."

"What about Lady Blessing?" Tony knew the answer to the question before he asked it. "Did her butler know she and her companion had vacated her house?"

"Yes, sir." Barnaby nodded. "He knew. The butler said he learned Her Ladyship and her maid were gone when they failed to come downstairs for supper. But he has no idea *where* they've gone."

Carlisle narrowed his gaze at Barnaby. "What about Rushton and Merrivale?"

"Lord Weymouth said they didn't appear to be overly concerned by Lady Blessing's absence," Barnaby replied. "But in all fairness to the gentlemen—"

"Which is more than they deserve," Tony grumbled, sotto voce. "Fairness."

"Most assuredly," Barnaby said. "But in fairness to the two gentlemen, we may have left before they learned of Her Ladyship's defection."

*"We?"*

"Lord Weymouth and I," Barnaby explained. "I drove him from Blessing House to this house, where I directed him to the back gate so he could pay his call on Lady Blessing." He nodded toward Tony's spyglass. "You'll be happy to know your reputation precedes you, sir."

"Oh?"

"Lord Weymouth was aware of your sharpshooting skill. He asked me to make certain you don't shoot him as he's traversing the garden."

Tony flashed a smile. He had been a cavalry officer in the Eleventh Blues and was known for his horsemanship, but he'd also won the Regimental Cup for sharpshooting two years in a row. "I didn't realize you knew the Wizard of the War Office, Barnaby."

"I don't, sir," Barnaby said. "I only knew what I'd heard about him over the years. All military talk. I never met him until tonight." He ran his hand over his closely shorn head. "But he knew a great deal about the two of us."

"Oh?" Tony arched an eyebrow.

"Called me by name, he did," Barnaby said. "And as far as I know, the gentleman had never laid eyes on me before. But he knew who I was." He met the major's gaze. "I found that impressive."

"Did he enlighten you as to how he knew who you were?" Tony was curious. Weymouth was Caroline's godfather. Had she spoken to Weymouth about him? Had she described Barnaby and the renovations taking place in the Carlisle House Gardens? Or the reasons for it? Carlisle wasn't naïve enough to think that Weymouth might be unaware of the injuries he had suffered at Quatre Bras. The Wizard of the War Office knew everything. Saw everything. Heard everything. And Tony had served with Weymouth's son during the Peninsular Campaign when Major Lord Griffin Abernathy, Viscount Abernathy, had suffered similar injuries to his own. Weymouth had to know his situation. The question was whether Lord Weymouth knew the full extent of Tony's injuries and if Weymouth had told Caroline what he knew. "How could he know your name and rank? You went to Blessing House disguised as a coachman and driving an unadorned vehicle with no connections to me."

"Except the horse," Barnaby said.

*"What?"*

"Lord Weymouth recognized the horse."

Tony's smile grew into a soft chuckle. "He should. He bred, foaled, and raised him." He related the events of how he had come to own Aeolus. "Weymouth and his in-law, Lord Tressingham, have the two best stables in England."

"I'm sorry, sir. I would not have asked the groom to harness Aeolus had I known his pedigree." Taking hold of the back of Tony's chair, Barnaby wheeled him to the divan across the room. He helped the major remove his boots and buff breeches and get into his robe and slippers.

"You've no reason to apologize, Barnaby. There's no way you could have known Weymouth would be at Blessing House tonight or that he would recognize a horse born in his stables nearly a decade ago." Tony gave another short laugh. "I didn't anticipate tonight's events, either, and if I had, I'm not sure I would have expected the Wizard to remember Aeolus after all this time." Wheeling himself back to the window, he whirled around and met Barnaby's gaze. "I am curious about one thing, Barnaby."

"What's that, sir?"

"Did Aeolus remember Weymouth?"

Barnaby roared with laughter. "He greeted Lord Weymouth the way he would greet you if you made an appearance in the stables."

Tony closed his eyes for a moment, remembering the sights and scents and sounds of horseflesh and hay, of leather and the jingle of harnesses. Suddenly, struck by how much he missed it, Tony longed to experience it again. *If only he could.* "What is he up to?"

"Lord Weymouth?"

Tony opened one eye and pinned Barnaby with a look. "Well, certainly not Aeolus."

Barnaby laughed louder, appreciating the major's sardonic tone. "Divining Aeolus's motives would be easier than Weymouth's. They don't call him the Wizard for nothing."

"That's true," Lord Carlisle agreed. He plowed his fingers through his hair. "Were you able to glean any hint as to why Weymouth was meeting with Lady Blessing?"

"'Fraid not, sir." Barnaby drew his brows together. "But this morning's *Ton Tidbits* column in the *Morning Chronicle* might provide a reason." Retrieving the morning edition of the paper, Barnaby folded it to the *Ton Tidbits* column and handed it to Tony, who read it aloud. "Caroline's Magnificent Folly? Has the Marchioness of Blessing gone too far? With the structures designed by John Nash and the gardens designed by Capability Brown nearly completed in her neighbor's, the Earl of Carlisle's, London gardens, the town is all abuzz, waiting to learn what the widowed marchioness is about. Will there be a spectacular garden party to reintroduce the earl to society? Or some other splendid fête to herald the season? The betting book at White's is filled with new wagers. Her recent purchase of Selby House and whispers of a wedding breakfast have tongues wagging all over town. What of the mysterious earl who has consistently refused all invitations and denied all callers entrance to Carlisle House? All callers except one. Have the earl and the marchioness formed an alliance? Or is he an unlikely recipient of Bountiful Lady Blessing's charity?" Tony handed the paper back to Barnaby. "According to this, I've become

Caroline's Folly." He paused momentarily to collect his thoughts. "That much is true. Perhaps I always was. But that doesn't give this newspaper the right to tarnish Caroline's reputation. The rest of the column is speculation and rubbish. Who's writing this? Where's the *Chronicle* getting their information?"

"The author of the *Ton Tidbits* column is a tightly held secret, sir. No one seems to know who he—"

"Or *she* is."

Carlisle snorted in disgust. He considered the popular column hearsay, gossip and innuendo and gave it very little credence. But Tony was under no illusions that the other members of the ton felt the same way about it. London society thrived on gossip and innuendo. He had no doubt that two parts of the article were correct—London tongues were wagging and the betting book at White's, the exclusive gentleman's club to which he belonged, was filled with recent wagers.

"Someone knows," Tony said. "Find out who it is."

Barnaby nodded.

"Is he staying the night?" Tony surprised himself by asking the question. He knew Weymouth personally and by reputation and understood the earl's relation to Caroline. Understood their closeness. There was no reason for him to feel the sudden, unreasonable surge of jealousy that shot through him at the thought of Weymouth spending the night beneath Caroline's roof. But it was there, nonetheless. Eating away at his peace of mind. Because Tony wanted to lie in bed and dream of Caroline in bed beside him. He didn't want to think of Weymouth as her houseguest. Tony wanted her all to himself. He wanted to be with her. In every way possible. Tony wanted to spend the night beneath her roof. *Beneath her*. God help him. He wanted her. Again. After five years, betrayal, and a broken heart, he still wanted her.

Training his spyglass on the back of the house, Tony detected the faint glow of lamplight across the garden.

"He wasn't carrying a valise," Barnaby said. "I assumed his visit would be a social call, not an overnight stay, sir. I offered him the loan of your horse and cab if he needed transportation elsewhere."

"Free with my expensive horseflesh, aren't you?"

"If the Earl of Weymouth can't be trusted with expensive horseflesh, who can?" Barnaby shot back. "And I knew you'd want to extend your hospitality."

Taking a sheet of paper out of his desk, Tony quickly penned a note. "You are right. I'm happy to extend my hospitality, not my horse and vehicle."

Carlisle's statement caught his former batman unawares. "Sir?"

"Send Kirby..." Tony wrinkled his brow. "No, wait, he and Fielder have been on duty since five or so this morning. Send Nelson next door to bring Lord Weymouth back here and have the green room made ready for him. He'll be our guest."

"I beg your pardon, sir, but are you inviting Lord Weymouth to stay the night here?" Barnaby couldn't quite believe what he was hearing. The major had been a recluse for weeks since his return to London.

"Yes, Barnaby." A smile played on Tony's lips. "I am extending my hospitality to the Earl of Weymouth rather than loan him a horse and vehicle he'll feel obligated to return as soon as possible."

"Are you going to receive him?" Barnaby asked.

"No." Tony glanced down at his legs. "Make him feel welcome. See that he has everything he needs. Extend my hospitality and my apologies. Lord Weymouth is welcome here at any time. But make it clear that I regret I will be unable to receive him." He paused. "If you think Nelson is trustworthy enough to be alone with Lady Blessing and her companion and is ready for the responsibility, have him relieve Fielder for the remainder of the night. If not, select someone else to do so."

"Nelson is young, sir, and not as experienced as Fielder or Kirby, but he's entirely trustworthy and more than capable of handling the responsibility." Barnaby frowned. "Have you reason to suspect Nelson mightn't be trustworthy, sir?"

"No," Tony said. "My only concern is his youth and inexperience around ladies. We haven't had any female guests since he began work with us. He's what? Sixteen? Seventeen?"

"I believe he just turned twenty, sir."

"He looks younger," Tony muttered.

"That he does, sir. But you needn't worry about his youth," Barnaby assured him. "Nelson's a handsome lad who seems to handle himself quite well among the female staff." He smiled. "The maids seem to be quite taken with him."

"How taken with him?" Tony asked, his tone more brusque than usual. "He understands the rules about dallying with the maids or ladies of quality, doesn't he?"

"Of course, Major," Barnaby said. "West is very thorough about explaining the rules of the house to the staff. Especially, the footmen. I can assure you Nelson is quite honorable and mature for his age."

Because footmen were the most visible servants in the household, serving the family and guests, they were generally tall in stature, strong and well-muscled, and pleasing to the eye. Freddie Nelson was no different. He was two or three inches shorter than Kirby or Fielder and slighter in build, but well-built and handsome in a fresh-faced, youthful sort of way. The young housemaids employed at Carlisle House were agog over him. But Nelson never seemed to notice. Barnaby frowned. If he didn't know better, he'd think the major was jealous of the young footman and worried Lady Blessing might find Nelson more attractive than she did him.

The major needn't worry. A man had only to look at Lady Blessing to know she only had eyes for Major Lord Anthony Carlisle. But the major couldn't seem to see what was readily apparent to other men because, Barnaby believed, the major was convinced he no longer had anything to offer a young woman. "Sir, do you want me to send Nelson or not?"

Tony closed his eyes once again, fighting his frustration at being unable to run his own errands, at being unable to entertain longtime friends and guests, at being unable to resume his life, at being unable to take Caroline in his arms... Opening his eyes, he thrust the message into Barnaby's hand. "I hate to ask it of you, Barnaby, but I would appreciate it if you'd accompany Nelson next door." He blew out a breath. "Fielder isn't going to want to abandon his post to anyone other than Kirby. But see that Fielder gets some rest and that Nelson understands the importance of his assignment. And tell Cook there will be one for breakfast in our morning room and a hamper for two delivered to Selby House."

"Only one?" Barnaby repeated the number. "Shouldn't it be two?"

"I won't be receiving Weymouth or joining him for breakfast." Tony was resolute in his decision. He liked Weymouth, admired him, but he was not prepared to entertain him. Or face the inevitable questions about his health, his future, his gardens, or Caroline. Nor was he ready to hear well-intentioned platitudes from a man he admired. Better to risk being rude and avoid the situation altogether. "I'll take breakfast in my room."

"As you wish, sir."

The note of disapproval in Barnaby's voice was impossible for Carlisle to ignore. "You disagree?"

"I thought you'd enjoyed breakfasting with Lady Blessing in the garden these past two days."

"I did," Carlisle admitted. "I do."

"But..."

"I prefer to keep my breakfasts with Lady Blessing private." He pulled his mouth into a wry smile. "As private as breakfast in the gardens amid fifty or so gardeners and builders, two footmen, and with one gentleman's gentleman looking on can be."

"When you put it that way, what's one more?"

"Not what," Tony corrected. "Who." He rarely offered explanations for his decisions or his behavior to anyone, but he offered one now because Barnaby's opinions mattered to him. "Weymouth sees too much. Discerns too much. I'm willing to offer my hospitality to him, but I'm not willing to face Weymouth over the breakfast table. And since I cannot ignore my guest in order to share breakfast with Lady Blessing in the garden, my best course of action is to take breakfast in my room."

"Then I'll do it, sir." Barnaby walked to the window. "If you'll do something for me."

Carlisle was wary. "What?"

Lifting the glass of whisky, he'd left on the table, Barnaby handed it to the major. "Drink this, sir. And get some rest yourself. You look done in. You were up earlier than Fielder or Kirby."

"Very well." Carlisle raised the glass to his lips and downed it in one swallow, grimacing as it burned its way to his stomach.

"And for the record, sir. You didn't ask me to do anything." Barnaby stepped to attention and snapped a sharp salute. "I volunteered."

# CHAPTER 22

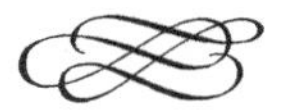

*"Be discreet in all things, and so render it unnecessary to be mysterious about any."*
—Arthur Wellesley, 1769-1852,
1st Duke of Wellington.

Caroline made her way down the stairs to the Selby House kitchen early the following morning. Sleep had been elusive. She'd spent the better part of the night tossing and turning, struggling to come to terms with what she'd learned about Tony's health and the challenges he faced. Challenges she faced as well, since she'd taken it upon herself to tackle them with him.

The fact that she'd managed to sleep at all surprised her. But she'd finally fallen asleep sometime after a clock somewhere upstairs chimed the five o'clock hour.

She'd slept soundly for two hours before suddenly coming fully awake. Fully awake and fully afraid of the consequences of the path she had chosen. Panicking at the thought of what lay ahead.

Caroline had been so sure of herself before. Now, she worried she might make a mistake. Might do the wrong thing. She worried she might do something to worsen Tony's condition and increase his pain. And an increase in pain would naturally cause an increase in his use of laudanum. After learning the extent of his injuries, Caroline was scared and full of doubt about her true motives and her decisions.

Did she want Tony to recover to absolve herself of the guilt she felt at professing her love for him and marrying someone else? Did she want him to be well for her or for him? Did she want him to recover to restore his health and independence? Or to tout the success of the Charlotte Society?

Did she want to restore his health so he'd be endlessly grateful to her? Or to make it possible for him to walk away and forget her? Or to make it possible for her to forget him with a clear conscience? Was she trying to help Tony fulfill his obligation to the Carlisle name and marry someone else? Could she live with herself if she did?

What did she know about helping Tony recover? The practice of medicine was an inexact one. A guessing game at best. Even for doctors with experience. She was neither a doctor nor an experienced nurse. The only experience she had was sitting with her late husband during the nights of his final illness and sending for the physician whenever he seemed to be taking a turn for the worse.

She hadn't doubted her course of action when she began it, but she was doubting it now.

With very good reason.

If everything Uncle Trevor had told her about Tony's condition was true, her plans for his rehabilitation were overly ambitious. Terribly naïve. And horribly depressing.

Caroline had lain in bed for hours, wide awake and weighing her options. She could abandon her plans for him and walk away. She could replace the gate in the wall, sell Selby House, and pretend the past few days had never happened.

She could admit that selecting Tony had been a mistake and a violation of the society rules. Major Lord Anthony Carlisle wasn't without means or support. He wasn't destitute or in need of assistance in re-entering society. If he wanted, Tony could return to society simply by accepting any one of the dozens of invitations he received every day.

Caroline could, and probably should, choose another soldier to be a beneficiary of The Charlotte Society. A soldier with less daunting injuries and no connection to her, someone who needed the charity she could offer.

But doing so would mean abandoning Tony and their shared past. It would mean letting him go and living with bitter regrets of what might have been.

It would mean breaking her promise to herself and to Uncle Trevor.

Caroline sighed. She'd already lived with five years of regrets. Could she endure five or ten or twenty more? Could she walk away from Tony again when every part of her ached to stay and fight for him? To fight for his well-being and for his love.

During her two hours of deep sleep, Caroline had dreamed of him the way he'd been five years ago—when he'd walked and danced and rode Ajax. When he'd been male perfection. She'd dreamed of his touch and his kisses, the look on his face when he spoke her name. She dreamed of the way he'd looked at her the night he'd asked her to be his countess...

When he'd loved her...

Feeling another rush of hot tears, Caroline squeezed her eyes shut. She could give up. On him. On herself. On her dream of their life together. Or she could get up, get dressed, go downstairs, and fight for him and, if needs be, with him.

Anthony Carlisle might be her magnificent folly, but Caroline couldn't bring herself to let him go. Not now. Not yet.

Crossing the threshold into the kitchen, she drew up short at the sight of a different footman in Carlisle livery unpacking a wicker hamper on the kitchen table. "Who are you?"

The footman looked up from his chore. "Kirby, milady."

"What happened to the footman who relieved Fielder?"

"I sent him home," he said. "I'll be serving you and seeing to your needs today."

Caroline frowned. "There seems to be a mistake. I generally take breakfast in the gardens with Lord Carlisle."

"No mistake, ma'am," Kirby told her. "Cook sent a hamper of breakfast over for you and your maid." He glanced around.

"She's still asleep." Caroline answered his unspoken question. "She was up far later than usual last night. I decided to let her sleep for another hour or two."

"Yes, ma'am." He removed one of the two settings he'd placed on the table.

"It was very kind of your cook to send breakfast for us. But Lord Carlisle will be expecting me next door and I hate to think of him dining alone."

"His Lordship ordered the hamper for you, Your Ladyship. He won't be breaking his fast in the gardens this morning."

"Oh." Glancing out the window, Caroline saw that the lawn between Selby House and the hole in the wall was shrouded in heavy fog for the third morning in a row. Recalling the cold and damp of the past two days, she asked, "Is he ill?"

"I'm not at liberty to discuss His Lordship's health, milady," Kirby told her.

"I'm not asking you to betray His Lordship's trust," Caroline said. "I'm only asking if he's ill. Please..."

Hearing the concern in her voice, the footman relented. "He was fine when I brought his shaving water this morning."

"Thank you." She squeezed her eyes shut and breathed a sigh of relief.

Kirby filled a cup with hot chocolate and set it on the table beside her plate, then pulled out her chair for her. "If you'll take a seat, milady, I'll serve your breakfast."

Caroline sat and allowed the footman to serve her a poached egg and toasted bread with her chocolate.

After finishing her meal, Caroline wrapped her hands around her cup, savoring the last of her hot chocolate as she relayed her schedule for the day. "The workmen will be here at eight to clean up and put the final touches on the new master bedchamber. They have their instructions and know what I expect." She glanced at Kirby as he busied himself tidying the kitchen. "Kirby, have you ever been inside Lord Carlisle's bedchamber?"

"Yes, ma'am," he said. "Fielder and I assist His Lordship."

"Assist him how?" she asked.

"We carry"—Kirby caught himself before he revealed too much—"and fetch—whatever Barnaby or His Lordship needs."

Caroline bit her bottom lip. "Perhaps you would be so good as to inspect the new master bedchamber to see if it meets Lord Carlisle's needs."

Kirby stopped. "I think Mr. Barnaby would be a better choice, ma'am."

"Barnaby isn't here," she pointed out. "You are."

Kirby threw a glance toward the stairs. "Lord Carlisle finds stairs difficult to negotiate at the moment, ma'am."

"The new master bedchamber isn't upstairs," Caroline said. "It's down the hall where the morning room would normally be." She gazed at Kirby. "The workmen will be here to finish up soon and I'm not sure it meets his needs. I thought..." She pursed her lips. "I thought you might give it a look and make notes on any changes or additions it needs while I'm otherwise engaged. But I understand your loyalty to Lord Carlisle and your natural reluctance to carry tales out of school."

Kirby debated a moment longer before answering. "I'll be happy to take a peek, ma'am."

"Thank you, Kirby," she said. "The interior workmen will be here at eight. I'll be in the Carlisle gardens until nine. The catering company will arrive at half-past nine. You'll need to have everything ready for them to prepare and serve the hired men on the back lawn. We have guests coming at eleven for luncheon. We'll require the drawing room be set for luncheon and the library for a private meeting. I'll need to be dressed by half past ten in order to greet my guests." She met his gaze. "Can you remember all that?"

The corners of Kirby's mouth turned up. "Workmen at eight. Gardens until nine. Caterers at half-past nine. Dressed by half-past ten. Collect you from Carlisle Gardens if you are not here by ten. Guests at eleven."

She gave a crisp nod to acknowledge him, then grabbed her apron, pelisse, and bonnet from the hooks at the back door. "I didn't say anything about you collecting me at ten, but if I'm not here by that time, please do." She smiled. "I must run. The plumbers and gardeners are waiting for me next door. We're filling the bathing pool today and I don't want to miss it." Opening the back door, Caroline hurried out, then turned back and retraced her steps. "Thank you, Kirby."

"Thank *you*, ma'am."

"I meant for breakfast."

"I meant for His Lordship." He opened his mouth to say more, then clearly thought better of it, and closed it again.

Beset by curiosity, Caroline asked, "What were you going to say?"

"I was going to mention the walkways, ma'am."

She drew her brows together, picturing the network of wooden walkways intersecting the garden. "What about them?"

"If it wouldn't be too much bother, I was going to suggest you extend one of the wooden paths through the garden to the cobblestones of the mews so His Lordship might…"

"Visit his horses!" She finished the footman's suggestion for him. "Were you in service at Carlisle House before Lord Carlisle went to war?"

He gave her a sheepish look. "No, ma'am. I've only been with him since his return to London, but I know he was an officer in the cavalry and I thought being able to see his livestock might do him some good."

"It would do him a world of good," Caroline said warmly. "I'm ashamed I didn't think of it myself."

"You've been busy thinking of everything else, ma'am."

Caroline gifted him with another smile. "I'll see to it straightaway." She turned back to the door.

"Half-past ten, Your Ladyship. Don't forget."

~

SHE DIDN'T. BUT SHE CAME CLOSE.

After overseeing the filling of the bathing pool, Caroline had half expected to meet Kirby coming through the hole in the wall to fetch her as she hurried to Selby House in time to bathe and change before her guests arrived.

Susan was waiting to help her out of her garments and into the tub.

"You're shaving it close, ma'am."

"I wanted to be there when they pumped the hot water into the pool for the first time. And it took longer than I thought it would." Caroline stepped into the tub, settled into scented bubbles up to her neck, careful not to get her hair wet as she bathed as quickly as she could. "If the workmen hadn't been on the grounds, I would have bathed there."

"Ma'am!" Susan sounded scandalized. "You wouldn't!"

"Oh, yes, I would." Caroline extended her right arm and soaped it. "Think about it, Susan. I could have bathed in hot water that didn't have to be heated elsewhere and poured into buckets and hauled up two or three flights of stairs and dumped into a tub, where it goes from hot to tepid to cold before a body can finish bathing." She washed her other arm, then slid down in the tub to rinse the soap off before standing up and wrapping herself in a length of toweling. "In Lord Carlisle's bathing pond, the water stays hot."

Holding a dressing gown open so Caroline could slide her arms into the sleeves, Susan gave a derisive snort. "I'll have to see *that* to believe it."

"You have seen it," Caroline reminded her. "The same hot water comes from the spring through pipes to the taps in the scullery."

"Where it has to be hauled upstairs in oak buckets." Susan laid out a stack of fresh undergarments.

Caroline slipped on drawers trimmed in lace and a matching chemise, hooked her half stays into place, then held her arms up as Susan dropped a dark pink morning gown over her head and smoothed it into place. Caroline sat on a chair at the vanity table and pulled on the stockings Susan handed her, tying them with pink garters, then turned to the mirror and began unpinning her hair.

"Here," Susan said. "Let me." She moved to stand behind her mistress and began brushing Caroline's hair.

"Nothing elaborate," Caroline instructed. "I'm already late."

Susan plaited Caroline's hair, fashioned it into an elegant coronet on Caroline's head, and pinned it into place. "There. All done."

Caroline stared into the mirror. Her face was pink from the heat of her bathwater and wisps of her normally straight hair curled at her forehead and the sides of her face. Standing up, Caroline faced her lady's maid. "How do I look?"

"Like a marchioness who spent the night in a house with no staff."

"I had *you,*" Caroline reminded her.

Susan grunted. "Only because I knew you'd get yourself into trouble without me."

The small ormolu clock chimed the quarter hour. Caroline had another quarter hour before she needed to appear downstairs to check the luncheon table, but Uncle Trevor was notorious for appearing, not only out of the blue, but *early*.

Caroline ran her hands over her skirts, smoothing imaginary wrinkles. "Just wait until tonight."

Susan was cautious. "What happens tonight?"

"You get to see hot water in a bathing pool for yourself."

Susan folded her arms over her chest. "How?"

"Easy," Caroline said. "After all the workmen leave for the day, we're going next door and I'm going to dip my toe in and test the water."

"Oh, no, you're not!" Susan exclaimed. "Not as long as Lord Carlisle can see you from his window."

He couldn't see her from his window. The design of the new pavilion covering the heated bath insured the privacy of anyone bathing inside it. The expensive frosted glass panes, framed by cast iron and forming the walls and roof of the building, made it impossible for anyone watching from the upstairs windows or balcony to see inside it. Including Tony, who had approved John Nash's design.

The only way for Tony to see who was in the pool was for him to watch from *inside* the building.

Caroline knew the choice of frosted glass had caused Tony considerable consternation. He had debated the merits of clear glass versus frosted, torn by the desire to watch the activities in the garden from the ballroom window and the necessity to conceal his injuries from the prying eyes of the household staff or anyone else who might be able to peer over the garden wall when he used the pool. He'd eventually settled on Caroline's choice.

She smiled. The frosted glass would afford her privacy in the daylight hours. But when illuminated from inside, as it would be at night, anyone bathing inside the pavilion would cast shadows. Tony wouldn't be able to see her nude. But he'd be able to see her silhouette quite clearly. Like watching a paper cut-out shadow play on the nursery wall.

Knowing her privacy would be assured didn't stop Caroline from teasing her maid. "Watch me," she challenged, with a saucy wink. "*He* will."

~

TREVOR, LORD WEYMOUTH KNOCKED ON THE FRONT DOOR OF SELBY House at a quarter hour to the appointed time. He'd arrived by cab, having left the War Office in time to run an errand before the weekly meeting of the Charlotte Society and his private meeting with Miss Dulcie Tennant.

When the footman in Carlisle livery answered the front door, he gave no hint of having passed the night as Carlisle's guest. Shifting the elegantly wrapped package he was holding from one arm to the other, Weymouth doffed his hat. "Good morning. I'm Weymouth. Lady Blessing is expecting me for luncheon."

"I'm Kirby," the footman said. "You're early, sir."

"Am I?" Weymouth's tone was disarming.

"If you will follow me, sir," the footman invited, "Her Ladyship is awaiting you in the library."

"Uncle Trevor!" Caroline greeted him as soon as he entered the library. "I had Kirby bring refreshments." She smiled. "I knew you'd arrive early."

"And have the ill manners to remark upon it," Weymouth teased as he leaned down to kiss her forehead.

Lifting a cup and saucer from the serving tray Kirby had brought, Caroline poured from a matching coffee pot. "It's my prerogative," she retorted. "As your goddaughter and as a marchioness."

"I feared the power would go to your head one day." Weymouth said, a twinkle in his eye.

"You feared nothing of the kind."

"Ah, but I did. First my son—" He paused a moment, deep in thought. "First my *eldest* son—" Weymouth had waited thirty years to have a second son and the idea that he now had two sons took a bit a bit of getting used to after all the years of having only Griffin to consider. "—becomes the first Duke of Avon. And you become a marchioness in her own right. The son I sired and the goddaughter I had a hand in guiding from a little girl to a young woman outrank me. I bow to both of you now. Not the other way around." He chuckled. "If the power hasn't gone to your head yet, it will at your first appearance at court."

"I've been to court," she said. "I don't much care for it." She smiled at him. "As you well know."

"You are your mother's daughter." Weymouth had grown up with Marianne Downing, daughter of the sixth Earl of Downing. Caroline's mother and Trevor Weymouth came from neighboring estates in Hertfordshire. "And are so very much like her."

"You cared for my mother very much," she said.

"I loved her," Weymouth said simply. "She was the sister I never had. And like an elder brother, I despaired of her taste in suitors. I never cared much for your father. And I never understood why she did. Henry, Viscount Hardage, as he was known then, wasn't nearly good enough for Marianne. She was genuine. He was—" Weymouth managed a Gallic shrug. "Less so."

"True. And quite diplomatic. My father has always been unduly impressed by influence, grand titles, and royal honors. Mother was not."

"Marianne cared about people. She placed little store in the titles they held," Weymouth said. "Which made her marriage to your father inexplicable."

"Mother always said being the eldest son and heir made my father take love and adoration for granted. She said it damaged his character. He knew how to accept love as his due, but he never learned to return it."

"And knowing he was a selfish rotter, she still married him," Weymouth said. "That sounds like Marianne. She always believed the best of him." He shook his head. "Although how a man could have a wife like Marianne and a daughter like you and never learn to return their love is beyond me."

Recalling something she'd once read, Caroline quoted. "You cannot persuade the heart to change course. The heart knows what it wants. She loved him."

Weymouth nodded. "The attraction between a man and woman cares nothing for logic."

"I miss her."

Her mother had died suddenly when Caroline was sixteen and life had never been the same. One day her mother was alive and well and three days later she was gone forever. A victim of the scarlet fever that had swept through London while they had been in town making the rounds of dressmakers, milliners, furriers, jewelers, and cobblers in preparation for Caroline's first season.

Her mother's death had left Caroline inconsolable. Life without her mother was bleak and colorless. Caroline cared nothing for the rituals of society. They had no meaning without her mother there to chaperone and watch her make her curtsey to the Prince Regent.

The loss of her mother and the period of mourning that followed had delayed her entrance into society by two years. Caroline would have foregone the whole thing, but Aunt Cicely wouldn't hear of it.

At the start of what would have been Caroline's third season, Aunt Cicely had sponsored her and served as her chaperone, proudly watching as Caroline donned court dress and ostrich feathers to make her formal curtsey before the regent.

Three weeks later, Caroline had met Anthony Carlisle at Lady Bessemer's ball and had fallen madly in love.

She had been over the moon when Tony proposed marriage and plunged into the depths of despair and disillusionment when she'd been promptly married against her will to the Marquess of Blessing.

"Mother wasn't impressed by society and neither am I." Caroline met her godfather's gaze. "I learned better when I was married to the previous Marquess of Blessing."

"I imagine you did." The empathy she saw in his eyes touched her deeply. He and Aunt Cicely had been as opposed to her marriage to Blessing as she had been, but Lord and Lady Weymouth's objections had fallen on deaf ears. Henry Hardage, ninth Earl of Rushton, was determined his only daughter would marry the marquess.

The Earl and Countess of Weymouth had had no say in the matter. Caroline's forced marriage to Blessing had only served to strengthen the enmity between Weymouth and Rushton.

"You tease me about holding the title in my own right," Caroline said. "But if I become hungry for power, you have only yourself to blame. You had a hand in the giving me that power. And Griffin's as well."

"No doubt you've been listening to rumors." Weymouth didn't admit his role in making her title possible, nor would he ever do so. "My influence in government and with the crown is highly inflated."

"If you say so, Uncle Trevor." Caroline played along with his fiction, allowing him to blame her knowledge on information that had come from rumors and innuendo when they both knew she put little store in rumors or innuendo.

Weymouth set his cup on the saucer, retrieved the package he'd brought with him, and handed it to Caroline.

Caroline examined the package, wrapped in the distinct brown paper and black ribbon and bearing the address of *Jonathan Meyer, Tailor. Thirty-Six Conduit Street.* The address and the name brought back a host of memories. "For me?"

"In a manner of speaking," Weymouth replied. "I paid a visit to his tailor to order the item you requested. He promptly provided it and was thrilled to do so. He's also exceedingly discreet."

Caroline sat back on her chair. "He did it in one morning."

"Forty-seven minutes to be precise," Weymouth told her.

She exhaled. "I thought it would take more time."

Weymouth's mouth turned up at the corners. "You thought you *had* more time."

Caroline met his gaze. "You're right, Uncle Trevor. I thought I would have more time to prepare."

"No time like the present."

She groaned at his poor play on words. "Now I have no choice but to get on with it."

"My dear, you never had a choice."

Caroline frowned at him.

"You cannot persuade the heart to change course. The heart knows what it wants," he repeated her earlier words. "Your mother wanted Rushton. You want Carlisle."

"And only you would have the ill manners to speak of it," she said, rephrasing *his* earlier words.

Weymouth pretended affront. "I'll have you know I have impeccable manners. I'm known for my manners."

"You're known for your bluntness," Caroline retorted.

He pretended shock. "Not my manners?"

"Hardly."

He laughed. "So very like your mother."

She would have continued her good-natured sparring with Lord Weymouth, but a knock on the front door interrupted them.

Glancing at his timepiece, Weymouth said, "That must be Miss Tennant."

"She's early, too," Caroline said. "I'll have Kirby bring fresh coffee and chocolate for Dulcie."

Weymouth nodded. "Go welcome your friend. I'll ring for Kirby."

"Would you rather meet with her in the drawing room?"

He shook his head. "Bring her in here. It affords more privacy. You may stay long enough to make the formal introductions, and then you're free to attend to your other guest and to other matters." He winked at her. "And no listening at the keyhole."

"I was six, Uncle Trevor!" she protested. "I know better now."

"Bad habits become ingrained very early," he teased. "Run along, little girl."

# CHAPTER 23

*"It is not so much our friends' help that helps us*
*As the confident knowledge that they will help us."*
—Epicurus, 341 BC-270 BC

"Oh, Caro, I couldn't believe it when I got your note!" Dulcie rushed across the marble entryway to greet her friend as soon as Kirby opened the front door. "I'm so excited and so nervous I'm shaking." She held out her hand so Caroline could see the tremors. "And being instructed to come here came as a complete surprise." Dulcie spun around with her arms outstretched. "Selby House. You're here. You said you'd do it, but I never dreamed you would do it so soon."

"Neither did I," Caroline admitted.

There was no hiding the fact that Caroline was in residence now. Dulcie's cab had dropped her off at the front door. With the staff returning tomorrow, the local tradesmen would resume deliveries and word would get around. Soon every resident of Park Lane would know Selby House's new owner had moved in.

Dulcie handed her bonnet and pelisse to Kirby. "What made you do it sooner than you planned? Tyson and the staff? Or something else? It wasn't yesterday's *Ton Tidbits* column, was it?"

"No," Caroline told her. "It was Lord Rushton."

"Your father? What has he done now?"

"He leased his Portman Square town house to a lord and lady newly arrived from the country for the season."

"Where's he going to live?" Dulcie asked.

"Blessing House," Caroline said. "He moved in yesterday afternoon. While I was in Carlisle's gardens. Rushton left before supper and was gone a short while before returning to Blessing House with Lord Merrivale."

"Merrivale?" Dulcie shuddered. "He's a fortune hunter of the first water. Why would your father cozy up to him?"

"According to Lord Weymouth, now that Lord Blessing is no longer with us, my father is feeling the loss..."

"Of Lord Blessing?" Dulcie was incredulous at the idea of anyone missing Lord Blessing. He certainly hadn't given Caro or Phoebe or her any reason to miss him.

Caroline gave a short laugh. "He is feeling the loss of his close association to the royal family. I'm told Lord Merrivale is one of the Gentlemen of the Bedchamber." Wrinkling her nose in distaste, she added, "And you can't get much closer to royalty than that."

Dulcie gave another exaggerated shudder. "Who would want to?"

"Other than my father?"

Dulcie laughed at Caroline's earnest expression and soon the two of them were giggling like schoolgirls, doubled over with mirth. "Oh, Caro, it's so good to hear you laugh again!" Dulcie hooked her arm around Caroline's and began pulling her from the foyer toward the drawing room. "Come on, show me the house. I can't wait to see it and hear all your plans for it."

"I'm afraid you'll have to," Caroline told her. "Uncle Trevor is waiting for you in the library."

"He's here? Already? I arrived early so I wouldn't run the risk of keeping him waiting."

Caroline shrugged. "Uncle Trevor arrived earlier."

Dulcie looked crestfallen. "And I so hoped to make a good impression..."

"How could you not?"

"By arriving late and keeping him waiting," Dulcie said.

Caroline took a deep breath. "Just because you didn't arrive early enough doesn't mean you were late or that you've kept Uncle Trevor waiting." She gave Dulcie a reassuring smile. "Unless we continue to debate the merits of arriving early."

Dulcie inhaled, then blew out the breath. "All right. I'm ready."

Caroline tapped on the library door before opening it. "Uncle Trevor?"

"Come in." Lord Weymouth rose from his seat when Caroline and Dulcie entered the room.

Although Dulcie had met Lord Weymouth in passing at various social events over the years, she had never been formally introduced to him. Caroline took the opportunity to remedy that. "Uncle Trevor, may I present Miss Dulcie Tennant, sister to the late Viscount Tennant?" She turned to Dulcie. "Dulcie, my beloved godfather, the Earl of Weymouth."

Dulcie extended her hand, then bowed her head and bent her knee in a polite curtsey. "Lord Weymouth."

Weymouth took her hand and helped her to her feet. "Miss Tennant."

She looked up. "Thank you, sir, for agreeing to help me."

Weymouth waved her to a chair. "I am glad to be of service. I knew your brother. He was an excellent soldier and an even better man." He glanced at Caroline. "Caro, my dear, if you would see to refreshments for Miss Tennant. Hot cocoa, I believe. And fresh coffee for me."

"I'll send Kirby in with them right away." Caroline gave Dulcie a reassuring smile. "I'll be in the drawing room if you need me." She exited the room, closing the door behind her.

Unable to bear the suspense any longer, Dulcie blurted the question out in a rush of breath. "Did you find him, Lord Weymouth? Is he —is he—dead?"

Weymouth leaned closer. "Oh, no, Miss Tennant, he's alive."

She exhaled. "Thank goodness." Thinking of Anthony Carlisle, she added, "Gravely injured? Maimed? I've made inquiries at every veteran's hospital and soldier's home in London."

"Rest easy." Weymouth chose his words very carefully. "At last report, he was holding up very well. The injuries he suffered in battle are healing nicely."

"Where is he?" she asked. "Do you know?"

"I'll tell you what you need to know," Weymouth promised. "Everything I can tell you, but first—" A tap on the door warned Weymouth that Kirby had returned with their drinks.

The footman entered the library, removed the empty coffee pot and dirty dishes and replaced them with a fresh pot of coffee, a pot of chocolate, and clean dishes and silver. He poured the beverages, then left the library as quietly and efficiently as he'd entered.

Dulcie took a small sip of her chocolate, then politely set her cup aside. Summoning her courage, she folded her hands in her lap and looked Weymouth in the eye. "The social niceties have been observed, Lord Weymouth. I believe it's time you break the bad news and tell me what you've come to tell me."

Weymouth swallowed a mouthful of coffee and set his cup beside Dulcie's. "I believe you're right, Miss Tennant. Forgive me for prolonging the suspense. But before I reveal what I've discovered about the gentleman in question, I need to know why you're determined to find him. London is filled with soldiers returning from war. Many of whom would make excellent candidates for the Charlotte Society." He removed the note on which she'd written the man's name from his pocket and waved it in the air. "Why this particular man?"

"He's my betrothed."

"I wasn't aware of your betrothal," Weymouth admitted.

"No one is," she said. "It's a secret."

"Between you and the gentleman in question?"

She shook her head. "No. He served with my brother in the regiment. He was my brother's friend," she said. "And my brother instructed me to get in touch with his friend should anything happen to him." She explained Geoffrey's promise that his friend had sworn to marry her, then glanced down at her hands, realizing she was nervously pleating the fabric of her skirt. She laced her fingers together to stop. "When my brother died, my uncle inherited his title. I don't understand quite how it happened, but I'm no longer welcome in the home in which I was born." She blushed at the idea that she was revealing such intimate details of her life to a stranger. But Caroline trusted Lord Weymouth and if Caro trusted him, Dulcie would trust him. "My uncle was only three years older than my brother and a dozen years my father's junior. As the younger son, Uncle Guilford greatly resented my father for being the viscount. He hated being a younger son with limited prospects and income and his bitterness grew worse when my brother was born."

She inhaled. "My uncle has made it plain that the only prospect I have for marriage is to marry whomever he chooses. The only money he's willing to spend on me is the dowry to marry me off." She frowned. "My uncle has expensive tastes and often indulges in games of chance. But he rarely wins. He's mortgaged our town house and the county seat in Surrey. I'm afraid I'm about to be betrothed to the mortgage holder to settle my uncle's debt. And if I refuse to marry him—" She met Lord Weymouth's gaze, willing him to understand. "And I *must* refuse so the best I can hope for is a position as a governess or a companion. Dulcie took another breath. "I know it seems horribly selfish of me, but I want more of a life than that. And I know Geoffrey wanted more for me. He trusted his friend to protect me. How could I do less?"

"Do you know who holds the mortgage on your family home?" Weymouth asked.

She shook her head. "I've no idea, but I know my uncle's friends are not the sort of men I would entrust with my future or my fortune."

"I see." Weymouth said. "How do you know the man your brother chose for you is any better?"

Dulcie smiled. "Because Geoffrey chose him. He was Geoff's friend and my brother, unlike my uncle, was an excellent judge of character. He wouldn't choose any man for me unless he was a gentleman."

"Was your brother aware of your uncle's resentment?"

"Of course," Dulcie said. "Geoff provided Uncle Guilford with a generous allowance, but it was never enough. Uncle Guilford never came to terms with the fact he was not only a younger son, but out of the direct line of succession to the title. He relished spending money he didn't have and begrudged having to ask Geoff to settle his obligations."

"Was your brother injured and dying when his friend swore to marry you?"

"No." Dulcie was adamant. "He wrote me of it on the eve of Burgos in the Peninsula. Geoffrey's friend added a few lines, attesting his willingness to marry me should Geoffrey be killed in battle. He signed the betrothal agreement of his own free will before Geoffrey was mortally wounded." She opened her reticule and took out several sheets of folded paper. "I have the letter here if you care to read it."

Weymouth took the letter, read it, and returned it to her.

"Well?" she demanded. "It's all there. Written out in Geoffrey's hand except for the lines the gentleman added and the signatures of the witnesses. He's to receive my dowry upon our marriage. The letter proves it. It's signed, sealed, dated, and legal. The gentleman in question, as you call him, is my betrothed. There's nothing my uncle can do to change that."

"Except marry you off to someone else." Weymouth tried to buffer his bluntness by gentling his tone. "The late viscount was desperate to see that you were protected from your uncle's cupidity. It's possible your brother made an error in judgment."

Dulcie remained steadfast. "Do you know where my betrothed is?"

Weymouth gave a crisp nod. "I've been apprised of his whereabouts."

"Tell me, please."

He did.

Stunned by Lord Weymouth's revelation, Dulcie sank back in her chair. "That can't be."

"I'm afraid it is."

"You were wrong about Lord Carlisle," Dulcie told him.

"Unfortunately, I'm not wrong about this," Weymouth told her. "I spent the afternoon at the War Office studying reports in an effort to locate him."

"Can you arrange for me to see him?"

He took a moment to consider. "I can."

Her voice was a mere whisper. "Thank you."

Reaching over, Weymouth took her hand in his, gently patting the back of it. "I'll make the arrangements and contact you."

"Not at home," she blurted out, doing her best to tamp down her rising panic. "My uncle will find out. And if he does, he'll stop me." She searched Weymouth's face. "I can't let him. He's taken my brother's title, his properties and fortune, his position as head of the family, and his home." She took a deep steadying breath. "I will not let him thwart my brother's last wish for me."

"Nor will I," Weymouth said. "I'll contact you."

"How?"

"I'll manage," he assured her. "And your uncle will be none the wiser and as long as you continue to attend the Charlotte Society meetings here at Selby House, I'll know where and how to reach you." He paused. "I'll arrange for you to see the gentleman…"

"In private," she stipulated.

"In private," he confirmed. "All I ask is that you not reveal any information I give you. You mustn't tell anyone, Miss Tennant. Not Caroline or your friend, Miss Osborne, until I've arranged your visit."

"I promise."

"If you might indulge me in one more matter…"

Dulcie didn't hesitate. "Of course."

Weymouth lifted her chocolate cup and handed it to her. "Finish your cocoa. You've gone quite pale. The sugar will do you good. So will a meal. Drink up and I'll take you into the drawing room so we can join Caroline and Miss Osborne for luncheon."

~

PHOEBE HAD ARRIVED BY THE TIME WEYMOUTH AND DULCIE ENTERED the drawing room for luncheon. Caroline performed the introductions, presenting Lord Weymouth to Miss Phoebe Osborne.

Weymouth shared their noon meal, then rose to take his leave. "Ladies, I thank you for allowing me to share your luncheon. Now, it's time for me to be about my business and leave you to your meeting."

"Will you be returning for supper tonight?" Caroline asked. "Or will you be dining at your club and staying the night there?"

"No." Weymouth shook his head. "I'm returning to Abernathy Manor today. I've been too long away from my wife and family."

Caroline walked him to the front door. "Please, give Aunt Cicely and the baby a kiss from me. And give Griffin and Alyssa and the twins my love."

"I will."

"Travel safely."

"I will." Weymouth leaned down and placed a kiss on Caroline's forehead. "I'll be in touch."

"Soon, I hope."

"In a day or two. And I expect to hear your staff has returned and that you and your maid are no longer alone in this house."

"They'll be here tomorrow morning."

"See that they are," he chided. "Or hire a new one. Don't remain in this house until you have a full staff."

She groaned.

"I worry about you," Weymouth said. "And, if you won't think of yourself, think of your maid and of Carlisle."

"Tony?"

"He kept watch over your house while you slept last night," Weymouth told her. "That's why he didn't breakfast in the gardens and why he sent a breakfast hamper to your house this morning."

"How do you know that?"

"I'm the Wizard of the War Office. I know things." Weymouth gave her a mysterious smile and a wave.

Caroline watched as he climbed into his coach and continued to watch until the vehicle rolled out of sight.

# CHAPTER 24

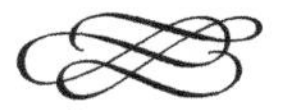

*"Enquire not what boils in another's pot."*
—Thomas Fuller, 1608-1661

"That was different," Phoebe said as soon as Caroline returned to the drawing room. "Interesting, but different."

"It's been a different sort of week," Caroline said.

"And you've been busy." Phoebe took a folded newspaper from her reticule and slapped it down on the table. "I've been exceedingly patient. Now, I want to know what you're doing at Selby House without a staff."

Caroline glanced at the newspaper and saw that it was folded to the *Ton Tidbits* column. "I didn't know you paid attention to rumors and gossip."

"I pay attention to the *Ton Tidbits* column." Phoebe gave an exaggerated sigh. "Everybody does."

"I don't," Caroline said.

"Everybody *except* you," Phoebe amended. "And since you don't read it, I'll read it to you. 'Has Another Suitor Claimed the

Marchioness of Blessing's Hand? Does the Earl of Carlisle Have a Rival? Is the Widow About to Be Wed? The Marchioness of Blessing is entertaining houseguests at Blessing House. Guests that include her father, the Earl of Rushton, and the recently widowed Earl of Merrivale. Has the widower found solace with the widow?'" Phoebe stopped reading and stared at Caroline. "Merrivale? Caro, what are you thinking? What is this all about?"

"Rumor and innuendo," Caroline said. "And Rushton's scheming."

Phoebe glanced from Caroline to Dulcie and back again.

"It's not all rumor and innuendo," Dulcie said. "Her father and Merrivale invited themselves to stay at Blessing House. Caro and Susan decided *not* to stay and entertain them."

"So, you moved in here? Alone?" Phoebe shook her head in disbelief.

"Selby House was the one place my father wouldn't think to look."

"Why not?" Phoebe asked. "Everybody in town knows you purchased it."

Caroline picked up the folded newspaper and dropped it back on the table. "And thanks to that, everybody in town knows the staff is on holiday while the house is being renovated."

"You didn't come here because Lord Rushton didn't know where to look. You came here because Lord Rushton would never consider staying in a house without a staff to attend his every whim." Phoebe understood Caroline's reasoning. "And because Carlisle is close by."

Caroline smiled.

"What about Carlisle?" Dulcie frowned. "Would your father consider looking for you at Carlisle's house?"

"The gardens, perhaps," Caroline said. "But not the house. Again, thanks to that"—she pointed to Phoebe's newspaper—"everybody knows Tony refuses all callers. Especially me."

"Does he really refuse all callers?" Phoebe asked. "Or are you the exception?"

"He hasn't made any exceptions for me," Caroline told them. "I've been inside the house twice. The first day I called upon Tony—"

"The day you were summarily dismissed and asked to leave the premises," Dulcie pointed out.

"And the day I barged in to see that Tony didn't dismiss Gerald for following my orders for the garden," Caroline said. "I wasn't invited in. I simply managed to outmaneuver the butler."

"What about the morning *tête á têtes* in the garden?" Phoebe asked.

"There are no *tête á têtes* in the garden. There are meetings while Tony is breakfasting," Caroline said. "I sometimes dine with him while we discuss the renovations and Tony makes it clear to the workers that his is the final authority. We are never alone," Caroline added. "There are workers around us from dawn to dusk. Including two of Tony's footmen." She gave a discreet nod in Kirby's direction. "Kirby is one of them."

"But the *Ton Tidbits*..." Phoebe persisted.

"Is fiction," Caroline said.

"Carlisle has never welcomed you into his house?" Phoebe asked.

Caroline shook her head. "His house *or* his gardens. I invited myself against his wishes." She met Phoebe's gaze. "Tony has been as rude and unaccommodating throughout this project as you say your churlish Scotsman has been to you."

Seeing Caroline's opening, Dulcie jumped into the conversation. "What about your Scotsman? Have you seen him since our last meeting?"

"What about you, Dulcie?" Phoebe asked. "Did Lord Weymouth locate your soldier?"

"Yes, he did," Dulcie said, holding up her hand to halt the flow of words when Phoebe began peppering her with questions. "I can't tell you more. I gave Lord Weymouth my word I wouldn't divulge any information to anyone—even my dearest friends—until he tells me I'm free to do so. I can tell you Lord Weymouth is arranging for me to meet my soldier."

"Then, he's not... He isn't..." Phoebe hesitated, unable to give voice to her greatest fear.

"Oh, no." Dulcie rushed to reassure her two closest friends. "He's alive and recovering nicely from his wounds." She tried to remember Weymouth's exact turn of phrase.

"Dulcie, that's wonderful!" Caroline exclaimed. "I'm so happy for you." Caroline lifted her cup of chocolate in a toast. "Here's to us, our gracious queen, and our soldiers!"

Dulcie and Phoebe raised their chocolate cups and clinked them against Caroline's. "Here's to the success of our Charlotte Society!"

~

CAROLINE STAYED IN THE DRAWING ROOM LONG AFTER DULCIE AND Phoebe departed for home. She was staring into the flames, considering the possibilities and the consequences of their decisions. Wondering about Phoebe's angry Scotsman, Dulcie's mystery man, and Tony's physical limitations, when Kirby entered carrying a scuttle of coal. Caroline watched as he added a scoopful of coal to the fire.

"Ma'am." Kirby completed his task, then turned to her. "If there's nothing more you require of me, I'll take my leave. Nelson will be on duty tonight."

Caroline looked up at him. "I was remiss in thanking you for your list of suggestions for the master bedchamber." She pulled the sheet of paper Kirby had handed to her before luncheon from her skirt pocket and read the ideas Kirby had jotted down. "I've been going over it and I can tell you gave the matter serious thought. I appreciate all your suggestions and I intend to discuss them with the project foreman." She met Kirby's gaze. "Of the items listed here, what would you say is the most important? The one thing that would enable Lord Carlisle to have more independence?"

Kirby didn't hesitate in his answer. "Bars of varying heights suspended from the ceiling above his bed would allow him to lift himself and give him more freedom of movement."

Caroline nodded. "Your attention to detail and your loyalty to Lord Carlisle is commendable."

"Thank you, milady." Kirby acknowledged her compliment with a slight bow.

"Do you think Fielder might also have suggestions for His Lordship's comfort?"

"I do, ma'am," Kirby said. "And Barnaby as well." He met Caroline's gaze. "We are the three who attend Lord Carlisle every day."

'I see." Caroline pocketed the list. "Would you be good enough to relay my invitations to them?" Rising from her chair, Caroline walked over to her writing desk and returned with two sealed envelopes she handed to Kirby.

"I'll be happy to, ma'am."

"Thank you once again." She smiled. "I'll be sure to commend your work to Lord Carlisle when next I see him—provided he's speaking to me."

Kirby forgot himself long enough to ask. "Why would he not, ma'am?"

"His Lordship is sure to be angry when he learns what I've done," she confided.

"What was that, ma'am?" Once again, Kirby forgot himself long enough to question the marchioness.

"I purchased a gift for him."

"Everything you've done—all the renovations to the gardens, the wooden paths, the heated pond, the glass pavilion, and the changes to this house have all been gifts for Lord Carlisle."

"This one is personal." Caroline watched the footman's expression change from concern to admiration to surprise.

Ladies did not purchase personal gifts for gentlemen who were not family members or intimate companions. Especially bachelors. And gentlemen did not accept personal gifts from ladies who were not members of their family. Especially young widows recently emerged from mourning for their late husbands. It was considered fast and scandalous and simply wasn't done.

Reaching down, Caroline retrieved the package from the floor beside her chair, where she'd placed it after Lord Weymouth gave it to her. Caroline handed it to Kirby. I would appreciate it greatly if you would see that Mr. Barnaby gets it before breakfast tomorrow morning. My note will explain what I require."

Kirby tucked the package beneath his arm.

Slipping her hand into her other skirt pocket, Caroline removed a set of iron keys and offered them to Kirby. "Give him these as well. They unlock the doors to the glass pavilion. I kept a set for myself and I'm giving these to Barnaby for Lord Carlisle. Give him the note, the package for Lord Carlisle, and the keys at breakfast tomorrow morning."

The footman took the keys, then tucked them safely inside his waistcoat pocket. "You'll be joining His Lordship in the gardens for breakfast tomorrow morning, won't you?"

"I doubt it," she said. "The work in the gardens is nearly finished. And the Selby House staff will be returning tomorrow morning. I'll need to be here to greet them." She managed a slight smile. "And there's Lord Carlisle's ire to consider."

"In that case, milady, may I say that it has been an honor to serve you?" Kirby clicked his heels together and bowed once more.

"Thank you, Kirby. For all you do for Lord Carlisle and for all you have done for me."

# CHAPTER 25

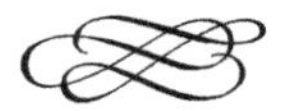

*"Audacity augments courage."*
—Publius Syrus, c. 100 BC

Caroline waited until full darkness to rouse her maid from her sleep. "Wake up, Susan. It's time to go."

"Go where?" Susan sat up, scrubbed at her eyes with the heels of her hands and complained.

"To Carlisle's heated pool." Caroline still wore the gown she'd worn at supper, while her lady's maid was dressed in a flannel nightgown and night cap, her hair tied in curling rags. In a reversal of roles, Caroline bent and retrieved Susan's slippers and shoved them onto her bare feet.

"Oh, ma'am, you can't mean it!"

"I do mean it." Caroline was adamant. "I worked hard to see the completion of the heated pool and I mean to be the first person to test it. Come along, Susan, I can't go by myself."

"Why not?" Susan grumbled. "You've done everything else by yourself."

Reaching down, Caroline took hold of Susan's arm and pulled her to her feet. Acting as lady's maid once again, Caroline held Susan's robe open so she could slip her arms into the sleeves. "Well, I'm not doing *this* by myself."

Susan groaned once again.

"You said you wouldn't believe it unless you saw it with your own eyes. Now's your chance. Let's get going." Lifting the lamp she had brought from her bedchamber, Caroline ushered Susan out of the room and down the hallway toward the stairs.

"Follow closely," Caroline instructed as she negotiated the Selby House Gardens. "I would hate to lose you in the flowerbeds."

"You don't have to worry about that, ma'am," Susan retorted. "I'm not letting you out of my sight."

They cleared the opening in the brick wall between Carlisle House and Selby House. A new wrought iron gate had been installed two days earlier, but Caroline had ordered it be left open so she could go back and forth through the two gardens. "I'm glad to hear it," Caroline called over her shoulder. "You grumble and complain a great deal..."

"Who? Me?" Susan's expression was the picture of innocence as she feigned shock at the idea that she had ever grumbled or complained in her mistress's presence.

Caroline gave her a hard look. "Yes, you. But you're an excellent lady's maid and I would hate to lose you. Good lady's maids are hard to come by. Especially during the season."

"That's because we're in great demand," Susan said. "If you're not careful, you might find I've been stolen by another lady. And you're already short one household staff."

"That's true." Caroline smiled as they stepped onto the nearest wooden walkway and began winding their way through the gardens to the pavilion. "But I still have my favorite lady's maid, peevish though she may be at times..."

"Oh, ma'am..." Susan stood transfixed at her first close-up look at the frosted glass and steel structure. "It's beautiful. Just like a fairytale castle!"

Manicured flower beds and topiary surrounded the structure, and the newly cleaned and refurbished Muses, lately returned from the stone masonry at Southwark, stood guard all around the structure. All the other statuary had been artfully placed around the gardens, including the center of the maze where Tony's koi fish were enjoying their new pond.

Stepping closer, Susan pressed her face to one of the frosted glass panes, trying to see inside. She turned to Caroline. "I can't see anything. I thought you said it was glass. I thought you would be bathing where he could see you."

"The glass is frosted for privacy. That's what makes it look like a fairy castle," Caroline said.

"So you knew he couldn't see you."

Caroline shrugged. "I'm bold, not brazen."

"You were teasing me."

*And hopefully, Tony as well.* "Just a little," Caroline admitted. "But not about Lord Carlisle. He'll be watching."

Susan was cautious. "But you're sure he won't be able to see us?"

"I'm sure," Caroline said. "The most he'll be able to see are shadows."

"That's not so bad," Susan pronounced. "I don't care if he watches my shadow."

Caroline smiled. *I'm counting on it.* "Neither do I."

Taking a key from her skirt pocket, Caroline unlocked the door to the pavilion and ushered Susan inside. Locking the door behind them, Caroline began lighting the lamps. She lit them all, enjoying the way the water in the pool sparkled as the lamplight illuminated the interior of the building.

The original reflecting pool had been two feet deep on each end and three feet deep in the center. The workmen had deepened it to three feet at each end, adding steps to the end near the door and four feet in the center—deep enough to walk, swim, and exercise without the danger of drowning. A stonework ledge had been added all around the pool to allow sitting on the edge of the pool. Four stone benches and two armless stone chairs were positioned around the pool. The benches on the sides and the two chairs at the end nearest the door.

A fountain had been added to the far end of the pool to circulate the water. Hot water from the spring in the Selby House garden ran through the fountain, mixed with cold water pumped from a collecting pond, then emptied into the pool, keeping the water a constant comfortably warm temperature. Containers of tropical plants—hibiscus and orchids—several varieties of palm trees and lemon and orange trees from the Carlisle House conservatory adorned the interior.

One corner of the room was partitioned off for use as a dressing or undressing area. There was no door on the room. It had been purposely left that way to allow Tony to wheel himself behind the partition to change his clothes and was fitted with a valet stand, shelves, and a low square table with a feather mattress atop it.

"Oh, ma'am, it's beautiful!" Susan exclaimed.

Caroline's smile was one of complete satisfaction in a job well done. For the first time in five years, she was glad to be the Marchioness of Blessing and have control of her fortune, proud of her accomplishment, and happy she could find a way to help Tony. "It is lovely, isn't it?"

"It's more than lovely, ma'am," Susan said. "It's the most beautiful thing I've ever seen."

"Let's see if it was worth all the trouble," Caroline invited. "Sit down." She indicated the stonework on the edge of the pool. "Tuck your nightclothes up, take your slippers off, and test the water."

Susan plopped down on the edge of the pool, did as her mistress instructed, and dipped her feet in the water. "It's hot."

"It's supposed to be," Caroline said.

Susan curled her toes as she splashed her feet in the water. "It feels wonderful."

Caroline smiled at her lady's maid as Susan began kicking her feet in the water. "It's supposed to." Watching Susan's expression, Caroline pointed to the steps. "Wade in if you like."

"No, ma'am." Susan shook her head. "I can't swim."

"Then stay where I can keep an eye on you," Caroline said.

"What about you, ma'am? Are you going to test the water, too?"

"I am indeed." Standing by the side of the pool, Caroline began removing her clothes. "I'm going to take a bath."

~

"MAJOR?" BARNABY TAPPED ON THE DOOR OF LORD CARLISLE'S bedchamber before he entered the room.

"In here." Tony wheeled himself to the open doorway of the ballroom and called down the hallway.

Barnaby followed the sound of his voice to the ballroom. "I left you in your bedchamber, Major."

"I was too restless after my bath to remain there," Tony admitted. "I've been confined to the house all day. I wanted to view the moonlight on the pavilion. Is there something you need?"

"No, sir." Barnaby carried a glass of whisky on a small tray. "Something *you* needed. I brought your evening libation."

"Thank you, Barnaby. Did you bring one for yourself?"

"No, sir, I didn't presume." Barnaby sounded affronted at the idea he would join the major in a drink without invitation.

"There's no presumption on your part, Barnaby. You have an open invitation. You know you're always welcome to join me," Tony told him. "It would be a pleasure to share an evening drink before retiring for the night. Like in the old days." He gestured toward his legs and chair. "Before all this."

"It would indeed, sir." Barnaby set Tony's glass of whisky on the bedside table.

"Did you add the usual dose?" Tony gazed at the amber-colored liquid in the short glass as if he could discern the two drops of laudanum mixed with the fine whisky.

"I thought I'd wait to ask your preference tonight." Barnaby retrieved the bottle of laudanum from the top of the armoire. "One drop or two?"

"One."

"Major, are you sure that's wise?"

Tony made a face that was half wry smile and half grimace. "It's not wise at all," he said. "But how can I know how much pain I can endure unless I know how much pain I'm in?" He met Barnaby's concerned gaze. "I can't continue to dull my pain and attend to my duties as earl."

"Understandable, Major," Barnaby agreed. "But you must take care of yourself first. You've exerted yourself more in the past ten days than you have since before Quatre Bras." He uncorked the laudanum and added a single drop to the whisky before handing it to Carlisle. "Drink up."

Tony tossed the whisky back. The liquor was familiar—smooth, warm, and soothing. The laudanum in it was bitter.

Like being home at Carlisle House. The house of his childhood and early adulthood was familiar, the floors and furnishings worn smooth in places by time and generations of Carlisles. The rooms he inhabited were warm, and after the cacophony of war, the atmosphere was soothing. But his homecoming had been bitter. His inability to traverse the multiple staircases or to walk from room to room or slide down the bannisters as he and his older brother and sister had done as children was bitter.

The vast emptiness of a large house without the siblings who had died of smallpox when he was ten, or his parents, who had died in the phaeton accident when he was thirteen, or a family of his own, was bitter. His parents, and three siblings—his older brother and one older and one younger sister and the child his mother had been carrying—were all gone. Of his family of six, he alone had survived. As the earl and the only member of his immediate family left alive, Tony had declined to go to war. He'd intended to marry and begin a new family. The irony of waking up aboard a ship bound for the war in the Peninsula with no memory of how he'd come to be there hadn't been lost on him. The final irony was that he had neither married or died in battle. He had no family and no hope for one in the future.

His memories of what had been and what might have been were like the whisky and laudanum. A blend of good and bad. Bittersweet.

He was the last of his family. What might have been—a wife and children—would remain a dream. Caroline would remain a dream. Carlisle lifted his glass. "How about another whisky, Barnaby?"

Barnaby shot him a concerned look. Since arriving in London, the major had limited himself to one drink with two drops of laudanum in the evening.

"One, Barnaby. One whisky without laudanum before bed," Carlisle said. "Pour one for yourself. We're celebrating."

"May I inquire the nature of the celebration, sir?" Barnaby added more whisky to Carlisle's glass and poured a measure for himself.

"The renovation of the gardens is finished." Tony accepted the glass Barnaby offered him and raised it high.

"I'm afraid I can't quite bring myself to offer a toast to that, sir," Barnaby said. "The chaos and the upheaval are over, but I confess to enjoying the few days of excitement. I'll miss the hubbub in the garden."

Tony frowned. "If you don't feel comfortable toasting the end of the chaos, we'll go with tradition. To the regiment!" He toasted the regiment, swallowed his whisky, and placed his glass on the side table.

Barnaby lifted his glass in salute. "To the regiment!" Tossing back his whisky, he slammed the glass down on the table. "Huzzah!"

Carlisle wheeled himself back to the window and picked up his spyglass. "I could have suggested a toast to the end of my indoor baths. Tomorrow morning, we can sneak down to the garden and christen the pavilion with a bottle of French champagne we shatter but don't drink before anyone else is up and about."

"That's a splendid idea, sir."

"Must be," Tony murmured. "Because someone has beaten us to it." He watched as the lamps inside the pavilion came on one by one, silhouetting the interlopers—one in particular. He recognized that willowy figure as soon as the lamps revealed it. "The pavilion is all alight."

"What?" Frowning, Barnaby hurried to the window and stood behind Carlisle's shoulder. "Should I send one of the footmen to investigate?"

"No." Tony lowered the spyglass but didn't offer it to his manservant. "No harm done. It appears our esteemed benefactress is performing a final inspection of the structure before she relinquishes the keys." He glanced at the mantel clock, taking note of the time. *Half past eight o'clock.*

"She did *build* it, sir," Barnaby reminded him.

"And finance it," Carlisle added. "Though, of course, I'll reimburse her expenditures on the project."

"Of course, sir," Barnaby said. "Under the present circumstances, I suppose she has every right to be the first person to enjoy the fruits of her labors."

"I suppose she does," Carlisle agreed, watching as the shorter of the two silhouettes sat down on the edge of the pool and began kicking her feet in the water while the taller, slimmer figure began removing her clothes. He glanced at his former batman. "Goodnight, Barnaby."

"Goodnight, sir." Barnaby started to withdraw from the ballroom, but paused mid-way to the door. "You will get some rest, won't you sir? You won't keep watch all night, will you?"

"No," Tony promised. "I'll go to bed as soon as I know our neighbor is safely tucked in her house once again."

Barnaby gave a brisk nod. "All right, then. Goodnight, sir."

"Goodnight, Barnaby."

Tony waited until Barnaby left the ballroom, then raised the spyglass to his eye for a closer look. "Until that time," he murmured to himself. "I intend to enjoy watching her enjoy the fruits of her labor."

# CHAPTER 26

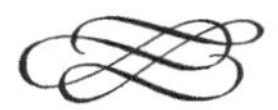

*Govern thy thoughts as if the whole world were to see the one and read the other."*
—Thomas Fuller, 1608-1661

Tony watched in complete fascination through the frosted glass panes of the pavilion as Caroline stood by the side of the pool. He couldn't see the particulars, but he could tell what she was doing from her movements.

Her hands went to her middle as she unhooked her short corset, dangling it from her fingers for a moment before letting it drift to the floor.

His mouth went dry.

His heartbeat increased.

The spyglass he held brought her silhouette closer, but it didn't reveal the details. He watched as Caroline untied the ribbon at the neck of her gown, watched as the fabric slid down her body, watched it glide over the slope of her breasts and the flat of her stomach, halting at the curve of her slim hips.

Tony couldn't see the features he knew so well—the red tint in the brown of her hair, the lapis blue of her eyes framed by thick, long lashes, the rosy hue and softness of her lips, the small scar on her fuller lower lip, the creamy ivory color of her skin, the slight scattering of freckles across the bridge of her nose, and her shapely calves and trim ankles. Shapely calves and trim ankles that had held him spellbound as she had waded in the pool days ago, driving the koi toward the net.

Gazing through the spyglass at the opaque glass of the pavilion, Carlisle strained to see the hundreds of tiny features that made Caroline who she was. The little details on her body only a lover or a husband would be privileged to know were there.

His heartbeat kicked up a notch.

Once upon a time, he had kissed those lips, felt their softness, and tasted the sweetness of her. He had caressed her breasts through the soft muslin of the spring frock she'd worn, felt the steady thump of her heart and the quick intake of her breath when he'd taken those liberties. He'd never shared her bed. Never seen her beneath him or felt the clench of her thighs around his waist, but watching her now, he could imagine the pleasure.

He leaned forward in his chair, a fine sheen of perspiration dampening his brow and upper lip as she used her foot to slide the gown onto the pile with the other garments. Suddenly, Caroline was standing in her stockings and brief chemise.

And she wasn't done.

Tony held his breath while she unbuttoned the row of tiny buttons on the chemise. He was anticipating the slow slide of the chemise down her body, when she caught the hem of the undergarment in her hands, raised her arms and tugged it over her head, surprising him.

She turned slightly as the garment cleared her head, and whether by accident or on purpose, Tony was gifted with a perfect silhouette of the topographical map of her body in profile. Caroline, wearing nothing except her silk stockings and garters.

He'd felt the weight of her breasts against the palm of his hand through layers of fabric on several memorable occasions. Now Tony could see the slope and the shape of them. He visualized their texture, the smooth creamy ivory color of her skin, the pink centers and the sensitive tips. He ached to touch them, to taste them, to flick his tongue across the tips and feel them pucker in reaction. He wanted to trace their contours with his tongue, feel their weight in his palms.

Tony shifted in his chair, groaning as she lifted her foot and placed it on the seat of a stone bench, leaned forward, untied the ribbon of her garter, and began rolling her silk stocking down her leg.

The silhouette she offered had changed, but it was equally tantalizing, if not more so. Suddenly, Tony had an idea of the landscape he'd only imagined before. The shadows concealing and revealing her frustrated him even as they tantalized him. He could see her movements, but was unable to see *her.*

Tony recognized the paradox. He was able to see more of Caroline than he'd ever seen before without seeing anything at all. And Tony desperately wanted—needed—to see her.

His imagination went to work at a furious pace, merging his memories with his desire. Blood that had barely circulated in the months since his injury suddenly rushed to his nether regions. The male part of him grew hot and hard and insistent, proudly standing at attention. He was lightheaded. And filled with images of what he wanted to do with her and what he prayed she would one day do with him.

Tony lowered his spyglass. He didn't watch Caroline peel off her remaining stocking or slip into the pool to bathe. Leaving his post at the window, Tony wheeled himself to the reclining couch. He transferred himself from his chair to the couch. Once there, he closed his eyes and indulged his imagination while Caroline took her bath.

Sometime later, Tony opened his eyes. He moved from couch to chair and wheeled himself back to the window. He expected to see the pavilion lit up, but it was dark, the lamps all extinguished. Retrieving his spyglass, Tony stared out over the darkened garden until he spotted the glow of two lamps moving along the wooden path to Selby House.

Tony waited until they were safely inside the house, then quietly wheeled himself to his bedchamber and went to bed, where he slept more soundly than he had in months.

The nightmares of war had been vanquished.

Lord Anthony Carlisle's dreams were all about Caroline.

"NOT ON YOUR BLOODY LIFE!" TONY'S OUTRAGED ROAR ECHOED OFF THE frosted panes of the pavilion in the Carlisle House gardens. "I will not consent to wearing those." He pointed to the box Barnaby held containing an article of clothing his tailor had fashioned for him to wear in the bathing pool—without his knowledge—and had had delivered to his door at breakfast.

He and Barnaby were in the dressing room of the pavilion where they had just completed the series of morning stretching exercises on his legs before making use of the heated bath.

Tony sat in a leather wing chair beside a large privacy screen, his right leg resting on the matching ottoman. He was naked beneath his flannel robe. "And you may inform Meyer that he will not receive payment from me for those...*things*."

Those *things*, as Carlisle called them, were an abbreviated pair of long underclothes knitted from a blend of white cotton and silk threads Barnaby had been attempting to persuade Tony to pull on.

Gentleman's long knitted underclothes generally began at the waist and ended at the ankle. The ones in the box from his tailor began at the waist and ended far short of the ankle. With his long legs, Tony realized he would be lucky if they reached the tops of his thighs. And damned if he was going to be seen in a modern loincloth designed to cover his male parts and buttocks and leave the rest of his body exposed. He had to look at his scarred and shriveled legs every day. He wasn't going to take a chance on anyone besides his manservant seeing them.

The manservant who didn't flinch at his display of temper. Barnaby had weathered far worse displays of temper on many occasions since Quatre Bras. "The tailor doesn't expect payment, sir," he said. "They're a gift."

"From *him?"* Tony sat back in his chair, stunned by Barnaby's revelation. He'd been measured, pinned, and chalked by the tailor more times than he could recall, but he hadn't been measured, pinned, or chalked since he'd returned from war. There was no reason for Jonathan Meyer, tailor, to gift him with an all-too-brief item of small clothes he hadn't ordered.

"Not exactly," Barnaby said, unwilling to mislead the major when he was bound to discover the truth on his own sooner or later.

Tony lifted his eyebrow and pinned his former batman with a look. "How exactly?"

Barnaby winced as he relayed the information. "Lady Blessing ordered them for you."

"She *what?"* Tony roared once again.

"She ordered..." Barnaby began.

"I heard what you said." Tony lowered his voice. "I just can't believe it. Has Lady Bloody Blessing taken leave of her senses? I cannot believe she ordered a personal garment for me from my tailor." He shook his head in dismay. "She knows better than that. It's bad enough that she's made us the topic of conversation in the newspaper, the gossip rags, and probably over every breakfast table in London. Has she no care for her reputation? Or sense of propriety?"

"I understand Lady Blessing had the sense to take great care for both, sir," Barnaby said.

"Not if she paid a visit to my tailor." Tony plowed his fingers through his hair. "She's a widow. What business does she have with my tailor? Or any tailor?"

"These days ladies often order their riding habits from Meyer's," Barnaby told him. "Lady Blessing's reputation is safe on that score, sir."

"When was the last time anyone saw Lady Blessing on horseback?" Carlisle's question was purely rhetorical. Tony already knew the answer. *Five years, two months, three days, and—he glanced at the mantel clock—eight hours.* The last morning he'd ridden with her on Rotten

Row. The morning he had asked Caroline to marry him. Tony pinched the bridge of his nose, then opened his eyes and stared at the table. "Word of her visit to my tailor to purchase a personal gift for me is sure to appear in that." He thrust his chin at the *Morning Chronicle*. "First my garden. Now my tailor. She seems hell-bent on ruining her good name. When did the package arrive?"

"Kirby brought the bathing attire home with him last night with strict instructions to give the package to me at breakfast. Along with this." Barnaby held up a ring with a key on it. "Instead of thinking Lady Blessing is hell-bent on ruining her good name, perhaps, you might consider that she's simply hell-bent on helping you."

Tony slid the box containing the bathing attire across the cushioned table toward Barnaby. "Send them back. I'm not going to wear a bloody loincloth to bathe." The white cotton and silk knitted clothing would reveal more than it concealed when wet. He'd rather go in the pool bare-arsed naked than be displayed. "When I bathe, I bathe the way God meant for men bathe. Bare-arsed. Heated water or not."

"It appears I've wasted my money," said a wry female voice. "Oh well, live and learn."

Tony looked up to find Caroline standing in the entrance to the dressing room. "What in the bloody hell are you doing here?"

"I thought I heard you shouting my name," Caroline said. "It turns out I was right." Caroline was relieved to find Tony sitting on the leather wing chair she'd had placed in the dressing room for his use. She glanced around. If Tony had wheeled himself into the pavilion, there was no sign of it.

"I wasn't shouting your name," he insisted in a voice just slightly lower than a shout.

"I heard my name halfway across the garden," Caroline informed him. "How was that possible if you weren't shouting?"

Ignoring her question, Tony asked one of his own. "What the devil were you doing in the garden? The work is completed."

"The pavilion has been completed, but there's still work to be done."

"Any work left to be done can be done by the gardeners and men in my employ," Tony said. "So what were *you* doing in my garden?"

She glanced down at the box on the table bearing the name of the establishment. "I could tell you that I was consulting with the carpenters' foreman because I decided to extend the wooden walkways to include other parts of the estate, but you wouldn't believe that." She took a deep breath and blew it out in a whoosh of air. "So I'll tell you the truth. I came over because I knew you would want to thank me for my thoughtful gift." She looked him in the eye. "As it turns out, I was wrong."

Barnaby gave a bark of laughter, but quickly covered it with a cough.

Tony glared at his manservant. "Goodbye, Barnaby."

"Sir?" Barnaby didn't budge.

"I would like to speak to Lady Blessing alone." Tony spoke slowly, carefully enunciating each word, trying to control his temper.

Barnaby shifted his innocent gaze to Lady Blessing. "Ma'am?"

"It's all right, Barnaby," she assured him. "I'll be fine."

Barnaby turned to leave the dressing room. "I'll be outside the pavilion door if either one of you requires me to intervene."

Caroline waited until Barnaby had bowed and left the building before speaking. She sounded as if she were addressing Barnaby, but her words were for Tony. "His Lordship's bark is fearsome, but he's too well-mannered to bite me."

*"Was,"* Tony muttered, sotto voce. "He's changed."

Caroline bit her bottom lip to keep from smiling as she met his silvery gray gaze. "Not *that* much."

"You may be surprised."

"I am surprised."

"Not as surprised as I was to learn you paid a visit to Meyer, the tailor. Must be time for a new riding habit..."

Caroline turned her attention back to the box bearing the tailor's name and address.

Tony followed her gaze. "It appears we share a tailor, my lady."

Caroline inhaled sharply, biting her bottom lip as the memories of another morning assailed her.

*"It appears we share a tailor, my lady."*

*Caroline exited the fitting room of Jonathan Meyer's tailor shop and ran squarely into Lord Anthony Carlisle. "It appears we do."*

*"Here for a new suit of clothes? Or a new ballgown embroidered with tiny blue flowers like the one you wore to Lady Bessemer's ball last evening?"*

*"I don't need another ballgown embroidered with tiny blue flowers," she said. "I already have one."*

*"What a shame," Tony said. "I liked the tiny blue flowers embroidered on your gown and the ones you wore in your hair. They match the color of your eyes."*

*She stared up at him. The pins Susan had used in her hair had been adorned with blue topaz and diamonds fashioned into the shape of tiny blue flowers. "You noticed."*

*"How could I not?" he asked. "Your eyes are rather unforgettable."*

*She blushed. "If I did need a new ballgown, this would not be the place to purchase it."*

*"Gloves?"*

*"No. Gloves come from the glover."*

*"Hat?"*

*She shook her head. "Milliner."*

*"Scarf?"*

*"Dressmaker or milliner."*

*"Fan? Parasol?"*

*"Harding, Howell and Company."*

*"Boots?"*

*She shook her head one last time. "Wood at Number Forty-seven Cornhill or Mr. Hoby."*

*He shrugged. "No suit of clothes and no ballgown," he said. "I can't imagine what you came to a gentleman's tailor to buy. Unless it's a waistcoat or a new cravat for me..." He'd waggled his eyebrows at her.*

*"It would be most improper for me to purchase a personal article of clothing for you as it would be for you to purchase a personal article of clothing for me."*

*"Why?"*

*"You know why. It simply isn't done," she reminded him. "You're an unrelated gentleman."*

*He'd raised an eyebrow at that. "An unrelated gentleman?"*

*"A gentleman who isn't a grandfather, father, uncle, brother or cousin," she explained. "I only just met you."*

*"We might be cousins," he suggested, a twinkle in his silver-gray eyes.*

*"We aren't."*

*"We could be," he drawled. "Kissing cousins..."*

*Caroline laughed. "Are you so desperately in need of a waistcoat or a new cravat, Lord Carlisle?"*

*"Not a waistcoat or a cravat." He focused his gaze on her mouth. "Something else. Something special."*

*Caroline blushed. "A riding habit, Lord Carlisle. I came to order a new riding habit. Mr. Meyer does the best work in town."*

*"You enjoy riding, Miss Hardage?"*

*"I do."*

*He grinned. "I ride along Rotten Row at eight every morning."*

*"Do you, Lord Carlisle?"*

*"I do. A handsome black stallion named Ajax. We cool down along the Row after our more strenuous stretch of the legs. You might meet us there if you happen to be up and about before the fashionable hours."*

It had been tantamount to an invitation and Caroline had taken him up on it, riding out on Mira every morning just in time to "accidentally" meet up with Tony and Ajax. Every morning until the announcement of her upcoming marriage to Lord Blessing appeared in the morning papers.

Caroline remembered her second meeting with Anthony Carlisle in vivid detail as she stared at the tailor's address printed on the brown paper wrapped around the box and heard Tony speak the same words.

"I thought you'd appreciate my gift."

"I did," he murmured, his voice lower and huskier than usual.

"Yet you refuse to wear them."

"That's not the gift I meant." Tony dropped his gaze to her lips.

"Oh." Her voice came out as a high-pitched squeak. "I'm afraid I don't know what you're talking about."

"You're afraid," he corrected. "Because you know exactly what I'm talking about."

She gave up the pretense. "You were watching."

"I was."

"I suppose you want me to relinquish my key to the pavilion." She moistened her dry lips with the tip of her tongue.

Tony felt the impact of that gesture from his head to his toes. He sat up straighter on the chair. "I want nothing of the kind."

"You sounded as if you d-did w-when I walked in."

He recognized the tiny hiccup in her voice, saw the beat of her pulse in her throat and the dilation of her blue eyes. "You were mistaken."

"Was I?"

He gave a sharp nod.

Her breath caught. "What do you want?"

Tony nudged the ottoman to the side and set his foot on the ground.

Caroline's mouth went dry.

He crooked his finger at her, beckoning her closer. "Come here, Caro."

Caroline moved closer until she stood near enough to touch him, drawn to him the way iron filings are drawn to a magnet.

Reaching up, Tony hooked his arms around the back of her thighs just below her bottom, and guided her between his legs, urging her to sit. "This. *This* is what I want."

"Tony, no. I'll hurt you." She tried to wriggle off his lap, but he held her in place.

Sliding his hand up her back, blazing a path from hip to neck, Tony buried his fingers in her hair, cupped the back of her head in his big hand, and closed the gap between them. "You'll hurt me far more if you don't."

# CHAPTER 27

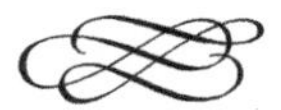

*"The wounds of love can only be healed*
*by the one who made them."*
—Publius Syrus, c. 100 BC

The sensation was like nothing she had ever felt. Or ever expected to feel. Caroline burned as hot as a flame in a tinderbox at the touch of his lips to hers. The surge of pleasure that swept through her took her by surprise and made it all but impossible for her to think of anything except the feel of Tony surrounding her—except the way *she* felt with his arms around her.

Until she'd met Anthony Carlisle at Lady Bessemer's ball, Caroline had never engaged in any manner of verbal sparring with a member of the opposite sex. But something about him gave her the confidence to be herself, to speak her mind and challenge him, not in an aggressive manner, but as an equal. Sparring with him made her feel special. He treated her as if he admired her intelligence as well as her looks. Tony challenged her, intrigued her, and excited her.

He was big and tall and handsome, and although he was injured,

Tony still made her feel safe and cherished and beautiful. Caroline knew she was attractive because she'd been told she was. While her father hadn't showered her with affection, Caroline knew she had worth in her father's eyes. He valued her looks and her accomplishments. They were commodities he leveraged against would-be suitors.

She had been bred to be an ornament used to decorate a man's home and occasionally, his arm.

Love had had no place in her future. Caroline hadn't felt loved or valued for herself since her mother died.

But Anthony Carlisle had changed all that. When Tony looked at her, Caroline felt beautiful and special and cherished. He might not be the man she had married, but Tony was the man she loved. He was the man she wanted. He was the man who *should* have been her husband, and in this moment, he was the man entitled to take whatever liberties with her person he wanted.

*Like the liberty he was taking now.*

His kiss was the most exhilarating and liberating thing she'd ever felt. It was Tony's kiss, but different. It wasn't like the kisses she remembered. His other kisses had been tender and gentle—the kisses of a gentleman wooing the innocent girl he wanted to marry. This kiss was intoxicating—hot and desperate and filled with pent-up passion. It was carnal. Tony kissed her as if he had never kissed her before and never would again. He kissed her as if he could never get enough of the taste and texture and feel of her mouth.

He didn't simply brush his lips against hers; he covered her mouth with his. The pressure he exerted should have been bruising, but it wasn't. He didn't bruise. He persuaded and coaxed. Thrusting his tongue through the seam of her lips, he raked the interior of her mouth, skimmed the surface of her teeth, and played an erotic game of thrust and parry with her tongue.

And Caroline never wanted it to end. She wrapped her arms around his neck, plunged her fingers into his hair, satisfying her curiosity as she kissed him back, matching him stroke for stroke, giving what he demanded from her and taking what she wanted from him. And all the while she marveled that she could have lived five years without his kisses, without the feel of his hands on her, without the passion Tony created within her.

Her friends had been correct. She had been wrapped in a cocoon for five long years, existing, protecting herself from the pain his defection had left, insulating herself from the horror of being married to an old man she could barely tolerate and would never like or respect, much less love.

She was like a butterfly that had suddenly emerged from its chrysalis and begun flexing its wings. She was free to explore the world and all its possibilities. And at this moment, her whole world was Anthony Carlisle. She kissed him with all the passion she possessed and moaned a throaty protest when he broke contact with her mouth and began to press kisses on her chin, her cheeks, the corners of her eyes, her eyelids, the center of her forehead, and the tip of her nose, before finally returning to her lips.

His second kiss was tender, filled with emotions he couldn't or wouldn't express. He brushed his lips against hers in an exchange of breath—hers for his and his for hers in the most incredible caress Caroline had ever felt. Or dreamed of feeling.

Tony knew he should pull away and put distance between them, but he didn't. He couldn't think of pulling away when everything in him urged him to hold her close. He forgot about releasing her and allowed himself to luxuriate in the pleasure of kissing her. Touching the tip of his tongue to the tiny scar on her bottom lip, Tony traced the seam of her mouth, entreating her to open it and allow him entrance once again.

She gladly acquiesced.

Moving ever-so-slightly, Tony changed the angle of their mouths and kissed her more deeply.

Caroline's heart pounded against her ribs. She gasped at the heat and the pleasure he gave her. She wasn't a complete novice when it came to kissing. She had been kissed before. *He* had kissed her before, but this one was, without a doubt, her best. The pleasure of this kiss was far greater than the pleasure she'd experienced the first time he'd kissed her. He swept his tongue inside her mouth and began to taste the warm recesses within.

She gasped.

Tony repeated the sweep several more times, each sweep more thorough than the one before. And after completing his exploration of her mouth, Tony began a delectable examination of her lower lip by nibbling on it, careful to give nothing but pleasure. Heat surged through him as Caroline pressed herself against his chest. Tony caressed her hair, then ran his hands down her neck, over her shoulders, and down her spine. Wrapping his arms around her, he cupped her bottom with his hands, kneading her beneath the delicate muslin of her gown.

Caroline molded herself against him, reveling in the taste of his mouth. She enjoyed the slight friction of his chin against the sensitive skin of her face and the warm, spicy scent she remembered as uniquely Tony. She'd never forgotten that scent. She'd know it anywhere.

He kissed her until she was lightheaded and gasping for breath, overcome by the depth of the emotions sweeping through her. Caroline pressed her hands against his chest, then opened her eyes, and found herself staring up into Tony's silvery gray ones.

She smiled at him and Tony leaned close to place another string of kisses from her lips to her forehead in an exact reversal of the way he'd just kissed her.

Tony placed his lips against her hair and inhaled her scent the way she'd inhaled his. Her hair and skin carried the scent of summer roses, a scent he remembered from the last time he'd held her in his arms. "Caroline. Caroline. Caroline," he whispered her name a dozen times as he nuzzled her hair.

The feel of her bottom moving against him was driving him to distraction. The thin flannel fabric of his robe and the equally thin muslin of her dress and unmentionables was the only thing keeping his naked flesh from hers. "I dreamed of this every day for five long years." Tony squeezed his eyes shut. "I missed you so."

"I missed you, too," she breathed. "Oh, Tony, I missed you so much it hurt. I thought I remembered your kisses and the taste of your mouth, but I never remembered anything as wonderful as this."

Tony's heart thumped against the wall of his chest. His eyes burned. He knew what it was like to miss her so much it hurt. He knew what it was like to lie on his cot at night and remember how it felt to hold her on the day he'd asked her to be his countess. He knew how it felt to remember the joy of that time and be compelled to recall his supreme disappointment at having her father refuse his suit, to remember every feature, every detail of her face, every kiss, every caress, every word they'd ever exchanged and not be able to forget the searing agony of reading the announcement of her marriage to Granville Blessing in the morning papers the following day.

He knew what it meant to love her.

He knew what it meant to lose her.

And he knew how it felt to lose hope of ever having her in his arms again.

When he'd awakened in that field hospital in Belgium and realized his body was as broken as his heart, Tony had sworn he would never allow himself to forget the sting of betrayal or the embarrassment of being taken for a fool by the person he had loved. He swore he would never forget how it felt to beg for the right to marry her and be refused—not once, but twice. How it felt to go to the man who had secured the right to marry her and ask that man to do the gentlemanly thing and step aside for a prior claim and find himself summarily removed from the premises and beaten for his efforts for having the effrontery to interfere in his better's personal affairs. Tony knew how it felt to awake and find himself a lieutenant in the cavalry, sailing with a regiment bound for Portugal and the guerilla war Lord Wellesley was waging against the French and Spanish forces there.

Holding her now, Tony realized none of those things mattered. He needed her. He wanted her. All the reasons he couldn't have her no longer mattered, including the days he'd marked off on the calendar. He couldn't stand on his own two feet for longer than seven seconds, but he didn't need to stand to make love to Caroline. All he needed was the right to do so. And only she could give him that right. If she would.

"I want you, Caroline." He murmured the words against her hair before he murmured them against her lips.

"I want you, too."

"Show me." He nibbled on the rim of her ear. "Show me what you've built for me. Show me my heated goldfish pond."

"I'm not wearing a pinafore," she teased, feeling emboldened enough to cover his face with kisses. "I'm not dressed for wading."

"You can be." He kissed an especially sensitive spot below her ear before he began undoing the buttons on the front of her dress.

"So can you." Following his lead, Caroline nibbled the rim of his ear before she found the sensitive spot. "You have swimming attire." She gently bit his earlobe. "Or you can go in the way I'm going in."

He shrugged her dress off her shoulders and began planting kisses along her collar bone and in the hollow of her throat before moving lower, placing random kisses along the top of her breasts. "How's that?"

Caroline shivered in reaction when he dipped his tongue into the crevice between her breasts. "Bare-arsed."

Tony looked up from his erotic exploration and grinned. "Not this time, my lady. We're both going to be clothed."

"Why?" She looked disappointed.

"Call it an experiment," he replied cryptically, before he began doing up the buttons on her chemise and the front of her dress.

She protested. "I thought you wanted me to show you the pool."

"I do." He rearranged the folds of his robe, then tightened the belt.

Frowning down at her dress, Caroline saw that she was completely presentable. "I don't understand."

"Fetch Barnaby," he instructed. "Then wait outside the door until Barnaby comes to get you."

# CHAPTER 28

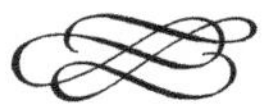

*"They are not wise, then, who stand forth to buffet against Love; for Love rules the gods as he will, and me."*
—Sophocles, 495-406 B.C.

Barnaby exited the pavilion to find Caroline sitting on the bench beside the statue of Terpsichore. "He's ready for you, milady."

She looked up and met the older man's gaze. "Barnaby?"

"He's impatient, milady. Best not keep him waiting too long," He motioned for her to go inside. "I'll lock the door behind me." He showed her the key. "And I'll return with breakfast presently."

Caroline slipped inside the pavilion, waited until Barnaby locked the door as promised, before turning to find Tony, naked from the waist up, treading water in the former fishpond. He kept one hand on the edge of the pool and his other hand over his groin.

"Come in," he invited. "The water's fine." The temperature of the water was perfect. The warmth of it surrounded him, easing the chronic pain in his muscles and bones without the need for laudanum.

Caroline sat on one of the benches and removed her half boots, then peeled her stockings down her legs. Once she'd dispensed with her boots and stockings, Caroline grabbed the hem of her dress and bent to tuck her skirts up as she'd done for wading during the netting of his koi fish.

Tony stopped her. "Haven't you learned your lesson about water and long skirts? The last time your skirt came untucked, you tripped and nearly drowned. Are you that eager to repeat the experience?"

Caroline secured the hem of her dress. "You said we were going in clothed. Can I help it if you've changed your mind?" She pointed to his bare chest.

"I haven't changed my mind," Tony retorted. "I'm wearing clothes."

"You are not!"

"Oh, yes, I am," he said. "Come in and see for yourself."

Caroline moved toward the steps.

"Oh, no, you don't," Tony called. "Not yet. Not until you take your dress off."

"Tony..."

"You're overdressed, my lady."

She reached for the top button of her dress, then hesitated.

"You weren't shy last night." The low, husky note in Tony's voice sent a thrill up her spine.

"I couldn't see you last night," she admitted. "I could feel you watching me. But I couldn't see you."

"Close your eyes then. And pretend I'm not here."

Pretending he wasn't there was out of the question. She could feel his heated gaze on her, as beguiling as a touch. But she closed her eyes and began disrobing.

She was down to her chemise and drawers when Tony called a halt to their game. "Open your eyes, my love. And come join me."

The 'my love' convinced her. Caroline opened her eyes and walked down the steps and into the pool where Tony was waiting.

Keeping one hand on the edge of the bathing pool, he kicked his way into deeper water.

Caroline followed, wading deeper. The water was below her chest, but it splashed her as she plowed forward, soaking her chemise until the only dry part of her undergarment was the straps.

Tony kept his gaze on her, savoring the way the wet muslin clung to her skin. Far from covering her, the transparent fabric enhanced the features he'd seen in her shadow play the night before. He kept backing away, using his grip on the edge of the pool to anchor him. The former goldfish pond was considerably deeper than before, but Tony's height kept his head well above water even if his legs wouldn't fully support him. Broadening his smile, Tony watched Caroline diligently making her way through the water to him.

"I can't wade any further," she told him. "It's too deep."

The water was hovering just below her breasts, the wet fabric clinging to their twin peaks, enticing him to do the same. He leaned against the pool wall and reached out his hand. "Hold on. I'll pull you to me."

Caroline hesitated once again. Unsure of her next move. "Why?"

"Because I want to thank you," he said.

Caroline touched her fingers to her lips. They were plump and swollen from his kisses. "You've already thanked me." She blushed. "Several times."

"I want to hold you." His voice dropped to the low, husky rumble deep in his chest that sent ripples of awareness through her. He answered honestly. "I want to feel you against me and the only way I —" Tony didn't finish his thought. He changed the subject instead. "I haven't thanked you for this, Caroline." He glanced around the pavilion at the table and chairs he and Caroline had used for breakfasting in the garden, the artful array of benches and potted plants scattered about, the fountain recirculating the water, the steps and incline plane she had added to give him access to the water, the dressing room with its privacy screen, padded table, leather wing chair and ottoman, every amenity thoughtfully arranged to accommodate the movement and height of the hated wheelchair Barnaby had secreted behind the privacy screen. Even his Muses were back, standing guard around the perimeter of the pavilion in their own little gardens, and looking better than ever. Tony turned his gaze back to

Caroline. "It's beautiful." He inhaled deeply, then exhaled. "It's magnificent."

Tears sparkled in her eyes at the gratitude she heard in his voice. "I'm happy you like it, Tony."

He swallowed the lump in his throat. "It's more than I could have imagined. And it pales in comparison to the extraordinary woman who made it all possible."

Caroline's breath caught at his words. She clutched her heart as if to hold it in. It was beating so hard she feared it might explode. Nobody had ever paid her such a heartfelt compliment. She gazed up at him, her eyes brimming with so many emotions. She had created everything around them for one purpose—to show him how much she loved him, how much she wanted to be a part of his life. No matter the obstacles he faced. "I love you, Tony," she said simply. "You are all I ever wanted. The man I dreamed of marrying. The man I wanted to father my children. The only man I've ever wanted to stand by my side and share my life."

Tony held onto the side of the pool as he took a step forward. Reaching out, he took hold of her hand and carefully pulled her against his chest. He wrapped his arm around her, holding her fast. "Caroline. My heart. My love. My beautiful Aphrodite." He buried his face in her hair. "I want to stand beside you, my love, but I cannot." His voice broke.

"You will," she promised him. "One day."

"For seven seconds." He squeezed his eyes shut.

"Seven seconds?"

"That's how long I can stand on my own."

"You don't need to stand on your own," she said. "You have me. We'll stand together."

"Caroline," he said, his voice firm. "I'm confined to a wheeled chair. I may never be able to stand by your side or walk again."

"I know, my darling," Caroline kissed the side of his neck, the hollow of his throat, and the scar on the underside of his jaw.

"How long?" His voice was throaty and raw, filled with unshed tears. He'd been so careful not to let anyone see him in his chair except Barnaby and Fielder and Kirby, so vigilant about clearing the household staff out of the area when Kirby or Fielder carried him and his chair downstairs, so wary of entertaining friends, relatives, or social callers.

"From the beginning."

"You've known from the beginning?" He wondered how he had managed to give himself away. How had she known his secret when he'd originally refused to speak with her?

She nodded. "I knew the moment I heard you'd returned to London in a closed sedan chair. Because you would never travel by sedan chair unless you feared being seen."

"I didn't fool you at all." He lifted his head and gave a short, ironic laugh, then leaned down to plant a kiss on her cheek. "My clever, clever girl."

Raising herself on tiptoe, Caroline placed her forehead against his. "If I hadn't known about the sedan chair, I would have known the first moment you failed to stand when I entered your study." She put her hands on his cheeks. "You're a gentleman. You never failed to behave in a gentlemanly manner before—"

*"Now."* He placed his hand on her bottom and pulled her against him.

She smiled at him. "Before you were injured in battle. I know you, Anthony Carlisle. I know you would stand if you could."

"Now that you know, what do you want from me?" He asked the question she'd asked him at breakfast three mornings ago.

"What I've always wanted." Her gaze locked with his. "I want you to love me again."

"I do," he said. "I love you, Caroline."

Caroline's smile lit up the room. "You love me again?"

"Not again," he breathed. "Always. I've loved you for five years, Caroline. I never stopped."

"Do you love me enough to make love with me?"

Tony hesitated.

Caroline was suddenly struck by a horrible thought. "If you... Can you... I mean... Are you able?"

"I wasn't sure," he admitted. "Until you rose up out of the water like Aphrodite the day you fell while herding the goldfish."

"Aphrodite rose from the sea completely naked."

"I'm a man, sweetheart. Once I realized you weren't hurt, I dreamed of seeing you like this. I *ached* to see you like this—" He glanced down at the transparent chemise and drawers that were plastered to her body and left little to the imagination. "With your wet clothing clinging to your body. I've been dreaming about it ever since." The tips of his ears reddened. "With predictable results."

She frowned. "What sort of predictable results?"

Reaching up, Tony covered her hand with his own and guided it beneath the water, gently pressing her palm against the rigid bulge in his swimming attire.

"You're wearing them." The knowledge delighted her.

"I am." He made a wry face. "And it seems you and I are in the same predicament."

As he released the pressure on her hand, she followed his gaze to see what he meant. "Oh."

The white fabric of his loincloth was only slightly less transparent than her fine muslin undergarments. It revealed as much as it concealed. Every part of him was prominently displayed.

Caroline was fascinated and repelled at the same time. Tony felt nothing like Lord Blessing. Tony was hard and big and straining against the wet fabric.

He closed his eyes and gritted his teeth, seriously doubting his wisdom in demonstrating the flaw in the design of her gift. "You are the only person who is ever going to see me in the water in these. I appreciate your thoughtfulness in buying them for me. But they're white. Just like the chemise and drawers you're wearing. My earlier objection to wearing them was because I was afraid they'd be indecent once they got wet." Tony opened his eyes.

Quickly withdrawing her hand from his, Caroline murmured. "I see." *More than she'd ever seen of any man.*

"Meyer should have known better," Tony said. "He's a tailor. He's made plenty of men's smallclothes."

"To be fair, I didn't tell Mr. Meyer you'd be wearing the undergarment in water. I simply told him you required it to accommodate your injuries."

"I refuse to wear these in the presence of Barnaby or any other man," he said. "And I require Barnaby's and Fielder's and Kirby's assistance."

"You were threatening to go in without anything on when I arrived," she reminded him.

"That wouldn't have worked out much better," he admitted. "Not if *you* were around."

"Oh." Caroline bit her bottom lip in consternation at her ignorance. "I understand. I didn't realize..." She stopped, then started again. "I apologize."

Tony frowned. She'd been married for three years, but failed to comprehend the workings of the male anatomy. "There's no need for you to apologize." He was quiet for a moment. "Caro, did Blessing ever kiss you or touch you the way I kiss and touch you?"

Caroline blushed. "Nobody has ever kissed me or touched me the way you do."

Carlisle was gratified to hear it.

"Certainly not Lord Blessing. He never kissed me. Or touched me in any but the most perfunctory way. Except at night."

The idea of Blessing touching Caroline at night made Tony a little crazy. Especially the image of Blessing touching her at night. "Go on." The two words were clipped and curt.

"Every month the housekeeper, Mrs. Tyson, reported the beginning and end of my monthly. Lord Blessing would appear in my bedchamber three days after it ended."

Recognizing her embarrassment, Tony led her to the steps. He sat down on the second one and pulled Caroline onto his lap the way he'd done in the dressing room. Only this time, he turned her, so they were face to face. Sitting in the water, Tony cradled her in his arms like a baby. "You can tell me," he promised. "Your secrets are safe."

She took a deep shuddering breath. "When he came into my bedchamber, he would climb in bed with me, pull up my nightgown, push my legs apart, and put that part of him on me." Caroline was too ashamed to look at Tony, so she squeezed her eyes shut and buried her face in the curve of his neck.

"What did he do?" Dozens of images of a variety of perversions filled his head.

"He would kneel between my legs and grunt and groan. It was awful," she said.

Tony didn't want to, but he made himself ask the question. "What happened when he finished?"

"My thighs were wet and sticky."

"How often did this happen?" Tony asked.

"Once a month. Every month for two years," she said. "I dreaded it because he blamed me. He blamed me every month for two years because I never gave him the heir he was promised." She lifted her head from Tony's shoulder. "I'm barren."

Her admission surprised him. *"What?"*

"I'm barren," Caroline admitted. "That means I cannot conceive children."

"I know what it means," Tony said. "How do you know?"

"Lord Blessing always cursed his misfortune in marrying two barren women. The first Lady Blessing and me." She tried to smile. "Perhaps, it was best that you purchased your commission in the cavalry instead of offering for me."

Tony recoiled as if she'd slapped him. "I did offer for you," he said. "I approached your father at the club the morning I proposed to you. I went straightaway after our morning ride." He smiled at the memory. "I met with your fa—" Remembering that Caroline addressed her father by his title, Tony did the same. "Lord Rushton. He refused my offer."

"You offered for me?" Caroline parroted Tony's statement as if she couldn't comprehend what he'd said.

"Twice," Tony said.

Caroline blinked.

He nodded. "That's right, sweetheart. I went to Lord Rushton to request your hand in marriage twice. The first time, I approached him at his club in front of witnesses." He sighed. "The second time, I was fool enough to go to the house on Portman Square without witnesses."

"You went to White's to ask Rushton for my hand in marriage?"

Tony nodded. "I'm ashamed to admit it, but there are several references to my offers being refused recorded in the betting books. Wagers on whether I would present a third offer. And whether Rushton would accept it."

Caroline groaned. The betting books at White's were legendary. In them a member could wager anything and wager *on* anything. Her marriage proposal had become gossip and a source of entertainment for inveterate gamblers. She pushed back from his chest to look him in the eye. "Phoebe and Dulcie were right. Why didn't Rushton tell me you offered for me?"

Tony sat up straighter. "He didn't tell you?"

"No." Caroline shook her head. "He told me Lord Blessing had offered for me, that he had accepted on my behalf, and that notice of our wedding would appear in the morning paper. I was to be the Marchioness of Blessing." She reached up and caressed Tony's cheek. "I told him that was impossible. I told him you had asked me to marry you, that *I* had accepted, and I would elope with you to Scotland before I would marry Lord Blessing."

"That bloody bastard!" Tony swore. "Rushton told me you weren't interested in being a countess, that you were determined to marry a marquess or a duke. And that you had begged him to refuse me."

Caroline's gaze flashed fire and fury. "You *believed* him?"

"No, I didn't believe him," Tony said. "I believed you. I believed *in* you."

She heard the hurt and the anger in his voice. "Then why didn't you come for me?" Her voice was rough sounding and unsteady. "Why didn't you come get me and take me to Scotland?"

Tony held her tighter, the anguish in her question almost too much for him to bear. "I was too late." He squeezed his eyes shut as he related the details of his meetings, both meeting with her father, and then with the Marquess of Blessing and how, after meeting with

Blessing, he'd awakened on a transport ship on its way to the Peninsula and learned he was a newly-minted lieutenant in the cavalry. How his papers had been authentic, and his commission purchased, but that he had no memory of any of it. "I didn't purchase my commission in the cavalry. I don't know who did. All I know is that I had been beaten to a bloody pulp when I arrived and commissioned into the Eleventh Blues rather than as a foot soldier." Tony dropped his chin to his chest, his forehead resting on the crown of her head. "By the time I became aware of what had happened, it was too late. I couldn't get back to you in time. You were married. And I was a thousand miles away in the middle of a war." His voice caught in his throat. He swallowed hard.

"Oh, Tony..." Caroline wrapped both arms around his head and pressed it to her breast. "I wanted so much to marry you. I dreamed of dancing with you at our wedding."

Tony squeezed his eyes shut. "It's all my fault. I thought Blessing would do the right thing and step aside. I thought he was a gentleman even if your—even if Rushton—was not. I expected honor from a man who had none. I expected honor and morality from *men* who had none. I should have eloped with you the morning I asked you to marry me." He kissed her tenderly. "I should have known Rushton would never accept me. I should have protected you from their schemes."

"How could you protect me from my father's ambition when he had parental and legal control over me. And you had none?"

"Forgive me."

"There is nothing to forgive," she said. "We've been granted a second chance, Tony. You're alive and I'm free of Lord Blessing's and my father's control. Lord Rushton can plague me with would-be suitors until the second coming, but he cannot force me to marry one. And he can't prevent me from marrying you."

"Caro, think about this." Tony raked his hand through his hair and rubbed his forehead as if trying to solve a great dilemma before pinching the bridge of his nose in a show of frustration. "I'm not the man I once was." He heaved a sigh. "You were married to an old man before. I refuse to tie you to a cripple now."

"Have you changed your mind about me? About us?" Caroline demanded.

"No. Yes. Dammit, Caro, I don't want you to settle for less when you deserve so much more."

"I could say the same thing about you."

"How?"

"I'm barren, Tony," she said. "I cannot give you an heir."

"That's debatable," he muttered.

"In what way?"

"What are the odds both of Blessing's wives would be barren?" he asked. "Perhaps, *he* was the problem not his wives." Tony was being very diplomatic. He'd heard whispers and bits of gossip over the years from men who had been at school with Granville Blessing, men who called him Hasty, including several peers attached to the Duke of Wellington's staff, and other peers who had been at court and had associated with him for years.

"Do you think that's possible?"

"I think it's quite possible," Tony said. "But only time will tell."

"You still want me?" Caroline didn't realize she was holding her breath until she heard his answer and released it.

"Of course I still want you," he said. "But more importantly, I want to marry you."

His answer stunned Caroline. She had been brought up by a father who believed having an heir was a man's first duty to himself, his family, and his country. Nearly every peer she'd ever known had married with that purpose and duty in mind. Her mother and the count and countess of Weymouth were the exceptions. They had married for love first and duty second. "Even knowing your Carlisle line dies with you if I am barren? And that your distant cousin will inherit?"

"Yes." He closed his eyes, counted to ten, and reopened them. He wasn't ready to confess his secret quite yet, but Tony understood his time on earth was rapidly expiring. He'd been marking off the days on the calendar for nearly nine months. Ever since he'd awakened in the Belgian field hospital and learned his fate. Tony also knew that soon his distant cousin would inherit his title and the Carlisle line would endure without him. "Even so."

"Why?"

"Because I love you, Caroline," he said. "Because I chose you to be my wife and my countess and if marrying you means my distant cousin will one day inherit my title instead of children born of my body, then so be it." He gazed at her face. "I'd rather have you than an heir to the title." Leaning closer, Tony kissed the corner of her mouth, then moved to her lips. The kiss began as a gentle, chaste meeting of the lips, a tender exploration, but he didn't stop with gentle and chaste. He slowly began to move his mouth over hers in a way that took them far beyond innocence. He nibbled at her lips, nipping, teasing, licking, sucking at the bottom one, asking permission, before demanding entrance.

Caroline parted her lips and allowed him to deepen the kiss. Tony didn't waste any time on finesse. His kiss was hot, hungry, and filled with desire. Caroline welcomed him. She copied his movements, imitating the way his tongue raked through her mouth, taking what he wanted, demanding she do the same. She met his challenge and reveled in the dizziness she felt under the fierce onslaught of pleasure he gave her.

He explored the contours of her body through her wet underclothes while he was kissing her, his big hands warming the places the wet clothing left chilled, and the things he did with his mouth and tongue and hands were incredibly exciting and enticing.

Caroline burned with need, feeling the insistent tug of desire pulling her in once again. Suddenly, kissing him wasn't enough. Even as she met him stroke for stroke, even as she learned the taste and touch of him, even as her tongue tangled with his, she wanted more. More of him. More of everything he made her feel…

Heart pounding, pulse racing, lips throbbing, Caroline fought to keep from crying out when Tony broke the kiss, pulling back to put some distance between them once again.

"What's wrong? Why did you stop?" She found her voice as she plummeted back to earth.

"Shh." Tony touched her lips with his index finger. "Listen."

She heard it then. The insistent knocking on the pavilion door. "It's Barnaby. Our lovely interlude is over."

"Only for now." Tony stole another kiss before he let go of her.

Caroline scrambled off his lap and watched as he levered himself to the top step, then used the rail to push himself to his feet. He wobbled once and Caroline wrapped her arm around his waist, placed her shoulder beneath his arm, and half-lifted, half-pushed him to the nearest chair.

Tony sat down hard, exhausted and exhilarated all at once. Gazing up at Caroline, he grinned. "Nothing to it."

# CHAPTER 29

*"We know truth, not only by reason,*
*but also by the heart."*
—Blaise Pascal, 1623-1662

Tony was wearing his robe and seated in his wheelchair when Caroline, completely dressed in everything except her wet chemise and drawers, and wrapped in her pelisse, opened the door to admit Barnaby with breakfast.

"I'm sorry to interrupt, milady." Barnaby inclined his head in deference to Caroline, then gave a quick nod in Lord Carlisle's direction as he set the butler's table down and began placing the food and beverages on the table. He lifted the coffee decanter to fill their cups. "Sir."

"It's quite all right, Barnaby." Tony wheeled himself to the table.

Barnaby froze mid-pour, his eyes widening and his mouth falling open. *"Sir?"*

Caroline closed the door behind Barnaby and moved to the table.

"That's right, Barnaby," Tony said. "She knows."

Barnaby glanced from the major to Lady Blessing and back. "I'm glad, sir." He turned to face Caroline. "I brought breakfast earlier than requested, milady, so I could inform you that the staff of Selby House has begun to return."

Caroline glanced toward Selby House, but was unable to see through the frosted glass of the pavilion. "How could you know that?"

"I took it upon myself to suggest to Mr. West that he instruct Nelson to extend a breakfast invitation to your maid, so she wouldn't have to dine alone. West returned with the news that the kitchen staff is beginning to report for duty."

Caroline turned to Tony. "I should be there to greet them."

Nodding his understanding, Tony said, "Go attend to your duties. I'm not going anywhere."

"I don't know when I'll be able to return."

"I'll be here this evening." He smiled at her. "After supper. About eight."

"Good. I have a surprise for you and we have something important we need to discuss." Caroline leaned down and kissed him in Barnaby's presence, using that intimate act to show Barnaby she appreciated his discretion and considered him entirely trustworthy. She had welcomed Barnaby into their private world, placing her trust and faith in him.

"How likely am I to like the surprise?" Tony asked, his eyes narrowing.

Caroline shot a glance at Barnaby.

Tony's former batman handed Caroline a folded sheet of paper.

*"Caroline?"*

She pocketed the sheet of paper, then leaned down and kissed Tony once again. "Very likely."

"How likely am I to agree to whatever it is we're going to discuss?"

"We'll talk about that after I meet with the Selby House staff." She gave him a jaunty wave as she hurried out of the pavilion.

"She's quite a lady, sir." Barnaby said, gazing after her in open admiration.

Tony grinned. "I see she has you wrapped around her finger, too."

"How could she not?" Barnaby flushed, his face and the tips of ears turning bright red. “She only wants the best for you, Major.” He brought himself to attention. “As do I.”

Carlisle faced his friend. “No need to explain, Barnaby. I fell in love with her during our first dance. Five years ago.” He ran his hand over his hair. “I believed I was over her.” He gazed up at Barnaby, the expression on his face clearly bemused. “But I was wrong. I’ll never be over Caroline Hardage. She has a firm grip on my heart.”

“Like I said, sir, she’s an amazing lady. I find it hard to believe you were ever parted.”

“*Were* being the important element in that statement,” came Tony’s cryptic reply. Recognizing the look on Barnaby’s face, Tony explained what he had learned from Caroline about their separation.

“Her father didn’t tell her you had asked his permission to marry her,” Barnaby repeated. “So she never knew.”

“She believed I received my commission before I had the opportunity to ask her father.” Tony snorted. “As if I’d chosen the cavalry and the excitement and glory of war over her.” He shook his head. “If I had been commissioned into the cavalry before I offered for her, I would never have left without seeing her, without explaining, without asking her to wait for me.”

Barnaby rubbed his hand over his close-cropped hair. “She didn’t believe it deep in her heart. Or she wouldn’t have written to you.”

Tony groaned, remembering the bundle of unopened letters he’d kept in his army kit. “I should have read her letters.”

“What would that have changed, sir?” Barnaby asked. “Except to increase your heartsickness and distract you from your duties?”

“I would have known she still loved me.”

“And was miserable in her marriage to someone else,” Barnaby said. “Which would have made you miserable. And angry.”

“Angrier. Because I couldn’t do anything to change her situation,” Tony agreed.

Barnaby thought carefully before speaking. “It’s possible your anger at her and your belief you’d been betrayed fueled your determination to survive and to triumph.” He met the major’s troubled gaze. “Anger and rage become necessary allies in war.”

"And revenge?" Tony asked.

"She was as much a victim as you were," Barnaby reminded him.

"I don't want revenge against Lady Blessing." He glared at Barnaby. "Never that."

"Perhaps right now," his former batman said. "But not before. I sat with you through the weeks of your delirium. I was privy to your anguish, your cries, curses, and damnations. A little over a month ago, you were urging Mr. West to remove her from the premises by any means necessary."

"So, I did," Tony admitted. "Fortunately for me, Mr. West was spectacularly unsuccessful."

"It is fortunate, sir."

"It goes to show just how wrong a man can be."

"And how right," Barnaby added.

Tony cast a sideways glance at him. "To want accountability from the man who saddled her with a husband she didn't want. Accountability from the man who forced me into war and into this blasted chair."

"Careful there, sir," Barnaby warned. "He may be a scoundrel, but he is her father. She may feel a loyalty to him and a willingness to forgive you don't share."

Tony was thoughtful. "She refers to him by his title. Never to his relationship to her."

"Remember the Hammersmith brothers, sir?" Barnaby asked.

Recalling a particularly vicious fight between Percy and Sidney Hammersmith that young corporal Chadwick had attempted to break up, Tony nodded. "They both turned on Chadwick and sent him to hospital."

"Aye, Major," Barnaby said. "Family is family."

"I see your point, Barnaby, but in this case, her *paterfamilias* may be planning to repeat his treachery against one or both of us."

Barnaby nodded his agreement. "Agreed."

Tony clapped his hands together. "So...what have we learned about the Selby House staff?"

"According to Nelson, the whole of the household is eager to go to work for Lady Blessing. They're excited about the changes to the house and gardens and eager to see which of their suggested changes she incorporated during the restorations."

Tony was surprised. "She asked for suggestions from the staff?"

"She did, sir. Just as she asked Mr. West, Kirby, Fielder, and me for suggestions on how to make your daily life more comfortable. The paper I handed her a few moments ago was my list."

Tony arched an eyebrow.

"I understand Mr. West, Fielder, and Kirby have already submitted theirs."

"Suggestions to make my life easier?" Tony smiled. "It seems I've become her newest project."

"You were always her intended project," Barnaby told him. "And I didn't say easier. I don't believe making your life easier will help you, sir. Easier makes soldiers softer. But small comforts can help make soldiers stronger."

"What small comforts did you recommend, Barnaby?"

"Lambswool seat cushions for your chair. Fine whisky. Mineral salts for your bath. A reclining couch, lap robes, and..." He glanced down at Tony's bare feet. "Slippers."

"Add bolsters," Tony told him.

"Bolsters, sir?" Barnaby wasn't sure he'd heard him clearly.

"For the bed. The added support would make it easier—" He shot a glance at Barnaby. "And more comfortable for me to sit up without assistance. A rocking chair might also be a comfort."

"Noted, sir," Barnaby said. "I'll make certain Lady Blessing is informed."

Tony laughed. "No, Barnaby, *I'll* make certain Lady Blessing is informed."

Barnaby smiled.

"I would appreciate it if you would see that none of the household enters the pavilion or the gardens adjacent to it after eight tonight." He gave Barnaby a wry look. "As I'll be availing myself of my heated bath."

"And Lady Blessing, sir?" Barnaby had the effrontery to ask.

"Lady Blessing may avail herself of the pavilion and the heated bath anytime she chooses. After all, she built it. And she was right to do so." He met Barnaby's quizzical gaze, then glanced at the small clock Caroline had thoughtfully left on the table. "According to that, I stood on my feet in the heated pool for twenty-three minutes this morning." Reading the expression on Barnaby's face, Tony added. "Before this morning, the longest I've been able to stand on my feet was seven seconds."

"It's the water," Barnaby said.

"It's not just the water," Tony said. "It's the woman who made it all possible. And I'm worried about her."

"You believe she may be making herself a target rather than you, Major?" Barnaby asked.

"I believe it's possible, though not likely."

"We know you were set upon and removed from London and Lady Blessing's life five years ago. There's no reason to believe they won't try to do it again."

Tony nodded. "I don't think Rushton would physically harm her. He needs her to achieve his ambitions. But there are other ways to harm her..."

"Chief among them would be harming *you*."

"She's stubborn." Tony's smile grew larger and brighter. "And she loves me. I don't trust what her father might do if she tries to thwart him."

Barnaby shook his head. He nearly bit out his words. "If you're out of the way, Lord Rushton won't have any difficulty controlling her. She loves you. With you gone, it won't matter to her who they force her to marry. You are Rushton's main target."

"I know," Tony agreed. "So we must be very careful and very vigilant. We need to know everything there is to know about her new staff. If Rushton and his allies remove me, there'll be no one to protect her from a forced marriage except the Earl of Weymouth."

"You could marry her, Major," Barnaby reminded him.

"It's my fondest wish, Barnaby," Tony confided. "But will that protect her or make the situation more dangerous by forcing Rushton's hand? If I were to marry her, there might be additional complications..." He gave Barnaby a meaningful look. "Welcome complications for me and Lady Blessing, but most unwelcome complications for Rushton." He sighed. "We need to know if there are any threats to Lady Blessing among her new staff."

~

"THANK YOU ALL FOR RETURNING PROMPTLY," CAROLINE SAID, addressing the Selby House staff, who were lined up in the foyer of the town house. "I hope you had a pleasant holiday."

"Yes, ma'am. Thank you, ma'am," the servants replied in unison. The male staff bowed, while the females curtseyed, in deference to their new mistress.

"Before you begin introducing yourselves to me, allow me to introduce myself to you." She smiled. "I am Caroline Hardage, Dowager Marchioness of the twelfth Marquess of Blessing and first Marchioness of Blessing in my own right. With me is my lady's maid, Susan Brown." She paused for a moment to allow the staff to acknowledge Susan. "Many of your families have worked for the Selby family for generations and many of you were in service to the late Viscount Selby for decades. I realize the change in ownership may be difficult for some of you." She swept her gaze down the line of Lord Selby's family retainers, beginning with the butler, Digby, and housekeeper, Mrs. Baldwin, and ending with the last scullery maid. "I don't doubt there will be changes in the way the house is run. As I'm sure you've noticed, the late Lord Selby and I are quite different." Caroline paused as titters of laughter echoed through the foyer. She understood their laughter; there was more than fifty years' difference in the ages of the late Viscount Selby and the Marchioness of Blessing.

Although the current Viscount Selby was younger than Caroline, his tenure as owner of Selby House had been mercifully brief. The staff, though loyal to the Selby family and name, held the younger viscount in contempt for living up to his great uncle's prediction that his young heir would end up wagering his family home on the turn of a card. And losing.

Caroline nodded to the butler. "Digby, if you'll begin..." She waited patiently as the staff members made their bow or curtsey before introducing themselves and their position in the household.

The household staff appeared happy to have Lady Blessing as the new owner. "Our households will also be different. I understand how hard that can be. Those of you who wish to seek positions elsewhere are welcome to do so," she continued. "That is not to say we wish you to leave, but we want you to be happy in your situation. If you are not happy working for me here, you are free to go elsewhere. If any of you wish to retire, I shall arrange for you to be pensioned off according to your years of service. I pay fair wages." She took a few minutes to explain the wages she offered for the individual services and the pensioner rates, including available retirement cottages on the Blessing country estate, Selby House acreage, and nearby homes in the mews behind Carlisle House for the head groundskeeper and head coachman and groom. "If you object to the renovations of the house or the gardens and refuse to recognize that Selby House has a new owner, tell me now. I believe you will find me a very amiable and fair mistress, but I require unquestionable loyalty and discretion from my staff. I assume those of you who have done me the honor of showing up this morning wish to remain. So it's only fair that I explain the rules of the house.

"Those of you who work here will be privy to my rather unorthodox comings and goings and that of my guests, including our near neighbor. There will be certain rules you'll be expected to follow. For reasons that may not be made clear to you. For that I apologize. But I tell you now, I will not tolerate breaches of my privacy or that of my guests. Or gossip of any kind. For *any* reason.

"Petty grievances should be brought to Mr. Digby's attention. Serious grievances should be brought before me. In my opinion, gossiping about the one who pays your salary is most unprofessional. And I am not interested in paying the wages of—or housing —unprofessional staff. Anyone caught gossiping or telling tales about the interior workings of Selby House, the gardens shared between Carlisle House and this one will be summarily dismissed. The question of references will be left to Mr. Digby, if he decides to remain, or to the housekeeper, Mrs. Baldwin, or Cook Enright, if they decide to remain, to review the dismissed staff member's performance of his or her duties before the occurrence of the transgression. Anyone caught gossiping or relaying rumors or divulging information to the editors or reporters in the employ of newspapers will be summarily dismissed without references." She took a deep breath. "I have plans for Selby House that require an excellent and unobtrusive staff. It is my wish that all of you stay on, but I will certainly understand if you choose not to do so." She took another deep breath. "Cook will lay out a cold buffet in the staff dining room for all of you. And I'll be in the yellow drawing room if you'd like to speak to me about retaining your position or leaving us." She smiled at the staff. "Thank you all."

After dismissing the staff, Caroline made her way down the hall to the yellow drawing room. Taking out the account books she had asked Digby to place on her desk, she turned to the listings of the names and duties of the staff to begin the individual interviews.

Susan brought Caroline her morning chocolate and a slice of toasted bread at nine. She took luncheon at one in the afternoon and was still interviewing staff when the butler interrupted her with a supper tray at half past seven in the evening.

"I brought your supper, ma'am," the butler told her. "And these arrived for you by special courier earlier this afternoon."

Caroline looked up from the notes she was making. "Thank you, Digby." She stood up and stretched, glancing up at the mantel clock as it chimed the half hour. "I didn't realize it had grown so late. Shall we schedule the remainder of the staff for tomorrow at nine?"

The butler shook his head. "Betty was the last of the household staff, ma'am. We've gardeners and the head coachman's staff scheduled for tomorrow."

Knowing the butler was keeping a tally of the number of staff to be replaced or added, Caroline asked. "How many did we lose?"

"Four, ma'am," he said. "One upstairs maid. One downstairs maid. One footman. And one laundry helper."

Caroline went down her list. "That's my tally as well."

"Then we are in accord, ma'am."

"Are we?" She met the butler's gaze.

Edward Digby was a distinguished-looking young man in his early thirties, a generation younger than Carlisle's butler, West, and the Blessing House butler, Tyson.

Digby had assumed the position as butler to the late Lord Selby four years earlier after serving as Under Butler for half a decade. He was well-respected by the housekeeper and cook and appeared to have a bright future before him. Caroline had liked him immediately and hoped he would choose to remain at Selby House.

"Most assuredly, ma'am." He bowed. "May I say it's an honor to serve you, Lady Blessing?"

"It's kind of you to say so, Digby."

He shook his head. "Households are small communities within a broader community, ma'am. I was born into service. My father served the late Viscount Selby and the one before that. I also served the late viscount and his heir. I was never asked if I wished to do so. It was my duty, so I served. You, Lady Blessing, have asked if I wish to continue my service in your household and the answer is a resounding yes. While I will do my utmost to curtail the repeating of gossip, I can do nothing to prevent the *listening* to it..."

"I realize that," Caroline told him. "I know belowstairs has an information gathering system with the belowstairs of other households. It's part and parcel of managing a household. I realize gossip between households cannot be eliminated entirely. My lady's maid is a fount of invaluable information for me. My wish is not to curtail the flow of information *to* Selby House; it is to prevent the flow of information *from* Selby House to the adjoining households and beyond. The only way I can do that is to inform the staff of the penalty for breaking the rules." She looked the butler in the eye. "If all goes well, Lord Carlisle may become the master here and his health and well-being, as well as his privacy, is paramount to me."

"Lord Carlisle, ma'am?"

"Surely you didn't think I purchased this estate because I had a burning desire to renovate?" She cracked a smile to show she was teasing.

Digby returned her smile.

"Or that I would reside here alone?"

"I've seen the papers, ma'am," he admitted. "Are best wishes in order?"

"Not at present," she said with a shrug. "He hasn't suggested a date on the calendar."

"Nor will he, ma'am," Digby told her. "Unless he feels he can make a full recovery."

Caroline arched an eyebrow in a close imitation of Tony's patented silent query.

"Lord Carlisle and I were childhood playmates before he went away to school and on holidays afterwards," Digby explained. "I knew him quite well at one time."

"Well enough to keep his secrets?"

"Well enough to keep both your secrets and to do whatever I can do to help."

"I hope you welcome a challenge, Digby." Glancing at the letters on the supper tray, Caroline recognized Uncle Trevor's handwriting on the smaller of the two missives.

Lifting Uncle Trevor's letter from the tray, Caroline slit the wax seal bearing the Weymouth family crest, removed the letter and read:

*My dear Caroline,*

*Please find enclosed an invitation for you and a guest to the private Thoroughbred sale at Tattersall's promptly at ten o'clock in the morning on the twenty-sixth day of April in the year of Our Lord eighteen hundred, sixteen.*

*Sincerely,*

*Weymouth*

The handwriting on the other letter was unfamiliar to her, but because it had come in the courier pouch with Uncle Trevor's letter, Caroline knew it must be from the Scottish physician, Sir James McGregor.

Opening it, she pulled out the letter.

*My dear Lady Blessing,*

*I've been instructed by Lord Weymouth to direct my reply to you.*

*Having read the medical reports of the injuries suffered by Major Lord Anthony Carlisle during the Battle of Quatre Bras and the treatment he received in the aftermath, I have concluded that with time, the major should make a full recovery.*

*His recovery would have progressed much faster had the field surgeons amputated his right limb (providing he did not succumb to blood loss or shock or general ill humors) as they wished to do, but I disagree with the prognosis of the previous physicians and surgeons. I do not consider the injury to his right limb a death sentence unless it fails to respond to treatment. In that case, the patient will surely die with or without amputation. Otherwise, the patient, with care, time, nourishment, and a regimen of exercise to rebuild strength, should make a complete eventual recovery.*

*I see no reason for surgical intervention unless his overall condition worsens, or if his pain worsens and his limbs continue to fail to support him. In the interim, I have taken the liberty of enclosing a recommended nutrition and exercise schedule for the patient.*

*If I can be of service in the future, don't hesitate to contact me.*

*Your servant,*

*James McGregor, Physician*

*Edinburgh, Scotland*

Folding the letter, Caroline looked up at Digby and sighed. "I hope you really *do* welcome a challenge, Digby. Because I'm about to give you one."

# CHAPTER 30

*"Below the navel there is neither religion nor truth."*
—Italian proverb

"I was afraid you weren't going to make it." Tony was waiting in the bathing pool when Caroline arrived in the pavilion.

"I'm sorry I'm late," she apologized. "Interviewing the staff took longer than I expected. Did I keep you waiting long?"

"No matter." He grinned. "Come on in. The water feels wonderful. I've already swum the length of the pool and back twenty times while waiting for you." He met Caroline's blue-eyed gaze. "I can't thank you enough for evicting my goldfish and renovating this pond for my use."

"Had I not," she reminded him. "Your goldfish would have been poached instead of happily swimming in a new pond in the center of the maze."

"I've missed being able to exercise my whole body, rather than just my arms and legs." He gazed up at her. "But what I missed most these last five years was holding you."

"How remarkable," Caroline replied. "Because what I missed most during these last five years was being held by you." Her voice wavered as she struggled to contain her emotions. "I feared you would never hold me again."

Tony's gaze seemed to see through the clothing she wore. "Then don't keep me waiting any longer. Let me hold you again."

Reaching up, Caroline unpinned her hair and loosened her plait before she unbuttoned her pelisse and shrugged out of it. Draping her pelisse over one of the stone chairs, she untied the ribbon at the neck of her dress, pushed it down her legs and let her dress fall to the floor, followed by her flannel petticoat.

And she wasn't done...

Tony's breath caught in his throat as she tugged her short chemise over her head and flung it aside, then untied the drawstrings of her drawers and stepped out of them.

Caroline blushed as she stood naked before him at the top of the four steps leading into the water.

"What? No undergarments?" He gazed at Caroline without the concealing veil of her wet and nearly transparent chemise and drawers. Studying her from head to toe, Tony was reminded, once again, of Aphrodite rising from the sea. But as far as he was concerned, Caroline was far more beautiful than any Greek goddess could ever be.

"According to my lady's maid, my supply of undergarments is seriously limited. I've been instructed not to get those wet until the others are dry." She glanced at the chemise and drawers on the pavement by the side of the pool. "And in this weather"—she gestured toward the frosted windowpanes that hid the dark low-lying clouds from view—"it takes longer for them to dry."

"I'm all in favor of saving your undergarments from further abuse." He fixed his gaze on the dark russet triangle between her thighs for a long moment before meeting her gaze. "In fact, now that I've seen you without them, I'm in favor of you always going without."

"Beneath muslin dresses? There would be nothing left to the imagination." She stepped down to the next step.

He grinned. "Exactly."

"And you'd be happy with me going about London like that?" She took another step deeper into the water.

"Not about town," he said. "Not where other people could see you. Only with me."

Her nipples formed tight, little buds beneath his steady silver-gray gaze.

"Cold?"

"A bit," she admitted, although she suspected her reaction was due more to nerves than cold. How could she be cold beneath his heated gaze?

"Come here." Tony's voice was a deep rumbling purr. Like the sound of a well-contented tom cat. "The water is warm." He winked at her. "And so am I."

Caroline worried her bottom lip with her teeth, then walked down the final steps until she stood chest deep in water.

"Don't be shy," he coaxed. "Not with me." Tony could feel himself growing thick and hard and very aroused.

Caroline widened her eyes at the sight of him. He was as naked as she was. "What? No undergarment?"

"It was wet."

Caroline giggled. "It was meant to be worn in water."

"It's damned uncomfortable wet." Extending his hand, Tony pulled her close. "Come here. I've missed you."

"You saw me just this morning," she reminded him.

There was a twinkle in his eye when he bent close, brushed her hair with his lips, and murmured, "Not as much of you as I'm seeing now."

She blushed brighter as he enveloped her in his arms. His body was big and warm and solid. Caroline went into his arms willingly. They were warm and welcoming. She felt safe and comforted and home.

Tony braced himself against the wall of his new heated bath and pulled her up against him, holding her tightly, warming her, his large hands against her naked bottom.

She relaxed, sighing her pleasure at being held close within the circle of his arms. Caroline felt him pressed against her belly, but this time, she didn't recoil in surprise or revulsion. She leaned into him, delighting in the weight and feel of him.

He crooked his neck so he could see the expression on her face. "Comfortable?"

A tiny upward curl started at the corner of her mouth. "Very."

He nuzzled her hair and neck, then bent his head and kissed her eyes, her cheekbone, her nose, the corner of her mouth, and finally her full lips, kissing her until they were both gasping for breath.

Skimming his hand over her bottom, her hip, the indentation of her waist, and up the ladder of her ribs where he discovered a ticklish spot, Tony paused. "Trust me?"

She didn't hesitate. "Yes."

"May I?" he asked politely.

"Please do," Caroline invited.

After seeking permission and having it granted, Tony lifted her right arm and then her left, positioning them around his neck.

The action brought her breasts in contact with his chest. Caroline giggled as the hair on his chest teased the tips of her breasts.

"Like that?"

"Mm-hmm," she murmured.

Tony ran the tip of his finger along the side of her breast, tracing an imaginary line from the slight crease below, along the lower slope, to the upturned tip. He smiled a knowing smile as her sensitive skin dissolved into a mass of gooseflesh and her nipples grew tighter.

Caroline moaned as he brushed his knuckle across the tip in a side-to-side motion. She moved forward, seeking closer contact, wedging her thigh against the hard ridge at the apex of his opened legs.

Tony pressed his back against the edge of the bath, easing the exquisite pleasure-pain of her creamy smooth thigh pressed against him. He slid his hands over her, mapping her contours, memorizing the feel of her soft skin and the ripples of awareness he awakened within her. And while he charted her body, he kissed her face, her hair, her eyelids, the curve of her cheek, the corner of her mouth, and finally her lips.

"Caro, you're exquisite. I dreamed of seeing you like this. Holding you like this. But I never dreamed you would be so beautiful." Tony meant it. She was beautiful, much lovelier than the girl he remembered. He fought to catch his breath and struggled to form coherent words as the magnificent pleasure-pain of holding her, kissing her, touching her, took its toll on his restraint. "My imagination didn't do you justice."

"You imagined me unclothed?" She was clearly surprised by his admission.

"Every night from the moment we were introduced." He smiled. "Five interminable years."

"Why?"

"Because I was a healthy young man who wanted a beautiful young lady." Leaning his forehead against hers, Tony breathed hard. "I still want..."

"What?" Caroline shivered in response.

"You," he said. "All of you."

"I'm here," she whispered. "You have me."

"And I want you so much, I'm almost afraid to touch you." He spoke in a soft, reverent tone. "Afraid I might hurt you. Or worse, disappoint you."

"Don't be afraid," she whispered. "Touch me."

Tony locked gazes with her, then slowly made his way to the second step, spread his legs and guided Caroline onto his lap. "Are you sure?"

"Quite sure." She plunged her fingers in his hair.

"All right." Tony paused long enough to gauge her reaction, then leaned close and slowly licked the underside of her breast, tasting the tiny droplets of water there before he moved upward and covered the sensitive tip with his mouth.

If she hadn't been sitting on his lap, Caroline's knees would have given way. But Tony held her fast, placing his hands on her hips to steady her.

Warmth, like the warmth of a hot rum toddy on an empty stomach, shot through her. But this warmth was a thousand times better than anything rum induced. Caroline gasped when Tony teased the tip of her breast, nipping and licking it with his tongue and teeth and his hot, wet kisses until her nipple grew harder and she ached in places proper ladies never admitted to having.

Caroline arched her back, filling the pavilion with the soft incoherent sounds she made deep in her throat. She wiggled in his arms as Tony continued to tease her with his wicked tongue, delighting in igniting spontaneous currents of hot desire that flared throughout her body.

Turning his head so that he might breathe once again, Tony slowly worked his way over to her other breast, nuzzling it first, then lavishing it with a rush of hot, moist air. After working his way from her breasts back to her lips, Tony plundered her mouth with his, tasting, devouring, wanting, raking the interior of her mouth with his tongue, as he gently smoothed his hand from her firm stomach through the soft hair at her delta to her bare thighs.

Breaking their torrid kiss, Tony leaned back against the top step, settled Caroline more firmly against him, and took a deep, steadying breath.

The hard, male part of him throbbed with each beat of his heart. Aching to sheathe himself in Caroline's warmth, Tony wrapped his arms around her waist, gently lifted her up and slowly, carefully eased her down onto him. Placing her hands on his shoulders, Caroline traced their contours, marveling at the strength she found beneath his hot flesh.

Groaning, Tony pressed himself against her, gauging her readiness by gently probing her entrance. Caroline bit her bottom lip as he penetrated her. Rising onto her knees, she lowered herself, wiggling against him, forcing him deeper, testing his reaction, tempting him past endurance.

"Darling, Caro, I'm not going to last if you keep doing that." He tightened his jaw against the exquisite pleasure. *Christ, he was about to react as badly as old Hasty Blessing.* Digging her nails into his shoulder muscles, Caroline urged him on, driving him to satisfy the ache building inside her.

Sucking her nipple into his mouth, Tony began toying with it as she rode him harder.

"I'm sorry, darling." Unable to wait one heartbeat longer, Tony released the suction on her breast, closed his eyes, bit his bottom lip and sheathed himself fully inside her.

Caroline cried out as he filled her completely.

Tony kissed her, swallowing her cry of pain as he felt, then pushed through her barrier. He knew the moment he breached it that he had been right about Blessing. Caroline had been married for three years and a widow for two, but she was still a virgin. Or had been, until he'd just claimed her as his own.

Tony shouldn't feel triumphant, but he couldn't squash the joy he felt at being her first, couldn't dampen the primitive rush of victory he felt at claiming his mate. That's how it was meant to be. He had wanted to marry her, had planned to marry her, and father her children.

As much as he rejoiced in being the first, Tony hated that Caroline had endured the fumbling attempts of an old man who had been unable to consummate their union. He hated the fact that she had been forced to submit to Blessing, who had continued to use her to satisfy his ambition and his destiny.

Tony could find a modicum of sympathy for a man desperately trying to continue his lineage and title, but he felt no sympathy or empathy for a man who blamed his young bride for his inability to do so.

And he wasn't much better...

Tony blamed himself for his clumsiness. It didn't matter that Caroline wanted, even encouraged, his lovemaking, he knew she was innocent. He should have made love to her with more finesse. She had tensed when he slipped inside her. She'd cried out in pain because he'd hurt her. And Tony was riddled with guilt and remorse because of it.

There was no excuse. He'd never made love with a virgin before, but he had had other lovers. He was the one with experience. He should have known better than to push past her barrier without regard to the pain he might cause. He should have known she wasn't ready. Should have anticipated.

But he was paying the price now. His body shook with effort as he strained to give her as much time as he could manage, struggling to allow her body the time needed to fit itself to his size and length. Tony waited until Caroline began to move before he surrendered the fight and granted her the right to set the pace.

Caroline squeezed her thighs against his, clenching her inner muscles, tightening them around him as she watched his face. The pain he'd inflicted had surprised her when he'd given her nothing but pleasure before, but she disregarded the momentary discomfort, braced herself against his shoulders and moved over him, reveling in the freedom and power of having Tony beneath her, giving of herself in a way she had never imagined, in a way that made everything they'd done—all the pleasure they had given and received—seem insignificant when compared to this…this miraculous joining.

He placed the heel of his hand against her, using his thumb to massage her in a steady, circling motion that created an avalanche of pure pleasure. Caroline squeezed her eyes shut. Tears of joy leaked from the corners, ran down her cheeks, and dropped into the water around her when Tony moved his hand from the place of their joining to her hip as the first tremors of passion rushed through her.

She gave voice to her pleasure, filling the air around them with sharp incoherent cries as Tony bracketed her hips with his hands, held her close, and exploded inside her.

TONY BRUSHED HIS LIPS AGAINST HER CHEEK AND BURIED HIS FACE IN the curve of her neck. Tasting the saltiness of her tears, he lifted his head, and met her gaze. "I'm sorry I hurt you."

"You didn't," she said.

"I heard you cry out." He had covered her cry with his kiss.

"I didn't expect it," Caroline told him. "Everything felt so wonderful before. Not at all like...with..." She frowned.

Tony reached up to smooth away her frown lines with his thumb and smiled when he dribbled water down her nose. "Now I've erased your worries and washed away your tears."

"My tears were tears of joy," she told him. "Because I was with you. Because this is the way it should have been from the beginning." Leaning forward, Caroline framed his face with her hands and kissed him, dripping water down the side of his face. "You washed away my tears. Now I've washed away your feelings of guilt because you weren't the first."

Tony shivered in reaction as a rush of emotions tore through him. "Oh, but I was."

"How could you be?" The frown lines he'd erased with his thumb were replaced by new ones. "I was married for three years to..."

"Lord Blessing." Tony finished her sentence. "Whose school chums nicknamed him Hasty."

"What has that to do with us?"

"Nothing." Tony palmed her breast, then let it go, watching as it bobbed atop the warm water of the bath. He did the same to the other breast, then recaptured it in his palm, reshaping it until the nipple pointed upward and begged to be kissed. He obliged. Then he turned his attention to its twin and did the same before he spoke again. *"Everything."*

"Tell me."

"Blessing earned his nickname because he got excited when he was with a woman. Too excited. Resulting in the release of his seed before the act of coupling was completed," Tony explained. "Or really started. In your case, he did it as soon as he touched you. My darling Caroline, you were a virgin until a few minutes ago."

"I was?"

He nodded.

"Oh, Tony! That's wonderful!" Caroline threw her arms around his neck and hugged him to her. "I always wanted it to be you and bitterly regretted that it wasn't."

Tony kissed her. Hard. Voraciously.

And Caroline kissed him back until they were both desperate for more.

She broke off. "How did you know?"

"I didn't," he whispered. "I guessed." He kissed the tip of her nose and smiled at her. "Forgive me for being the man that I am, because I know you suffered anguish when he blamed you, but I hoped. I hoped he hadn't truly touched you. I hoped he didn't have your heart or soul."

"He didn't," she said. "He could never have what already belonged to you."

Tony squeezed his eyes shut. "I should have been gentler," he said. "I should have spoken words of love instead of passion. I should have taken my time instead of pushing you to fulfillment. You deserved better."

"I don't think you could ever give me more pleasure than this."

"Oh, but I can," he promised. "Much more."

"Now?"

Tony laughed at her eagerness. "I need a moment of recovery and a bed would be nice."

She arched an eyebrow at that. "I thought the water helped."

"It does," he agreed. "And I needed it to find out if what we just did was possible." He shrugged. "But I'm turning into a prune..."

Caroline glanced down and saw that he was right.

"Not that part." He laughed. "That's normal." He held up his hand to show her the wrinkling caused by submersion in the bath. "This part."

She raised her hand and showed him her wrinkly fingers. "Mine, too." *And she'd spent less time in the bath than he had.*

"It's a shame we don't have a bed close by." He cast a glance toward the dressing room and the padded table beyond. It would do in a pinch, but he wanted something more comfortable. "And it's a shame these lovely fingers are going to get prunier." Taking her hand, Tony brought it to his mouth and began sucking her fingers.

Caroline felt the impact in her woman's place. "I have a bed."

"So, do I," Tony remarked. "Unfortunately, I have to climb a mountain of stairs to get there."

"No, you don't," Caroline corrected. "You only have to make it into your chair." She nodded toward the chair he hadn't bothered to hide from her.

"Help me up."

# CHAPTER 31

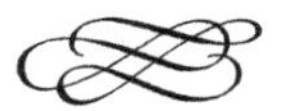

*"I loved you at your darkest."*
—Romans 5:8, New Testament

"Why are you bringing me here?" Tony asked as Caroline pushed his wheelchair up the ramp to the terrace entrance of Selby House.

"I thought you wanted a comfortable bed," she said.

"I do," he confirmed. "It's my second greatest desire in life."

"Second?" Caroline pressed a kiss against the crown of his head. "What's the first?"

"You."

Warmth swept through her at his words. "You're in luck," she said. "This house has one."

There were a hundred concerns Tony could have voiced. His concern for her reputation chief among them. A hundred questions he could have asked. But he asked only one. "How are you going to get me upstairs?"

"You'll see." She unlocked the doors to the orangery with a key she took from her pelisse pocket.

"You're using a key." He remembered the trouble she'd had the first time she'd unlocked the kitchen door with a key.

"I didn't think it fair for Digby to have to unlock the door at all hours to accommodate my comings and goings," she said. "Which I explained to him was my business and nobody else's."

*"Digby?"* Tony was clearly surprised. "Selby's butler? Good heavens! He must be closing in on ninety by now."

"This Digby is about thirty," Caroline said. "And a childhood friend of yours."

"Eddie? He's your new butler?" Tony frowned.

"He is. And he's called by his surname now, like his father before him," Caroline told Tony as she pushed the wheelchair inside the terrace room.

"Are you sure you want him as your butler?" Tony asked. "He used to cut a wide swath through the housemaids when he was younger."

"I do want him as butler," Caroline said. "I like him. Digby told me about his past romantic pursuits. And you've nothing to worry about on that front. He's reformed. Now...close your eyes."

He was skeptical. "Why?"

"Because I have a surprise for you."

"I don't care much for surprises," Tony warned her.

"You'll like this one," she said. *I hope*. After locking the orangery door behind her, Caroline wheeled Tony into the master bedchamber and stopped.

"Does my surprise include a bed and a beautiful, willing marchioness?"

"Open your eyes and see." Caroline found it hard to keep the excitement out of her voice.

Tony opened his eyes only to discover Selby House's new master's chamber.

The room was massive, with Palladium windows on the wall overlooking the gardens and a marble fireplace at the opposite end. There was a fire burning in the grate, taking the chill out of the air. Between the door and the fireplace was a bedchamber, a sitting area, and a washroom containing a sink with hot and cold running water, plus a privacy closet that could be reached by a man in a wheelchair.

The entire room was designed to facilitate the movement of his chair. Interior shutters covered the windows. The shutters were closed at night, but Tony knew the room would be flooded with sunlight once they were opened. The knobs on the doors were set lower, so a man in a chair could wheel himself from the bedchamber to the orangery and through to the terrace and down the ramp into the gardens. Brass handrails were attached to each wall to allow him to grab and hold on if necessary or to pull himself along.

Tony used the rails to make his way around the suite. The bed was large and made up with a quilted coverlet and matching bolsters for support. A large rocking chair bore matching back and seat cushions. Tony had forgotten to mention his requests to Caroline during the heat of passion, but Barnaby—bless him—had remembered.

Mounted above the bed, suspended from the ceiling was a brass grid. Tony studied it. "Whose idea was this?"

"Kirby suggested it," Caroline told him. "You can use it to sit up or to transfer from bed to chair or bed to your feet. Or just to steady yourself when you're doing your morning exercises."

Everything that could possibly help in his recuperation had been included in the master suite. He turned to Caroline. "You built this for me?"

"Of course I did."

"Why?"

"Because I wanted to help you regain a bit of your independence," she told him. "Because I didn't want you to be dependent on someone carrying you up and down stairs for the rest of your life."

He shot her a look.

Caroline read his mind. "Barnaby, Kirby, and Fielder kept your secret, Tony. Nobody had to tell me."

Reaching up, Tony took hold of her hand and brought it to his lips. "You created a bedchamber in *your* house for me." He shook his head in wonder. "As well as the heated bath and the renovated gardens. I don't know what to say."

"You don't have to say anything. I *purchased* the house for you because you needed access to the hot spring."

He was clearly surprised by her admission. "Your man of business refused to meet with mine about the possibility of purchasing this house from you."

"I instructed him to refuse all offers—including yours." She locked gazes with him. "When it came."

"Why?"

"Because you would have purchased Selby House to keep me out and away from you. When I desperately needed to be close to you." This time, she brought their joined hands to her lips and kissed the back of Tony's hand. "And you needed to be close to me."

"I have a house next door," Tony reminded her.

"That you can't use," she said. "And I have a house across the park."

"That you can't use." He glanced around, still shaking his head in wonder. "It's a good thing you were wise enough to buy one we both can use."

"Wisdom had nothing to do with it."

"I beg to differ." The look in his eyes was intense. Meaningful.

Caroline smiled. "I originally intended to renovate *your* house to accommodate your injuries." She gave him a stern look. "And I would have, if you had allowed me inside it."

"I seem to recall you stormed it twice." He grinned at the memory of her managing to get past the venerable West. "Getting past West took some doing."

"A lot of good it did me. You threatened to have me rolled up in a carpet like Cleopatra or to use my pretty, little backside to dust the marble floor."

"Forgive me." He kissed the back of her hand again. "I had no idea how pretty your little backside is."

"You're forgiven."

"Thank goodness," he breathed. "Because I want to wrap you up in my arms and pay homage to your backside and your frontside, and all the pretty parts in between."

Caroline unbuttoned her pelisse and shrugged it off her shoulders. The garment crumpled to the floor.

Tony sucked in a breath.

She was naked except for her slippers.

He wondered if he would ever tire of the sight of her.

Turning her back to him, Caroline wiggled her hips. "Get on with it."

He grinned. His shy Caroline was rapidly developing a confident sassy side he adored. The difference between a girl and a woman.

"My pleasure." Tony snaked his arm around her waist and pulled her to him to plant a devilishly wicked kiss on the small of her back. "Mm." He smacked his lips. "Delicious."

Caroline's knees wobbled at the sensations he evoked.

Sensing her lapse of control, Tony urged her backwards until she plopped down onto his lap. Holding her firm, Tony wheeled them to the bed. Caroline flipped back the covers, climbed into bed, and waited for Tony to join her. He levered himself out of his chair, grabbed hold of one of the brass rails above the bed and pulled himself to his feet. "One, two, three, four, five, six..." He counted quietly.

"What are you doing?"

"Counting the seconds I'm on my feet," he replied.

"Oh." Caroline moistened her lips with the tip of her tongue. "One, two, three..."

"What are *you* doing?"

"Counting the seconds until you're off your feet, in bed, and making love to me."

She didn't make it to five.

Tony amazed her with the speed at which he shed his robe and slippers and rolled into bed beside her.

"I thought you would never get here," Caroline teased when he began covering her flesh with kisses.

He took his time. Teasing. Tempting. In no particular hurry to finish.

"There's nowhere I would rather be." The look in his eyes mirrored the desire in his voice.

"Flat on your back and in bed with me?" Caroline asked, running her fingers through the hair on his chest and stomach. She circled his navel with the tip of her finger, then traced the arrow of dark brown hair below his navel.

"Flat on my back. Lying on my side. Upside down. Or kneeling above you. I don't care as long as you're here."

"You did assure me you could do it again," she reminded him. "With a brief respite and a comfortable bed. I've provided both."

The look he gave her was devilishly wicked and matched the kiss that quickly followed. "Then I shall endeavor to keep up my end of the bargain."

IN THE END, HE KEPT HIS BARGAIN THRICE MORE.

Tony taught her everything he'd learned about lovemaking. Every temptation. Every trick. Every kiss. Every touch. He surprised himself with the positions he was able to achieve and maintain. The most difficult being the traditional face-to-face position because it required him to pump with his hips. He had faltered a time or two, but Caroline had simply rolled with him until she was atop.

He had pleasured her in other ways, too. Ways that didn't require such exertion. Tony had brought her to completion more times than he could count and had spent himself inside her time and time again.

And Caroline assured him he'd done it perfectly each time.

Lying on his back with Caro nestled beside him, Tony fell into his first deep sleep since awaking in the field hospital after Quatre Bras. His first without the whisky and laudanum.

Caroline opened her eyes to find herself cradled against Tony's chest, her arm lying across his flat belly, one breast pressed against his side, the nipple of her other breast almost touching his, while her head rested against his shoulder.

She felt the rise and fall of his even breathing as he slept and listened to the steady beat of his heart beneath her ear. She shifted slightly, moving closer to him, seeking the warmth of his body. He tightened his arm around her, mumbling something incoherent before sliding his big, warm hand over her ribs and the curve of her waist, skimming the line of her hip. Maneuvering his hand lower, Tony flattened his palm again her bottom and pressed her against his thigh.

As she lay, relaxed and sated, luxuriating in the heat Tony generated, Caroline realized his eyes were open. He was wide awake and very aroused. She inched her hand lower, plowing her fingers through the arrow of hair below his belly button, then watched as the blood rushed to the male part of him, engorging it.

Tony sucked in a breath as his body tightened and the bulge beneath the corner of the sheet draped across his hip grew so insistent it began to tent the fabric, staining it with drops of moisture that appeared each time he looked at her.

"Good morning." His voice was gruff from slumber as he pulled her close enough to plant a kiss on her forehead and to snag a strand of hair caught in the corner of her mouth.

Caroline sighed. Sleeping with Tony, being held in his warm, protective embrace through the night was the best feeling she'd had in five long years. She hadn't felt safe and cherished since she'd learned Tony had gone to war and that she was about to be married to Lord Blessing. After her marriage, no amount of telling herself Lord Blessing wouldn't hurt her had made her feel any safer or loved. She'd been devasted to learn Tony had been killed at Quatre Bras and was never coming back to her, but lying here within the circle of his arms, pressed against his body, listening to his heartbeat, banished all the worry and anxiety she'd felt since her marriage.

"Sleep well?" he asked.

"Hmm..." She stretched against him. "Better than I have in years. Is it always like this?"

He kissed her bare shoulder. "No. I think this only happens with someone special, someone you care deeply about, someone you trust. Someone you love..." He kissed her again. "I've had other women and I admit those encounters were physically satisfying, but this is a first for me. I've never stayed the night with any woman. I've never awakened the next morning with a woman in my arms. I've never felt for anyone what I feel for you, Caroline. I've never loved anyone else."

"Anthony Carlisle," she breathed. "I love you so much."

He tightened his arms around her and began tracing a series of circles on her back with his thumb.

"The things we did last night..." she began

"And this morning..." Tony was quick to point out.

Caroline smiled at the memory of kissing every scar on his body. The slicing scar beneath his jaw. The bayonet scar between his ribs. And another in his left shoulder. And dozens of others. Caroline had kissed the unscarred parts as well. "And this morning. The things we shared. Do other couples do that?"

Tony took his time answering. And when he spoke, his answer was thoughtful. "I suppose lovers do. I'm not sure about married couples." He thought of his parents, who had died together in the phaeton accident. He hadn't realized until he was nearly grown that his mother had been expecting a baby when she was killed. Over the years, he'd forgotten many details about his childhood and remembered others. Tony remembered when he was old enough to leave the nursery to share breakfast with his parents, there had been several mornings when his father and mother had appeared later than usual and had only had eyes for each other.

Thinking back to the morning of his parents' fatal accident, Tony recalled that morning had been one of those mornings at breakfast when he'd been eager to relate some tale from school, some bit of gossip he'd heard, and had been frustrated by his parents' inattentiveness to him.

He gazed at Caroline. He hadn't understood when he was on the cusp of thirteen. But he understood now. His parents had loved each other. Desired each other. When he'd asked Caroline to marry him,

Tony had wanted with her what his parents had had. For however long it lasted. And he still wanted it with her. His soulmate. The love of his life. Instead of counting down the days until he was no more, he should be counting down the days he could have with Caroline. Tony had been granted a second chance at life when he survived the battlefield. Barnaby was right. He should be living his life, rather than waiting for death.

"Except love matches," Tony said, at last. "I think couples who marry for love are exactly like us. The Duke and Duchess of Avon, Viscount and Lady Grantham, the Marquess and Marchioness of Shepherdston." He paused, considering. "I'm told my parents were a love match. Even your godparents, Lord and Lady Weymouth." He smiled. "I read that Lady Weymouth recently gave birth to her second child."

"Yes," Caroline said. "After thirty years. Imagine how thrilling *that* must be." She thought of Weymouth's letter and invitation. "That reminds me. I received a letter from Uncle Trevor yesterday."

"Oh?" Tony wondered if Weymouth had mentioned spending the night as his guest at Carlisle House.

"He's invited me to a private thoroughbred sale at Tattersall's three weeks from now." Caroline was idly twirling the hair on his chest with her fingers. "At ten in the morning on the last Friday in April."

Tony raised his head to look at her. Weymouth's private sales were rare and very exclusive. The earl and his in-law, Lord Tressingham, were discerning as to where they sold their horseflesh and to whom. Tony had bought Aeolus and Ajax from Weymouth. *Ajax.* He closed his eyes. Would he ever be able to think of Ajax without remembering his last breath on the battlefield? And how the villagers and battlefield plunderers had savaged Ajax's carcass in an effort to get to him? They would have finished him off and scavenged his body like they'd done to Ajax if they had been able to move Ajax off of him. Fortunately for Tony, there had been plenty of other dead and wounded men for the soulless scavengers to murder and strip and rob. The scavengers had given up on him and moved on to easier pickings. For the time being…

He relived those harrowing hours on the battlefield in his nightmares, lying pinned beneath Ajax, breathing in the scent of the blood and gore and mud surrounding him, covering him, listening to the cries of the dying and the screams of the wounded, listening to the murders of the wounded…

Waiting. Hoping. Praying he'd be found by his comrades before the scavengers returned to dispatch him. Fearing the odors of blood and sweat mingled with the smell of food—cabbage, onions, leeks. Praying Barnaby would find him before the looters did. Deciding to provoke the scavengers if Barnaby didn't find him before they did, so his death would be swift, and he would not have to endure the indignities he knew they would inflict upon his corpse.

"I'd like to attend," Caroline was saying. "I haven't kept a horse in town since I married."

"Ladies can't attend the sales without an escort," Tony said.

Caroline nodded. "I know. I'll need an escort. Someone who knows horseflesh. I'd like that someone to be you."

"Weymouth will never sell you one of his horses on my recommendation," Tony said. "He values his horseflesh too highly. And I…" He broke off.

"You what?"

*I was foolish enough to take Ajax with me to war. Even though he didn't remember how it came about, how Ajax came to be there. He was filled with guilt for not protecting him. Ajax had deserved better.* "It doesn't matter." Tony rubbed his hand over his face. "Weymouth won't lead you astray."

"Uncle Trevor may not be there," she said. "He's subject to be called away on government business at any time. Lord Tressingham may be there instead." She grimaced. "And you know how *he* feels about ladies attending the horse sales."

"I haven't been around horses in some time, Caroline. I don't know that I would make a suitable escort for you." Because the date circled on his calendar was the twenty-fourth of April. According to the prognoses of six surgeons and physicians, he would be dying or dead by then.

Caroline hid her crestfallen expression from him, but she couldn't keep the disappointment out of her voice. "I understand."

"It's not that I don't *want* to escort you," he told her. "I'd be proud to do so, but..."

Caroline managed a slight smile. "I understand. Don't fret about it. The sale is nearly a month away. I have time to find someone else. I just hope no one offers to buy Achilles before I have a chance to see him."

*"Achilles?"* Horses bearing the names of the Greek gods and demigods were Weymouth's best prospects. The best-bred horseflesh in all of England.

"Yes," Caroline said. "He's a three-year-old colt out of Apollo and Ariadne. Uncle Trevor says he's a spirited beauty."

"You haven't ridden in five years." Tony's tone was sharper than he intended. "You don't need a spirited three-year-old colt. You need a sweet-natured little mare." *Like the one currently residing at his county seat in Yorkshire. The last horse he'd purchased at Tattersall's the morning he'd learned Caroline was marrying someone else.*

"I'm not planning to ride him," Caroline said.

"Then what are you planning to do with him?"

*Give him to you.* She almost spoke the words aloud, but something forced her to hold her tongue. "I could race him," she said. "Or I could use him for breeding stock. He has some of the best bloodlines in the country."

"You can't race him unless he's broken to saddle and trained," Tony said. "And you can't breed him unless he's trained, either."

"There's no guarantee Uncle Trevor will sell him to me. But if he does, I'll find *someone* to train him," she assured him. "I'm sure Uncle Trevor or Lord Tressingham can recommend a trainer." She propped herself on her elbow, then leaned over and kissed Tony. "Don't worry. Everything will work out."

Tony reached up, tangled his fingers in her silky hair, and pulled her face down to his. He kissed her with a hunger that seemed to explode around them. And when kissing no longer satisfied either one of them, Tony did the impossible.

He made love to Caroline for a fourth time.

TONY GROANED. HIS RIGHT ARM WAS TINGLING FROM HAVING BEEN USED as Caroline's pillow for most of the night. His right leg was aching from the exertion he had given it during his swim the evening before. Not to mention all his amorous exercise. But he needed to move... "I hate to leave a warm, comfortable bed and a warm, willing woman, but..."

"Just a woman?" Caroline pretended to be affronted. "Is that all I am to you? Just a woman?"

He flashed his grin. "Not just a woman. A warm, willing woman." He kissed her. "A beautiful, warm, willing, woman."

"There are plenty of beautiful, warm women willing to share your bed," Caroline said.

"Where?" Tony glanced around.

Caroline punched him lightly in the side.

"Ouch! I'm recovering from war wounds, remember?"

She was instantly contrite. "Tony, I'm so sorry. I didn't mean to hit you so hard. Where did I hurt you?"

"Here." He pointed to the offending spot.

Caroline leaned down and kissed it.

"And here." He pointed again, this time to the arrow of hair below his navel.

Caroline looked up and met his gaze. "I didn't hit you there."

"You sat on me," he accused. "Me. A man wounded in battle."

"You asked me to," she retorted.

"No, I did not," he countered with an engaging smile. "I believe I begged you to."

Caroline giggled. "Yes, you did, and very nicely I might add, for an earl unaccustomed to it."

"I'm more than willing to do it again," he said.

"You could do something for me..." she began.

"I'm all ears."

She glanced down the most prominent part of him. "Not *all* ears."

"You can't blame a man for wanting."

"I want you, too, Tony," Caroline said. "But first I need to ask another favor of you."

"Anything,"

"You haven't heard it yet."

"Anything except Tattersall's." Tony couldn't promise something he wasn't sure he could deliver.

"Carlisle House."

"What about it?" Tony shifted from his back to his side so he could see her face and read her expressions.

"Trade houses and households with me."

Tony frowned. "Carlisle House is my family home. I can't simply divest myself of it."

"I'm not asking you to divest yourself of it," Caroline said. "I'm simply asking that you allow me to live there."

"With me?" he asked.

She shook her head. "You need to live here. I designed it for you. To use during your recovery. You can't do that at Carlisle House." Caroline sighed. "And you can't get better if you're distracted."

"By you?"

She nodded. "But not just by me. By everything." Reaching up, Caroline framed his face between her hands. "I promise to take care of your family home. I promise to run it as if I were the mistress of it. And I want you to promise that you'll do the same here. I'll take care of all the necessary details. I'll consult with you on the important issues, but otherwise, I'll use my best judgment."

"And this?" He ran his hand down her naked thigh.

"I'll come to you in the pavilion and I'll come to you here." She paused. "Anywhere. As long as you want me."

"I'll always want you," he vowed. "And that will cause a scandal."

"Not if nobody knows."

"My darling, people will know." Tony gently smoothed her hair away from her forehead. "They always do. And they will talk. Two households already know. And *you* know what will happen.

Everyone will believe you're living with me. They'll think we're lovers."

Caroline smiled at him. "Aren't we?"

"We're much more than that," he said. "You are the love of my life. And I don't want to damage your good name."

"I don't care about my reputation or my good name," she told him.

"I do."

"And I love you for that. But my reputation doesn't matter."

"It matters, Caroline," he said. "It matters to the people who care about you. To the Weymouths and the Avons, to Phoebe, to Dulcie, to Susan, to all the workers who worked to bring your plans to fruition, to all your friends, and to the future of the Charlotte Society."

"My friends and family love me," she argued. "They know me, and they know my love for you."

Carlisle arched his eyebrow at that.

"I never tried to hide it from my friends. Or yours." She gave him a meaningful look. "And what the ton thinks means nothing to me. Despite my father's scheming, I'm not going to marry...."

Tony cut her off with a passionate kiss. "That's a shame," he said, after kissing her breathless.

She blinked. *Tony thought it was a shame she wasn't going to marry any of her father's matrimonial candidates?* "Oh."

"Because I was about to ask you to marry me. *Again.*" He grinned. "Caroline, will you marry me? Will you be my wife? My countess? And God willing, the mother of my children?"

"Yes!" Caroline threw her arms around his neck and covered his face with kisses. "When?"

"The twenty-third of April."

"The twenty-third of April?" She met his intense gaze. "Why that date?"

"It's the day you chose five years ago." Tony answered honestly.

"You remembered."

He nodded. "I remembered." He'd never forgotten the date and had noted the irony of dying one day after what would have been his fifth wedding anniversary with Caroline when he'd circled the date of his impending demise on the calendar.

If everything worked out the way the surgeons and physicians predicted, Caroline would become his countess twenty-four hours before she became his widow. Tony would keep his promise not to tie her to a cripple for the rest of her life. She would only be tied to him for the rest of his. She would be protected. Caroline would retain the title of Marchioness of Blessing, but she would become the Countess of Carlisle as well and would have his name. And she would have a full nine months from the date of his passing to make plans for her future and that of any result of their lovemaking, who would be born legitimate and a posthumous heir.

It wasn't the outcome he wanted. Tony wanted to live a long full life with Caroline and the children they might have, but seven doctors had told him otherwise. And after months of being unable to stand or walk on his own, Tony was inclined to believe them.

"It's a date," Caroline told him.

Tony shook his head. "Not yet."

Caroline frowned.

"There's something I need to tell you before you agree."

"Tell me." Caroline pinned him with a fierce gaze.

He did. He told her about the predictions of the seven surgeons. He told her what his future and hers, held in store. He didn't tell her he'd circled the predicted date on his calendar.

"I can't guarantee a long life for us," he finally said. "Only a happy one. Seven surgeons and physicians have examined me. Six of them have told me I won't live to see thirty."

"I know what the surgeons and the physicians predicted, Tony."

"Barnaby?" he asked.

"No. Uncle Trevor," she said. "I asked for your medical reports. He procured them, read them, and told me what they said."

"And knowing that, you still want to marry me?"

"None of us are guaranteed a long and happy life. We move forward on faith." She framed Tony's face with her hands. "I would marry you if I only had one minute as your wife. One minute of belonging to you. Of you belonging to me. Of us belonging together. Of sharing your name. Your name, Tony, not the title. I love you. You are all I've ever wanted. And I'll gladly take whatever time God grants us."

"It isn't just for you, my darling," he said. "It's for the child I may have given you. A child that should be born as my son or daughter, not Blessing's."

"There's no guarantee I can have a child," she reminded him.

"And no guarantee you won't." He grinned. "Especially after last night."

"And this morning." Caroline beamed her joy at the thought.

"Then you may have Carlisle House until our wedding day," Tony said. "With two caveats. First, that you go out of your way to win West's respect and trust. And second, that you do not begin any renovations on it without my approval." He extended his hand. "Agreed?"

"Agreed." Caroline accepted his hand and firmly shook it. "So when may I move in?"

# CHAPTER 32

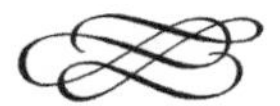

*"I love you with so much of my heart that none is left to protest."*
—William Shakespeare, 1564-1616

The three weeks that followed were the happiest of Tony's life.

And the most frustrating.

West was not happy with the earl's current living arrangements. After nearly forty years of service at Carlisle House, West had threatened to quit when he learned Caroline, Marchioness of Blessing, was moving in.

"My lord, it's unseemly," West had protested when Tony informed him of the switch. "For Lady Blessing to move in here with you." He had puffed out his chest and drawn himself up to his most indignant posture. "It simply isn't done, sir. A gentleman does not bring his ladybird into his ancestral home."

"Lady Blessing is not moving into Carlisle House with me," Tony explained, choosing to ignore, for the moment, West's disparaging comment about Caroline's status. "She and her lady's maid are moving in here. Barnaby and I are moving into Selby House."

"But this is your home, sir," West protested.

"Yes, it is," Tony agreed. "Unfortunately, Carlisle House isn't suitable for my present situation. The majestic staircase and my wheelchair are incompatible. And I will not consent to renovations that would make them compatible."

West recoiled. "Carlisle House was designed by Wren himself."

"Which is precisely why I won't allow it to be changed," Tony said. "But Selby House is different. The present viscount had no true attachment to it and sold it to Lady Blessing, who had it renovated for my needs."

"But Selby House's butler is young and inexperienced."

"Eddie Digby grew up at Selby House," Tony reminded his butler. "He was trained from the cradle to inherit the position. He knows every inch of that house the way I know every inch of this one."

"Sir, how can you bear to leave your home?" West appeared to be truly mystified by Lord Carlisle's contemplation of such a thing.

"I don't want to leave my home, but those blasted stairs make it impossible for me to stay. I cannot go on as a prisoner trapped on the upper floor of my house."

"My lord, we have footmen to assist you up and down the stairs."

"I don't want footmen to carry me up and down the stairs like a bloody invalid. I'm a man. I want to walk through the halls of my house and climb the stairs on my own. And if I cannot do that in Carlisle House, I choose to do it in a house more suited to my needs. Lady Blessing has given me a house that makes it possible for me to regain at least a part of my independence."

"But to allow her to live in the house that was home to your mother." West shook his head. "Sir, if that woman moves into this house, I fear I shall have to give my notice."

Tony pinned his butler with a sharp gaze. "I should hate for that to happen, West. You've been here since before I was born. You served my parents well. And you've served me well since I became the earl.

But you must understand that I asked, and Lady Blessing has consented, to become my wife."

West's normally unreadable expression was marked by surprise. He opened his mouth to speak, but no words came out.

"From this moment forward, a word spoken against Lady Blessing is a word spoken against me. Lady Blessing is not my ladybird. She is not a trollop. She is the remarkable young woman I love, the same remarkable young woman I loved and asked to be my wife five years ago. She is the remarkable young woman my mother would have been proud to have as a daughter-in-law. She asked to stay here and promised to do her best to win your trust and your regard. I suggest you allow her the opportunity. But if you choose not to do so, I will regretfully accept your notice and arrange for you to receive your pension and a pensioner's cottage at Carlisle Court or one of my other estates."

"Understood, sir," West said, his mouth still pinched into a disapproving line. "I shall see that Lady Blessing has no reason to find fault with my performance of my duty."

"Thank you, West," Tony said. "And West..."

"Sir?"

Tony narrowed his gaze at his butler. "Lady Blessing will know nothing of this conversation. Or the reason for it."

"Yes, sir."

~

West was as good as his word. Carlisle House ran as it always had, like clockwork.

Caroline went out of her way to be kind and considerate to the elder family retainer. There were minor disagreements, all of which were brought to Tony's attention in one way or another, but he didn't interfere. He allowed Caroline to handle things and noted that she never showed West up and did her best to allow the butler to retain his dignity and his position of authority in their petty disagreements.

Caroline began the healing process by apologizing for making

West's job more difficult than necessary when Lord Carlisle was in residence and consulting West on every decision she made for Carlisle House. She asked his opinion on menu suggestions and together, they worked out a schedule in which the two houses alternated meal preparation.

The first week, Carlisle House prepared breakfast and luncheon and Selby House prepared supper, and the second week, Selby House served breakfast and luncheon and suppers were prepared at Carlisle House.

Lord Carlisle and Lady Blessing shared breakfast in the pavilion every morning and a bed at Selby House every night. Soon, Tony was able to stand unsupported for minutes at a time instead of seconds, and began to regain the muscles he'd lost in his arms and legs during his long recuperation.

Although his nightmares loomed at the edges of his dreams, Caroline's presence reminded Tony he was safe at home and the battlefield was far away. The exhaustion he experienced after bouts of energetic lovemaking brought peaceful, blissful slumber. And the whisky he enjoyed each night came without the added drops of laudanum. His appetite had returned, and he was steadily regaining the weight he'd lost. But he was still unable to walk more than a step or two without excruciating pain or the threat of falling on his face.

Barnaby helped Tony with his exercises every morning and evening just as he'd been doing since the earl awoke in the field hospital. After his exercises, Caroline would watch as he swam the length of the heated pond and back for an hour each morning, and although he preferred his chair to the agony he endured with them, Tony soon learned to walk with crutches, practicing every day after his swim.

Despite the hard work and physical exertion, the weeks leading up to the thoroughbred sale at Tattersall's were the happiest Tony had ever known. And it was all because of Caroline.

Caroline also had her hands full with a bit of rebellion from Susan, who had been grumbling over their latest move for nearly a fortnight.

"I don't see why we had to move again," her maid complained as she helped Caroline dress. "I just got used to Selby House."

"Just got used to the hot and cold running water, you mean," Caroline corrected.

"I don't see why we have to go back to hauling buckets of water up and down stairs again." Susan picked up a hairbrush and began to brush Caroline's hair.

"I thought you admired Carlisle House and hated this one."

"I changed my mind," Susan said. "I've decided I like the conveniences of a modern house better."

"Then you're in luck," Caroline told her. "We're moving into Carlisle House to see what modern conveniences might be added to improve His Lordship's life."

"Other than you?" Susan shook her head. "Not much. Fielder explained the layout of the house to me. It's full of twists and turns and *architectural* marvels. Fielder's words for it, not mine."

Caroline winced as Susan hit a snarl. "Ouch! Easy. I'd like to keep as much of my hair as possible."

"Then tell His Lordship to keep his fingers out of it," Susan retorted.

"I'll do no such thing." Caroline smiled. "I like having His Lordship's fingers in my hair."

Susan snorted her disapproval.

"You're just out of sorts because, for the time being, Fielder has to remain here with His Lordship and Barnaby."

Caroline and Tony had decided to keep the households separate except for Barnaby and Fielder, who would move with Tony to Selby House. Kirby and Nelson would remain in service as footmen at Carlisle House.

Unfortunately, Fielder and Susan had formed an attachment during the time he'd spent guarding them.

Susan snorted again.

"Don't think I didn't notice," Caroline teased. "I've seen the way you look at him. And the special care you take with your hair and dress when he's on duty."

"And I've noticed the lack of care you've been taking with yours," Susan drawled. "Coming in at all hours in a pelisse, carrying soaked undergarments and crumpled gowns. Speaking of which..." She shot her mistress a meaningful look in the mirror. "You've run out of fresh ones."

"What?"

"Dresses," Susan said. "I only packed enough for a few days. And your wading in them in the heated bath isn't helping me keep them fresh and dry." She frowned at the overcast sky visible in the top windowpanes. "It's nearly impossible to get anything dry in this damp and cold."

Caroline couldn't disagree. It was a wonder Tony hadn't caught his death of pneumonia with as much time as he'd spent in the water.

Shuddering at the thought, Caroline made a decision. She didn't like it, but it had to be done. She could order a few dresses from her dressmaker, but the dressmaker wouldn't have enough time to complete them before she needed them. Caroline loathed the idea, but she needed her wardrobe. And that meant returning to Blessing House. "It's Wednesday. My father will be at his club most of the day. We should be able to get in, get our clothes, and get out before he returns."

"It's tricky, ma'am." Susan sounded as daunted by the prospect of returning to Blessing House as Caroline did.

Their gazes met in the mirror. "Have you a better idea?"

"No, ma'am."

"Please help me dress then. We need to hurry."

"THE POST HAS ARRIVED, MAJOR."

"Put it there." Tony nodded toward the corner of the desk. He knotted the sash of his robe and shoved his feet into his slippers. He was dressed for the heated bathing pond. "Thank you, Barnaby." He finished reviewing the household account book, then glanced up at Barnaby. "Who is Sanders?"

"The new groom," Barnaby replied. "He started work a fortnight ago."

Tony frowned. The name sounded familiar, but he couldn't put a face to the name. "Who hired him?"

"Latham, Major." Barnaby went about the room tidying up and opening shutters. Recognizing the note of discord in Carlisle's voice, he stopped and turned to look at him. "He came with exceptional references including recommendations from a number of peers."

"Which peers?"

"Easterly, Weston, Milford, Tennant."

Tony nodded. The peers he named were all known to be boon companions to Rushton and the late Granville Blessing. "I see."

"What, sir?"

"It seems Rushton has put a spy in our household." Tony turned to Barnaby. "Has Lady Blessing already left for breakfast in the pavilion?" They shared a bed, but when the household began stirring in the early morning hours, Caroline returned to Carlisle House.

She did so, she'd told Tony, to spare the staff the embarrassment of being asked to shield her from her actions. She need not have worried. Most of the staff at Selby House believed she could walk right across the water of his heated bath and could do no wrong. And he was universally appreciated by the staff at Carlisle House. Some of the staff might object to their unusual arrangement, but no one would complain.

"No, sir," Barnaby said. "She sent word through Nelson that she could not share breakfast with you this morning as she had urgent errands to run."

Tony met Barnaby's gaze. "The last urgent errand she had was Weymouth. Have you heard if he's back in town?"

"No, sir. But Nelson said he was accompanying Lady Blessing and Miss Brown to help load her trunks."

"Trunks from where?" Tony frowned. "Bloody hell! She's gone to Blessing House to collect her clothes and all she took with her for protection is the youngest, most inexperienced footman we have." Tony hefted himself out of his chair, took three steps forward, and nearly collapsed. "Damnation!" He grabbed at the rails overhead to keep from falling, then pulled himself upright and back to his chair.

He banged the arm of it with his fist. "What good am I? How can I protect her? What good am I to her like this?"

"I'll go, sir," Barnaby volunteered. "I'll see that she comes to no harm."

"We'll *both* see to it," Tony said. "I'll be damned if I'm waiting here."

"Sir?"

"I'm going with you, Barnaby. As soon as I find my blasted crutches."

~

"LADY BLESSING."

Caroline stood facing her former butler at the front door of Blessing House. "Good morning, Tyson. Is Lord Rushton in?"

"I'm afraid he and Lord Merrivale have already left for their gentleman's club," Tyson said, before stepping back to close the door.

"Good." Caroline placed her hand on the door. "Now step aside, Tyson. I'm coming in."

Tyson stood his ground. "Lady Blessing..."

She frowned. "I own this house, Tyson. My father is living here on my largesse, but this house belongs to me. I can leave it open and the staff in place or I can close it and dismiss the staff. It's up to me." Caroline didn't give an inch. "We've already had this distasteful conversation once. See that you don't give me reason to have it again. Now step aside. We're coming in to retrieve our possessions." She glanced over her shoulder at Susan. "Come along, Susan, we have work to do."

The two of them hurried upstairs and began packing Caroline's clothes and personal items. When they had finished packing Caroline's belongings, they began stuffing Susan's things into a separate trunk.

Susan brushed her hands together. "That's the last of them, ma'am."

Caroline eyed the open door of the mahogany wardrobe, satisfied with everything she and Susan had accomplished.

"Are you leaving those?" Susan gestured toward the interior of the wardrobe, where Caroline's black mourning and half-mourning clothes still hung inside.

"They belong here," Caroline replied. "In the past." She would need mourning clothes again one day, but not these. Not the ones she had worn for Lord Blessing or for Tony.

That chapter of her life was over.

"Call Nelson to load the trunks," Caroline instructed. They had arrived at Blessing House in a plain, black cab. Nelson had followed in an estate dray large enough to hold whatever she decided to fetch.

Caroline watched as Nelson finished loading the trunks onto the dray. Realizing he was wearing Carlisle livery, Caroline ordered him to return to Carlisle House with the dray. She was unwilling to chance her father arriving earlier than expected and recognizing the Carlisle regalia.

"I shouldn't leave you, ma'am," Nelson protested.

"Susan and I will be right behind you." Caroline lifted a gloved hand to signal the cab.

The driver pulled behind the dray. Susan was stepping into the vehicle when she suddenly stopped, dismay darkening her expression. "Oh, ma'am, I forgot your bonnets! They're in the hat boxes on your bed upstairs."

She scrambled to get out of the cab, but Caroline held up a hand to stop her. "I'll get them. You go ahead. Send the cab back when you get there."

Susan shook her head. "I'll wait here for you."

"Very well," Caroline replied. "I won't be a minute." She turned, reentered the house, and lifted the hem of her skirts to hurry up the stairs.

She found the hat boxes in her former bedchamber, right where Susan said they would be. Collecting them from the bed, Caroline left her room and started down the stairs. She had made it as far as the foot of the stairs when her father stormed into the house, waving a newspaper in the air.

"Tyson! What the devil is going on here?" Rushton shouted. "I had barely opened the newspaper and settled into my favorite chair when Pruitt"–he nodded toward the footman who'd followed him inside the house—"came running after me. Where the devil is my daughter?"

Caroline could have slipped out the front door, but she refused to skulk out of her own house. She set the hat boxes on the settee beneath the staircase and faced her father. "Here I am."

Rushton stomped up to her and flung the newspaper in her face. "What is the meaning of this, missy?"

"What is the meaning of this, *ma'am?"* Caroline corrected as she caught the newspaper against her chest. "Or, if you prefer, what is the meaning of this, *Lady Blessing?"* She met her father's scathing gaze without flinching. "I don't answer to *missy*. Or to you." She didn't look away until her father dropped his gaze, then she held the paper up to the light and saw that it was folded to *The Ton Tidbits* column. Bracing herself for what she was about to find, Caroline began to read: *"The Marchioness of Blessing has left her late husband's magnificent home and taken up residence in the home of her new neighbor, the Earl of Carlisle. Has Caroline's Folly brought the young widow into Lord Temptation's lair? Can she escape with her virtue intact or is Lord Merrivale in for an unpleasant wedding surprise nine months hence?"* She tossed the newspaper back to her father, scorn tightening her lips.

"Is it true?" Rushton demanded.

"Parts of it resemble the truth, parts are insinuation that impugn my honor, and the last is an outright lie. Lord Merrivale has nothing to do with me now or nine months from now."

Rushton was shaking with rage. "Are you staying alone with Carlisle at Carlisle House?"

"I am a guest at Carlisle House," she said. "But we're hardly alone. The place is fully staffed and Susan is with me."

Lord Rushton, reacting swiftly and without warning, raised his arm and backhanded his daughter across the face. "How dare you flaunt your love affair in the newspapers? How dare you besmirch your late husband's name? How dare you besmirch Merrivale's name? How dare you besmirch *my* name?"

Caroline staggered backward several steps beneath the force of her father's wrath, but she didn't hit the floor. She kept her feet. "How dare *you* come into my house and try to bully me into doing your bidding? I buckled beneath your will when I was a girl. I didn't fight back when you forced me to marry Lord Blessing. I didn't fight for the man I loved because I didn't want to fight against you. Not because I knew you were stronger than I, but because you're my father. You are the man my mother loved, and as her daughter, I thought I should honor her choice because to do otherwise seemed disloyal. Not to you. But to *her.*" A trickle of blood escaped from the corner of her mouth, but Caroline stubbornly refused to wipe it away. "But I don't owe you anything, Lord Rushton. I don't owe you love or respect or honor. Nor do I owe you a place to eat and sleep now that you've leased your home to someone else. And I certainly don't need to sacrifice the rest of my life on the altar of your ambition. I married the first time to suit you. I will not do it again."

More incensed than ever, Rushton raised his hand to backhand her a second time.

"I wouldn't do that if I were you."

"Tony!" Caroline cried.

He stood, balanced on crutches, in the foyer behind Lord Rushton, Barnaby at his side. "Sorry I'm late." He shrugged and gave her his most engaging grin, his silvery gray gaze never leaving hers. "I've come to take you home, my sweet. Are you ready to leave?"

Caroline collected her hatboxes. "Now I am."

"Go with Barnaby, my love. Wait for me outside," Tony said gently. "There's no need for you to witness what passes for conversation between your father and me."

She glanced from Tony to her father and back again. *"Tony?"*

"I'll be all right," he assured her. "We're going to talk. Go with Barnaby."

Caroline crossed the foyer to Barnaby's side. Rushton turned to follow her as Tony's manservant led her outside and into the waiting cab.

Tony leaned against the wall and lifted his right crutch. "Stay where you are, Rushton."

"Don't presume to threaten me." Rushton attempted to push past him. "You're a helpless cripple, Carlisle. What can you do to stop me?"

"I can even the odds by making *you* a cripple."

Moving faster than he thought possible, Tony whacked Rushton as hard as he could across both shins with his crutch.

Caroline's father dropped like a stone.

"I've been waiting five years for the opportunity to do that." Tony whacked Rushton again, this time across the shoulder. "That's for my horse, Ajax."

Rushton moved, groaning as he attempted to get up. Tony whacked him a third time as hard as he could across his ribcage. "And that's for Caroline." He bent closer. "Listen to me, Rushton, and listen well. If you *ever* lay a hand on Caroline again, I'll do far worse than beat you."

"My leg," Rushton whined. "It's broken!" He glared at Tony. "You *broke* my leg!"

"*I* broke your leg?" Tony gazed at Rushton with wide-eyed innocence. "I'm a cripple, Lord Rushton. And as you pointed out, entirely harmless."

"The Prince Regent will hear about this!"

"Don't threaten me," Tony warned. "You got off lightly. You get to wake up in a bed in this house instead of on a boat headed across the Channel to war in Spain." He glared at Rushton. "If you ever touch your daughter again in anger or frustration or greed or because of your twisted ambition, I'll kill you."

"I'm a belted earl!" Rushton yelled. "You've no right to threaten me."

Tony looked at him and through him. "You are mistaken, Lord Rushton. I didn't threaten you." Tony smiled. "I gave you my word. And I never go back on my word."

# CHAPTER 33

*"It is not in the stars to hold our destiny but in ourselves."*
—William Shakespeare, 1564-1616

Tony whistled a cheerful little ditty as he entered the mews to check on his wedding gift to Caroline two mornings later. The stable was bustling with activity. Stableboys fed and mucked, while grooms groomed and exercised the mounts and carriage horses. Tony absorbed the sights and sounds and smells of everyday life in the mews, wishing he could pitch in to help. He had become much more proficient in the use of crutches during the past few days, but he wasn't up to pitching hay or mucking stalls or exercising the horses. He frowned. Or even leading them.

But he reminded himself that he was making progress. Baby steps instead of strides, but progress nonetheless. The crutches gave him far more freedom than his wheeled chair. And Tony was determined to enjoy it as he made his way down the cobblestone aisle, stopping at each stall to greet the horses stabled there.

"Good morning, Aeolus." He propped one crutch against the front of the stall, then braced his hip against the wall. Reaching into the stall, Tony smoothed his hand from the horse's forelock down his face to his velvety nose and lips. "My good boy, you haven't forgotten me, have you?" Tony laughed as the horse nuzzled his hand before going in search of a bit of a treat—a piece of carrot, or apple, or lump of sugar purloined from Cook's worktable. "You haven't forgotten that, either." Tony produced a lump of sugar and offered it to Aeolus, who quickly demolished it. Tony sighed, breathing in Aeolus's scent. He'd missed that smell, the mingling of sweat and hay and heart that made them unique. He had missed that communion with horses while he lay flat on his back in the hospital. He had grieved for Ajax. And the grief he felt for his beloved horse was secondary to the constant ache of losing Caroline. He dreamed night after night of riding Ajax, of flying across the open fields at his country house and of his more sedate jaunts through Hyde Park with Caroline and her little mare, Mira. Only to wake in a cold sweat, awash in horrifying memories.

Aeolus nuzzled Tony's hand again, then moved to his pocket, searching for more sugar. Tony smiled. "Don't be greedy. Save some for your friends." Aeolus nickered and Tony relented, palming another lump of sugar for him.

"Good morning, sir."

"Good morning, Latham." Tony returned his head groom's greeting.

"I see you're still spoiling the horses."

"I am, indeed," Tony replied. "There's no harm in a bit of dessert after breakfast. It's been years since I've been able to spoil them and they seem to enjoy it as much as I do."

"I'm pleased to hear it, sir." Chester Latham grinned. "As long as they mind their manners."

"No horse in your care would do otherwise," Tony said. "Where's the new addition? I was told she'd arrived and I came to see for myself. Is she settling in nicely?"

"She's fine, sir. I put her at the far end of the stables. Far enough away from the other horses to be safe, but close enough to hear and smell them," Latham said. "Give me a moment to store this," he nodded toward the wooden wheelbarrow he was pushing, "and I'll take you to her, sir."

"Go ahead," Tony invited. "I'll follow behind you."

"Are you certain?" Latham glanced from Tony to his crutches. "It's a bit of a stretch. And amid the morning bustle..."

Tony smiled. "You lead. I'll follow."

Latham touched the brim of his cap. "Very well, sir."

The groom led the way, pushing the wheelbarrow to the storeroom, where he stowed the cart until the evening feeding. Tony followed at a more leisurely pace, pausing to observe the horses munching their grain and hay.

He reached the last stall, resting his crutches against it as he watched the newcomer. He called the mare's name and she looked up from her hay and nickered softly. He turned to his groom. "She looks good, Latham. No trouble during the journey?" Latham and several grooms had brought her from Tony's country estate, transporting her by canal and by roadway.

"None, sir. We took turns leading her."

"You did a fine job, Latham. I'm pleased."

"Thank you, sir." Clearly made uncomfortable by his master's praise, Latham cleared his throat. "I'd best be getting back to my duties. Are you going to be here awhile, sir?"

"Just a few more minutes to get reacquainted." Tony made a face. "If I'm late for breakfast Lady Blessing will come looking for me and I want her surprise to stay a surprise. So mum's the word."

"Of course, sir," Latham said. "I'll see that no one says anything to Lady Blessing and that you're not disturbed."

Tony watched the mare as she demolished her hay, then gathered his crutches and carefully made his way through the mews. He had reached the open courtyard when he saw a groom heading toward him, leading one of the carriage horses.

The man was dressed in Carlisle livery, and while he looked familiar, Tony didn't recognize him. He was not one of the grooms who had worked at Carlisle House before Tony left for war and he wasn't one of the grooms to whom Tony had been introduced since he'd begun visiting the mews. "You must be Sanders," Tony said, suddenly recalling the name of the newest hire as the groom drew abreast of him.

"Aye, I am," Sanders said.

"Welcome to Carlisle House. I hope your service here will be a long and happy one," Tony said.

"It won't be long." Sanders dropped the carriage horse's lead line. "But it will be happy once I collect the bonus promised me."

The hairs on the nape of Tony's neck prickled, much as they had on that hill overlooking Quatre Bras on the day of the battle that had cost him so much. "I beg your pardon?"

"You should." Without warning, the groom gave Tony a hard shove, sending him spilling to the ground along with his crutches.

Tony's head hit the cobblestones. Hard. Stars flashed in his vision, but he still saw the groom lift one of the crutches high above his head. The crutch came down once, then again. Tony counted five sharp blows before the stars faded and the world went black...

"TONY!" CAROLINE CALLED AS SHE LEFT THE SUMMERHOUSE IN SEARCH of him. She glanced toward the mews, her heart constricting as she spotted him lying at the top of the path. Lying flat on his back, sprawled on the pavement, his crutches out of reach. "I knew it was too soon for crutches," she muttered as she hiked up her skirts and headed for the pavement at a full run. "Please, God, let him be unharmed. Please," she repeated over and over, like a monastic chant. "I can't bear to lose him again. Please let him be unharmed. I can't bear to lose him again."

Reaching him, Caroline dropped to her knees with enough force to leave bruises and began running her hands over his beloved face, tracing his lips, feeling for his breath. "Please, Tony. I can't bear to lose you again."

He opened his eyes and blinked up into her face. "What are you doing here?" he whispered. "Why are you scowling at me like that?

And why does my head ache like the very devil?" He tried to reach up to touch his brow with a shaky hand, but Caroline caught it in hers. She didn't want him to be alarmed by the sight of fresh blood on his fingers.

"You were late for breakfast, darling. I missed you and came looking" She gave him what she hoped was a reassuring smile. "What on earth happened to you?"

He blinked again. "I seem to have run into some trouble."

"Do you think you can sit up if I assist you?"

Still clutching her hand, he tried to push himself into a sitting position. But the effort was more than he could endure. A cry of pain escaped from between his clenched teeth.

Caroline glanced around frantically. "Barnaby! Fielder! Kirby! *Somebody help me!"*

Tony winced at the sound of her shouts.

Barnaby and Kirby came running from the summerhouse.

"What happened, ma'am?" Barnaby asked, reaching her first.

"I found him like this," she said. "I think he fell."

Turning to Kirby, Barnaby began to snap orders like the sergeant major he'd been. "Quickly! Let's get him to bed."

Kirby sprang into action. "Hold on, sir. This is going to hurt."

Tony gritted his teeth anew, bracing himself as his footman lifted him. His muted groan of agony seemed to tear through Caroline's heart. But he clung to consciousness and her hand, even when she might have wished him the respite of a fresh faint.

Caroline didn't let go of his hand until Kirby and Barnaby had carried him into his room in Selby House. Gently easing her fingers from his grip, she flipped the covers of his bed aside so Kirby and Barnaby could settle him onto the welcoming softness of the feather mattress.

Turning to Kirby, Caroline said, "I want you to fetch Sir Walter Grimm right away. He's the closest and most highly recommended physician. Go! *Now!"*

~

Much to Caroline's relief, Grimm arrived promptly and immediately set to work. Her heart still racing, she paced outside the closed door of the master bedchamber while she waited for him to emerge. Barnaby stood at attention just down the corridor, keeping her company in her vigil. Her heart plunged when the door opened and she saw the resigned look on the physician's weathered face.

"After examining Lord Carlisle," Sir Walter said as he drew Caroline aside, "I feel the best course of action is amputation of his right leg."

"No." Clenching her hands together to still their trembling, Caroline shook her head. "Absolutely not.". And remembering Weymouth's comments about his daughter-in-law, she added, "And there won't be any blood-letting, either."

"Lady Blessing, *I* am the physician. And I can assure you that I know what's best for my patient." He pulled a card from his medical bag and handed it to her. "You must send a footman at once to collect a surgeon at this address."

She shook her head again. "No. I won't allow it.

The physician frowned at her. "Lady Blessing, perhaps you do not understand that it's imperative we perform the operation before he awakens."

"What I understand is that you wish to remove Lord Carlisle's leg."

"That is correct. And the longer we tarry, the more difficult the procedure will become."

"Is anything freshly broken?" she asked.

"No, my lady."

"Then what's best for *this* patient is keeping his blood inside his body and his leg attached to his torso."

"He'll recover much faster without it," Grimm told her.

"He's in no hurry," Caroline said. "And I'm sure he'd rather keep his leg."

"But he could very well die without treatment," the physician insisted.

"He could die *from* the treatment just as easily." Caroline turned away from the physician and began to pace the width of the corridor. "Or from fever. Or loss of blood."

"If you wish to seek another opinion, I should warn you that all the physicians of my acquaintance will make the same recommendations."

"Are you acquainted with Sir James McGregor of Edinburgh?" she asked.

Dr. Grimm frowned, giving her question some consideration before answering. "I don't believe I've had the pleasure of meeting a McGregor from Edinburgh."

"Well, then, thank you for coming so quickly, sir. But I fear I must bid you a good day. Barnaby will see you to the door and present you with a purse containing your fee."

"Well," Barnaby said after he returned from seeing Dr. Grimm out. "Number eight was aptly named."

Caroline managed a rueful smile at Barnaby's observation.

"The doctors all say the same." Barnaby frowned. "Six of the previous seven all declared it would be easier or kinder or better for him if we cut off his leg." He fixed his gaze on Caroline. "But easier or kinder for whom?"

"What did the seventh physician say?" Caroline asked.

"He thought Lord Carlisle might survive without the amputation, but he would never make a full recovery."

"Perhaps we'll get a better course of treatment from the next one."

"The next one?" Barnaby followed her into the study, not sure he'd heard her correctly.

"Yes." Caroline sat down at the desk and picked up the pen. "I'm sending for number nine. Lord Weymouth recommended him. He only amputates as a last resort."

"That will be a refreshing change," Barnaby said. "All the other physicians and surgeons predicted he'd be de—" He broke off.

Caroline frowned at Tony's former batman. "He'd be what?"

Barnaby lowered his eyes. "I cannot say, milady."

"I'm well aware of what the medical reports from His Lordship's physicians and surgeons said, Barnaby."

"I figured as much, milady," Barnaby said, "when the major told me you had agreed to marry him on the twenty-third of April. I was pleased to hear you'd convinced him to forget about the twenty-fourth." He glanced at the wall calendar, where the major had circled the twenty-fourth of April. "He's been marking off the days for nearly a year."

"Why?" Caroline asked, growing even more bewildered. "What happens on the twenty-fourth?"

Barnaby hesitated.

"Barnaby, what happens on the twenty-fourth?"

Barnaby drew in a deep breath and slowly released it. "He dies."

*"What?"* Caroline could feel the blood drain from her face as the pen slipped from her fingers. Clearly alarmed, Barnaby reached across the desk to steady her.

"Six surgeons and physicians calculated the major would be dead or dying from the effects of his injuries before the year is out," he gently explained. The twenty-fourth of April is the date they calculated."

"That's utterly ridiculous! He's not going to die," she vowed. "They're wrong."

"Do you truly think so?" Barnaby asked, clearly wanting to hope, but afraid to do so.

"I *know* so," she pronounced in a voice that sounded far more confident than she felt. "Lord Carlisle is healthier and stronger than he was when he first arrived back in London. And Sir James McGregor is going to prove it."

MAKING GOOD ON HER PROMISE TO BARNABY, CAROLINE FINISHED penning a letter to Sir James in Edinburgh, which was to be delivered by one of her footmen to the War Office to be included in Lord Weymouth's courier pouch.

Then she waited for three interminable days for McGregor to arrive.

During those three days and nights, she refused to leave Tony's bedside. She stayed with him, listening to his nightmares and his screams and his rambling thoughts as he relived the pain and horrors of war. She listened to his secret fears and his doubts for his future.

Barnaby also stubbornly refused to leave Tony's side. During those three days and nights, Tony's batman proved invaluable to Caroline. Barnaby had been through hell with Tony before. He knew what to do for Tony to calm him and make him comfortable. Caroline watched and learned.

She was afraid Tony would never open his eyes again, but a few hours after Sir James finally arrived, he did. "Caroline?" he whispered.

"I'm here, darling." She leaned over the bed so Tony could see her.

"Barnaby?" His voice came out as a croak this time.

"He's here with me," Caroline assured him. "We haven't left your side since I found you."

"You found me." He had known she would find him. He had never doubted that for a second. The only question was if she would find him in time.

"Yes." Caroline gave him what she hoped was a reassuring smile. "Do you remember? Do you know what happened to you?"

Tony gave a slight nod. "I received word that my wedding gift to you was in the mews. I went to check on it using my crutches instead of my chair."

"My wedding gift is in the mews?"

Tony gave a strangled laugh. "Yes. I had Latham send to Carlisle Court for it a week ago."

"Carlisle Court? What is it?" Hoping to distract him, Caroline scooted to the edge of her chair and leaned closer.

"Do you want to know what caused my fall? Or are you more interested in your gift?"

"I want to know what caused your accident, of course..." Caroline glanced down at her lap. "But..."

"But you also want to know what I got you for a wedding present," Tony teased.

Caroline blushed as she met his silvery gaze. "I do."

Tony took a deep breath. "Then I shall tell you I was in the mews checking to see how Mira had fared during the trip…"

"Mira? *My* Mira?"

*"Your* Mira," he confirmed.

"How?" Caroline blinked down at him in disbelief. "How on earth did you find her?" Unable to resist the temptation, she leaned down and began covering Tony's face with grateful kisses.

"She's been at Carlisle Court for the past five years. One of the grooms at Tattersall's alerted me to her sale the day I approached Rushton about marrying you. My agent bought her and had her delivered to the country house."

"Tony." She breathed his name. "You saved her for me."

"I believed Rushton had put her up for sale to punish you for our secret morning rides."

"But now we know he sold her to pacify Lord Blessing," Caroline said. "And to prevent me from eloping with you."

Tony moved his head from side to side on the pillow. "I didn't want you to lose her. Little did I know…"

"That I would be forced to marry Lord Blessing." She finished his thought for him.

*That I would lose you. And my ability to ride*. "No matter," he said. "Mira proved to be a good investment. She's already foaled several quality prospects."

"It mattered, Tony." Caroline choked back tears. After the betrayal he'd suffered at the hands of her father. After the betrayal she had inflicted upon him by marrying her father's partner in betrayal, Tony had still thought of her. Had still worried about her loss. "It matters to *me*."

"How did you come to fall, sir?" Barnaby rose from his chair and moved to stand beside Caroline, providing her with a moment to collect herself. "Can you tell us what happened?"

"One of the grooms bumped me while leading a horse," Tony said, avoiding Caroline's earnest gaze. "He was already past when I lost my balance and fell onto the cobblestones." One of the grooms had *pushed* him. The new one. Sanders. The one Tony had not met. The one who had once worked for Rushton. But there was no need to upset Caroline by telling her. He reached up and gingerly touched the side of his head where a large bump had formed. "I must have hit my head on the way down as well." *Tony distinctly remembered seeing the groom wield his crutch against him before his world had gone black. The groom had meant to maim or kill him. But men had tried to kill him before and had failed. Maiming was something else.*

Tony didn't want to alarm Caroline, but as soon as he could get Barnaby alone, he would make sure his batman summoned a constable and had the groom arrested. Although he suspected the villain had already fled like the coward he was, believing his job completed. A job no doubt contracted by Rushton. Or even Merrivale. If the man was still foolish enough to be lurking around, Tony might even give Barnaby leave to mete out his own brand of justice...

Tony closed his eyes, then slowly opened them again. His head throbbed like the devil, but he was more concerned with the damage done to the rest of his body, especially his legs. His apprehensive gaze traveled between Barnaby and Caroline as he braced himself to learn the worst. "What did I break this time?"

"Nothing, Lord Carlisle."

Tony didn't recognize the Scottish burr or the ruddy face of the man who suddenly melted out of the shadows. "Who are you?"

"James McGregor. Physician and surgeon from Edinburgh. And rest assured, as far as I have been able to ascertain following my cursory examination, this fall, as bad as it was, didn't cause further damage to your hip or your legs." He bent closer. "It did, however, compound your previous injuries."

"You can go straight back to Edinburgh. Or to hell," Tony said grimly. "I won't allow you to cut off my leg. Either leg."

"I'm not interested in removing your leg," McGregor explained. "What I'd like to do, if you'll allow me, is to save the limb and repair the previous damage so you can walk again."

Tony narrowed his gaze. "How do you know I can't walk?"

"I told him," Caroline said.

"Why?" Tony asked.

"Because he can help you," she said.

"How do you know?"

"Because Uncle Trevor recommended him." She met Tony's gaze. "I wrote him about you after Uncle Trevor sent him your medical reports."

Tony frowned. "What day is it?"

"April twenty-second."

*He had been asleep for three days.*

"I'd like to do surgery tomorrow morning," McGregor said.

Tony eyed the doctor suspiciously. "What kind of surgery?"

"I specialize in shrapnel wounds. I'm going to remove the bits you collected at Quatre Bras. I suspect they are what is preventing you from walking."

Tony shook his head. "I won't agree to more surgery."

"Tony!" Caroline exclaimed in dismay. "You must! Didn't you hear the man? Dr. McGregor believes his surgery will enable you to walk again!"

"And six other physicians believe I'll die unless I agree to let them remove my legs," he said. "How do I know he"—Tony nodded toward McGregor—"won't change his mind while I'm helpless and unable to protest and cut off my legs?"

McGregor stepped in. "I believe the surgery will be successful without the need for amputation."

"No." Tony was adamant. "No surgery. I've worked too hard to get this far. I won't risk having to start over."

Caroline took a deep breath. "I love you, Tony. There is nothing I want more than to be your wife. But I won't marry you unless you agree to let Dr. McGregor perform surgery. Unless you agree to allow him to help you."

"And if I allow him to perform surgery on me and it fails? What then?"

"Then I'll pledge my troth to you with all my heart," she said. "And we'll begin again."

"I don't want to begin again just to get where I am today. I don't want to start over in order to make it back to a wheeled chair. I'm already confined to a damned chair. And I refuse to tie you to a man in my position."

"I don't care that you're in a chair," Caroline insisted. "You're the man I love. The man I adore. The man I want above all others. Please, Tony, if you won't do this for yourself, then do it for me."

Tony sank back on the pillow. How could he undergo the surgeon's knife once again? How could he face another of his biggest fears? He hated the idea of failing. But he hated the idea of disappointing Caroline more. She had done so much for him and had asked for nothing in return—except that he love her. And she had never had to ask for that. She'd had his heart almost from the first moment he'd laid eyes on her.

Tony glanced around. "Barnaby?"

Barnaby hurried to Tony's side. "Yes, major?"

"Find West and have him bring the contents of the silver box in the safe at Carlisle House, then tell him to send for my solicitor. I need to make changes to my will should I not survive Dr. McGregor's surgery."

"This conversation is unnecessary, Lord Carlisle," McGregor said. "You aren't going to die or lose your leg. You may walk with a limp for the rest of your life. But I guarantee you'll walk."

"Outlook?" Tony asked the doctor. "Risk?"

"There are always risks to surgery. Blood loss. Complications. But your outlook is quite good. Barring complications, you should be up and walking about within a fortnight or two."

"Walking within a fortnight?" Tony wasn't sure he'd heard the doctor correctly. The man must be quite mad.

"Yes. And riding within a month or so," McGregor said. "Riding will take longer because it will require more exercise. But you'll be able ride again as well. After the surgery, you should be able to do everything you did before your injury. We'll do the procedure first thing in the morning."

"No." Tony's voice was strong and firm. "We won't."

"No? You still refuse the surgery?" McGregor asked.

Tony shook his head. "I'll allow you to perform the surgery. But not first thing in the morning." He seized Caroline's hand and brought it to his lips, his gaze as determined as his expression. "I'm getting married in the morning."

McGregor scowled.

"We planned to marry on the twenty-third," Caroline explained to the glowering physician before she turned to Tony. "Tony, our wedding can wait until you're well again."

"No, it cannot. No wedding. No surgery." He had an obligation to Caroline and a duty to his family. He wanted her protected. If he should die tomorrow, she would be his countess and well provided for. There was no reason to delay and every reason to follow through. He already had the wedding contracts and a special license he'd purchased five years ago. "I'm not waiting any longer. I've already waited five years."

McGregor heaved a weary sigh. "Have the wedding at nine, then. I'll operate at twelve."

Tony nodded.

"Oh, my darling, Tony, I love you so." Caroline blinked away her tears as she leaned over to tenderly brush her lips against his.

"And I love you, Caro. Always have. Always will." He smiled. "And I promise, one day soon, to dance at your wedding."

# EPILOGUE

*"One word*
*Frees us of all the weight and pain of life:*
*That word is love."*
—Sophocles, 495-406 B.C.

Anthony Carlisle, third Earl of Carlisle, awoke from surgery as a married man. Married to the woman of his dreams. The woman he loved. The woman who loved him. Despite everything.

He had planned to walk her down the aisle, but he married her while he was flat on his back and unable to walk.

But, according to Dr. MacGregor, the surgery had been a success.

A small piece of metal, shrapnel from his original injury, had lodged in his hip causing the excruciating pain he felt when he tried to walk, preventing healing which kept him from supporting his weight except in the heated bath his wife—his beautiful, wonderful wife—had built for him.

Tony sighed.

Dr. McGregor had removed that bit of metal and several other pieces that had migrated from bone and muscle to the thin layer of fat beneath the skin above his pelvic joint. His prognosis was excellent. McGregor expected him to be walking within a week. Two at the most.

Tony wasn't convinced it would happen that quickly, but he was convinced it *would* happen. Eventually. Like Caroline, Sir James was a force of nature. If he declared Tony would live to walk again, he would.

But the Earl and Countess of Carlisle had missed Lord Weymouth's special auction at Tattersall's. Tony had been unable to escort her after undergoing surgery and Caroline had refused to go without him.

"Tired?" Caroline laid her left hand on his chest. The three-carat sapphire he'd bought all those years ago as a betrothal ring and the matching sapphire band sparkled on the third finger of her left hand.

West had retrieved them from the safe in Tony's study at Carlisle House and presented them to Barnaby, who had stood up for Tony as best man. West had given the bride in marriage. Dulcie had served as maid of honor. Phoebe and Susan were bridesmaids, while Kirby and Fielder served as groomsmen.

"Amazed," he whispered. "It isn't every day a man gets married to the love of his life *and* regains the ability to walk."

"Uncle Trevor sends his best," Caroline said, reading a message that had arrived by special messenger from Lord Weymouth. "He says to tell you his wedding gift to us is munching hay in the mews as we speak."

"Achilles?" Tony guessed.

"The same." Caroline smiled. "Achilles was in London. Uncle Trevor figured he'd do better here with Aeolus than at Tattersall's."

"That was kind of him," Tony said.

"Yes, it was," Caroline said. "He says he hopes Achilles will help ease the pain of losing Ajax."

Tony swallowed the lump in his throat, unable to speak. Remembering Ajax's fate still hurt. Tony imagined it always would.

"Were you ever going to tell me?" she asked.

"Tell you what?"

"That you believed you were going to die the day after our wedding and leave me a widow."

"No," Tony said.

"Why not?"

"I didn't want to spoil the wedding,"—he waggled his eyebrows at her—"or the honeymoon by dying. I didn't think you'd want that, either." He frowned. "By the by, I thought you might like to know your betrothal to Merrivale appeared in this morning's paper."

*"What?"* Caroline was clearly stunned. "But I'm not betrothed to Merrivale. I'm married to you!"

"Barnaby read it in the *Ton Tidbits* column this morning."

"He's at it again!" she exclaimed. "And this time, I'll demand a retraction."

"Who?" Tony feigned a nonchalance he was far from feeling.

"You know very well who. My father. *Lord Rushton,"* she corrected, no longer able to bear thinking of the ruthless bully as her father.

Tony sighed. "I don't suppose it would be good form to sue my new father-in-law…"

"You won't have to," Caroline said, her expression fierce. *"I* will. He deserves it for meddling in our lives. Not once, but twice."

"Using the same tactic," Tony added. "If not the same accomplice." He smiled up at his wife. "Fortunately, I'm proving hard to kill. I've survived thrashings at the hand of your father and your late husband, abduction, the French army, eight"—he glanced toward the connecting door to the room McGregor had appropriated for his use during Tony's recuperation—"no, *nine,* surgeons, Barnaby, and you."

"Barnaby?" Caroline echoed in surprise. "He's devoted to you."

"He is," Tony agreed. "So devoted he nearly killed me when he first began manipulating my limbs. But, you, my darling…" He took a deep breath. "Wanting you and fearing you would never be mine sent me to the brink of despair. I'd fought so hard to survive everything else, but my survival meant nothing if I couldn't have you."

"Silly man." Caroline placed her hand against his cheek. "I had no intention of letting you get away again."

"No danger of that," he whispered. "I'm not going anywhere."

"Yet," she promised. "But you will."

Tony lifted an eyebrow at that.

"And I'll be right beside you. Wither thou goest…" Caroline kissed his bare shoulder. "I'm so glad we don't have to sneak about anymore or pretend the staff doesn't know I've been sharing your bed for weeks. I belong here beside you, and yet I want to pinch myself because I'm still afraid it's a dream. I can't believe we're finally married."

"I fear you're stuck with me now," Tony said.

"And you're stuck with me," she told him. "For better or worse."

He smiled down at her, drinking in the sight of her snuggled beside him. "Why do you think I invited you back into my life?"

"You didn't invite me into your life," she reminded him. "On the contrary, you threatened to throw me out. I invited *myself* into your life."

"Part of the plan," he teased. "I threatened to throw you out because I knew you couldn't resist a challenge. I knew you would return."

Caroline laughed. "It was a lovely wedding, wasn't it?"

"The loveliest," Tony agreed. "Especially the bride. It was a shame your father couldn't make it, though." He pressed a kiss against the crown of her head and sighed innocently. "Who would have thought he could slip and fall in a marble entryway and break his leg in two places?"

"Yes, who would have thought?" Caroline eyed her husband suspiciously. She'd never asked, and he had never told her what had taken place at Blessing House after Barnaby had escorted her out, but she wasn't an idiot and she didn't believe Rushton's convenient fall had been innocent…or coincidental. But she couldn't bring herself to feel sorry for him, either. His ambition had cost her five years with Tony and had cost Tony years of pain and the ability to walk. Caroline moved closer, molding her body to his. "As it turned out, I much preferred West to Lord Rushton. Although I admit I was surprised West consented to give me away."

"Surprised?" Tony snorted. "West was overjoyed at the prospect of giving you away.

He was eager to get you out of his domain and away from Carlisle House. Even temporarily."

Caroline laughed once again. "I suppose he was. There's only one problem."

"What's that?"

"He gave me to you."

"What can I say?" He shrugged. "The man wants me to be happy."

"Are you?"

"Deliriously."

Caroline placed her hand on his forehead to check for fever. Tony grasped her wrist and guided her hand to his mouth, where he planted a tender kiss against the pulse of her inner wrist. "There's no fever," she said, although she was beginning to feel a bit overheated herself.

"Oh, there's fever." He gave her a wicked grin. "But it's further south." He guided her hand to the sheet draped over his groin.

"You are incorrigible!" she accused.

"I am that," he agreed. "Because I'm married to an incredibly intelligent and desirable woman."

"I'm so happy."

"You should be, Lady Carlisle. It's not every day a woman fulfills the mission of The Charlotte Society," he said.

"What mission is that?"

"Adopting a lost soldier and taking him from a nightmare of pain and despair and loneliness to a life of infinite possibilities filled with love."

"Is that what I did?"

Tony kissed her. "You performed a miracle, Lady Carlisle. You brought a man back from the dead." He met her sparkling gaze. "You loved me back to life."

"What else could I do?" she murmured against his roving lips. "You're the love of my life and all I ever wanted."

He chuckled, the warm rumble sending a fresh shiver of desire deep within her. "I was hoping I could tempt you into making just such a confession."

She lifted her lips from his just long enough to lean back and give him a tender smile. "Of course, you could. After all, you are and always shall be…my Lord Temptation."

*The End*

Keep reading for a Sneak Peek at *Lord Dare*

by Rebecca Hagan Lee

Book 2 in "The Charlotte Society" Series

Sneak Peek

*Lord Dare*

*by Rebecca Hagan lee*

Book 2 in the "The Charlotte Society" Series

Coming Soon!

*25 March 1816*

"Do you be daft, woman?" The big Scotsman shouted at Phoebe Osborne as she pushed the tea cart laden with cakes and cups of tea through the rows of beds in the ward at the Returning Soldiers' Hospital in St. Martin-in-the-Fields, London.

Phoebe looked up and met the furious gaze of the surly Scot she had hoped to see. "I beg your pardon?"

"You would do well to," he muttered.

"What did you say?" she demanded.

"I asked if you were daft, woman?" he repeated, his Scots burr thick with disgust. "Are ye?"

"For politely speaking to you? Probably. But to do otherwise would be rude. And I am not a rude woman."

"Only *séolta* for coming here," he said. "Where no decent Sassenach lady should be. For wandering unescorted through the wards of a hospital full of men your own Lord Wellington called the scum of the earth."

"I'm here on behalf of the Charlotte Society."

"The what?"

"The Charlotte Society," she repeated. "I represent our patroness, Queen Charlotte. I'm here to minister to the needs of those less fortunate than myself."

He raked his gaze over her, noting the fine muslin of her gown with its dyed-to-match pelisse trimmed in lace. "With tea and cakes?" He scoffed. "Or with something more substantial?"

"With tea and cakes," she replied. "And human kindness."

His look spoke volumes.

"If you don't want to partake," Phoebe said. "You may refuse. But you've no right to spoil it for the others."

"I don't want what you're offering," he said, his green eyes flashing equal amounts of fire and disdain.

Phoebe's mouth dropped open, forming a perfect 'o' of surprise. "I don't understand why you're so angry with me."

"You're a woman in a place where a woman should not be. What's more you're a Sassenach lady. This is a place of men. Injured men. Dying men. Coarse men. Angry men. You should be taking care of your family, tending home and hearth with a *bairn* at your feet and a babe at your breast. Not catering to strangers."

"I don't have a home of my own or a hearth to tend. If I did, I would offer refreshments to guests who came to call. I'm doing the same here as I would do there. No more. No less."

"Except we're not your guests," the Scotsman said. "We're here until we heal or expire." He fixed his attention on a young soldier three beds down. "You're the guest. And if you had the brains God gave a sheep, you'd know you've come where you aren't wanted."

Phoebe lifted her chin a notch higher. Then nodded toward the men enjoying the refreshments she'd served them. "I *was* invited. By the hospital trustee. He asked me to come as a representative of the Charlotte Society and your fellow patients seem glad to see me." She looked him in the eye. "They seem to want me here. Even if you do not."

"They—" He shot a glance at the patients in his ward. "Want to enjoy tea and cakes and the company of a female to break up the boredom of their day." He pinned his gaze on Phoebe's face. "What do you want?"

"I want to adopt a soldier."

"Of course, you do." He laughed. "Every Sassenach lady wants a war hero. We're like gladiators to the high-born females of Rome. We're all the rage this season." The Scotsman opened his arms wide to encompass the occupants of the ward. "There's one of everything—Londoners, Welshmen, Cornish, Yorkshire, Midlothian, Lowlander, Irish, even a Hessian or two…Take your pick."

Phoebe glanced around the ward, taking note of all the faces of the men confined there, half hoping to find someone she knew, someone she recognized. But these men were all strangers to her. On her previous visit, she had served refreshments in the common room for ambulatory patients. She had never been in the wards. And none of the men here had been in the common room last week.

*With one exception...*

"Well?" he demanded.

"Well what?"

"Take your pick," he ordered. "There's one of everything except a gentleman."

"How about an angry, churlish, highlander?" Phoebe looked him in the eye. "Have you one of those?"

"Only one," he said. "And I am not for sale."

"You were a soldier," Phoebe said. "You took the king's gold once."

"Aye." He glanced around the ward before pinning her with his sharp gaze. "I did. And I'll not make that mistake again. Look where that one landed me."

*Lord Dare* by Rebecca Hagan Lee
Book 2 in "The Charlotte Society" series
Coming Soon!

## ABOUT THE AUTHOR

After arming herself with a degree in fine arts and experience in radio, television, and film, Rebecca Hagan Lee wrote her first novel *Golden Chances*. Since then, she's published numerous bestselling and award-winning novels and three novellas.

She's won a Waldenbooks Award, a Georgia Romance Writers *Maggie* Award, several *Romantic Times* awards, been nominated for an RWA *Rita* Award and has been published in nine languages.

She currently lives in Georgia with her husband, her two beloved Quarter Horses, and a miniature schnauzer named after literary icon Harper Lee.

Visit Rebecca's website http://www.rhaganlee.com

Join Rebecca on Facebook at http://www.facebook.com/rebeccahaganleeauthor

CPSIA information can be obtained
at www.ICGtesting.com
Printed in the USA
LVHW102136021122
732257LV00022B/351